ELM BROOK MANOR

IWAN ROSS

1

To my wife, Marna, the heartbeat of my life. Your love is the melody that inspires every word I write, the suspense that keeps me on the edge of my seat, and the twist in every tale. You are the romance in my drama, the vivid color in my world. This story is but a mirror reflecting the beauty and mystery of our love. With all my heart, this book is for you.

Mister Jones,

In the dimly lit room, shadows dance, their movements casting an eerie atmosphere. The air hangs heavy, filled with a palpable sense of foreboding. This is the tale of Mister Jones, a narrative woven from threads of reality and dusted with the allure of the unknown. Each word you are about to read holds more than ink; they carry echoes of sights, whispers of sounds, and imprints of scents. The essence of this chronicle is interwoven with the very fabric of your senses. Some fragments are raw truths, laid bare, while others have been meticulously crafted to fill the gaps that time's relentless teeth have gnawed open.

Chapter One

Coby leaned to the side, his eyes scanning the length of the line, taking in the bustling scene of eager readers. His stature was neither imposing nor insignificant, standing at an even 5'11", yet it was his undeniable aura that drew eyes towards him. A crown of tousled dark hair sat upon his head, a hint of silver streaks peppered at his temples. He exhaled softly, a sense of relief washing over him, like a gentle breeze on a warm summer day.

His Scottish accent gave each word he spoke a comforting and captivating quality, like a beautiful melody. Only three more people stood before him, their presence a reminder of his impending task. With a stroke of his chin, he mulled over the words he would write when he finally signed the book. Ideas had eluded him for some time now, leaving him feeling a sense of emptiness.

Yet, he took solace in the fact that he had sold all his books, with the empty boxes standing as a testament to his success. A flicker of annoyance crossed his expressive face, the lines around his eyes deepening as he remembered his wife's promise to bring more boxes, a promise left unfulfilled. The mall buzzed with activity, a symphony of voices and footsteps creating a vibrant backdrop. Bargain seekers rushed from store to store, their presence akin to an avalanche of humanity descending on the shops.

In an effort to maintain order, the shop assistant had closed the doors of the bookstore, shielding Coby from the clamour outside. Lost in his thoughts, Coby's keen gaze remained fixed on the book before him, oblivious to the curious onlookers peering through the windows.

Some of them contorted their faces and hurled insults, their words bouncing off him like pebbles hitting a shield. The sound of their jeers filled the air as they called him "Scrooge," a mocking reference to his wealth and tightfisted ways.

He inhaled deeply, his senses tingling with anticipation. The taste of whisky lingered on his tongue, its rich, woody notes intertwining with his thoughts. Finally, he found the words he sought. With deliberate movements, he wrote, 'Dear Christie, Happy reading,' signing it with the initials M. Jones. As each person in line received their signed book, the line gradually dwindled until only one remained.

A fiery redheaded girl, her determination etched on her face, abruptly slammed the book down in front of Coby, startling him.

Nerves tinged his voice as he asked, "Who should I make it out to?"

The girl's eyes blazed with fury as she spat out the name, "Gordon Snape!" Recognition flashed in Coby's eyes, sending a shiver down his spine. In an instant, the veil of time lifted, transporting him back to a haunted house. The echoes of laughter and the scent of death filled his senses. The flashback was so vivid, so real, that his present surroundings felt like a mere dream in comparison.

"Mister Jones!" snapped the young girl, her voice sharp and piercing, cutting through the quiet of the bookstore. Her eyes bore into him with intensity, fixing him with a gaze that seemed to penetrate his very soul. The fury in her expression snapped Coby out of his daydream, causing him to jump slightly in surprise. Without wasting a moment, he hastily picked up the pen and signed the book. His hand trembled slightly as he scrawled his name. 'Dear Gordon,' he began, 'I hope you find comfort in the pages of this book. My deepest sympathy, M. Jones.'

As he closed the cover shut with a soft thud, a sense of reluctance washed over him, as if the book held the key to his own redemption. The faint scent of aged paper and ink mingled in the air, reminding him of the countless stories trapped within those pages. The fiery red of the girl's hair stood out vividly against the dimly lit backdrop of the bookstore, adding a touch of vibrancy to the scene.

With determination, she clutched the book tightly, her fingers curling around the cover as she snatched it from his grasp. Before she left, her disdainful gaze lingered on him, a silent reminder of the pain and regret he carried within him. His reputation as a 'Scrooge' seemed to weigh even heavier on him in that moment, a stark contrast to the joy and success of his book signing event. In that moment, his past surged back to haunt him, a familiar feeling that seemed to never fade away.

As the thick fog slowly unfurled over the misty Scottish moors, Coby McTavish wearily trudged back to his quaint stone cottage. The grey mist created an eerie ambiance, engulfing the surroundings in a haunting veil. Inside, the cottage emanated a comforting warmth, a beacon of solace amidst the encroaching gloaming.

Waiting for him within was his wife, Elaine, a captivating presence whose beauty seemed as timeless as the rugged highlands themselves. Elaine was petite and delicate, with an air of frailty that belied her powerful spirit. Her auburn curls, soft and slightly wavy, framed her face perfectly, giving her an almost pixie-like appearance. Her eyes, a soft hazel, were large and expressive, holding a profound depth that was both comforting and mystifying to Coby. They spoke volumes of the understanding they shared, a silent testament to the years they spent entwined in their shared passion for weaving tales of the supernatural.

Her laughter, like delicate wind-bells, often echoed through the cosy home, casting a melodic counterpoint to the eerie silence that enveloped their world. Yet today, something felt amiss. Coby's unease heightened as he noticed the straw boater playfully perched on the side of Elaine's head, accompanied by white opera gloves. The sight gave him a foreboding sensation, as if she were preparing for a journey. The scent of vintage perfume lingered in the air, adding a nostalgic touch.

Coby's gaze shifted to Elaine's side, and there it was, her hand grasping the handle of a large suitcase. With a scoff, she lifted the suitcase and disappeared through the door, leaving Misty, her beloved Scoodle, behind. The proud canine stood poised, her hair adorned with a dainty pink ribbon, seemingly aware, or perhaps presuming, her regal lineage.

"You forgot your dog!" Coby called out, his voice filled with concern.

"It's not a dog!" Elaine reminded him, her voice fading into the distance. The abrupt slam of a car door resonated through the foggy air as the engine roared to life, signalling her departure.

Resigned and with his shoulders slumped, Coby ascended the creaking stairs, his weary feet dragging along the worn wooden floor. A chilly breeze slipped through the cracked window, causing him to shiver involuntarily. As he reached the top, his eyes caught sight of a small rock lying on the floor, surrounded by shards of broken glass. He picked up the rock and tossed it outside, patching the resulting hole with an old, threadbare woollen jersey, its warmth providing some solace amidst the growing cold.

His eyes lingered on the pristine white envelope, its smooth surface reflecting the dim light of the room. Bearing only his first initial, C, for Coby, it exuded an air of mystery. With a mix of apprehension and curiosity, he tore the flap open, the sound of the paper tearing echoing in the stillness. Hastily unfolding the letter, he could almost feel the delicate texture of the paper between his fingertips.

Coby hesitated, his heart pounding in his chest, as he put the letter down beside his keyboard. Needing a moment to gather his courage, he fixed himself a double Scotch, the rich aroma of the liquor filling the air. With each sip, the warmth spread through his body, granting him the strength to face the cruel words that awaited him.

The letter was short and succinct, written in Elaine's unmistakable handwriting. As he read her words, he could almost hear her voice in his head, dripping with an eerie malice. A mix of anger and sadness washed over him, causing him to crumple the letter in his hand until his knuckles turned white. In a moment of defiance, he tossed it into the hearth; the flames casting a golden glow on his face, making his eyes sparkle with determination.

As the fiery tongues licked the side of the letter, a crackling sound filled the room, accompanied by the faint scent of burning paper. The flames devoured the contents of the letter, releasing rising embers into the air, a symbol of the remnants of their shattered relationship.

Coby's gaze locked with Misty's, their eyes meeting in an intense moment. She panted heavily. The sound resembling a roaring locomotive as she lay next to the crackling fire. A thin smile formed on her lips, sending a shiver down his spine. It felt as if the black-coated creature took pleasure in his misfortune. Ignoring the dog, he shifted his focus back to the familiar sight of his keyboard, a source of comfort and peace. His fingers gently rested on the cool keys, his eyes fixed on the blank document before him. The story he had in his mind seemed to slip away, elusive. His thoughts kept drifting to the memory of the fiery young red-headed girl from the bookshop, her harsh words still stinging in his mind. He could almost feel her anger enveloping him, radiating hatred. Coby shivered and shook his head, trying to push those thoughts away.

Like a scanner, his eyes swiftly scanned his emails until he spotted it. RE: ELM BROOK MANOR – PROPOSAL FOR SALE. Excitement surged through his veins, a newfound freedom energising him. With a decisive click of the reply button, he typed out his message, his fingers dancing across the keys. The offer he made contained enough zeros to make anyone's jaw drop. After hitting send, he strained his ears and heard the satisfying swoosh sound, feeling a sense of accomplishment. Rubbing his hands together, he couldn't help but shoot a mischievous glance at the dog, who observed his every move.

"Who's laughing now, eh?" he asked, his tone dripping with sarcasm.

Coby carefully lifted the frameless, all-glass tailgate of his Volvo P1800 ES, marvelling at its sleek design. He tossed his few belongings into the spacious hold, the metallic clinks echoing in the quiet garage. The car's robust build, clear in its sturdy body, gave him a sense of security as he prepared for the journey ahead.

As he placed his laptop on the passenger seat, he couldn't help but notice the cool touch of the leather against his fingertips. He carefully tucked it under a soft towel, ensuring its safety during the trip.

Negotiating with two enthusiastic boys, their voices filled with excitement, Coby secured his prized desk onto the roof rack of the car's extended roofline. The weighty thuds of the desk hitting the metal rack served as a reminder of the task at hand. In the end, their eager help came at the cost of all his loose change, the jingling coins slipping through his fingers.

Examining the desk, he couldn't help but notice how its legs were rigid, pointing skywards like a lifeless creature. The sight sent a shiver down his spine, a strange mixture of fascination and unease.

Before departing, Coby placed a heartfelt letter on the console table, its surface smooth beneath his touch. It was a message to his wife, a loving greeting mixed with an explanation of his whereabouts. He knew she would disapprove, her previous warnings about the risks involved with the manor still fresh in his mind. But he couldn't ignore the pull he felt towards the mysterious estate.

His mind wandered to the looming manor, its ancient stones exuding an aura of mystery and foreboding. It was a place that seemed to hold secrets, its dimly lit corridors inviting him to explore their depths. Lost in thought, he conjured up the subtle aroma of mustiness, a fragrance that whispered tales of the past.

Coby was determined to uncover the hidden stories within those walls, his fingertips tingling with anticipation. The manor's haunted embrace beckoned him forward, a chilling sensation that thrilled and chilled him in equal measure.

He embarked on the lengthy journey filled with bubbling anticipation, his lips vibrating with a cheerful melody. A heavy, sombre grey curtain veiled the heavens, ready to unleash its wrath upon the world. Before long, it released torrents of rain, cascading down in relentless sheets. Coby swiftly silenced the radio, his grip on the steering wheel tightening, causing his knuckles to pale under the pressure. Each fat raindrop violently hammered against the windshield, while his desk securely clung to the roof. The monotonous swishing of the windshield wipers added to his growing frustration. He cast a scowl towards the gloomy skies, muttering curses under his breath.

Many long and solitary hours passed by agonisingly slow, like a snail inching along. The relentless rain intensified the feeling of loneliness inside the car as it drowned out the rhythmic chug of the engine. While he patiently waited on the narrow road for a flock of sheep to leisurely pass, he meticulously examined his worn-out map. The scent of dampness filled the car, mingling with the scent of the old leather seats. He had never quite grasped the concept of modern navigation systems, even though his sleek smartphone supported it. Frustration tugged at him as he traced the twisting blue line that snaked its way across the map, leading from his former sanctuary to his eagerly awaiting abode. Judging by his estimation, he was only an hour's drive away from his destination.

Coby carefully folded the worn map and tossed it into the cluttered glove box. The incessant baaing of the sheep gradually faded into the distance, replaced by the distant sound of the herder's commanding whistle and the occasional bark of his two loyal border collies. With a quick wave at the herder, he eagerly lunged forward, the engine purring beneath him. It always irked him when people failed to wave back after he greeted them, a sense of disappointment settling in his chest.

He followed the winding road, the lush green scenery stretching out before him under the ethereal glow of the clear blue skies. As he approached a junction, a contented smile played on his lips, the corners of his mouth tingling with anticipation. And there it was, the weathered road sign proudly displaying the name 'Serenity Falls,' accompanied by an arrow pointing left. The soft click of the indicators filled the car, blending with the gentle hum of the engine. Without hesitation, he obediently followed the direction showed by the arrow, his hands gripping the steering wheel with a mix of excitement and relief.

Nestled deep within the Highlands, where the echoes of ancient tales mingle with the pulse of existence, resides a town veiled in a mysterious serenity. Serenity Falls, it's called, a name that rolls off the tongue as soothing as the lilting melodies of a lullaby. Here, time seems to slow, as if the universe itself has paused to take a breath, its pulse echoing in the gentle babble of brooks and the soft sigh of the wind.

This is a place where shadows dance with the light, where the ordinary mingles with the extraordinary. Nestled amidst emerald hills and silver streams, Serenity Falls is cradled within the verdant arms of age-old woods. These woods, they stand sentinel, their gnarled branches reaching out like spectral fingers, their leaves whispering tales of yore in the hushed, sacred silence.

Here, the air is heavy with the scent of pine and wet earth, a heady perfume that weaves an intoxicating spell. The sky overhead, a canvas of ever-changing hues, reflects in the shimmering surfaces of the brooks, painting portraits of the heavens in the heart of the earth. Coby carefully navigated the twisted, serpentine path that wound its way through the eerie, foreboding shadows cast by the towering hemlock trees. His intense gaze fixated on each bend, desperately trying to commit the route to memory. Over a year had passed since he had fortuitously stumbled upon the captivating stronghold. Deep in contemplation, his forehead creased with furrowed concentration, while his eyes strained against the blinding rays of the descending sun.

And there was Elm Brook Manor. It rose, abruptly and imposingly, from the tranquil landscape like an ancient monolith. A monument to a bygone era, it loomed over Serenity Falls, casting long, creeping shadows that merged with the twilight. Its stone walls, weathered by time and tempered by history, stood resilient against the elements, every groove and crack a silent testament to tales untold.

Finally, Coby turned into the rising driveway of his new sanctuary. The gravel crunched under the weight of his tires, sending a satisfying sound that echoed through the quiet air. A sense of pride washed over him like a crashing wave, filling the air with a subtle feeling of accomplishment. The sun bathed the scene in a warm glow, casting long shadows across the driveway.

His face beamed with pride, a wide smile spreading across his lips. The fresh scent of cut grass mingled with the earthy aroma of the nearby trees, creating a pleasant fragrance that filled his nostrils. His eyes gleamed with joy, reflecting the excitement and contentment he felt in his heart.

Under the strain of the rising incline, the engine chugged noisily, its rumbling sound blending with the symphony of nature that surrounded him. The chirping of birds and the rustling of leaves added a melodic backdrop to the scene, creating a serene ambiance. The aged, moss-covered stone walls of a quaint cottage emerged from the dense forest, wisps of smoke dancing from its chimney. Against the backdrop of beige stone, a woman's silhouette stood, diligently hanging laundry on the line. As she glanced at the newcomer, the wind whispered through the trees, carrying the scent of pine and damp earth. Ignoring Coby's friendly wave, she kept her attention fixed on her task.

The sight of the manor captivated Coby, his eyes inevitably focusing on the left wing wrapped in scaffolding. Construction work was obvious in the air, as tools clinked and hammers thudded intermittently. The scaffolding rose all the way to the mansard roof with its dormer windows, creating a striking visual against the blue sky.

In his mind, Coby imagined Rapunzel appearing at one of the dormer windows, her long, golden hair cascading down. However, his fantasy was shattered as he saw workers clambering down the scaffolding, resembling a busy army of ants. They wore worn-out overalls and dusty boots, their tired faces showing the signs of a hard day's work. The sight brought a smile to Coby's face, appreciating their dedication to completing the renovations.

Amidst the workers, a long ladder extended across the rooftop, leading a man who was busy fixing a dish to the roof. The clinking of metal against metal accompanied his every move as he meticulously adjusted the equipment. It was a reassuring sight for Coby, knowing that the new internet service provider was diligently installing their equipment.

In front of the entrance, a group of branded vans were parked, their engines occasionally humming and emitting a soft rumble. Each van bore the distinct insignia of the companies they represented, showcasing the diverse range of services involved in the renovation process. The air in the manor was a blend of fresh paint and the subtle aroma of gas, a testament to the various trades at work.

Just like the real estate agent promised, Coby made a mental note to write her a thank you note and reward her with a bunch of vibrant flowers. The anticipation of settling into his new sanctuary grew stronger as the sights, sounds, smells, and feelings of the scene enveloped him, making him feel even more grateful for this new chapter in his life. He didn't mind the inconvenience of workers surrounding him, their loud voices echoing through the old house. The sound of hammers and saws filled the air, drowning out the silence he used to share with Elaine and the ever-arrogant Misty. And, Coby was certain, Elaine would also agree that the old house was better with him out of the picture. His mind drifted back to the previous evening, the memories now distant and hazy.

There was a persistent annoyance that plagued him throughout the entire journey. And now, finally, he knew what it was the distinctive scent of Elaine's alluring perfume. A delicate floral fragrance that always lingered when she went out with her lover. She openly admitted to an affair, and Coby wondered which one of his friends it could be. For some reason, the name Niall Preston shot into his mind, and the premonition sent an icy shiver down his spine.

"You sneaky little bugger," Coby whispered, his breath forming a cloud in the chilly air. His head shook involuntarily, as if trying to physically dislodge the mental image of Elaine and Niall entangled in a lover's embrace. Slowly, the memory flooded back to him, enveloping him like a thick fog.

"Yes!" he exclaimed, his eyes widening as realisation struck him like a bolt of lightning. One late night, as he waited for Niall at the dimly lit bar, the scent of that same perfume wafted towards him, mixing with the faint aroma of alcohol and stale cigarette smoke.

Chapter Two

Coby's anticipation grew as he neared the entrance, and he could feel a tingling sensation spreading through his veins. The two lion head sculptures, carved with intricate detail, stood proudly beside the towering wooden doors of the grand entrance. The faint scent of age wafted from the rusty knocker, a testament to the manor's long history. He had heard whispers of the manor's enigmatic past, of ethereal apparitions that roamed the halls and spectral voices that reverberated in the stillness of night. But his insatiable curiosity pushed him forward, undeterred. Holding his breath, he pressed against the freshly painted arch-shaped doors, feeling the coolness of the wood against his fingertips. The creak of the rusty hinges pierced the silence, casting an eerie echo down the empty hallway.

Within the walls of Elm Brook Manor, secrets whispered in the corridors, hidden in the nooks and crannies of its majestic architecture. The manor's opulence was undeniable, with ornate chandeliers casting dancing patterns of light and sweeping staircases that seemed to beckon him further. But it carried an air of mystery that captivated all who dared to enter.

With each step, the aged floorboards groaned, their timeworn voices urging him to delve deeper into the mysteries that lay ahead. The manor seemed to possess a life of its own, its history interwoven with the very essence of Serenity Falls.

A wave of nostalgia washed over Coby, as though he had walked these familiar paths in a previous life. The portraits adorning the walls appeared to come alive, their eyes following his every move. The echoes of laughter and tears seemed to linger in the air, as if the spirits of the past were still present. He could sense their presence, a tingling sensation at the back of his neck. However, he couldn't accurately determine their exact number. Only time would reveal the truth. While exploring the space, he caught fleeting glimpses of their elusive forms. Their shadows swiftly disappeared behind bookshelves, doors, and into dusty cupboards. They trailed behind him, their curiosity ignited by his unfamiliar arrival. Their existence was so palpable that he could feel their whispers brushing against the back of his neck, causing goosebumps to rise and a knowing smile to dance on his lips. Continuing his exploration, he meticulously examined every nook and cranny, searching for the places where their presence felt strongest. Little did they know, he was well aware of their presence and could sense them with every fibre of his being. Their hushed whispers penetrated deep into his bones, creating an indescribable sensation within him.

He stumbled upon a dusty library, the scent of aged paper and leather filling the air. The shelves, lined with books that had withstood the test of time, beckoned him closer. Running his fingers along the spines, he could almost hear the stories they held, patiently waiting to be unravelled.

After hours of meticulous exploration, Coby finally stumbled upon the perfect spot to set up his workstation. An old, desolate room greeted him, adorned with towering windows that provided a breathtaking panoramic view of the outside world. Sunlight streamed in, illuminating the room and casting dancing shadows on the worn floorboards. The air held a hint of mustiness, a testament to the room's abandonment.

Through the open doorway, he gazed upon the vast hallway adorned with two grand staircases that gracefully swept upward. The sight was awe-inspiring, a testament to the stately home's former glory. From this vantage point, he knew he could catch a glimpse of anyone who dared to approach from any direction.

However, a sense of disappointment washed over him as he realised that his new office was in the west wing, where maintenance work was still ongoing. Undeterred, he enlisted the help of a window washer, who diligently aided him in transporting his desk inside. With determination, he carried the rest of his meager belongings himself.

Opting for a modest, small bedroom on the lower level, he marvelled at the furnishings left behind by the previous owners. They had lovingly adorned the entire manor house. The bedroom stood as a silent testament to their hurried departure, with only the faint echoes of their footsteps lingering in the air. But white sheets draped over the furniture had preserved them from the ravages of time and dust. As he removed the sheets, he could almost smell the faint scent of history, mingled with a touch of nostalgia.

Rumours about the former owners' mysterious disappearance swirled through the air, shrouding the estate in an air of intrigue. The most plausible explanation, whispered amongst the townsfolk, was that they fled because of the eerie whispers of haunting spirits that seemed to linger in the air. But questions continued to haunt him: Why had they abandoned their cherished possessions and never come back? It was this enigmatic puzzle that fuelled Coby's irresistible urge to purchase the estate. To uncover the truth hidden within its walls. Drawing upon his past experiences as Mister Jones, he was determined to embark on a journey of discovery once again.

With a crystal-clear double Scotch whisky by his side, the rich amber liquid shimmering in the soft light, Coby powered up his sleek silver laptop. He plugged in the password and connected to the new wireless internet, feeling an immediate sense of relief wash over him. Finally, he could catch up with his work undisturbed, free from the constant hindrance of Elaine's incessant chatter and Misty's distracting presence.

His publisher had been nagging him for a sample of his work, a looming deadline that had been hanging over his head. Yet somehow, he always managed to find an excuse, a way to postpone it. Deep down, he knew that something significant was on the horizon, a momentous event waiting to unfold.

Bringing up a vivid map of Serenity Falls on his screen, the vibrant colours and intricate details filling his vision. Coby familiarised himself with the layout of the town, the various shops and establishments that lined the streets. The liquor store conveniently nestled beside the old-fashioned barbershop, their close proximity catching his attention.

His eyes skimmed the map, tracing the intricate pathways, until he spotted it – the local pub, aptly named the Stag's Head Inn. The sight of the name sent a ripple of anticipation through his body, his stomach growling in response. Glancing at his watch, he realised that there was still ample time to visit the pub. A chance to indulge before his fiftieth birthday arrived. An occasion he had no intention of spending alone.

Before he left, he felt a surge of determination as he carefully crafted a questionnaire, eager to address his most burning inquiries. The clickety-clack of the keyboard echoing in the room. It would serve as his excuse to strike up conversations with the strangers at the pub, a way to gather valuable information. After all, pubs were renowned for being a treasure trove of local knowledge. A hub where the residents shared their secrets and insider tips. They would surely have the inside knowledge to guide him to exactly what he required.

In the peaceful Serenity Falls, the Stag's Head Inn stood as more than just a pub. It embodied a sense of community, radiating warmth and camaraderie amidst the rugged surroundings. Its weathered stone structure, adorned with glowing windows, exuded a humble charm. The lively melody of a fiddle resonated through the air, enveloping Coby in the joyful sounds of traditional Celtic tunes. The enchanting strains of a classical Scottish lullaby called to him, drawing him closer to the quaint pub's entrance.

Underneath the wooden sign of the Stag's Head Inn, a symbol of the noble animal that has roamed these lands since time immemorial, Coby stepped into a world steeped in tradition and camaraderie. The stag, revered in local lore for its wisdom and strength, seemed to cast a protective aura over the inn and its patrons, making it a haven amidst the rugged beauty of Serenity Falls. The burning peat in the fireplace mingled with the aroma of hearty food being prepared in the back, creating a comforting olfactory symphony. Laughter and animated conversations filled the room, forging a joyful connection among the patrons. Local residents and weary travellers alike gathered around worn wooden tables, their faces bathed in the soft glow of antique lamps.

The fiddle player, a talented musician with nimble fingers, continued to serenade the crowd. The enchanting melodies carried the weight of tradition and the echoes of distant lands. Coby found himself captivated by the music, transported to a world where time stood still, and worries melted away.

Behind the bar, the skilled publican poured generous measures of whisky, his practiced hand conveying a warm hospitality. His eyes crinkled with a friendly smile as he engaged in pleasant banter with his customers. In one corner, a group savoured plates of traditional Scottish fare – haggis, neeps, and tatties – providing nourishment and comfort against the chilly night. A distinguished gentleman, his greying hair matching the hue of his immaculate white suit, sat solitary at a table. His polished top hat rested on the chair beside him. The ominous gleam in his eyes exuded an aura of superiority. His lips, forever poised in a subtle, enigmatic grin, hinted at a wealth of knowledge.

Coby's eyes scanned the room, and a smile spread across his face as he spotted an inviting empty chair. Hastening to the bar, he settled into the welcoming seat. Taking in his surroundings, he assessed the potential for connections. One peculiar observation stood out – the absence of a dartboard. Furthermore, he noticed the lack of women, save for the buxom barmaid, whose vivacious presence enhanced the atmosphere. With her infectious laughter and playful interactions, she charmed and entertained the patrons. It became clear to Coby that this establishment was more than just a pub; it was a sanctuary, a haven where stories were shared, friendships were forged, and lasting memories were created.

He took pleasure in the silky smoothness of his whisky and relished the mouthwatering local delicacy – bangers and mash – as the lively conversations swirled around him, tickling his ears. The name Elm Brook seemed to be on everyone's lips, accompanied by the typical pub rumours surrounding the new owner. Amidst the chatter, a story caught his attention: the new owner, a Yank rockstar, had supposedly acquired the estate as a secret love nest for himself and his mistress. The rumours brought a mischievous smile to Coby's face. Although tempted to reveal himself, the delectable food held him in his seat, its flavours captivating him. He labelled the evening as a 'slop,' a term commonly used in the game of darts. Despite not hitting the target, he found solace in the delightful flavours of the food and the exquisite taste of the local whisky. Settling his bill with a generous tip, he firmly believed in leaving an impression as a good tipper. As he walked away that night, under the watchful gaze of the stag on the sign, Coby knew he would return. After all, he was understanding the wisdom of the stag – to observe, to adapt, to find strength in solitude. And above all, to enjoy the journey.

Chapter Three

With the avalanche of maintenance workers arriving, Coby embarked on a shopping spree, frantically grabbing items off the shelves. The absence of a refrigerator took skilful planning, but the anticipation of his online order arriving soon filled him with excitement. He visited the barber, Niamh, a young woman with a vibrant smile and the scent of freshly cut hair filling the air. There, amidst the buzz of conversation, he gained valuable information about his new town and its influential people. From the barber, he ventured to the liquor shop, the inviting aroma of aged whiskey greeting his senses. Then to the bustling grocery store, where the vibrant colours of fresh produce beckoned him. Finally, he reached the veggie market, its earthy scent mingling with the sounds of haggling and laughter.

To his surprise, nestled within the town, stood a charming little bakery named 'Sweet Serenity.' Inside, the warm fragrance of baked goods filled the air, and a friendly, sturdy lady behind the counter greeted him with contagious laughter, especially when money changed hands. Coby couldn't resist and ordered a mouthwatering chocolate birthday cake.

Returning home, he unloaded his shopping bags, feeling the weight of the items in his hands. The window washer, always reliable, assisted him as usual. His presence brought a sense of calm and reassurance to the task. They carried everything to the oversized kitchen, which had only one appliance – a rusty old kettle sitting on the gas hob.

Wasting no time, Coby hurried to his office, the click of his footsteps echoing in the empty hallway. He settled in front of his computer, the blank screen staring back at him, its glow casting a pale light on his face. With a deep sigh, he rested his fingers on the keyboard, feeling the cool touch of the keys beneath them. A moment of hesitation passed before he wrote, the soft tapping of the keys filling the silence. 'The early days at Serenity Falls,' he typed, the words forming a visual image on the screen.

His mind kept drifting to Elaine as he wrote, her presence lingering in his thoughts like a vivid memory. He couldn't help but recall her connection with Misty, her loyal companion. Now, however, Coby couldn't escape the image of her and Niall Preston, her lover, entangled in his mind. The memory of shaking Niall's hand after winning a darts game against their opponents sent a pang of bitterness through him. The thought of that very hand caressing Elaine's body, their passionate moments together, sent a chilling shiver down his spine.

Suddenly, a loud clatter from above startled him, jolting him out of his contemplative state. The sound reverberated through the room, breaking his concentration. A furrow formed on his brow as he assumed it was a maintenance worker dropping a hammer, their presence a constant reminder of the repairs needed in his new home.

The air abruptly grew colder, sending a shiver down Coby's spine. He knew what was coming and braced himself. His heart raced with anticipation, yet he refused to look away from his screen. Suddenly, an ethereal figure materialised before him, her monochrome image slowly fading into view like a gentle mist. Her lips formed a tight line, and her fingers twitched by her side, aching for connection. The vibrant, dark curls cascaded freely down her exposed shoulders, pulsating with life that mirrored her spirited nature. Each movement of her hair created a graceful symphony of waves, adding a touch of untamed elegance to her persona. Her bangs, perfectly straight and precise, framed her face like a carefully crafted portrait, drawing attention to her delicate features.

Overwhelmed by her captivating allure, Coby's lips parted in awe, yet he restrained himself, not wanting to startle her. She stood there, her sorrowful gaze fixed on him. The urge to meet her eyes consumed him, but he fought it with all his might. Her attire harmoniously blended elegance with practicality. Clad in a fitted bodice of muted tones, its high collar and long sleeves paid homage to the modest fashion of the era. A wide belt, crafted from dark leather, cinched her waist, contrasting beautifully with the soft hue of her dress. The skirt, a cascade of fabric adorned with a rich tartan pattern, swirled gracefully around her ankles. Her leather boots, worn and weathered, whispered secrets of the countless miles they had journeyed.

Coby's fingers danced across the keyboard, magnetically drawn to its touch. The rhythmic clacking filled the air, as if composing a symphony of words. With swift precision, he captured the ethereal beauty of the young creature before him, his fingers flying across the keys. He had christened her the 'dark angel,' her name still unknown. Pausing, he stole a glance at her, his eyes distant and longing. Her brow furrowed with curiosity, and she rose on her tiptoes, her presence captivating.

The room seemed to buzz with an electric charge, as if the very air around him crackled with energy. A sudden realisation struck him like a crashing wave – she had never seen a computer. The sleek, modern device intrigued her, its silvery form sparking her curiosity. Inspiration surged through him, a powerful force. Tilting the laptop screen, he framed his face in the camera app and took a picture. Sending it to the printer, he watched as it whirred to life, slowly producing a printed image. The apparition darted towards the printer, her eyes fixed on the paper, wide-eyed with awe. Her parted lips revealed her sense of wonder. Unfazed, Coby continued typing, knowing the image would captivate her. Sneaking a glance at her, he saw the amazement lighting up her once sombre face.

But amidst the fervour of his creative surge, a sudden thump shattered the atmosphere, jolting Coby from his trance. His head snapped towards the sound, his eyes narrowing as he spotted the fallen candlestick. A knowing smile tugged at his lips, a hint of mischief dancing in his eyes. He had sensed her presence all along, an invisible force observing his every move. With unwavering confidence, Coby met the apparition's gaze, his voice filled with conviction. "I know you're there," he declared, the words carrying a weight of certainty.

The apparition's jaw dropped, and a gasp escaped her lips, whispering like a hiss. She retreated into the shadows, fading away like a wisp of smoke. Coby's lips curled into a mischievous smile, his eyes gleaming with a sinister twinkle. He knew she had only slipped away from the view of people, leaving behind an empty space.

"See you later," he sang, his voice taking on a high, lilting tone. He rubbed his hands together, relishing in the anticipation of what was to come. Silence filled the room as the air grew still, interrupted only by the rhythmic tapping of his keyboard. The words flowed effortlessly from his mind to the screen, each keystroke resonating with a sense of purpose. His fingertips held a newfound power, a testament to his abilities. His heart raced in sync with his thoughts, the adrenaline surging through his veins. A bead of sweat formed on his brow, a testament to the intensity of his inspiration.

Without hesitation, Coby swiftly poured himself a generous serving of smooth, amber-hued whisky. The rich aroma of the golden elixir wafted up, enticing his senses. It was a moment of triumph, the culmination of his investment in this place finally paying off.

With his vast experience and a track record of success in dealing with apparitions, Coby pondered his encounter with the enigmatic 'dark angel.' As contemplation filled his mind, he cast a thoughtful gaze outside. And there, once again, he caught sight of the chubby ginger-haired boy who had been surreptitiously observing him through the windows ever since his arrival.

Startled, the boy emerged from his hiding place behind the thick, overgrown thicket and swiftly darted into the safety of the surrounding woods. Coby furrowed his brow in deep concentration and resolved to inquire about the enigmatic boy.

A sudden chill permeated the air, causing a shiver to run down his spine. Even after all these years in the trade, the mere presence of these apparitions never failed to give him goosebumps.

From the ethereal shroud of shadows, the dark angel materialised before him, accompanied by two equally captivating, otherworldly beings. Their monochrome appearances took Coby's breath away, the absence of vibrant colours only adding to their mystique. As his fingers hovered over the keyboard, he felt an unexplainable pull, as if he was being drawn into an enigmatic trance.

'A tableau of women,' he began typing, his words flowing effortlessly as he described them. 'Each one unique, radiating an allure that is distinctly her own. Amidst the whisper of silk and the gentle rustle of wool, the glimmer of jewellery and the vibrant hues of fabric, their individuality shines through.'

Pausing for a moment to appreciate the awe reflected on their ethereal faces, Coby continued his description. 'One woman's dress, adorned with delicate lace, showcases her refined tastes, the intricate patterns a testament to her elegance. The other embraces boldness, her tartan skirt a riot of shades that speak of her vibrant personality. And then there is the dark angel, standing out like their personal Florence Nightingale. Their dresses bear a striking resemblance, hinting at an era between the late nineteenth and early twentieth century.'

Once again, Coby paused to take in the mesmerising sight before him. The ethereal trinity stood poised, their unique hairstyles catching his attention. Coby's eyes focused on the dark angel's hair, which cascaded in stunning curls that framed her face with an air of mystery. The second apparition's preference for extravagant updos, decorated with ribbons and flowers, stood in stark contrast to the third apparition's neatly braided tresses. The practicality of the latter hinted at an attitude that left no room for frivolity.

Filling the air, the rhythmic clacking of the keyboard created a symphony of sound. The dark angel leaned in close, her delicate hands cupping her companion's ears as she whispered softly. Even though Coby knew they were watching him, her gestures implied that she thought he could also hear her. In unison, the ethereal trinity rose on their tiptoes, their graceful movements reminiscent of ballerinas preparing for an elegant pirouette.

Understanding the message she had conveyed to them, Coby tilted the screen, framing his face. Their eyes widened in astonishment as the camera flash illuminated his features. He swiftly sent the captured image to the printer, which whirred into action, filling the air with a gentle hum. The ethereal beings hurried to the printer, their whispered gasps creating an ethereal melody. They studied his likeness, their faces filled with a mixture of wide-eyed excitement and reverential awe.

Their swift return to their positions was a display of seamless grace, akin to a synchronised performance. They struck elegant and graceful poses, their bodies poised like works of art waiting to be immortalised. The mere sight of them ignited a fiery desire within Coby. The gleam in his eyes testified to their otherworldly divinity. An impish chuckle escaped his lips, and he felt compelled to explain himself.

"I cannot take your picture," he said, his voice filled with regret. "A camera works by capturing light, and you, my ethereal friends, do not reflect light." With their hands still on their hips from their previous poses, they scowled at him, urging him to capture their likenesses. Yielding to their requests, Coby turned his laptop so that the camera faced them and took a picture.

Yet, when he sent the image to the printer, it only displayed the entrance, with the grand hallway behind them, failing to capture their ethereal elegance. Disappointment replaced their once-beautiful expressions, and they retreated into the shadows, disappearing like a wisp of smoke.

And that is when Coby noticed her, sitting all by herself on the cold marble staircase. A fourth apparition, not as enchanting as her counterparts, but still intriguing, somewhat sinister. The soft glow of the chandeliers illuminated her face, casting a warm, ethereal glow upon her delicate features.

With her dark hair cascading down her shoulders, she wore plain clothes that seemed to blend into the background, as if she belonged to a different time. The stark contrast between her companions' pristine footwear and her worn, tattered shoes was hard to ignore. Coby couldn't help but feel that she belonged to a different social class, which explained her solitude.

Enchanted, he slowly rose from his chair, the floorboards creaking beneath his weight, and approached her cautiously, his steps measured and deliberate. The air carried a faint scent of old books and forgotten memories. Her fingers moved with grace, tracing intricate patterns on the stairs that were covered in a fine layer of dust. Her lips parted slightly, and a gentle hum resonated from her throat, like a distant echo from a forgotten realm. The melody, a hauntingly familiar Celtic tune, weaved its way through the air, whispering tales of ancient lore and timeless love.

Vibrations from the melody created a symphony of emotions rippling through the silent hallway. The sound of the weary maintenance workers' labours blended into the background, drowned out by the peacefulness of the surroundings. The melody acted as a magnet, drawing Coby closer, and he absentmindedly reached out, his fingers hovering just below her face. As if trying to touch the ephemeral beauty of the moment.

But as if startled by his presence, the harmonious serenade abruptly ceased. With a gasp, she rushed up the stairs, her footsteps so quiet they could be mistaken for a whisper. With a quick, mysterious gaze over her shoulder, she receded into the veil of shadows, disappearing like a wisp of fog before the brilliance of the rising sun.

Coby christened her 'the siren,' mesmerised by her ethereal voice that danced through the air like a delicate melody. Hurrying back to his office, he sought solace in his plush leather chair, pouring and swiftly downing a neat whisky to calm his racing thoughts. The room exuded a sense of comfort, with the scent of aged wood mingling with the subtle aroma of leather. With the memory of their encounter still vivid in his mind, he painstakingly captured every detail, from the way she looked to the heavenly timbre of her voice.

With each keystroke, the temperature in the room seemed to drop, sending a chilling sensation down his back. A hauntingly alluring fragrance, reminiscent of vintage perfume, wafted through the room. The intoxicating blend of pepper, lotus flowers, and a hint of saffron hinted at the presence of the enigmatic dark angel. Ignoring the urge to glance behind him, he succumbed to her magnetic pull, her presence hanging over him like an enchanting force. His fingers hovered over the keyboard, poised to continue expanding on the allure of 'the siren's call,' the enchanting serenade still echoing in his memory.

However, a surge of inspiration crashed over him like a powerful tidal wave. Saving the document as 'the siren,' he opened a new blank page, selecting a large font size. The word 'Hello' sprawled across the page, its size nearly consuming the entire length. He waited, his gaze fixated on the blinking cursor, hoping for a response. His fingers rested on the keys, and he typed out the words 'My name is Coby McTavish.' The intoxicating fragrance of her perfume grew stronger, filling the air around him, amplifying her presence. Yet, the cursor continued its relentless blinking, urging him into stillness. 'What is your name?' he typed, leaning back in anticipation. Time stretched on, but no response came. Though her scent lingered in the air, and he knew she was there, nothing happened.

He rose from his worn leather chair, the creaking sound echoing through the dimly lit room. With deliberate movements, he poured a generous amount of amber liquid into a crystal glass, the scent of aged whisky filling the air. His eyes were fixed on the frosted window, where the unmistakable silhouette of a red-headed figure caught his attention, peering through the tangled thicket. A sly smile tugged at the corners of his lips, and he shuffled back into the comforting embrace of his well-worn chair.

Lost in thought, he absentmindedly stared at the flickering screen, his fingers tightly gripping the glass. Just as he took a long, throat-burning sip, Coby's throat convulsed, causing a wet cough to erupt. The sound filled with the struggle to breathe. Startled, he glanced down at the screen, where garbled letters formed an undeniable word beneath his name. Tilting his head from side to side, he tried to decipher the ethereal message: 'Sine.' Recognition sparked in his eyes, assuming she had observed him typing earlier. With a simple response, he typed, 'Siren?' because he believed she enjoyed the sound of it. But nothing happened.

Disappointment settled over him like a heavy cloud, causing his brow to furrow in confusion. Starting anew, he greeted her with a simple 'hello' and inquired about her name. This time, the dark angel's response came swiftly, the word 'Sine' appearing on the screen. An urge to shout at the screen welled up within him, but he restrained himself, knowing better. Coby's gaze intensified, fixated on the monotonous blinking cursor as he recalled every detail he had learned about these apparitions. Their numbers, hairstyles, shoes, and clothing.

Suddenly, a revelation struck him like a bolt of lightning from the heavens. He swiftly typed the word 'Sine' into the search engine, discovering its mathematical function. Correcting himself, he added 'Sine, Gaelic name meaning,' into the search bar. And there it was, right in front of him. Sine, Gaelic for Jane. Excitement coursed through his trembling fingers as he typed, 'Hello Jane, I am so very happy to meet you.'

In a fleeting moment, Jane, the enigmatic dark angel, materialised before him, her radiant smile illuminating the room, before vanishing like a wisp of smoke.

With a triumphant smile, Coby reached into the top drawer and pulled out his sleek silver Dictaphone, its cool metallic surface glinting under the soft glow of the desk lamp. With his finger on the record button, he felt a rush of anticipation, causing his arms to break out in goosebumps. The room filled with the sound of his voice, capturing the heartfelt message. "Contact made," he announced, excitement lacing his words. He meticulously recorded the sights, sounds, and smells around him, as well as his strategic plans to tame the ethereal trinity.

Chapter Four

That night, Coby's dreams transported him to a realm of enchantment. In his mind's eye, he watched Jane gracefully dance, her body moving with a serpentine fluidity that wove an intricate tapestry of desires. The ethereal music accompanied her every movement, filling the air with a symphony of enchanting melodies. The dream unfolded, and Coby could almost sense the delicate scent of lotus flowers, blending with the intoxicating fragrance of passion. Suddenly, the loud thuds and thumps reverberated through the house, jolting him awake. The sounds of the maintenance workers reverberated through the walls, filling the space with clanging and banging.

Cradling a steaming cup of bitter black coffee in one hand and a crispy, buttery rowie in the other, Coby meandered through the grand hallway towards his sanctuary – his office. His footsteps echoed against the marble floors, creating a rhythmic symphony that reverberated through the expansive hall. He paused momentarily at the grand staircase, his eyes scanning the surroundings on a quest for 'the siren.' She was absent, yet her sweet, entrancing serenade echoed within the chambers of his mind, a symphony of ethereal notes that haunted his senses.

Humming the alluring tune under his breath, he quickened his pace, drawn towards his office by the enticing aroma of ancient perfume. The moment he stepped inside, a cold sensation crept down his spine, and the room emitted an uncanny sense of serenity. His eyes couldn't resist being pulled towards his laptop, where the spectral trio had gathered, creating an eerie luminescence with their ethereal images.

Their eyes remained fixated on the screen, completely engrossed in the captivating digital spectacle. The room held its breath, shrouded in a cloak of anticipation.

"Good morning, ladies!" Coby greeted, his voice brimming with enthusiasm. Their eyes remained glued to the screen, oblivious to his greeting, that was swallowed by the silence. Jane's hands moved fluidly, like a serpent dancing to the beat of an unseen drum. Her voice, a soft hiss, was reminiscent of a gentle summer breeze whispering through the leaves. With unwavering focus, their eyes stayed locked on the screen, immersing themselves in the content. Coby's curiosity flared up, pulling him into their circle. His eyes locked on the empty screen, eagerly awaiting any supernatural activity.

He listened attentively, entranced by the captivating melody that flowed from Jane's lips. Each word she uttered was akin to the soft rustle of heather swaying across the highlands, a sound that resonated with the very essence of the earth beneath his feet. The consonants twisted and turned, mirroring the gnarled branches of an ancient oak, while the vowels flowed like the ceaseless rhythm of a babbling brook. It was as if he could discern the whisper of the sea in every 's', the caw of a raven in every 'r', and the sigh of the wind in every 'h'. The words, like threads in a tapestry, carried the weight of time and bore witness to the collective heritage, creating a sense of unity beyond his comprehension.

Coby sank into the plush, supple embrace of his worn leather chair, revelling in its comforting touch against his skin. He reached out and pressed the power button on his sleek laptop, its soft hum filling the air. As a blank document appeared on the screen, he eagerly began typing the word 'Hello Sine,' watching the letters sprawl across the white canvas.

Raising his gaze with anticipation, Coby hoped for a flicker of recognition, a sign that he wasn't alone. Instead, he found himself greeted by the inquisitive gazes of the ethereal trinity, their eyes twinkling with otherworldly wisdom. Their presence lingered in the centre of the room, almost tangible. They struck poses, their bodies poised and ready, waiting for him to capture their likeness.

Amusement bubbled within him, a joyous chortle escaping his lips as his face illuminated with inspiration. Urgency propelled him out of his office, navigating the labyrinthine corridors until he reached his bedroom. Returning moments later, he cradled a full-length mirror in his hands, its cool surface glinting in the light. Carefully, he positioned it against the back of his desk, facing the trio.

With animated gestures, Coby signalled that something magical was about to unfold. "Now look," he exclaimed, pointing at the mirror. Stepping in front of it, he watched as his image reflected from head to toe before stepping back with a sense of satisfaction. The spectral threesome gasped, their whispers reminiscent of hisses, as they mimicked his movements. However, they did not see their own reflections. Instead, they drew their gaze to the grand hallway behind them, which mirrored what they saw within the looking glass.

Suddenly, the mirror caught a bright ray of sunlight, transforming into a radiant beacon that rivalled the gleaming windscreen of a passing car. Curiosity piqued, Coby stole a furtive glance outside, spotting a sleek charcoal Range Rover ascending the steep driveway. He furrowed his brow, pondering the identity of its occupant.

The magnificent spectral trinity followed his gaze, their faces etched with awe, as the car came to a halt near the front doorway. Slowly, the door swung open, revealing a man with meticulously groomed silver hair neatly combed back. His bright red tie, flawlessly aligned, added a vibrant splash of colour against his crisp, white suit. A matching white top hat rested on the chair beside him, while a slick black walking stick with a polished brass knob completed his ensemble.

With the grace and poise of a debonair on a first date, the man placed the hat atop his head, its brim casting a shadow over his piercing grey eyes. Retrieving his walking stick, he firmly closed the car door and ascended the staircase leading to the entrance, exuding an air of authority that demanded attention.

Coby exchanged a fleeting gaze with the apparitions, his wide eyes brimming with unspoken inquiries. Their piercing stares remained fixed on the grey-haired man, their eyes betraying a profound sense of dread.

"Sassenach!" Jane exclaimed, the word slipping out like a venomous whisper, reverberating against the cold stone walls. A shrill, ear-piercing shriek sliced through the air, only to fade away as the spectres retreated into the enveloping shroud of shadows, vanishing like a phantom ship in the mist. An eerie silence settled in the wake of their departure, leaving Coby lost in his contemplation, his gaze drifting into the distance.

A thunderous knock on the door shattered Coby's thoughts, jolting him back to the present. He hurried across the grand hallway, the sound of his footsteps echoing against the polished marble floors, and swung open the imposing wooden doors. The man in the immaculate white suit lifted his hat upon seeing Coby, his voice filled with a mix of surprise and familiarity.

"By Jove," the visitor exclaimed, "If it isn't the esteemed Mister Jones himself." He extended a weathered hand, adorned with gleaming golden rings.

"Coby McTavish," Coby corrected him, his voice tinged with a hint of frostiness as he clasped the man's chilly hand in his own.

"Sinclair, Alistair Sinclair's the name. The pleasure is all mine," replied the grey-eyed man, a sinister glimmer dancing in his eyes, his words laced with a chilling undertone. Coby's gaze was fixated on the golden wedge that adorned the space where Alistair should have had a tooth. "Where are my manners?" Coby asked, gesturing for him to enter.

Alistair's cane tapped rhythmically against the marble floor as he followed Coby to his office. Coby could feel his pulse quicken, the rhythmic thumping echoing in his ears. The flickering fireplace cast dancing shadows on the walls, filling the room with an eerie ambience that mirrored the unease in Coby's heart. Coby made a beeline for the sideboard, the scent of aged Scottish whisky wafting through the air, filling the room with its rich aroma. He reached for his prized bottle, its label bearing the marks of time, offering a drink to his guest. Alistair paused momentarily, his eyes drawn to his own reflection in the mirror leaning against the desk. His face contorted into a smug smirk as he adjusted his tie.

With a resounding double tap of his cane, he remarked, "Ah, such exquisite taste," his head nodding in approval of the fine liquor collection, the rich aroma filling the room.

Coby poured two generous shots into crystal glasses, their weight and clarity a testament to their craftsmanship, and motioned for Alistair to take a seat, his hand trembling ever so slightly. A sense of unease settled in the pit of Coby's stomach, causing it to churn with anxiety. He felt suffocated by the palpable tension in the atmosphere, which grew more oppressive. The room felt suffocatingly small, as it seemed to close in around him. Coby forced himself to take a deep breath, to steady his nerves as he prepared to uncover the truth behind Alistair Sinclair's unexpected visit.

But despite the physical discomfort, Coby maintained a facade of composure. His face remained stoic, betraying none of the turmoil raging within him. He knew he had to tread carefully, to navigate the treacherous waters that lay ahead. Alistair Sinclair may have appeared friendly on the surface, but there was something about him, something ominous and unsettling that Coby couldn't quite put his finger on.

"So, what brings you to my humble abode?" Coby asked, his voice trembling with a palpable quiver.

Alistair fixed Coby with a penetrating stare, his eyes as cold and grey as a winter storm over the North Sea. They concealed more secrets than a crypt. He raised his glass, the clink of ice against crystal resonating through the room, and took a mouthful of the golden elixir. With a sip, he put on a fake charming smile, his teeth dazzling in the low lighting.

"It is quite simple, you see," he began, his voice smooth and calculated. "What an extraordinary turn of events has led our paths to cross."

With a furrowed brow, Coby challenged Alistair's gaze, his eyes narrowing with suspicion. "What events?" he asked, his tone tinged with curiosity.

"Your amazing stories!" exclaimed Alistair with a chuckle, the sound echoing in the room. "What else?"

The air seemed to grow colder, as if an icy breeze had swept through the room. Coby felt a shiver run down his spine, his skin prickling with goosebumps. The intoxicating scent of saffron wafted through the air, hinting at Jane's presence. Her spectral image materialised, flickering in and out of sight, like a ghostly flame. Her gaze, full of scorn, locked onto Coby, her eyes ablaze with fury. With a long, bony finger, she pointed menacingly at Alistair Sinclair. Coby shifted uncomfortably, feeling trapped between two worlds. His eyes nervously shifting between the flickering image of Jane and Alistair, who sat there with his trademark smug smirk.

"And how did my stories make our paths cross?" Coby asked, his voice trembling with nervous energy.

"You are a man of many questions, Mister McTavish," Alistair replied, a mischievous glint in his eyes.

"Writer's habit," Coby defended, his tone sharp and frosty.

A pensive silence hung in the air, the only sound being the faint crackling of the fireplace. Alistair tore his gaze away from Coby and took in the breathtaking scenery, his eyes wandering to the ornate mirror leaning against the desk. It seemed to fascinate him, as if he found something captivating within its depths. Perhaps it was his own reflection that intrigued him, Coby wondered. Jane's apparition had vanished into the shroud of shadows, leaving a lingering sense of unease in the room. Coby contemplated her actions, determined to find a way to ask her about it. Without warning, Alistair forcefully slammed his empty glass onto Coby's desk, the resounding thud startling Coby. Without a word, he abruptly stood and headed for the door. Coby leaped up from his chair and trailed behind him, his heart racing as he swung open the imposing wooden doors.

"Beware the shadows, my dear scribe," said Alistair with a lift of his hat, his words carried away by the whispering wind. He stepped outside and slid into his car. The engine roared to life and echoed against the distant sounds of the maintenance workers.

Coby felt a knot tighten in his stomach as he watched Alistair's car fade into the distance. The weight of unanswered questions hung heavy in the air, causing his pulse to quicken and his palms to grow clammy. The encounter had left him with a mix of anticipation and apprehension, his mind swirling with possibilities.

He turned back towards the room, and the deafening silence swallowed him whole. The once welcoming ambiance now felt tinged with an eerie unease. Coby's footsteps echoed through the silence as he returned to his desk, his fingers tracing the edges of the ornate mirror that had captivated Alistair Sinclair moments before.

The mirror's surface reflected a distorted image of Coby, his face etched with a furrowed brow and eyes filled with determination. He wondered if there was a connection between Jane's sudden disappearance and Alistair's cryptic warning. It was as if the room itself held secrets waiting to be unveiled, secrets that intertwined their lives in ways he couldn't yet comprehend.

With a deep breath, Coby gathered his thoughts and resolved to seek answers. He glanced at the empty glass that still bore the imprint of Alistair's forceful gesture, a reminder of the tension that had permeated the room. The intensity of the moment had left him momentarily shaken, but his writer's instinct pushed him forward, fuelling his determination.

Leaving the confines of his study, Coby ventured out into the cool morning air. The rising sun cast a soft glow over the estate, its ethereal light casting elongated shadows across the landscape. With each step he took, he couldn't shake the feeling that the forest was alive, whispering secrets that only it could understand.

The distant sounds of maintenance workers gradually receded, making way for the gentle symphony of leaves rustling in the wind and the occasional melodic chirp of a bird. Coby's steps quickened, his heart pounding with a mix of trepidation and curiosity. He needed to think, to untangle the truth behind Alistair's unexpected visit and the enigmatic connection it held to the secrets of the stately home.

The further he ventured into the woods, the stronger the nagging feeling grew – as if someone or something was silently observing his every step. Shadows danced at the corner of his vision, whispering secrets just beyond his reach. A chill ran down his spine, but he pressed on, determined to unravel the mysteries that entwined their lives.

The wind carried Alistair's warning to his ears once more, a haunting reminder of the dangers that lurked in the shadows. Coby's steps faltered for a moment, uncertainty gnawing at his resolve. But he shook off the fear, his writer's curiosity burning brighter than ever.

Beneath the watchful gaze of the sun, Coby forged ahead, his path illuminated by the glimmer of uncertainty and the flickering hope of discovery. The shadows may have been lurking, but he was ready to face them head-on, armed with nothing but his words and the burning desire to understand the intricacies of their intertwined fates.

Chapter Five

The irresistible allure of the hidden mystery that lay in front of him captivated Coby. A charming stone cottage nestled among the tranquil forest, emanating a rustic elegance with its sturdy stone walls, wooden windows, and shingled roof. The vibrant yellow and green foliage created a stark contrast, enhancing the cottage's beauty. He noticed a cobblestone pathway leading to the entrance, its surface worn smooth from years of use. In the foreground, a gentle brook flowed gracefully, its melodic whispers adding to the peaceful atmosphere of this picturesque setting. Coby's attention shifted to the ginger-headed boy, who he had previously seen concealing himself in the thickets. Now, the boy was busy hanging laundry on the line, creating a sense of domestic tranquillity in the air.

Since he quit smoking, Coby always carried chewing gum in his pocket. His fingers, searching in his pocket, made contact with the sleek wrapper of a piece of chewing gum. He carefully unwrapped it, the crinkling sound filling the air, and placed it in his mouth. The enigmatic charm of the cottage tugged at him, beckoning him forward. With each step, the soft earth beneath his shoes emitted a satisfying crunch. A sudden snap, the sound of a twig breaking under his shoe shattered the silence. Startled, the redheaded boy pivoted, his wide eyes meeting his gaze, filled with surprise and intrigue. The boy gasped, his breath catching in his throat, as he watched Coby approaching.

"Hey laddie," Coby said, his voice warm and friendly, "what's your name?"

"G'afternoon, sir, my name is Ewan Drummond, Mister MctT...

McTa..." stammered the boy. Ewan Drummond, a young lad whose spirit is as vast as the boundless skies. His plump cheeks, speckled with a constellation of freckles, glowed with the warmth of his ever-present smile. His eyes, mirrors of the emerald highlands, sparkled with a lively curiosity that reflects the wild beauty of his homeland.

"McTavish," said Coby, helping the young lad out, his voice laced with kindness, "where's your parents at, then?" he asked, his tone brimming with concern. He reached into his pocket once again, the crinkle of the wrapper filling the air, and pulled out another piece of chewing gum. The scent of mint wafted through the air, a refreshing aroma that mingled with the earthy smell of the surrounding countryside.

Ewan Drummond couldn't tear his wide eyes away from the chewing gum in Coby's hand. His gaze was almost tangible, a palpable force filled with longing and anticipation. His rosy, freckled cheeks flush a deeper hue, an adorable testament to his unabashed desire for the delight.

"Want some chuddy?" asked Coby, his words accompanied by the rustling sound of the chewing gum packet being opened. He pulled out a few pieces, the crinkling sound growing louder, and offered it to the young boy. Ewan moved impressively fast for his size, his small hand reaching out and snatching the chewing gum from Coby's palm. He wasted no time shoving it into his mouth, the sound of chewing filling the air.

"Mum's feeding them workers over at your house," Ewan said, his words muffled by the mouthful of chewing gum, pointing towards the elegant country house.

Coby smirked, his eyes gleaming with curiosity. "So your mum's a baker then?" he asked, his tone laced with intrigue.

"Naw!" exclaimed the young lad, his voice brimming with pride. "She bakes for the money. Ever since you bought this place, she's been out of a job."

"Ewan!" cried a female voice behind Coby, making him jump. He turned around and saw a graceful woman approaching, adorned in a flour-dusted apron, cradling a basket of freshly baked goods. With each step, her dress rustled softly, and a faint floral perfume wafted through the air.

She tugged at the hem of her dress to avoid collecting dirt, revealing a glimpse of her slender, toned legs. With each step, her dark, silky hair flowed behind her, dancing gracefully in the air. Her sapphire eyes, like the deep ocean, pierced Coby's soul with their depth and intensity.

"What did I tell you about talking to strangers?" she snapped at her son, her voice tinged with concern. She took his hand firmly and swiftly dragged him into the cosy cottage.

"I'm so sorry, Missus Drummond, but—" Coby explained, but she cut him off, slamming the door shut in his face. Standing there, he could feel his heart pounding in his chest, a rapid rhythm that matched his racing thoughts. The abruptness of the door closing on him left him feeling a mix of disappointment and confusion. He could feel a flush of embarrassment creeping up his neck, his cheeks turning a shade of crimson.

Coby took a deep breath, trying to steady himself, as he glanced at the closed door. His eyes, once gleaming with curiosity, now reflected a hint of sadness. The intensity of her reaction took him by surprise, and a wave of unease washed over him.

His gaze shifted, and he found himself fixated on the sprawling manor in the distance. Its imposing presence seemed to mock him, a reminder of the stark contrast between their lives. Coby couldn't help but feel a tinge of guilt, knowing that his wealth had inadvertently affected Ewan's mother, leaving her without a job. The weight of his privilege settled heavily on his shoulders, causing a knot of guilt to form in his stomach.

He took a step back, distancing himself from the closed door. He could still taste the disappointment lingering on his tongue, the offer of friendship abruptly denied. The sound of his own breath seemed louder now, filling the silence left by the absence of conversation. He couldn't shake the image of Ewan's prideful proclamation about his mother's baking, a small glimmer of their resilience despite the hardships. He noticed the workers perched on the scaffolding, enjoying their delectable pastries.

With a sigh, Coby turned away, his footsteps carrying him towards home. The crinkling sound of the chewing gum packet resumed as he absentmindedly chewed on a piece, the act providing a slight comfort amidst the lingering emotions. His mind replayed the encounter, trying to make sense of it all, while a part of him hoped for a chance to explain and bridge the divide that had unexpectedly formed.

The essence of his sanctuary, once alluring, now waned. Coby poured a generous measure of amber whisky, its rich aroma wafting through the air, calming his frayed nerves. Disheartened, he sank into the plush leather chair, its softness embracing him. His gaze fixed upon the empty computer screen, the cursor blinking ominously, as if taunting him. Suddenly, a single word on the document captured his attention. 'Ruith' sprawled across the white canvas. He squinted, furrowing his brow in deep contemplation, the screen casting an eerie blue glow upon his face. Initially dismissing it as a typing error, he considered the possibility that 'ruith' might have been intended as 'Ruth.' However, he couldn't help but recall that Jane, who went by 'Sine' in Gaelic, was the only ghost he had ever met who was tech-savvy. A spark of inspiration illuminated his features. With nimble fingers dancing across the keyboard, he sought the Gaelic meaning of 'ruith.' And there it was, 'ruith' meant "run" in Gaelic.

The weight of the word's meaning hit Coby like a sucker punch, leaving him breathless. His heart rate quickened, causing a slight tremor in his hands as he continued to type furiously. Filled with a mix of excitement and curiosity, he acted with renewed vigour, leaving behind the discouragement that had burdened him mere moments before.

The amber whisky in his glass sat untouched, forgotten for the time being. The rich aroma still hung in the air, but it was now overpowered by the electric atmosphere that filled the room. Coby's anticipation grew, making the softness of the leather chair feel suffocating instead of comforting.

He kept his gaze fixed on the screen, but now determination filled his eyes instead of despair. The cursor, once taunting, now seemed to beckon him forward, urging him to uncover the truth behind the mysterious word. The eerie blue glow cast upon his face highlighted the intensity of his focus, accentuating the furrowed brow that deepened with each passing moment.

Coby's research consumed him, and he could physically feel the tension building in his shoulders and the knot forming in his stomach. Beads of sweat formed on his forehead, glistening under the soft glow of the computer screen. His breathing became shallow and rapid, matching the rhythm of his racing thoughts. The anticipation coursing through his body made his muscles coil with tension.

With each keystroke, he felt a surge of energy, as if he was running alongside the meaning of 'ruith' itself. The combination of the whisky's aroma, the plushness of the leather chair, and the blue glow of the screen seemed to fade into the background as he became consumed by his quest for answers.

In that moment, his sanctuary transformed once again, filling with the vibrant colours of a new dawn. It was no longer a place of fading allure, but a space filled with possibility and intrigue. The physical world around him became a mere backdrop as he delved deeper into the realm of words and meanings, his frayed nerves now replaced by a renewed sense of purpose.

His fingers danced across the keyboard, his eyes fixed on the screen in front of him. The faint hum of his computer filled the room as he tirelessly searched for any trace of Elm Brook Manor. He tried different combinations of words, hoping for a breakthrough.

But his efforts were in vain. The search results yielded nothing but real estate listings, mocking him with their past offers. Frustration washed over him like a wave, but he refused to give up.

A novel idea sparked in his mind, and he swiftly typed in 'Serenity Falls.' The screen transformed, displaying a detailed map of the quaint town. His eyes eagerly scanned the digital representation, desperate to find a clue. And there it was – the library, the municipal office, and the Stag's Head Inn.

He reached for his glass, the smooth weight of it comforting in his hand. The scent of whisky wafted up to his nose, a warm and inviting aroma. Memories came rushing back as he took a sip, instantly transporting him to a different time. His tongue tingled with emotion as he savoured the golden elixir.

The room around him faded away as the past engulfed his senses. Before him, the inn appeared, brimming with laughter and the tempting aroma of homemade food. The sensation of being transported back in time engulfed him, rendering the present as nothing more than an illusion.

In his mind, he heard the whispers of the townspeople, their gossip swirling in the air. They spoke of the arrival of the new owner of the haunted estate. The realisation hit him like a thunderbolt, and excitement filled his voice. He exclaimed, "That's it. Hemlock Manor!"

The man's voice echoed in his head, a haunting reminder of the past. He couldn't help but wonder why they called it Hemlock Manor instead of Elm Brook Manor, the name he knew and had acquired. The curiosity consumed him, driving him to uncover the secrets hidden within the walls of his home.

The thoughts raced through his mind, causing an involuntary shiver and a ripple of goosebumps on his skin. A chill crept into the room, despite the warmth of the whiskey in his hand. His heart raced, pounding in his chest like a drum, its rhythm matching the frenzy of his thoughts.

The room grew dim, as if the light itself was being swallowed by the shadows that danced along the walls. They seemed to hold secrets of their own, whispering tales of forgotten lore. The air carried a faint scent, a mixture of old books and the mustiness of memories long past.

An ethereal voice, delicate and haunting, floated through the air like a melody. It was a Celtic tune, familiar yet distant, weaving its way through the room. The melody gently whispered tales of bygone eras and eternal romance. Coby felt a surge of emotions, like a symphony, as the vibrations from the melody filled the room. He knew it was 'the siren', serenading him, urging him forward, guiding him with an invisible hand.

The air grew heavy with anticipation, making it difficult to breathe. Each inhale was a struggle, as if the very atmosphere conspired against him, trying to keep the truth hidden. With a deep breath, Coby steadied himself, his fingers trembling slightly as he reached for the keyboard once more. The soft glow of the monitor bathed his face in an ethereal light, casting long shadows across his determined expression. He typed in the words 'Hemlock Manor,' his hands moving with a mix of anticipation and trepidation.

His eyes scanned the page, eagerly searching for any mention of the mysterious estate among the search results. But to his dismay, the results were once again disappointing. It appeared Hemlock Manor was just as elusive as Elm Brook Manor, a name lost in the annals of time. The only details he discovered were that a British peer purchased the estate as his family's 'Hunting Box'. Game sport enthusiasts flocked to the stately home, drawn by its reputation for offering exceptional hunting experiences – high-quality pheasant and partridge shoots, duck flighting, wildfowling, and deer hunting. These thrilling activities had become a popular trend among aristocrats since the early nineteenth century.

However, these magnificent estates were more than mere playgrounds for the wealthy; they stood as symbols of status and power. They were tangible representations of wealth and influence, granting their owners an unofficial membership into British nobility, a privilege only reserved for the world's elite.

A surge of frustration threatened to overwhelm him, but he refused to let it consume him. He was determined to uncover the truth, to peel back the layers of history and reveal the secrets that lay hidden within the walls of his home. The weight of the past pressed upon him, urging him forward, as if the spirits of those who had come before were guiding him on this quest.

With renewed determination, he took another sip of whiskey, feeling the warmth spread through his body, emboldening him to continue. The memories of the past, though hazy and fragmented, fuelled his curiosity, urging him to delve deeper into the enigma that surrounded Hemlock Manor.

Lost in his thoughts, he wondered about the whispers of the townspeople, their hushed conversations echoing in his mind. What had they known that he didn't? Why had they chosen to name it Hemlock Manor instead of Elm Brook Manor? The mystery consumed him, its relentless grip driving him to uncover the truth.

With a resolute glint in his eyes, he sprang to his feet, snatched his Dictaphone from the table, and hastily made his way to the waiting Volvo. The powerful engine roared to life, filling the air with a symphony of raw energy, as he accelerated down the steep driveway, stirring up a cloud of dust. The wind whipped through his hair, carrying the scent of freshly cut grass and the promise of adventure. Determination surged through his veins, propelling him forward towards the unknown, fuelled by an unwavering thirst to unveil the enigmas concealed within the very walls of his abode.

Chapter Six

Coby effortlessly discovered an unoccupied parking spot just steps away from the bustling town centre. Immersed in the tranquil ambiance of the quaint village, he could hear the cobblestone streets whispering tales of bygone eras beneath his feet. The air was heavy with the intoxicating fragrance of petrichor, transporting him to a nostalgic realm. This unseen veil enveloped the charming houses and the undulating landscape, adding to the allure of the surroundings.

Nestled within the rustic allure of this town, he stumbled upon the heart of its history – the library. A weathered stone edifice, it stood as a silent sentinel, safeguarding the tales of the town and its inhabitants. The arched wooden door creaked open, revealing an awe-inspiring sight of rows upon rows of timeworn books, their spines aligned like disciplined soldiers.

For a fleeting moment, Coby stood frozen, absorbing the scene and finding his bearings. In a secluded corner, he spotted a section dedicated to archival records beckoning him towards its allure. Amidst the musty scent of aged parchment and faded ink, the legacy of his estate lay dormant. A microfiche reader, affectionately dubbed 'fish' by Coby, patiently awaited his exploration. This antiquated contraption, a relic of a forgotten era, held the key to unlocking the enigmatic secrets of his property.

Coby carefully fed the reel of microfilm to the 'fish', mesmerised by the soft hum that resonated through the room. The projected images flickered on the screen, ethereal echoes of the past, each document a vital piece yearning to be connected in the grand tapestry of his estate's history.

His heart raced with anticipation as he navigated through the image, the warm glow from the reader casting elongated shadows that danced around the room. With every click, every rotation of the film reel, he inched closer to the elusive truth. The atmosphere crackled with electric energy, the tranquillity occasionally interrupted by the rhythmic ticking of the ancient grandfather clock and the gentle rustle of turning pages.

Desperately, Coby's eyes scanned the illuminated images on the screen, his heart pounding in anticipation. His fingers trembled as he clicked through the images, his gaze darting from one to another, searching for any clue, any hint of Hemlock Manor.

Suddenly, like a flash of lightning, his eyes caught something buried amidst the sea of images. It was as if a secret message had been subtly embedded, reminiscent of subliminal advertising. With a quick, almost frantic movement, he hastily flipped back to the previous image, his heart racing.

And there it was, in bold letters that seemed to jump off the screen, sending chills down his spine. The headline read: "LORD LUCAS VANISHES: NANNY FOUND MURDERED." The words, though faded, still held a haunting power, as if they were screaming out the chilling tale of a sinister past.

Filled with a mix of excitement and trepidation, Coby's gaze darted around the screen, devouring every line, every word, in his quest for answers. In his elation, he couldn't contain himself and exclaimed, "I found it!" Disrupting the hushed atmosphere of the library, drawing disapproving murmurs and shushing from the other patrons. But Coby's unwavering focus remained, his eyes fixed on the screen, determined to uncover the secrets hidden within.

The article provided a chilling glimpse into the horrific events that unfolded on that fateful November day. Sandra River, a dedicated nanny to the Lucas family, was tragically found brutally bludgeoned to death in the basement of the grand Hemlock Manor. The murder weapon, a lead pipe, was left behind at the scene, serving as a silent and ominous testament to the brutal violence that had occurred.

The prime suspect in this heinous crime was none other than Lord Lucas himself, who mysteriously disappeared following the incident. His sudden vanishing only added to the speculation and scandal surrounding the case.

Despite extensive manhunts and investigations, Lord Lucas was never located, leaving behind a trail of unanswered questions and a mystery that would captivate the nation for decades to come.

Coby's body tensed as he took in the grim details, and a chilly feeling of dread consumed him. The echoes of the past seemed to seep from the yellowed pages, filling the dimly lit room with a palpable tension. The air was heavy with the smell of the microfilm reader, its dusty aroma blending with a delicate touch of mildew. In the image on the screen, the flickering shadows playfully danced across the peeling wallpaper, creating eerie shapes that appeared to whisper secrets. The tale of Lord Lucas's alleged crime and subsequent disappearance was more than just a chilling chapter in Hemlock Manor's history – it was a haunting spectre that continued to cast a long, dark shadow over its present.

Richard John Biggans, famously known as Lord Lucas, captivated Coby with his story. As a writer, he meticulously absorbed the intricate details, contemplating the idea of writing about it one day. Little did he expect that fate would lead him to acquire Lord Lucas's opulent estate. As he sat there, he felt an undeniable pull towards the place, a mysterious and enigmatic force that now made sense to him. Deep in thought, he pondered over what this force was and why it had chosen him.

Lost in his musings, Coby beckoned the overeager librarian, who hurriedly approached him. He inquired about the availability of modern newspapers, yearning to uncover more about his newly gained property. The librarian eagerly shared all the newspapers they had, neatly stacking them on a wooden table. He sank into the rigid seat, the unyielding surface pressing against his back, as he rummaged through the stack of papers, the sound of crinkling filling the air.

His eyes scanned each headline and article with fervour, seeking any mention of 'Elm Brook Manor.' The anticipation grew within him, his senses heightened. With sudden astonishment, his eyes widened as he stumbled upon a headline that read 'ECHOES OF THE PAST: THE UNSOLVED MYSTERY OF ELM BROOK MANOR.' Trembling with excitement, he eagerly devoured every word, the paper quivering slightly in his shaky hands.

Within the hallowed halls of Elm Brook Manor, a chilling tale unfolds, once the grand residence of an esteemed lineage, now standing as a monument to a haunting past. Its opulent rooms echo with secrets that refuse to be silenced.

Left to grapple with the shadows of a history he never asked for, Mr Coby McTavish, the Manor's present owner, inherits more than just the sprawling estate and its ancient walls. It is a legacy steeped in mystery, scandal, and a crime that has left an indelible mark on the Manor's reputation.

Decades ago, the gruesome discovery of a body in the Manor's dank and gloomy basement sent shockwaves through the local community. The victim was none other than the family's devoted nanny, a woman whose life was cruelly snuffed out in the prime of her youth. Her lifeless form had been found sprawled on the cold stone floor, a grim testament to the violence she had endured.

The circumstances surrounding her death remained shrouded in mystery, creating a dark and unsettling atmosphere at Elm Brook Manor. Rumours of a brutal murder circulated, leaving a lingering pall over the entire estate. Despite extensive investigations, no one was ever held accountable for the crime. As time passed, the case grew cold, but the tragic end of the nanny continued to haunt the manor, serving as a grim reminder of the violent act that had occurred within its walls.

Coby's eyes remained fixated on the article, his gaze unwavering even after he had devoured every word. The soft murmur of his voice escaped his lips as he muttered to himself, his breath mingling with the scent of aged paper.

"And so the whole town knows," he whispered. Frustration surged through him, causing his hand to slam the newspaper down on the table with a thunderous thud. The sudden impact reverberated through the air, making him flinch at the unexpected noise. He stole a fleeting gaze around him, feeling the weight of disapproving stares from the surrounding people. Their piercing gazes bore into him, silently conveying their message – "this is a library." His face twisted into a grimace as he absorbed the scornful looks, his heart sinking with a mix of embarrassment and regret.

Seeking solace, he stole a glance at his watch, the subtle ticking sound permeating his ears, a constant reminder of the fleeting time. He gasped, a surge of realisation flooding his senses, as he knew he had immersed himself in the library's vast realm for over five hours, tirelessly conducting his research. The relentless gnawing in his stomach intensified, a desperate plea for nourishment. A seed of an idea took root in his mind, fuelling his determination. With purposeful strides, he embarked on his journey towards the exit, eagerly anticipating a visit to the renowned Stag's Head Inn. The tantalising aroma of a neatly poured whisky and the comforting familiarity of their cherished in-house delicacy, bangers and mash, beckoned him. However, before indulging in his well-deserved treat, he had one swift detour to make, a fleeting pause on his path.

Cradling a dartboard and four dart sets, Coby confidently strolled into the Stag's Head Inn. The bustling crowd paid no attention as he entered. A cacophony enveloped the air as the football game roared on, captivating the local fans. Coby's arrival with the dartboard caught the attention of the swamped publican. Coby glanced briefly at the television, catching the intense rivalry between Aberdeen and Inverness Caledonian Thistle. The spectators' voices blended together harmoniously, punctuated by the piercing shrill of the referee's whistle. The pub erupted in a cacophony of boos and a barrage of insults aimed at the referee. Nearby, a man's exclamation of "Offside my arse!" earned him a round of applause and jovial back pats from his friends.

Navigating through the crowded bar, Coby carefully set the dartboard and dart sets aside and ordered a perfectly poured double Scotch and a plate of mouthwatering bangers and mash. The voluptuous barmaid strutted around, her infectious laughter filling the space as she served delectable food to the eager patrons. Coby's plan was working. During halftime, curious glances were cast at the secluded dartboard, leading to a clever plan being devised to mount it on the wall. The air came alive with the clinking of beer glasses and daring challenges. Coby quickly finished his meal and enthusiastically joined in on the fun. He teamed up with a towering silver-bearded man, aptly nicknamed 'bullseye.' Together, they achieved victory after victory, earning rounds of free drinks. Coby graciously declined the drinks, offering them to the losing teams, subtly winning their respect and trust. Soon, he earned the moniker 'Bogey' and proudly wore his new bar name.

Many players were bestowed with comical nicknames in recognition of their awe-inspiring achievements. Coby particularly enjoyed the sound of a man dubbed 'Lipstick' and another called

'Robinhood.' As the barman announced "last rounds," he had forged many friendships and vowed to return regularly. Moreover, he had gathered valuable information about the notorious Mister Sinclair and his mob linked to a mysterious goldmine. With newfound determination, Coby felt a fire ignite within him, filling him with a surge of energy and propelling him forward into the day's challenges.

Chapter Seven

The moon, shining brightly, cast a silvery glow over the grand estate, illuminating its majestic presence. In the darkness of the night, Coby ascended the staircase until he halted abruptly before the ominous front door. The rusted knocker, worn and irritating, caught his attention, grating on his nerves.

His gaze fixated on a paper plate that held an assortment of tempting baked treats. His eyes darted around, searching for any sign of the enigmatic person who had left him the gift. With a puzzled expression, he searched the area, the absence of any human presence adding to his confusion. He raised an eyebrow and muttered, "What the...?" before cautiously bringing the plate to his nose. The tantalising aroma of the pastries filled the air, making his mouth water. Cradling the plate, he fumbled with the lock, causing the front door to creak ominously as it swung open, revealing the grand hallway.

He held his breath; the anticipation gripping him as he cautiously stepped inside, his footsteps echoing on the cold marble floors. Amidst the array of treats, it was the white envelope, carefully tucked under a baked pie, that caught his attention. With eager anticipation, he opened it, unfolding the neatly written letter. The words, written in elegant cursive handwriting, brought a twinkle of joy to his eyes.

"Dear Mister McTavish. Please accept my apologies for my rudeness yesterday. Little did I know you were the new proprietor. Accept this gift as a token of my regret. Kindest regards, Gracie Drummond."

"So your name is Gracie, eh?" Coby exclaimed, his voice filled with astonishment. A wave of relief washed over him as he tucked the letter into his pocket, ready to set out on his journey.

He hurried outside, following the same path he had taken yesterday, traversing through the dark woods. The occasional hoot of an owl interrupted the stillness of the night, its haunting calls reverberating through the air. The sound of his own breathing and the crisp snap of twigs under his feet filled his ears.

In the distance, a faint light beckoned him forward, guiding his way. His heart raced with excitement, urging him to quicken his pace. The constant flow of the nearby brook provided a soothing background melody for his journey.

He spotted white smoke billowing out of a chimney, illuminated by the soft moonlight. A path leading up to the house beside the brook came to his mind, but in the darkness, he struggled to find it. Desperately seeking an entrance, he felt the cool night air brush against his skin as he searched for a door at the back of the house.

He rounded the corner and approached the quaint cottage, feeling the warmth emanating from its cosy windows. He hugged the wall, feeling its rough texture guide him into the enveloping darkness. A dim light seeped through a nearby window, casting a delicate shadow on the ground before him. The image tugged at his curiosity, pulling him forward, and he paused, his breath catching in his throat. Gracie stood inside what appeared to be her bedroom, steam filling the air, billowing out from an adjacent door. With a graceful movement, she pulled her jumper over her head, revealing her dark curls cascading over her supple porcelain breasts.

Coby stood frozen, his eyes fixated on the mesmerising sight before him, his heart racing. With each breath he took, a misty cloud materialised in the crisp, chilly air. The way she elegantly wiggled her hips and effortlessly slipped out of her jeans sent a jolt through Coby's heart. She gracefully let the delicate lace thong slip from her body, revealing her bare skin. Coby's eyes widened in disbelief.

Gracie's discarded garments pooled around her bare feet. With a gentle shake of her head, her hair fell loose, framing her slender figure. The soft light delicately caressed her smooth skin, imparting a subtle radiance. Coby's eyes involuntarily traced her form, captivated by the neatly trimmed, dark mystique – a tantalising secret nestled in the cradle of femininity. His excitement grew, causing his pants to become snug, a clear sign of his intense desire. His fingers twitched, yearning to touch her velvety skin, to cup her breasts in his hands. She moved with a dancer's grace, her silhouette casting long shadows on the humble walls of their home. He watched intently, feeling a powerful longing tugging at his heart, a desire for something elusive.

In the stillness of the night, the air carried a sense of tranquillity, undisturbed by any sound. But suddenly, a voice pierced through the silence, youthful yet tinged with a hint of mockery.

"So you're checking out my mom, eh?" The words lingered in the crisp evening air, their echo sending a jolt of surprise through Coby.

Startled, Coby spun around, his heart racing in his chest. He froze to the spot, his body immobilised as if time had come to a standstill. Illuminated by the gentle glow of the moon, Ewan stood in the clearing, a mischievous smile dancing upon his lips. The moonlight bathed his face, revealing the playful mask he wore. His eyes, filled with an undeniable vibrancy and curiosity, sparkled under the moon's gentle gaze, reflecting a spirit untouched by the harsh realities of their world.

Around Ewan's slender neck, a worn leather catapult hung, its rough texture a testament to years of use. It dangled there, a tangible symbol of his defiance and resourcefulness, catching the glimmer of moonlight. In his dirt-streaked arms, he cradled two lifeless coneys, their once vibrant fur now matted and dull. The silence hung heavy in the air, broken only by the distant hoot of an owl and the soft rustle of leaves beneath Ewan's worn boots. Ewan stooped down and laid their limp bodies on the cold, hard ground.

The earth, damp from recent rain, seemed to absorb their fading warmth, leaving only a faint musky scent in its wake. It mingled with the crisp, cool air that swept across the highlands, carrying the fragrance of damp soil and distant pine trees.

When Coby locked eyes with Ewan, his heart raced with anticipation, the intensity of the moment palpable. He couldn't help but feel a surge of admiration for the young lad, his heart swelling with respect. Despite their harsh circumstances, Ewan remained undaunted, his spirit unyielding, like the untamed winds that danced through the rugged landscape.

"Evening Mr McTavish." Exclaimed the young lad, a sinister glint playing in his eyes.

Coby's lips parted, attempting to explain himself, but the words eluded him, lost in the air like smoke. In the stillness, a soft creak sliced through the silence, shattering the tranquillity.

"Ewan, who are you speaking to in the eerie darkness?" Gracie Drummond's voice, velvety and alluring, flowed through the air like a sip of smooth whisky. Coby turned, his eyes drawn to her presence in the kitchen doorway, a towel enveloping her enticing figure. With a graceful movement, she adjusted the towel, accentuating her sensual curves, captivating his attention.

"Oh, hello Mr McTavish!" she exclaimed, her voice filled with surprise, caught off guard by the presence of a stranger. "Please pardon my rudeness and come inside," she invited, her voice carrying a touch of warmth. Invited by her kind gesture, he entered the kitchen, feeling the warmth and intimacy surround him.

The flickering flames in the fireplace cast a warm glow, illuminating the room with a comforting ambiance. A large pot simmered on the black cast-iron stove, filling the air with the fragrant aroma of boiling vegetables, teasing his senses.

Young Ewan gently laid the lifeless bodies of his prized coneys down on the cold, slate surface in the dimly lit scullery. The faint aroma of iron and earth hung in the air as he sauntered into the warm, cosy kitchen. With a soft pull, he retrieved a gleaming boning knife from a drawer, its sharp blade catching the glint of death under the soft glow of the kitchen light. As he effortlessly busied himself, the rhythmic sound of the knife slicing through flesh filled the room, accompanied by his faint humming of a merry Celtic melody. The gentle melody danced through the air, caressing Coby's ears and filling him with a sense of tranquillity as he settled into a worn, creaky chair at a small round table.

A collection of framed photographs adorned the wall above the countertop, capturing a series of joyous moments. Each image emitted an overwhelming sense of warmth and happiness. His gaze meandered over the cherished memories, and he couldn't help but notice a raven-haired man standing tall and protective next to Gracie. The man's hazel eyes held a spark of pride, and a knowing smile played on his lips, igniting a pang of jealousy within Coby's heart. A constellation of smiles stretched across all the images, capturing the essence of the moments frozen in time. Startled, Coby's attention snapped back to the present as Gracie's voice sliced through the silence.

"Giles," she said, her words surprising him. "My late husband." Gracie entered, her tone legs elegantly showcased by the woollen jumper she was wearing. In a moment of reflex, Coby leaped up from his chair, steadying himself against the table.

"I'm sorry, Mrs Drummond," he quickly apologised, averting his gaze. She scoffed dismissively, waving his apology off with a graceful gesture.

"Please call me Gracie," she said, effortlessly pouring whisky into two small glasses as if it were a familiar routine. Coby's eyes scanned her body, fixating on her graceful legs, imprinting the image in his memory. Her legs were a study in elegance and strength, sculpted like marble by a master craftsman, seeming to stretch endlessly towards the sky.

Placing his glass before him, she met his eager gaze, and he quickly took a sip, relishing the warm, smoky flavour that danced on his tongue.

"Coby's the name," he said, his voice tinged with both nervousness and intrigue, extending his hand in greeting. Gracie's slender fingers curled around his palm, their touch electrifying, sending a jolt of desire coursing through his veins. Their hands, locked briefly, intertwined in a soothing embrace, before reluctantly letting go. Her fingertips glided off his palms, leaving a delicate and affectionate touch that lingered, teasing his senses and leaving him yearning for more.

"Giles was the Factor," Gracie said, her eyes shimmering with his memories, the soft glow of nostalgia reflecting in her gaze. Coby was at a loss for words, but his gentle, affectionate look conveyed his response. She nodded at him, her eyes filled with understanding, and continued speaking.

"A hunting accident, right here in this desolate place." Her finger pointed in a specific direction, as if tracing the path where her husband met his untimely end.

"I am so sorry for your loss, Gracie—" he attempted to console her, his voice tinged with empathy. But she cut him off, her words rushing out before his courage faltered.

"I still remember the haunting sound of the gunshot that ended his life," she revealed, her hands instinctively covering her ears as if trying to block out the echo that lingered in her memory. A tremor ran through her fingers, and tears welled up in her eyes, threatening to spill over. Seeking solace, she took a long sip of her whisky, its smoky aroma filling the air.

"It was such a tragic and peculiar event," she continued, her voice quivering with emotion, her delicate touch wiping away the tears that escaped. "Anyway, what brings you to my humble abode?"

Gracie locked her dreamy gaze onto Coby's, her eyes filled with curiosity and a hint of longing. Coby cleared his throat, his voice cracking as he struggled to find the right words in response to the unexpected question.

"I came to express my gratitude for your kindness and to extend an invitation to my birthday celebration," he responded, his words carrying a mix of appreciation and anticipation. Ewan sauntered into the cosy kitchen, his footsteps echoing softly on the worn linoleum floor. A melodic tune escaped his lips, filling the air with an enchanting melody. With a graceful motion, he dropped the diced cubes of freshly cut coneys into the simmering pot, the sizzle and aroma of the cooking meat wafting through the room.

Effortlessly, he reached for the assortment of fragrant herbs and spices, their vibrant colours dancing in the dim light. As he added them to the pot, the enticing scent intensified, mingling with the warm aroma of the simmering stew. With a wooden spoon, he stirred the stew, the rhythmic motion creating a gentle symphony of clinks against the pot.

Gracie sat in silence, her eyes fixed on Ewan, as if she anxiously awaited his departure. The weight of anticipation hung heavy in the air, causing Coby to almost repeat his question. Just as he was about to speak, Gracie leaped up, her movements swift yet graceful, and refilled their glasses with the golden elixir of their choice. The liquid glugged into the glasses, breaking the silence with a soothing sound.

Gracie's lips curled into a thin smile as she delicately placed Coby's glass in his hand. He raised his glass in a gesture of gratitude, the clink of glass against glass echoing softly. Taking an eager sip, the smooth liquid danced on his tongue, a symphony of flavours that brought a smile to his face.

While Ewan busied himself with the stewing pot, Gracie turned her attention to Coby. Her eyes held a dreamy gaze, captivating him, and her thin smile held a hint of mischief. Time seemed to slow as they exchanged glances, a subtle connection forming between them.

Finally, Ewan gathered a roll of pie dough and flour. With expertise, he spread the dough on the floured surface, the gentle sound of the dough gliding against the rolling pin echoing in the scullery.

"Why would you invite a hapless girl like me to your birthday party?" Gracie asked, her voice tinged with a shy chuckle. A soft red hue crept up her cheeks, adding a touch of colour to her delicate features.

The question caught Coby off guard, momentarily rendering him speechless. He searched for a plausible excuse, his mind racing.

He finally replied, his voice filled with sincerity, "I am new in town and don't know many people. I have invited anyone I know, including my new friends from the pub." Recognition flickered in Gracie's eyes at the mention of the word 'pub', but she quickly composed herself. A soft giggle escaped her lips as she teasingly said, "I would love to be there and meet your silly mates."

The sound of her laughter was like a sweet melody, stirring a whirlwind of emotions within Coby. His lips curled into a bright smile, his heart feeling lighter.

He responded with genuine gratitude, "Thank you. And I would be very happy to have you and young Ewan around." With the last sip of his drink, a surge of excitement coursed through his veins, causing a tingling sensation.

Rushing towards the kitchen door, he felt the chill of the cool metal handle against his fingertips, causing a slight shiver to run through him. Stepping out into the chilly night breeze, he could feel it seeping through his clothes. The earthy scent of autumn leaves filled the air, gently reminding him of the changing season.

Chapter Eight

Coby jolted awake, his heart racing. He fixated on the mesmerising patterns of the ceiling, the intricate designs dancing before his eyes. Memories of his intense dreams flooded back, particularly the one featuring Elaine, their bodies intertwined in a passionate embrace. Weary and sluggish, he dragged his exhausted body out of bed and stepped into the shower. A string of expletives escaped his lips as the icy water hit his skin, sending a shockwave through his senses. Recalling the maintenance manager's words about the arrival of plumbers today, he felt an unexpected surge of energy. In the kitchen, he ignited the gas hob and stove, filling the room with warmth. He heated the pie Gracie had given him and brewed a pot of strong, bitter coffee, its aroma enveloping the air.

Entering his office, Coby unfolded the blueprint of the manor house, a sprawling document that covered his entire desk. Squinting, he scrutinised the intricate details, searching for the ominous basement. Tracing his finger along the blueprint, he located the path from his office to the entrance. Equipped with a powerful torch, he embarked on his journey, navigating the dimly lit corridor. Finally, he reached the end, revealing a concealed trapdoor underneath a carpet. The aged, weathered wooden door protested with a creak as it swung open, revealing a narrow, winding staircase that echoed with the faint sound of footsteps from years gone by.

The unmistakable scent of earth accompanied his descent into the basement, creating a cool and musty atmosphere. Upon reaching the bottom, he flicked on his flashlight, illuminating the vast expanse of the basement beneath the manor. On the wall beside him, an ancient switch awaited his touch. He flipped it, causing the old ceiling bulbs to flicker to life, casting an eerie, dim glow against the ancient walls. A labyrinth of rooms and corridors sprawled out before him, filled with forgotten relics and echoes of bygone eras. History's weight was burdensome, with each brick and cobweb-laden beam holding untold stories.

The ethereal beauty of an ancient Celtic lullaby filled the air, guiding him forward with its mesmerising notes. A shiver ran down his spine as he carefully took each step, his fingers tracing the weathered texture of the old walls. Coby stumbled into the buttery, a small room with a staircase leading up to the back of the kitchen. His eyes widened with surprise and he let out a gasp as the apparition materialised before him. And there she was, 'the siren,' her melodic voice and enchanting presence drawing his attention, perched on the bottom step. Memories of the newspaper article bearing the name Lord Lucas flooded his mind, and he instantly recognised her. Whispers of her name escaped his lips, "Hello Sandra," his voice filled with a mix of reverence and wonder, as her intense grey eyes blazed like fiery pools, fixated on him. Her body jolted upwards, her hand thrusting forward with determination, directing her gaze towards a shadowy corner.

Coby's curiosity deepened as he followed her outstretched finger, noticing neatly grouped piles of sacks in different colours.

Making a promise, his eyes conveyed a sense of warmth and tenderness. "Sandra, I will find who did this to you. I always do."

Sandra's lips parted, and she hissed the word "pears" over and over, the sharpness of her tone sending a chill down his spine.

Coby's hand trembled as he shone his torch into the dimly lit corner and up the staircase, desperately hoping to uncover any significant clues. But to his dismay, he found nothing of importance. With each empty sack he rummaged through, his hopes of finding any clues dwindled. The scent of dust mingled with the musty air, filling his nostrils and adding to his growing frustration. He could feel the weight of disappointment settling upon his shoulders, threatening to crush his determination. However, he was resolute and unwilling to surrender. In the dimly lit buttery, silence shrouded its secrets, punctuated only by the soft exhale of his breath and the rapid thumping of his heart.

Defeated, Coby trudged back to his office, his shoulders sagging. A bone-chilling breeze swept through the room, sending shivers down his spine. With a whoosh, the ethereal trinity materialised, their ethereal forms casting haunting shadows on the wall. His heart raced, its beats echoing in his ears as the intensity of their penetrating eyes pierced through him. True to his expectations, they reappeared without explanation after the surprising visit from Alistair Sinclair. The memory of Alistair Sinclair, cold and gripping, sent shivers cascading down his spine, making his body shudder uncontrollably.

Determined to uncover the truth, Coby launched a full-scale digital assault on the Lucas family, offering an astonishing reward for any information that would lead to Sandra River's demise. He swiftly emailed his expert researcher, detailing everything he had learned and pleading for help, promising a generous bonus.

By some fortunate twist of fate, his editor called him, curious to know how his writing was going. Coby eagerly shared the details of his investigation, listing the facts he had uncovered. The editor's voice crackled with excitement as he eagerly announced the indefinite extension of the deadline for Coby's latest work. Relief flooded Coby's senses, and he reached for the bottle of Scotch, pouring himself a generous double, savouring the moment of triumph.

Sensing his relief, Jane moved closer, her breath escaping in a soft hiss as she whispered the word "pears" as a gentle reminder.

Coby's face suddenly lit up with recognition, and he snapped his fingers in realisation. "That's it!" he exclaimed, his voice filled with excitement.

Jane's lips curved into a knowing smile, adding to her ethereal beauty. Coby's mind raced, desperately trying to decipher the cryptic message. The word 'pears' echoed in his ears, lingering with a faint resonance. It held a weighty significance, like a missing puzzle piece that couldn't find its place in the larger picture.

With a determined resolve, Coby swiftly typed 'pears' into the search bar, but alas, it provided no meaningful connection to the Lucas family. Undeterred, he combined the word 'pear' with the name Richard John Biggans, yet still found himself empty-handed. Then, a sudden inspiration struck him. He merged the title of Lord Lucas with the word 'pear', and an astonishing discovery unfolded before his eyes. The search engine, in bold letters, crossed out 'pear' and replaced it with 'Showing results for Lord Lucas' peer', highlighting the prediction. Coby squinted his eyes, the crinkles in the corner revealing his mild irritation. As he perused the search results, the description below caught his attention. It read: 'The 6th Earl of Lucas, commonly known as Lord Lucas, was a British peer who...' Without hesitation, Coby clicked on the link, and in that very moment, realisation hit him like a bolt of lightning. "Pears means peeress!" he exclaimed, his voice filled with astonishment. 'Sandra mentioned his wife.' With his eyes locked on the screen, he leapt from his seat, a resounding "no!" escaping his lips as the shock settled in. Cupping his hands over his mouth to stifle his surprise, he struggled to process the newfound revelation.

He's heart pounded fiercely in his chest, its rhythmic thumping echoing in his ears. The surge of adrenaline raced through his veins like a powerful, rushing river, electrifying every fibre of his being. His senses, heightened to an almost painful degree, made every sound seem louder, every movement seem sharper.

The ethereal trio's flickering presence slowly vanished, leaving behind a lingering sense of mystery in the air. It felt as if they knew they had accomplished a monumental task, at least for the time being. As the room temperature returned to normal, a sense of calm washed over Coby, albeit briefly.

Coby's hands trembled as he kept his gaze fixed on the screen in front of him. The haunting display of search results sprawled across the screen, leaving him in awe. He knew he needed to gather himself, to summon the strength to delve further into the enigmatic world of Lord Lucas and his elusive peeress. However, as he stood there, his mind in turmoil, an unsettling feeling crept over him, whispering that he was on the brink of unearthing secrets that were better left buried.

Coby embarked on a relentless search, immersing himself in every detail he could find about Lady Lucas. He wanted to know everything about the Dowager Countess of Lucas, or Vanessa, as she had once been known. He delved into the tragic tale of her dying peacefully in her sleep, but it only led his investigation to a dead end filled with unanswered questions. But then, a glimmer of hope emerged when he stumbled upon the news that Scotland Yard had reopened the cold case, prompted by recent evidence concerning Lord Lucas. Astonishingly, people reported sightings of him, even in far-off

Australia, despite his legal declaration of death. Now Coby grappled with the idea of contacting Scotland Yard, although he knew it would likely result in an onslaught of futile questions.

Instead, he meticulously looked up the contact details of his associate at New Scotland Yard and composed a detailed email, outlining the reasons for his inquiry. Having done all he could, Coby was left with nothing but anticipation lingering in the air. While mentally going through his checklist of tasks, memories of his conversation with Gracie Drummond momentarily disrupted his thoughts. Glancing at his watch, he resolved to visit the library, seeking solace and answers within its hallowed walls.

The librarian, known for her warm and inviting demeanour, seemed distant and aloof, a stark contrast to the friendly woman Coby had met just yesterday. Her temper was short, and her movements elusive, creating an atmosphere that made him feel unwelcome. With a forceful thud, she slammed the stacks of newspapers onto the table; the sound echoing in the quiet library, and quickly retreated to her desk. Her mood soured, and a noticeable air of detachment surrounded her as Coby asked about any details on Giles Drummond.

Fingers swiftly sifting through the papers, Coby's eyes scanned the bold headings and detailed articles, searching for any mention of the elusive name 'Giles Drummond.' When his gaze finally settled on an article, a rush of relief flooded through him. The headline, bold and captivating, displayed the words, 'HIGHLAND TRAGEDY: GILES DRUMMOND MEETS FATAL END AMIDST AUTUMN'S RUT.' Eagerly, he delved into the article, dated October nine years ago, immersing himself in the vivid details it provided.

In the heart of the Scottish Highlands, a tragedy unfolded amidst the annual rut of the red deer stags, sending shockwaves through our tight-knit community. Giles Drummond, a respected local factor, was found lifeless amidst the heather-clad moorlands on Monday.

Drummond, known for his deep connection to the wild landscape and its creatures, met his untimely end during a time of natural spectacle and beauty. The stark contrast between the primal passion of the rut and the grim finality of death has left our community in a state of stunned disbelief.

The initial investigations suggest a tragic accident, an unfortunate casualty of the unpredictable wilderness that Drummond loved so deeply. However, as the misty Highlands mourns their fallen son, questions seep into the narrative like a chilling Highland wind. Does a darker truth lurk in the shadows of the glens, or was Drummond's death merely an accident?

As we bid farewell to Giles Drummond, we are reminded of the raw, unforgiving beauty of the Highlands – a place where life and death dance their eternal waltz. Our hearts go out to Gracie Drummond, who must now navigate the rugged terrain of grief while grappling with the enigma of her husband's death. The autumn leaves may fall, but the memory of Giles Drummond will remain as enduring as the mountains he called home.

Coby's heart clenched with a sharp pang of pity as he thought of Gracie Drummond. Carefully, he pulled out his phone from his pocket, its sleek screen catching the reflection of the bright overhead lights. He captured the article, and for a brief moment, the bright flash of the camera illuminated the worn wooden table.

However, his actions did not go unnoticed. The disapproving scoff that escaped the librarian's lips cut through the silence of the library, adding to the weight on Coby's heart. Her groan reverberated in the stillness, amplifying the sound of her hastening footsteps as she approached the table.

The librarian's eyes scanned the scattered newspapers, her disapproval clear in the way she furrowed her brow. With an air of authority, she gathered the papers in her arms, her movements swift and efficient. The anger that radiated from her was palpable, tangible in the way her gaze locked onto Coby's, her eyes burning with irritation.

Coby could feel the librarian's glare searing into him, intensifying the already heavy burden of pity he carried. It felt as though her anger had taken on a physical form, weighing him down and making it difficult to meet her gaze. His own eyes dropped to the floor, unable to bear the full force of her disapproval.

He stole a quick glance at his watch, feeling the pressure of time. The perfect moment had arrived to venture towards the Stag's Head Inn, where the aroma of a hearty pub lunch would envelop him. He imagined the cold lager, its condensation dripping down the glass. And, of course, the sound of darts hitting the board, the excitement lingering in the air.

When Coby stepped into the dimly lit pub, he immediately noticed a vibrant announcement of a darts match, which ignited a spark of excitement within him. The sight of the grand prize intensified his anticipation, but his enthusiasm quickly waned as he discovered that the prize money was merely a donation from Alistair Sinclair.

However, his excitement re-surged as he noticed a group of eager players huddled around the dartboard, their voices filled with animated chatter. As Coby hurriedly consumed his savoury shepherd's pie, the tantalising aroma of the dish mingled with the familiar scent of beer in the air. The cold pint glass felt cool against his palms as he cradled it, preparing himself for the upcoming game.

Placing his name on the board, Coby struck up a conversation with the fellow players, his eagerness palpable in his voice. With each interaction, he skilfully guided the discussion towards the topic he had in mind. What he uncovered only solidified his suspicions.

The players revealed that Giles Drummond, a man with a history as a union leader at a local silica sand mine, had secured the position of the estate's Factor. The mine had shut down, but a Japanese bottling company, desperate for the silica-rich sand, had provided the funding to reopen it, employing a workforce of two hundred. Despite everything, the workers decided to retain Giles as their union leader.

Enter Alistair Sinclair, who had acquired controlling shares in the mine and outsourced the workers, a decision that left them discontented and planning a strike. Giles Drummond, with his intricate knowledge of the situation, had overseen the strike and handled the complex details. However, his role extended beyond the mine. He also took charge of organising and overseeing hunting events at the estate.

It was this tangled web of connections that led the locals to suspect foul play in Giles Drummond's untimely demise. They believed that his death was no accident but a deliberate act, orchestrated to safeguard the mining company from substantial financial losses.

The aura surrounding Giles Drummond was palpable, a tangible fog of respect and admiration that clung to the very air he breathed. His presence was an unspoken command, a silent sermon preached from the pulpit of his own existence. The locals revered him, their eyes lighting up with a blend of awe and deference whenever his name graced their conversations.

But Gracie Drummond was the whispered secret, the forbidden

fruit in the Eden of their small town. The locals reacted to her name with apathetic shrugs, avoiding any eye contact, and a silence that echoed their indifference. Her name was an unspoken taboo, a haunting tale that circulated in hushed whispers.

When Coby dared to utter her name in the local bar, the barmaid responded with a scornful scoff. "Tart," she spat out, the word slicing through the air like a venomous dart. It struck Coby's ears with a force that left him reeling, a cruel echo that lingered in the caverns of his mind.

Suddenly, the puzzle pieces fell into place. Gracie's desperate attempts at securing employment, her humble endeavour selling homemade treats, the wolf whistles and lewd remarks from the maintenance staff – they all painted a picture of a woman grappling with adversity, a testament to her resilience in the face of societal judgment.

A cold, merciless grip tightened around Coby's stomach, sending chills down his spine. It was as if he could feel Gracie's pain, her desperation, mirrored in his own gut. A wave of remorse washed over him, filling him with a profound sense of empathy for Gracie and her son. The injustice of their situation was a bitter pill to swallow, a stark reminder of the harsh realities that lurked beneath the surface of their seemingly idyllic town.

Chapter Nine

The powerful roar of the Volvo engine reverberated through the air as it ascended the steep driveway. From a distance, Coby could see scaffolding slowly climbing up the walls of his majestic estate, filling him with a deep sense of pride. A glimmering red reflection caught his eye as he approached his grand residence, causing him to squint. He soon recognised the unmistakable figure of Ewan Drummond, perched on the steps in front of the imposing doors. A warm smile spread across Coby's previously sombre face, a rush of endearment washing over him. Ewan approached, carefully holding a plate filled with irresistible treats – buttery pies and crunchy shortbreads.

"Good afternoon, Mr Mac... M... Mac..." Ewan's determination wavered as he struggled to pronounce Coby's name. His voice trailed off in resignation, and a deep shade of red coloured his speckled face, betraying his embarrassment. However, he pressed on, extending the plate towards Coby. "My mum sent me up with some leftovers. She said a busy man like you must make time to eat."

Coby's face filled with affection as he gratefully accepted the plate from the young boy's hands. Playfully, he ruffled Ewan's hair and replied with genuine warmth in his voice, "Thank you. Please send my regards to your mum."

Ewan bobbed his head excitedly and darted off towards the woods, eager to return to their cosy cottage. However, he abruptly stopped and spun around, exclaiming, "The next time you visit, use the front door!"

Coby scoffed and chuckled, a sly smile playing on his lips. "Go home now, little man!" he retorted, his voice filled with playful amusement. The vision of Gracie's exposed mystique haunted him, the vivid image lingering for a moment before he forcefully dismissed it. He stepped into the grand hallway, immediately sensing an icy chill in the air, as if it were embracing him with an eerie presence. Setting the plate aside in the kitchen, he couldn't help but notice the fresh breeze coming in through the open back door. Concern etched itself across his face as he noticed the cracked doorframe, a silent testament to a forced entry. Gasping, he hurried towards his office, a sense of urgency gripping him.

Anger boiled up inside Coby like a seething volcano, threatening to erupt. The sight of his ransacked office, with its dishevelled drawers and overturned furniture, left him feeling a mix of shock and anger. Frantically searching for his laptop, his eyes darted around the room, but all he found was a vacant spot, leaving him with a sense of unease. Paperwork lay scattered haphazardly across the floor, a chaotic mess. Rushing to his desk, his heart pounding in his chest, he realised his Dictaphone was nowhere to be found. Frustration coursed through him, making him slam his fists down on the desk with a resounding thud. The resounding thud echoed through the room, intensifying his fury. Coby's eyes burned with an unquenchable fury.

Storming outside, his tightly clenched fists trembled as he stared up at the imposing scaffolding above him.

"Did any of you witness someone entering my house?" he bellowed, capturing the attention of the workers. The foreman swiftly descended while the others nonchalantly shrugged.

"What happened, Mr McTavish?" asked the foreman, his concerned expression clear as his brow furrowed. "You are as pale as a ghost," he said, his voice filled with concern.

Coby spat angrily, his teeth clenched tightly, and exclaimed, "Someone burgled my house!"

The foreman's expression grew serious as he removed his safety helmet, revealing his flowing, golden hair that tumbled down his strong shoulders. Inside the dimly lit hallway, he anxiously waited for Coby to lead him to the scene of the crime. Coby pointed towards his study, now a scene of utter chaos. The foreman surveyed the ransacked room, taking in the broken furniture and scattered papers, shaking his head in disbelief.

"I swear to you, Mr McTavish," he declared with unwavering

conviction, "none of my men would be responsible for this." With his safety helmet cradled under his arm, he ran his fingers through his golden locks. "They must have gained entry from the rear," he said, his voice filled with certainty. "No one entered or left during your absence. I give you my word, sir." With those words spoken, he turned and departed, his heavy footfalls echoing through the opulent hallway.

Coby reached into his pocket and pulled out his phone, feeling the cool metal against his fingertips. He dialled the number of the local police station, the sharp clicks of each number reverberating in his ears. A friendly and helpful young constable answered, her voice soothing and comforting. Coby eagerly explained the grim details, his words filled with urgency. After promising to send an investigating team soon, she ended the call, leaving Coby with a sinking feeling in his gut.

A sudden chill filled the air, causing goosebumps to rise on his skin. The ethereal trinity materialised before him, their translucent forms sending a shiver down his spine. Gloom etched itself across their faces, their expressions conveying a sense of foreboding. In perfect synchrony, their ghostly, skeletal fingers extended towards the entrance as they all pointed at it.

Coby furrowed his brow, his mind racing with thoughts as he followed their outstretched fingers. Each step he took towards the doorway amplified the creaking sound of the worn wooden floor beneath his feet, shattering the eerie silence that hung in the air. Yet, as he scanned the dimly lit area, his eyes strained to find anything sinister, only to be met with confusion.

He raised his gaze, and a shiver ran down his spine as he came face-to-face with the ghostly apparitions. They stood there, their ghostly figures translucent, still pointing their bony fingers, urging him forward towards the unknown.

He obediently followed their guidance, his footsteps resonating through the deserted hallway as he entered the kitchen. The smell of leftover food lingered in the air, mixing with the dampness that seeped in from the outside. Once again, astonishment surged through him as the ghostly figures materialised, leaving him breathless. Their skeletal fingers gently guided him out through the creaking door, down the dimly lit service alley, and into a cramped parking bay.

Coby noticed footprints etched into the muddy ground, evidence of someone else's presence.

His gaze locked onto the deep-seated tire tracks, the marks leading him further into the woods. He felt a mix of determination and anger coursing through his veins as he followed the parallel lines, disappearing into the darkness. He realised the men wore rain boots and used a four by four to gain entry to his property. His frustration grew, his anger mounting with each step, until he couldn't contain it any longer and kicked the ground in frustration.

As he walked back to his dimly lit office, the ethereal trinity floated silently behind him, their faint whispers sending a chilling breeze down his spine. With each step, his muscles tightened, his hands clenching into tight fists at his sides. The smouldering anger within him threatened to erupt, fuelling his unwavering determination to unearth the truth. His jaw locked, teeth grinding together, as he pressed forward, refusing to be swayed by fear or uncertainty. Coby poured himself a potent whiskey, the amber liquid cascading into the glass, its soft splashing breaking the stillness. He downed it in one swift motion, feeling the fiery burn as it glided down his throat. The intensity of his anger lessened, but not entirely, as he poured himself another drink.

Out of nowhere, a gentle hiss pierced the silence, evoking a hauntingly beautiful tune. He felt an icy shiver as he glanced at the ghostly figures, his eyes full of inquiries. The ethereal creature, with her delicate lace dress and elaborate updo, parted her lips and whispered, her voice filled with a haunting beauty. The sound seemed to hang in the air, filling the room with an otherworldly presence.

Coby's gaze locked onto the ethereal creature's monochrome eyes, their intensity filled with a motherly sincerity. He couldn't believe what he was experiencing, his disbelief clear in his tone as he asked if she had seen who had committed the act. She slowly nodded, a hint of shyness flickering across her face. Coby gasped, completely baffled by the revelation, and sank into his office chair, the worn leather creaking beneath his weight.

The loud crunching noise of tires rolling over the gravel shattered the silence. The spectral trio cast their curious gazes towards the source of the sound, their ghostly forms shimmering. Coby, assuming it was the police officers arriving, remained seated, his heart pounding in his chest.

"Don't go anywhere," he demanded sternly, but the apparitions remained oblivious, their faces frozen in awe.

The sound of approaching footsteps on the gravel echoed ominously, sending shivers down his spine. The front door swung open with a bone-chilling creak, instantly filling the room with an unsettling aura. Coby's unease grew as the distinct clacking of heels resounded through the hallway.

"Jacob Struan McTavish, show yourself!" serenaded the shrill voice of his Elaine, her high, lilting soprano cutting through the tension. Gasping in surprise, Coby's body jolted, causing him to nearly lose his balance on the chair.

"In here!" he spat angrily, his frustration mounting. With each step, the clacking of her heels became more pronounced until she finally entered his office. Sporting a wide-brimmed fedora and black opera gloves, she appeared ready for a day at the races. Her gaze scanned the disarray of his office, a sinister glint playing in her eyes.

"I see you made new friends already," she taunted, her words cutting through the air and causing him to flinch. The ethereal trinity gathered around her, their amazement palpable. A chorus of hushed whispers filled the air, mingling with the hisses of anticipation, as their hands reached out in a yearning to touch Elaine's impeccable outfit. Their eyes lingered on her, taking in every detail of her appearance, their admiration palpable.

Elaine forcefully slammed a manila envelope down on his desk, causing the apparitions to jolt in surprise and emit menacing hisses. "This is a love letter from my attorney," she said, her distinct Yank accent adding a sharp edge to her words.

"It's called a solicitor!" Coby spat, causing the apparitions to gasp and hiss menacingly.

Elaine dismissed his correction with a wave of her hand, intensifying his irritation. "Please adhere to the conditions outlined in the divorce decree," she said, her voice dripping with icy coldness. With a graceful whirl on her heel, she left the room. The apparitions trailed behind Elaine, swirling around her as she reached the front door, their envy palpable in the air.

Coby sprang up, his pulse racing, and hurriedly followed behind, desperate to catch up. But just as he reached the front door, Elaine slammed it shut in his face, leaving him feeling a mix of frustration and despair. He swiftly yanked it open, his heart pounding in his chest. Parting his lips to protest, he caught a glimpse of his best friend Niall Preston behind the wheel of his sleek silver Porsche Carrera, further fuelling his frustration. Sunlight danced off the gleaming body of the car as a group of maintenance workers gathered around, their tools glistening in the light. Niall glanced nervously at them, his eyes darting back and forth, as Elaine joined him inside the car. They swiftly sped up, the engine emitting a satisfying roar that resonated in the air, drowning out the cheering of the workers, their excitement palpable.

Coby hurried to his sleek metallic champagne Volvo, the leather seats cool against his skin as he leaned inside. With a determined motion, he pulled out his worn map, the crinkling sound echoing in the silence. Hurrying back to his office, he flung open the map and spread it across his chaotic desk. He strained his ears and caught the faint sound of another car approaching from outside.

"Stay," he sternly commanded the ethereal apparitions, his voice echoing through the empty room. Their mischievous giggles, reminiscent of delicate tubular chimes, filled the air around him.

Greeting the two officers, Sergeant Cole and Chief Inspector Beatie, at the front door, Coby guided them through the empty hallway to his dimly lit office. The flickering fireplace cast eerie shadows on the wallpaper, adding to the tense atmosphere. The auburn-haired sergeant diligently scribbled notes in her pocket-sized notebook, the scratch of her pen echoing softly in the cramped space. Meanwhile, the chief inspector, a formidable presence with his receding hairline and prominent nose, meticulously combed through the ransacked study, searching for any clues. His hazel eyes, sharp and penetrating, explored every corner, filling the air with their unwavering intensity. With each "yes inspector" Coby uttered, the man in charge corrected him with a stern "chief inspector," his voice reverberating with authority. Sergeant Cole would exchange a knowing smile with Coby, their unspoken camaraderie providing a brief respite from the intensity of the investigation. Her deep blue eyes sparkled with intelligence, drawing Coby in.

Impressed by their efficiency and teamwork, Coby couldn't help but admire their dedication. Yet, he couldn't ignore the growing annoyance emanating from the ethereal trinity. He was certain he understood why.

With the apparitions trailing behind them, Coby escorted the officers outside. They assured him that a team would arrive soon to carefully examine the tire tracks and footprints. Camera shutters clicked as they captured detailed images of the cracked doorframe, preserving the evidence.

Returning to the sanctuary of Coby's study, Sergeant Cole politely declined his offer of a whisky, while her male companion gladly accepted. The chief inspector made a brief phone call, his voice confident and authoritative, informing Coby that a team would arrive early the next morning to dust for fingerprints.

Coby, understanding the gravity of the situation, agreed to not use his office or tampering with any evidence. A sense of relief washed over the room as Coby concocted a tale, falsely claiming to have witnessed the culprits. With a fleeting glance at the ghostly figures, he quickly explained that he had cowered behind the door out of sheer terror. The apparition with the elaborate updo emitted a knowing smile, her spectral eyes shimmering with a mischievous glint.

As the chief inspector inquired about the details of the incident, a surge of inspiration ignited within Coby, compelling him to recount every detail that was still fresh in his mind. Glancing inquisitively at the spectre with the intricate updo, Coby noticed a newfound radiance on her cheeks, a rosy hue that seemed to illuminate her ethereal form. Agreeing with a graceful nod, she raised her hand, elegantly extending two fingers in confirmation.

Coby urgently informed the chief inspector that he had witnessed two perpetrators. The elegant apparition, with her ethereal presence, nodded gracefully, understanding the gravity of the situation. To Coby's keen eyes, she comprehended her task with utmost clarity. Chief Inspector Beatie, realising the significance of the information, swiftly motioned for his sergeant to capture every detail in her notes.

With the help of the mystical figure, Coby vividly recounted the appearances of the culprits. There were moments when she startled him, causing his words to falter and his guesses to emerge. She described the glasses as "transparent portals shielding his eyes." One miscreant bore a cross tattoo on his upper arm, which she described as "a verdant cross etched into his sinewy muscles." The term "oily hair" showed a slicked-back hairstyle. As for the mention of "recent divorce," Coby understood it as a faded indentation on the finger where his ring used to be. And last, "a nose like the back of a camel" translated to a nose that bore the marks of many fractures, with jagged contours.

Together, they meticulously provided detailed descriptions of the perpetrators, painting a vivid picture for the investigating officers. Time and again, Sergeant Cole would furrow her brow in deep concentration or arch an eyebrow inquisitively. A spark of recognition lit up the chief inspector's face upon hearing a whispered revelation from his sergeant. Coby, keenly attuned to their conversation, overheard the captain muttering, "Sinclair's thugs," displaying a lack of surprise, indicating a deeper connection to the case.

Coby carefully poured the chief inspector a last shot of the shimmering elixir, its rich fragrance permeating the room, enveloping the air with a comforting warmth that conveyed his profound gratitude for their exceptional service. As he bid the officers farewell, Coby noticed a graceful apparition with an elaborate hairstyle gliding silently by his side. Positioned like a guardian on the threshold, their hands raised in a solemn farewell, a wave of nostalgia washed over him as the officers' silhouettes slowly disappeared into the advancing horizon. Coby's eyes, brimming with curiosity, reflected the soft glow of anticipation, mirroring the ethereal figure that stood beside him.

The apparition's lips curled into a tantalising smirk, an enigma wrapped in mischief that beckoned him into the unfathomable depths of her allure. An intoxicating fragrance seemed to bloom from her, filling the air with the heady scent of lilacs. It was as if she exuded this perfume as effortlessly as a breath, akin to the female panda and lemur who emit their own symphony of floral and fruity scents to ensnare potential mates.

As if under a spell, he found himself drawn towards her, his senses captivated by her enchanting aura. Each breath he took was laced with her essence, a potent cocktail of intrigue and desire that stirred within him a longing as ancient as time itself.

Back in his office, Coby carefully traced the route from his abode to Inverness on the map, the touch of the smooth surface giving him a slight tingle of excitement. The distance, a daunting fifty-six miles, loomed in his mind, prompting him to swiftly calculate the time it would take to reach his destination, the weight of anticipation settling in his chest.

With a quick glance at his watch, its ticking sound echoing in his ears, Coby set off on the journey. The raw beauty of the Highlands served as a majestic backdrop, its towering mountains and rugged terrain mirroring the turmoil within his heart. The crisp air filled his lungs, carrying with it the scent of heather and earth, invigorating his senses.

As he drove along the winding roads, the landscape unfolded before him in all its splendour. The tranquil lochs glistened under the sunlight, their still waters reflecting the vibrant colours of the surrounding hills. The sound of his tires against the tarmac and the occasional bleating of sheep added a rhythm to the journey, a melody that harmonised with the breathtaking scenery.

Amid his thoughts, Coby dialled his maintenance foreman, the touch of the phone's buttons providing a reassuring tactile sensation. The foreman's voice on the other end of the line brought a sense of relief as he assured Coby of a reliable contact for security systems. Tomorrow morning, a solution would be in motion.

But this journey was more than just a means to an end. It was an odyssey, an adventure through Scotland's dramatic landscapes. The roads curved and dipped, inviting Coby to surrender to their allure. Ancient mountains stood tall, casting shadows that danced with his emotions, reminding him of the challenges that lay ahead.

Despite his urgency, Coby couldn't help but marvel at the simplicity of the interruptions caused by flocks of sheep crossing the narrow roads. The sight of fluffy white creatures scattered across the path brought a smile to his face, a brief respite from the weight on his shoulders.

With only twenty miles remaining, fate dealt its blow as a flat tire forced him to stop. In stark contrast to the peaceful surroundings, the hiss of escaping air filled the silence. The rough texture of the tarmac pressed against his hands as he swiftly replaced the deflated tire, a tactile sensation that fuelled his determination. The minutes ticked by, each second slipping away, as he glanced at his watch with a mix of determination and hope.

Setting his foot firmly on the gas pedal, Coby continued his journey, the wind rushing through his open window, carrying with it a sense of anticipation. He knew that every passing moment brought him closer to his destination, closer to facing the challenges that awaited him.

With only two minutes left before the store closed, Coby's silver Volvo came to a screeching halt in a loading zone marked with red paint. He hastily leaped out of his car, the cool air hitting his face, and hurried into the brightly lit electronics store. The salesman, with his immaculate white shirt and hair that gleamed like a raven's wing, welcomed Coby eagerly. With his fair complexion and bold eyebrows, he exuded an air of eagerness, signalling his desire to make a quick sale. The salesman's technical jargon didn't deter Coby, who carefully considered his options before settling on a small, sleek silver laptop. Coby's request for two identical computers left the salesman in disbelief, his eyes widening. Coby, feeling a sense of urgency, shared his cloud account details with the tech-savvy man. With nimble fingers, the salesman quickly signed in and set up the computer. While he waited for his valuable details to download and install, Coby noticed the delicious aroma of freshly baked bread as he darted across the road to the nearby bakery. The warm, inviting aroma of freshly baked treats enveloped him as he entered. He purchased several delectable pastries and refreshing sodas as a gesture of gratitude for the salesman's wonderful help.

Despite the hefty price tag, Coby reassured himself that the investment was necessary after years of needing an upgrade. Eventually, even Elaine nicknamed his old computer 'Noah's calculator' as it became ancient and outdated.

Now, he possessed a state-of-the-art machine, although he only utilised a fraction of its functions. Faced with a crossroads, he pondered whether to drive home while it was still light or satisfy the tingling sensation on his tongue with a taste of whiskey.

The allure of the whiskey ultimately triumphed. Coby swiftly placed his newly gained items into the trunk of his sleek Volvo and set off, leaving behind the gleaming glass facades of the technology shop. As he drove through the metropolis, the grandeur of the Highlands' capital unfolded before him.

The fading rays of sunlight painted the Victorian architecture with a warm glow, casting long shadows that danced upon the cobbled streets. The River Ness flowed serenely, its waters glinting as they wound their way through the heart of Inverness, mirroring the city's vibrancy in its shimmering surface. Historic stone bridges arched over the waterway, connecting the bustling urban centre with the tranquil green spaces beyond.

As he navigated through the city, his eyes scanned the surroundings, searching for a pub. The sight of an ancient castle perched atop a nearby hill, its sturdy walls a testament to the capital's storied past, momentarily distracted him. But the promise of a good drink steered his focus back onto the quaint pubs lining the streets.

Across the road, a wooden sign with the name of a tavern caught his eye. Coby skilfully maneuvered his car into a conveniently vacant parking spot. Just as he was about to cross the road, the unmistakable sound of a dog's bark caught his attention. His gaze fell upon a cage where a lively golden retriever puppy stood upright, its fur shimmering in the light, barking with boundless energy. The sight of the adorable creature tugged at his heartstrings, beckoning him forward and into the nearby pet shop.

Pity coiled her icy fingers around his heart and squeezed the heat out of it. His own saying, "A dog and house choose you, not the other way around," echoed in his mind, haunting him. He needed no convincing; the irresistible puppy, a fine example of the Scottish breed, instantly melted his heart. With a warm smile, the pet shop owner, her curly orange hair bouncing with each movement, emitted the potent scent of hairspray. Her hands were sturdy and substantial, their touch akin to well-crafted sculptures, a testament to a life of abundance. She gently handed over the puppy, its velvety fur brushing against Coby's fingertips, eliciting a soft tickle. Coby joyfully counted out the bills, carefully placing them in her outstretched hands. Her fingers, reminiscent of cigars, skilfully wrapped around the stack of cash before discreetly tucking them away in her bosom. She subtly gestured towards a royal blue box with a narrow slit, encouraging Coby to leave a generous donation for the local animal shelter.

Convinced by the kind pet shop owner, Coby splurged on costly dog food, feeling the weight of the premium bag in his hands. "No good deed goes unpunished," he murmured to himself, a hint of amusement in his voice, as he manoeuvred through the shop, juggling the puppy and the shopping bags.

In the end, he splurged on a plush bed for his furry friend, along with shiny feeding bowls and a vibrant collection of toys. Coby affectionately named the puppy Janie, and carefully placed her on the passenger seat of his Volvo.

Coby's voice filled the car as they began their journey home, creating a cheerful melody that resonated alongside the steady hum of the engine. Janie's head poked out of the window, her ears flapping in the wind, and Coby couldn't help but grin at the sight. He could almost feel the wind rushing against his face, mirroring the joy he saw in Janie's eyes.

Chapter Ten

Janie's relentless barking pierced through Coby's ears, assaulting him with its sharpness as the morning sun filtered through the windows, casting a calming, cool glow on the walls. Weary and groggy, he reluctantly pulled himself out of bed and freshened up before embarking on his quest to calm his new furry family member. Janie, stationed at the foot of the staircase, sent out a series of echoing barks that reverberated off the walls of the grand hallway. Understanding her agitation, Coby diverted her attention. The tantalising aroma of flavoured dog food wafted through the air, a mouthwatering mix of savoury goodness that made Coby's senses come alive. Janie eagerly devoured every delectable morsel, her paws skidding on the smooth marble floors as she hurried back to the hallway. Her excited yapping filled the space, creating a symphony of joyful chaos. Suddenly, she skidded to a halt, leaving behind a pool of excitement on the floor. Annoyed, Coby let out a grunt and quickly grabbed a paper towel to tidy up the messy sight.

The morning quickly escalated into a whirlwind of activity. The security company arrived. Their presence felt as Coby guided them through the house, pointing out the perfect spots for the installation of cameras. Meanwhile, Elaine's solicitor called, seeking an update on Coby's progress with signing the divorce papers. Amidst the chaos, Chief Inspector Beatie and his friendly sergeant arrived bearing exhilarating news – Coby's detailed description had led to the arrest of two suspects. The officers handed Coby his recovered belongings and informed him they were still working on extracting a confession from the uncooperative thugs. Overwhelmed with gratitude, the chief inspector gladly accepted a double whisky as a token of Coby's appreciation for his help. Despite being friendly, the sergeant politely turned down the offer and focused on the area behind the door, where Coby said he had been hiding during the burglary. And amidst the dimly lit room, the enchanting apparition of Jane and her ethereal companions materialised.

The one with the intricately arranged hairdo sensed the sergeant's suspicion and devised a swift diversion. With a resounding thud, a book plummeted to the floor, capturing the sergeant's attention. The sound reverberated through the room, echoing off the walls. Startled, Sergeant Cole emerged from her concealed position behind the door. Her face lost all colour, and her eyes grew wide with shock. She excused herself and hurriedly dashed outside, her pallid complexion revealing a heightened sense of urgency.

Amidst the echoing laughter of the maintenance workers, one of them playfully taunted, "What's the matter?" he jeered. "You seem as if you've seen a ghost!" His pun ignited a chorus of boisterous laughter from his companions. Coby's eyes widened as Jane, the ethereal trinity's ever-present godmother, hurried over to the apparition with an elaborate updo. She took her hand and pulled her out from the shadows behind the creaking door. Her voice, filled with menace, reverberated through the room as she wagged her finger and scolded her spectral companion. The moment he heard her name, Vivienne, Coby's heart raced, the hiss of it hanging in the air like a foreboding omen. The elegant French words spoken by Jane were foreign to Coby, leaving him puzzled. Meanwhile, Janie sat nearby, her tail wagging excitedly as she watched.

The air turned frigid, sending a chill down Coby's spine. Janie let out a sharp bark and dashed across the grand hallway towards the front door. The atmosphere buzzed with hushed murmurs and soft hisses, creating an unsettling ambiance that lingered in the air. Coby noticed the sheer gravity of the situation in the apparition's grave expressions, betraying their dread. The word "Sassenach!" slipped out of Jane's mouth like a venomous hiss, echoing through the air. A shrill, ear-piercing shriek sliced through the silence, only to fade away as the spectres retreated into the enveloping shroud of shadows, vanishing like a wisp of smoke.

Amidst the haunting scene, Coby heard the distinct sound of tires crunching over gravel, and he cast his glance outside. The sound created an unsettling tension in the air. "The devil is in the details," Coby uttered under his breath as he glimpsed Alistair Sinclair's land drover screeching to a stop before the doorway.

"Time to hit the road," Chief Inspector Beatie remarked, the thump of his empty glass reverberating in the room. Coby trailed him to the front door, where he greeted him and expressed his gratitude for his help. As they stood there, Coby couldn't help but notice the heavy tension between Alistair Sinclair and the inspector as they brushed shoulders. Alistair Sinclair lifted his hat in greeting, but the inspector fixed him with an icy glare.

The atmosphere grew even colder as Coby snapped, "What's your business here?" He stood his ground firmly, blocking the doorway.

Alistair Sinclair stopped abruptly, his breath visible in the chilly air from the brisk walk up the steep staircase. Clutching his walking stick, he took off his hat, revealing a sinister glint in his eyes. His signature fake smile, laced with malice, appeared on his face.

"No need for hostility, Mr McTavish," he said, his voice dripping with venom. "I came to pay my condolences. Rumour has it you were burgled." His smile transformed into a knowing one, sending a chilling shiver down Coby's spine. Janie, sensing something unsettling about Alistair Sinclair, emitted a low growl that reverberated from deep within her chest.

Coby gently stroked Janie's soft, furry head, hoping to soothe her. "And how is it any of your business?" he asked, his tone frosty.

"You know what, Mister McTavish?" Alistair asked, his face turning a deep shade of crimson, and his tone filled with unmistakable agitation. His voice echoed ominously through the luxurious hallway, intensifying the palpable tension.

"None of this shit ever happened before you came," he contorted, his words laced with frustration, as if holding Coby responsible for the chaos.

"Bugger off," Coby snapped, his voice filled with hostility and a sharpness that could cut through ice. In a swift motion, he slammed the heavy doors in Alistair's face, the resounding echo filling the hallway. Leaning against it, he could feel the coolness of the polished wood against his back, providing a sense of temporary refuge.

Coby stood there, fully immersed in his surroundings, his ears picking up every subtle sound. He heard the distinct clacking of Alistair's walking stick as it contacted the steps, each tap resonating in the silence. The jeers of the maintenance workers echoed in his ears, their mocking laughter piercing the air as Alistair drove off.

Janie's adorable expression tugged at his heartstrings as her bright, innocent eyes met his. Without prevailing, he gently guided her to the cosy kitchen, where the aroma of delectable dogwood filled the air, its rich beef gravy enticing his senses. She eagerly gobbled up every morsel, her tail wagging with delight.

While Coby savoured the moment, a chilly breeze drifted in through the open door, bringing with it the subtle sound of a worker meticulously sealing the newly replaced window with putty. He turned his attention to the steaming coffee, the boiling water creating a frothy, aromatic blend that warmed his hands as he handed a cup to the worker. The worker's grateful grin spoke volumes, a wordless exchange of kindness.

With Alistair taken care of, Coby's mind shifted to his next task – organising his to-do list. The memory of Jane's venomous hiss, calling out the name "Vivienne," lingered in his thoughts. He swiftly scrawled the name 'Vivienne' on his whiteboard, anticipation bubbling as he yearned to unravel the mysteries surrounding her and her acquaintances. Checking his emails, disappointment washed over him as he found nothing from his researcher.

But amidst the mixed results, the day brought a significant breakthrough. An email from his contact at New Scotland Yard confirmed his suspicions, reopening the cold case involving Lord Lucas after a positive sighting in Australia. The news of Lady Lucas's tragic fate weighed heavily on his mind, the mystery of the Sandra River adding to his unease.

Flagging the email for follow-up, Coby couldn't help but feel a surge of anticipation. "Jane, Vivienne," he crooned in a lilting tenor, his voice carrying a hint of excitement. "Show yourselves."

His social accounts were abuzz with activity, filled with responses teeming with rumours and speculations about his inquiries regarding the prominent Lucas family. Each comment seemed to add fuel to the growing intrigue. Coby's heart raced with anticipation as he scrolled through the comments on his social accounts, his fingers tapping anxiously on the screen. The screen before him seemed to pulsate with the intensity of the emotions conveyed through each response. Excitement and curiosity coursed through his veins, fuelling his eagerness to explore.

The once calm atmosphere now crackled with an electric energy, as if the collective thoughts of the online community had manifested into a tangible force. Coby's eyes darted back and forth across the screen, devouring every word, every hint that could potentially unravel the mysteries surrounding the enigmatic Lucas family. His mind raced, connecting dots and forming theories, his thoughts echoing in his head like a chorus of whispers.

With each comment that appeared on his feed, the intensity of the intrigue deepened. It was as if the virtual world had become a pressure cooker, and Coby found himself caught in its grip. The weight of the unanswered questions bore down on him, causing a knot to form in his stomach.

The comments, once mere pixels on a screen, now had a physical presence. They seemed to dance before his eyes, their words etching themselves into his mind. Coby's heart pounded in his chest, almost drowning out the sounds of the outside world. The growing fascination with the Lucas family had taken hold of him, consuming his thoughts and seeping into his very being. His pulse throbbed in his veins, a tangible reminder of the exhilaration that surged within him.

With the online buzz intensifying, Coby's emotions swung between anticipation and unease. The allure of the unknown and the thrill of unravelling the truth propelled him forward, despite the mounting pressure and the increasing complexity of the situation.

Like a sudden bolt of lightning, an epiphany jolted him, making him realise he had unknowingly become a small piece of a much larger puzzle. The virtual realm had transformed into a battleground of speculation and curiosity, and he was at the centre of it all. With every comment and rumour that surfaced, the intrigue surrounding the Lucas family grew, intensifying the emotions that coursed through Coby's veins. His face lit up like a lightbulb as inspiration sparked a fire in his mind.

"Jane, in your name, I summon the ethereal trinity; their presence felt in the whispering wind," Coby intoned, his voice resonating with a deep, haunting melody.

The scent of lotus flowers permeated the air, its alluring fragrance embracing Coby in a moment of pure bliss. With a whoosh, Jane's apparition broke through the shroud barrier and materialised before him. Vivienne and the nameless presence materialised slowly, their ghostly figures merging seamlessly with Jane's. Their expectant eyes, shimmering like saffron embers, pierced into his soul, daring him to disrupt their ethereal slumber.

A cautious smile appeared on Coby's lips as he gazed at them. "I need your help," he said, his voice steady and determined. Jane exchanged a curious glance with Vivienne before uttering something in French, her words laced with intrigue.

"Speak," Vivienne hissed venomously, her voice bouncing off the walls and sending a chill down Coby's spine. Filled with excitement, Janie let out a shrill yelp and quickly scurried for shelter.

In that moment, Coby's keen observation skills caught sight of an interesting trend unfolding. Whenever Alistair Sinclair visits, the ethereal trinity turns hostile. The clue was like a precious gem, a key that held the potential to unravel the enigma surrounding these mystical creatures. He knew what he had to do, but for now, he had other plans to set in motion.

"Follow me," Coby said with conviction, his voice echoing through the empty hallway. As they strode through the dimly lit corridor, he noticed a mushy heap on the floor where Janie had unleashed her excitement. The putrid stench assaulted his nostrils, forcing him to pinch his nose tightly shut. The supernal beings giggled mischievously behind him, their laughter reverberating off the cold stone walls. He resisted the urge to turn around and question their amusement, knowing it would only lead to more confusion. They continued their journey, following the path until they reached the end of the corridor. Coby lifted the heavy trapdoor and descended the spiral staircase into the musty abyss below. As he flicked the switch, the sudden illumination startled him, causing him to jump and gasp. There they were, standing right in front of him.

"Stop doing that!" he exclaimed in a hushed whisper, frustration clear in his voice. The spectral threesome exchanged curious glances, their eyes filled with bewilderment.

"Never mind," Coby assured, sensing their confusion. He motioned for them to follow him, his hand gesturing them forward.

They slowly made their way down the path to the buttery, entranced by the melodic sound of Sandra's voice echoing through the air. The vibrations from her angelic melody created a symphony of emotions that rippled through the eerie basement. And there, on the bottom step, sat Sandra, her finger delicately tracing intricate patterns in the layer of dust. The room fell into an eerie silence as her jaw clenched shut, silencing her enchanting melody. Jane and Vivienne's faces twisted in surprise as they both turned sharply towards Coby. They protested with a cacophony of French and English, their words blending into a bewildering symphony. In a last-ditch effort, Coby raised his arms in surrender, his voice cracking with desperation as he pleaded for them to halt.

"Dearly beloveds," Coby began, his voice filled with a mix of determination and concern. He hesitated, his brow furrowing as the familiar words escaped his lips. Sensing their amusement, he took a deep breath and started over. His eyes locked onto Sandra, as if she held the key to the truth he sought. With a pleading gesture, he implored, "Please, help me speak to Sandra."

Vivienne and Jane shook their heads dismissively, crossing their arms over their chests in a defiant stance. The unnamed apparition, her neatly braided tresses and vibrant tartan skirt speaking of her lively personality, glided over to Sandra and sat beside her, wrapping her arm around her shoulder in a comforting gesture.

"Non Josephine!" exclaimed Jane, her voice filled with concern, as she reached out to comfort her friend. Coby observed the distress on Jane's face, while his ears picked up the urgency in her tone. The scent of anxiety hung in the air, mingling with the faint aroma of jasmine perfume emanating from Josephine. Coby, having a basic understanding of French, recognised that "non" meant "no." The revelation of Josephine's name added a mischievous sparkle to his eyes. Sensing an opportunity, he swiftly acted before Josephine's motherly kindness could fade away.

"Josephine," Coby said urgently, his voice filled with determination, "please ask Sandra who killed her." His words hung in the air, accompanied by a nervous silence. Coby's heart raced as he anxiously awaited the response. He sensed a lingering curiosity in Sandra's eyes, a subtle clue that piqued his interest.

"Now look here, sugar," Josephine's voice, soft and angelic, floated through the air, bringing a sense of calm to the room. She affectionately rubbed Sandra's back. "Please," she pleaded, "tell this man who ended your life." Her words, sharp as a celestial sword, shattered the silence, whispering with a hiss.

Sandra's fearful eyes locked onto Vivienne and Jane, instantly filling the room with tension. In an eerie hiss, Jane said something to Sandra that Coby couldn't make sense of. In that moment, something truly extraordinary happened. Right before his eyes, Sandra leaned forward, her finger gracefully gliding across the dusty surface. Coby, Jane, and Vivienne inched closer, their curiosity piqued. The sound of Sandra's finger brushing against the dust filled the room, creating a soft, shuffling noise. Coby strained his eyes, trying to decipher what she was writing, but it remained frustratingly out of sight.

Josephine, ever the guide, sat beside Sandra, her fingers delicately spelling out each letter. Coby watched in awe as Sandra's movements formed the shapes of the alphabet. The anticipation in the room was palpable, causing Coby to hold his breath. Finally, he saw a name etched into the dusty surface – "V-A-N-E-S-A" - which instantly triggered a distant memory.

With each letter completed, a wave of relief washed over him, escaping with an audible sigh. He scanned the room and couldn't help but notice the inquisitive stares of those around him, all directed at him. The weight of their curiosity pressed upon him, but he remained determined. It may not make sense yet, but he knew he would uncover the truth. Sandra's eyes were fixed on him as she leaned forward, her hand swiftly scribbling another word in the dusty ground. "H-A-S-B-U-N-D," she wrote, just below the previous word. Coby raised his eyebrow, his curiosity piqued. Leaning forward again, Sandra delicately etched shapes into the layer of dust with her finger, the fine particles tickling her skin. The soft scraping sound of her writing broke the hushed silence filling the room. Coby could feel a strange electricity in the air, a charged anticipation that made his heart race. Sandra leaned forward once again, and Coby could feel the rush of excitement coursing through his veins, making his chest tighten.

With meticulous care, she etched the word "L-O-V-R-E" onto the dusty surface, leaving behind a delicate trail of particles with each stroke. Coby silently repeated the words to himself, his lips moving in a faint murmur as he sought to decipher their meaning. Suddenly, a triumphant realisation washed over him, and he couldn't contain his excitement any longer.

"Vanessa's husband was my lover!" he exclaimed, his laughter echoing through the quiet. Sandra's eyes, bright and shimmering like saffron pools, fixed on him, and she subtly nodded in approval.

"Yes!" Coby cried out, his voice filled with triumph, punctuating his exclamation with a victorious fist pump. In his eagerness, he quickly pulled out his phone and stepped forward, aiming the camera at the words etched into the dust. Just as he raised the phone to take a picture, he felt a tremendous gust of air escape from Jane's lips, creating a swirling sensation in the room. The force of it blew over the dust, leaving behind a clean slate with no trace of words.

Coby lowered the camera, his gaze turning hostile as he stared at Jane in disbelief. "What did you do that for?" he asked, his tone laced with frustration. Jane's fierce response was straightforward as she bared her teeth and emitted a menacing hiss, her eyes glowing like fiery embers. The chilling air of her breath brushed against his skin like the kiss of death, sending shivers down his spine.

"Sorry!" Coby shouted, panic coursing through him. He whirled around and sprinted to safety, scared out of his wits by the wrath he had inadvertently unleashed.

He scribbled the words 'Vanessa, husband, my lover,' on his whiteboard in red, feeling a surge of excitement. His hands trembled slightly as he analysed the phrase from every angle, the anticipation building. The possibilities seemed endless. But one thing was clear: Sandra had confessed to being Lord Lucas's mistress. At least, that hinted at an undeniable motive for her murder.

With a sense of purpose, he eagerly shared the breakthrough with his contact at New Scotland Yard. Just as he was lost in thought, his phone chimed with a text notification, and Elaine's name appeared on the screen. Irritation consumed him completely, clinging to him like a damp towel. Coby tapped on the message preview and read the words. "Hey cowboy," she began, using her teasing nickname for him, a play on his name Coby's resemblance to Cowboy. "Happy birthday, from us here at the sunny Maldives. PS. Have you signed the divorce papers yet?"

Coby's heart sank at the word 'us', a heavy disappointment settling in his chest like a weight. The image of his wife on his birthday sent a sharp jolt of remorse through his body. Memories flooded his mind of how she used to surprise him with a seductive outfit on his birthday, her alluring curves and slender legs enticing him, filling him with excitement. The sound of her voice, evocative and sultry, sent a ripple of anticipation down his spine, causing goosebumps to spread across his skin. Leading him upstairs, she moved with a hypnotic sway, each step accentuating the allure of her backside. Her slender fingers skilfully unbuckled his belt and unbuttoned his shirt, causing his heart to pound in his chest. With skill and confidence, she took control, mounting him and guiding their movements with the grace of a seasoned rider on a wild, untamed horse. Elaine performed her special trick, a teasing pinch that caused him to jerk violently, desperate to shake her off, but she held on firmly to his shoulders. He listened intently to the rhythm of her desires, eagerly awaiting her repeated cries of "Yes, yes, yes," as he prepared himself, attuned to the sound of her panting breaths.

In a powerful climax, their shared desires reverberated through the bedroom, their euphoric screams filling the air. Their bodies intertwined; she collapsed onto him, savouring the lingering scent of their passionate love that permeated the air as he tenderly caressed her silky hair. Time seemed to freeze as they lay there, lost in each other's embrace.

Suddenly, a thud from a worker upstairs jolted Coby out of his lustful haze. He could feel his excitement growing, his pants winding tightly around his waist, a testament to his longing.

"Shit!" he exclaimed, glancing at his watch in disbelief. He had forgotten his own birthday. Moving swiftly, he leaped up and hurried into the hallway. With a quick whistle, Janie appeared from her cowering spot below the staircase. He knew she would eventually get used to the apparitions that were an almost everyday occurrence in his life. She just needed time. He jingled his Volvo keys, and the puppy barked excitedly, chasing her tail in circles. With a forceful swing, he opened the door, only to be met with Janie's swift exit as she darted towards his waiting car. Without waiting for an invitation, she leaped onto the passenger seat, her head popping out of the window, eager for their adventure into town.

Chapter Eleven

His first stop was at the delectable bakery, Sweet Serenity. Coby rushed inside, but not before leaving the car window slightly open for Janie. When he walked by a parked car, his blood boiled as he saw dogs trapped inside, panting and desperate. The air inside the bakery was thick with the tantalising scents of freshly baked treats and pastries, tickling his nostrils with their mouthwatering aroma. The friendly and sturdy lady behind the counter handed him a cake box, the anticipation building in his chest as he felt its weight in his hands. He couldn't help but steal a sneaky glance at the chocolate cake, its decadent, dark frosting adorned with elegant white letters that spelled out '50', causing a warm smile to spread across his face.

With a quick stop at the local liquor store, Coby asked the cashier about the preferences of the local women. The cashier's demeanour turned hostile as soon as he mentioned the name Gracie Drummond, his cold shoulder leaving Coby feeling an unexpected chill. Undeterred, Coby purchased various flavours, the bottles making a soft clinking sound as he carefully placed them into the roomy trunk of his Volvo. With determination, he sped towards the Stag's Head Inn.

The bustling atmosphere left no time for a darts game, but Coby settled for a pint of frothy beer, the golden liquid glistening in the dim light of the pub. As he waited for his take away shepherd's pie, he requested a pen and paper from the barman. He carefully wrote a concise birthday invitation and secured it to the notice board with a pin. Thoughts of Elaine and her lover, his best friend, relentlessly invaded his mind. He pictured them on the idyllic island, their bodies entwined on the pristine white sands, the moonlight casting a heavenly radiance on her bare skin, as they listened to the soothing sound of waves caressing the shore.

His knuckles turned white as he squeezed the beer glass, the sharp edges digging into his palm. The rage coursed through his veins, making his heart pound in his chest. Every thought of them together felt like a stab to his core, igniting a fire of jealousy that threatened to consume him whole. The room around him seemed to blur as his mind played out vivid scenes of their forbidden union. He could almost hear their laughter carried by the gentle sea breeze, their whispers of affection mingling with the sound of crashing waves. The image of Elaine's radiant smile, a smile he thought she reserved only for him, taunted him relentlessly. The bitterness in his mouth matched the bitter taste of the ail he held in his hand.

The taste of bitterness filled his mouth, mirroring the bitter taste of betrayal that had seeped into his soul. He could no longer ignore the ache in his chest, the ache of a heart torn between love and betrayal.

Despite the overwhelming anger, a profound sadness crept into his heart. The realisation of losing both his lover and his best friend felt like a crushing weight upon his shoulders. Tainted with betrayal, his once cherished memories now leave him adrift in a sea of conflicting emotions.

The curvaceous and amiable barmaid returned, delicately placing the steaming pie in front of him, abruptly halting his tumultuous thoughts. In a moment of anguish, he let go of the glass, envisioning the fragmented shards scattering across the floor, mirroring his broken trust.

Coby wasted no time in gulping down the last of his pint, enjoying the invigorating flavour that tingled his palate. With a sense of purpose, he headed to the groceries store, the fluorescent lights overhead illuminating the aisles filled with an array of tempting food. He selected a platter of delicate pastries, the flaky crusts practically begging to be devoured. Next, he chose a savoury platter, the aroma of seasoned meats and spices filling the surrounding air. Remembering the dietary preferences of some guests, he carefully picked out something for the vegans and vegetarians, the vibrant colours of the plant-based options catching his eye.

With his car now loaded with an assortment of delectable treats,

Coby glanced at his watch, feeling a sudden recognition dawn on him. Without hesitation, he turned back towards the pub, the anticipation in his chest growing stronger. He relished a swift pint, savouring the alluring amber liquid as it danced gracefully in the glass. With a stretch, he reached up and plucked his birthday invitation off the notice board, meticulously adding his address before carefully reattaching it.

Just then, Alistair Sinclair swaggered into the dimly lit pub, drawing everyone's attention. His walking stick clacked ominously against the polished wooden floor, creating an eerie echo. He stopped and gazed intently at the faded noticeboard, the flickering fireplace casting eerie shadows on his weathered face. With a grunt, he settled into a solitary table, the creaking chair adding to the hushed atmosphere. His presence shrouded the pub in a pensive stillness, as if a heavy fog had descended upon it. The once lively atmosphere turned sour, matching the lingering smell of stale beer that hung in the air. Even the ever-friendly barmaid lost her smile, her usually cheery demeanour replaced with an air of unease.

Coby paid him no heed, his attention captured by the dartboard, where a fierce competition was raging. With two quick gulps, he finished his pint, the bitter taste lingering on his tongue, and headed towards the exit. Just as he was about to step outside, a sudden, piercing sound reached his ears – the unmistakable call of his name, "McTavish," in Alistair's distinct, rough English accent. Coby stopped abruptly and whirled around, facing his nemesis. "Remember," Alistair cried, his voice cutting through the noise of the bustling pub, his words lingering in the air like an ominous reminder, "there are always eyes observing." He pointed a menacing finger at Coby, his gaze filled with a sinister gleam, and let out a chilling, maniacal laugh. Coby shrugged off the ominous warning, his heart racing, and headed towards his Volvo.

The engine growled as it ascended the steep driveway of his stately home, its powerful roar echoing through the air. He parked his car right next to the stairs, making it convenient to unload his heavy shopping bags. Janie, filled with anticipation, eagerly scratched at the door lever, sensing their arrival home. A feeling of excitement washed over her as she pondered the mysteries that lay within this place.

Bathed in the cool rays of sunlight, the manor's freshly painted exterior shimmered, as if it had been given a new lease on life. Each day brought a renewed sense of pride to Coby, and he couldn't help but fall in love with this magnificent estate.

The diligent window washer, always eager to lend a hand, assisted Coby in carrying his shopping inside. His services, as expected, required a small fee. Coby carefully placed the drinks in the shiny new silver fridge, which boasted an impressive capacity, as if it could accommodate a truck, in theory. They gracefully transported his desk and a few chairs into the grand hallway, finding their rightful place. With great attention to detail, they meticulously organised a plethora of platters, each one filled with irresistible treats.

Amidst the preparations, Coby's birthday cake took centre stage, adorned with the number 50, serving as a not-so-subtle reminder of the passing years. Together, they set the table meticulously with gleaming forks, sparkling glasses, and soft serviettes. However, Coby discovered he had a limited supply of party candles. Thinking quickly, the resourceful window washer suggested six candles, one for each decade of Coby's life. With the transaction complete, the window washer bid farewell, his footsteps fading away as he disappeared from sight. Coby stood alone, surrounded by the vibrant colours and playful decorations of the party area. As he took it all in, a sense of excitement and anticipation washed over him, filling his heart with joy.

The lit candles flickered and danced, their flames swaying to the rhythm of the cool breeze that caressed the spacious hallway. Coby recognised this familiar sensation, the signature scent of the house, a blend of age and history, which seemed to permeate every corner.

A faint scent of lotus flower permeated the air, delicately tickling his nose. Coby's body immediately tensed, anticipating their arrival. Jane's ethereal form materialised, flickering ominously in front of the birthday cake. Vivienne's ghostly apparition slowly appeared beside Jane, their eyes locked on the dancing flames of the candles. The soft candlelight cast a gentle glow on their awed expressions, accentuating the depth of their haunting monochrome eyes. Coby furrowed his brow, pondering Josephine's absence. Then, a rush of warmth enveloped him as he remembered Sandra and the comforting embrace from Josephine. He hurried down the dimly lit hallway, taking the stairs and flicking the switch, following the dark corridors that led to the buttery. Goosebumps formed on his skin as the chilly air clung to him, reinforcing his resolve to invest in a fine wine collection.

Stepping into the buttery, a mix of excitement and trepidation flooded Coby's chest, making his heart flutter like a trapped bird. The sombre atmosphere hung heavy, as if it were physically clinging to his skin. Each step he took echoed through the vast space, amplifying the anticipation building within him.

The ghostly figures of Josephine and Sandra materialised before him, their translucent forms illuminated by an ethereal glow. They sat side by side on the bottom step, enveloped in a heavy, ominous silence. Josephine's eyes, as dark as a moonless night, flickered with a curious gleam, while an unsettling silence replaced Sandra's enchanting melody. Coby couldn't help but wonder what had happened to Sandra's enchanting melody, and a wave of concern washed over him.

Their ethereal gazes shifted towards him as he approached, their eyes filled with uncertainty, questioning why he had intruded upon their space. He sensed their curiosity, their ethereal presence almost tangible, and he couldn't shake off the feeling that they held secrets within their ghostly forms.

Summoning his courage, he spoke up, reminding the apparitions of his birthday celebration and inviting them. The words hung in the air, weighted by the intensity of the moment. Josephine and Sandra exchanged a brief glance, their ghostly features frozen in contemplation, before finally nodding in agreement.

With a flicker of their ethereal forms, Josephine and Sandra disappeared into the darkness, their figures transforming into wisps that floated effortlessly, like tendrils of smoke. Coby hesitated for a moment, feeling his heart race and his breath hitch, before tentatively trailing the intoxicating cloud of jasmine perfume.

With each step into the shadows, a bone-chilling feeling coursed through him, causing his arm hairs to prickle. The darkness enveloped him, swallowing him whole, until he emerged into the grand hallway. Josephine and Sandra reappeared, their spectral bodies taking on a more substantial presence, standing alongside Jane and Vivienne.

The air seemed to shimmer around them, as if charged with an otherworldly energy. Coby couldn't help but feel captivated by their presence, as their haunting beauty stood out against the opulent surroundings. Their ethereal presence turned the grand hallway, with its intricate tapestries and sparkling chandeliers, into a mesmerising scene.

With each step closer to his celebration, Coby's anticipation grew, mingled with a hint of unease. He couldn't shake off the feeling that there was more to Josephine and Sandra than met the eye.

An idea took root in his mind, blossoming into a well-formed plan. Coby eagerly made his way to his bedroom, the polished wooden floor cool beneath his feet. He reached for his sleek Bose docking station, its glossy surface reflecting the soft glow of the room. With a satisfying click, he placed his sleek phone into the cradle and brought up his favourite playlist. When the music started playing, the room filled with a vibrant tapestry of sound that brought it to life.

Coby's eclectic taste in music was like a kaleidoscope, each genre representing a different chapter of his life. The melodies, like colourful threads, wove together in harmonious unity. The timeless classics resonated with him, melodies that had stood the test of time, just like him.

"It's party time," Coby sang in a high, lilting tenor, his voice filling the air with excitement. Marvin Gaye's soulful voice crooning "I Heard It Through The Grapevine" echoed through the grand hallway, the smooth notes evoking memories of days long gone. Nostalgia washed over him, a gentle nod to his youthful years.

The deep and mysterious bass line slithered into the room, filling the air with an enchanting aura that surrounded the ethereal gathering. It was a sound that both fascinated and disturbed, a paradoxical melody that made the blood run cold. Jane, moving with a serpentine grace, danced between the notes, her fluidity sending shivers down Coby's spine. Her movements held the attention of everyone in the room, even Janie, who barked excitedly, momentarily caught up in the enchantment.

As the song faded, Stevie Wonder's "Superstition" took its place, its infectious rhythm and iconic clavinet riff filling the room. The soulful melodies and harmonious instruments resonated deep within Josephine, as if seeping into her very marrow. The beat compelled her to move, her feet tapping out the quick, intricate steps of the Charleston. Her movements flowed with grace, perfectly in sync with each note.

It was a fusion of old and new, a celebration of music and dance that broke through boundaries and united people. As Josephine gracefully danced, the others stood in amazement, their ghostly hands clapping in perfect rhythm with the enchanting music. The chant of "banana" filled the room, adding to the vibrant energy of the scene. The song abruptly ceased, and the resounding applause that followed Jane's performance filled the hallway. Much to everyone's surprise, Sandra joined in the celebration.

Coby stood in awe, his eyes fixed on the mesmerising dance performances unfolding before him. The room buzzed with the murmurs of excitement. With his double Scotch in hand, he savoured the sensation of the smooth amber liquid flowing over his tongue.

The ethereal trinity, connected through the magical realm of music and dance, seemed to float effortlessly across the marble floor. Coby could almost taste the anticipation in the air, a blend of excitement and curiosity. They entranced him, his senses heightened, as he carefully etched every key moment into his memory.

Vivienne, her body swaying to the opening notes of Dire Straits' "Walk Of Life", found her rhythm. The room seemed to come alive as she burst into an explosion of energy. Her high kicks and rapid skirt twirling added a visual spectacle to her dance, while her movements effortlessly synchronised with the beat of the song.

Intriguingly, Vivienne cleverly adjusted her pace, seamlessly blending vigorous can-can steps with graceful, fluid movements during the song's calmer sections. The fusion of styles created a dance like no other, a feast for the eyes that held the spectral audience in rapt attention.

Coby's eyes were fixed on the performers as the music filled the room, its pulsating beats reverberating through his chest. The energy of the performance enveloped him, transporting him into a world where time stood still. He could smell the faint scent of perfume mingling with the polished aroma of the marble dance floor, creating a sensory symphony that heightened the experience.

In that moment, Coby knew these performances held the key to unravelling the mysterious events that bound them all together. And as Vivienne danced her heart out, he felt a surge of determination, knowing that he was one step closer to solving the enigma of Sandra's untimely demise.

Chapter Twelve

Before the ornate brass knocker reverberated through the grand hallway, startling Coby, the ethereal figures sensed the interference. They whirled around, their ghostly forms glaring at the entrance, eagerly expecting the arrival of the newcomers. And then, with a resounding echo, the knocker jolted Coby into action. Filled with excitement, Janie let out a joyful bark, hurried to the front door, and slid to a stop, her tail wagging with enthusiasm. The mere thought of Gracie Drummond made Coby's heart flutter, and his stomach twisted with a kaleidoscope of butterflies. With a swift motion, he turned down the vibrant music, and as the sound faded, a chorus of astonished whispers and disappointed hisses filled the air. With a determined swing, he flung open the front door, revealing a breathtaking view of the outside world.

Gracie's sensual lips curved into a wide grin, revealing a flawless set of pearly white teeth. A warmth crept up Coby's cheeks, suffusing them in a deep shade of crimson.

"Hello Gracie and son!" he exclaimed, his voice filled with genuine excitement. "Welcome to my party." With an inviting gesture, he urged them to step inside. Ewan's eyes widened in delight as he caught sight of the adorable puppy, and with excitement, he rushed inside. Janie's excited barks filled the air as he lifted her into his arms, her wet tongue leaving a trail of slobbery kisses on his face, a perfect pairing that warmed Coby's heart. Gracie greeted him with a soft peck on his lips, igniting a spark of excitement within him. As she handed him a beautifully adorned gift box, his fingertips tingled with anticipation.

"Happy birthday, Mister McTavish," she serenaded in her angelic voice. With envy etched across their ethereal faces, the spectral quartet silently observed the living beings. As the spotlight fell upon Gracie, she emerged from the shadows, every inch a walking, talking, living doll. Her porcelain skin shimmered under the soft glow of the chandelier lights, casting an ethereal glow upon her. Her cerulean eyes sparkled with a mesmerising light, captivating all who beheld them. The subtle scent of her perfume wafted through the air, a delicate floral fragrance that added to her allure. Her lips, painted a perfect shade of rose, curved into a smile that held the apparitions captive, their admiration palpable.

With every step she took, Gracie moved with a grace that bordered on the surreal. Each movement was measured, every gesture deliberate, as if choreographed by a higher power. It was as if she had stepped out of the pages of a fairy tale, embodying the epitome of perfection and beauty in a world that often fell short.

"Please call me Coby," Coby said, his voice carrying a hint of warmth as he followed Gracie's graceful footsteps towards the inviting aromas of the Kitchen. "Or Cowboy, but it's up to you."

With a coy glance over her shoulder, Gracie responded, her eyes twinkling mischievously. "Coby it is," she said, her words accompanied by a playful smile. "But not cowboy like your ex-girlfriend."

Coby couldn't help but chuckle, impressed by her foresight. Meanwhile, young Ewan, his cheeks rosy and his smile bright, lingered in the hallway, his gaze fixated on the tantalising display of treats. With the help of the seasoned window washer, Coby had already sliced the alluring chocolate cake into eight equal, mouthwatering pieces.

Ewan's hand reached out, his fingers itching to steal a slice, his mouth watering in anticipation. His eyes gleamed with a hint of mischief, reflecting the flickering candlelight. Just as his stubby fingers sank into the velvety texture of the slice, he caught a whiff of Jane inhaling deeply before blowing out the candles.

Her breath escaped her lips in a chilly puff, brushing against his fingertips and sending a shiver down his spine. His sturdy frame faltered, his feet buckling beneath him. The blood drained from his face, revealing the constellation of freckles that adorned his cheeks.

Wide-eyed, his emerald orbs resembled saucers, filled with a mixture of surprise and fear. In a high-pitched shriek, he cried out, "mummy!" The sound pierced through the air, echoing off the walls as he darted towards the kitchen, seeking solace and safety.

Coby could hear the mischievous chuckles of the apparitions emanating from the dimly lit hallway, their eerie sounds echoing through the air. He did not need to ask. He could see the mischievous glint in their translucent eyes, knowing they had pulled a nasty prank on young Ewan. But from his experience, he guessed the lad must have done something to deserve such treatment.

"What's wrong?" Gracie cooed, her voice as gentle as a summer breeze. She tenderly wiped away the tears streaming down her son's glossy cheeks, soothing him with her touch. Janie looked on with adoration, her bright eyes darting back and forth between Ewan and Gracie, her tail wagging eagerly, as if she held a secret to share.

"There's a go... ghost!" Ewan cried out between his sobs, his voice trembling with fear, as he pointed a shaky finger towards the eerie hallway. Janie yapped incessantly, as if trying to substantiate the young lad's claims.

Coby hurried to the hallway, determined to have a word with Jane and her mischievous accomplices. In the background, he could hear Gracie softly saying, "There is no such thing as ghosts." He scoffed, dismissing her skepticism, but as he reached the hallway, his eyes widened. There, before him, he noticed a slice of cake, its perfect wedge now out of place, with indents where Ewan's fingers had sunk into the softness. He let it be, realising that Jane had only done what any caring mother or mature woman would have done in her position. He cast a quick glance their way, and caught sight of the mischievous smile on Jane's face, daring him with her intense, fiery gaze. *Good for her*, he thought, and joined his guests.

Coby poured Ewan a tall glass of bubbling, hissing Irn-Bru, and the sight of the fizzy orange liquid brought a sense of comfort to the young lad. Gracie, seeking solace, found comfort in the rich aroma of a Drambuie, the golden elixir swirling in the delicate liqueur glass. Coby's eyes were fixed on her as she delicately touched the glass to her lips, her expression filled with pleasure. The aroma of the rich beverage filled the air, teasing his senses and igniting a sense of anticipation.

Janie barked excitedly, the sound echoing through the air as she followed Ewan out through the front door. Watching Ewan and Janie together amidst the lush landscape, Coby felt a bittersweet ache in his chest. He could smell the fresh scent of the outdoors as they ventured on their hunting adventure. Ewan aimed his catapult at imaginary birds, and the sharp twang of the elastic echoed through the air, blending with Janie's excited barks.

Meanwhile, Coby turned up the music slightly, filling the room with the gentle melodies of Celtic music. He and Gracie settled into chairs, feeling the weight of Jane and Vivienne's ethereal presence. The sound of murmurs and whispers filled the space, bouncing off the walls.

Gracie, dressed in blue jeans and a champagne silk blouse, captivated Jane and Vivienne with her sleek collar bones stressed by the Celtic knot pendant swaying from her neck. The pendant's interlacing lines represented eternity and continuity, mesmerising the ethereal duo. They couldn't help but whisper and hiss in astonishment.

With a hint of anticipation, Gracie asked, "Who else is coming?" Her words hung in the air, and Coby found himself enchanted by the shapes her lips made as she spoke. He tore his gaze away from her mouth, snapping out of his trance.

"Ach," he managed, "I put an invitation up at the Stag's Head Inn." The name of the pub held significance, causing Gracie to flinch.

She carefully arranged an assortment of mouth-watering treats on a paper plate, their enticing aroma instantly filling the room.

"Ewan!" she called, her voice carrying a mix of urgency and excitement. Her son, with Janie eagerly by his side, stormed into the hallway. Coby could see the eagerness in his wide eyes as he snatched the plate and stuffed the treats into his mouth.

"Thank you, mum," Ewan exclaimed, his voice brimming with excitement. "And thank you, Mister Mac... Mac... Ta..." he mumbled, his words muffled by the food. He settled on the stairs, sharing his treats with Janie. Tears of pure joy welled up in Coby's eyes, glistening like tiny diamonds, as he looked at Ewan and Janie happily sitting on the worn-out steps. He carefully pulled out his sleek phone and aimed the camera at them, hoping to capture the vibrant moment forever. Just as he was about to press the shutter button, a gentle whisper caressed his cheek, accompanied by a subtle fragrance of lilacs. Gracefully, the ethereal trinity stepped in front of his lens, their luminous figures shimmering like a mirage. Yet, with a mischievous smile playing on his lips, Coby defiantly snapped the picture, feeling a surge of excitement course through his veins. The moment his eyes met the screen, a heightened sense of anxiety consumed him. Gradually, the ethereal figures materialised, their translucent forms taking on substance and evoking a sense of wonder. "Good god!" he exclaimed, flinging the phone away as if it burned his hand.

Coby's heart pounded in his chest, the rapid thumping reverberating in his ears. He took a step back, his breath hitching in his throat. The room seemed to swirl around him, colours blending together in a dizzying whirl. He felt trapped by the heavy and suffocating air, as if it tightly embraced him. The spectral trio remained suspended in the air, their ethereal forms pulsating with an otherworldly glow. Their eyes, filled with wisdom and mystery, bore into Coby's soul, their presence overwhelming and captivating. His spine tingled with a shiver, causing goosebumps to rise on his arms.

Fear and curiosity warred within him, each emotion battling for dominance. His mind raced, trying to comprehend the inexplicable sight before him. Frozen in awe and terror, he felt a gentle breeze caress his cheek, carrying with it the delicate fragrance of lilacs. It was as if the spirits were reaching out to him, their intentions unknown but undeniably powerful. Coby's thoughts jumbled together, his rationality slipping away as a sense of wonder and unease consumed him.

With a shaky hand, he reached down and picked up his phone, the screen still displaying the captured image. The apparitions, now fully visible, seemed to emanate an energy that pulsed through the photograph. It was a moment frozen in time, a glimpse into a world beyond his comprehension.

Taking a deep breath, Coby's curiosity overcame his fear. He couldn't let this opportunity slip away. With determination in his eyes, he focused on the image, his mind racing with questions and a new found sense of purpose.

Gracie, unaware of Coby's distress, shattered the silence with her comforting voice. "Don't forget, Ewan's birthday is approaching," she said, her hand finding comfort on his shoulder. Lost in his thoughts, the sudden and unexpected touch jolted him back to reality, leaving him momentarily disoriented.

Lost in thought, he absentmindedly asked, "When?" and as he did, the familiar sights of the room snapped back into focus.

Gracie's lips curved into a sensuous smile as she radiated satisfaction in response to the question. "November ninth," she replied, her face clouded with regret. "He will turn eight. It's exactly a month after Giles died." Her expression became enveloped in a shroud of sadness.

The words hung heavy in the air, mingling with the ironically familiar melody of Elton John's "I'm Still Standing" playing softly in the background. Memories flooded Coby's mind, as if a veil had been lifted, revealing a vivid tapestry of the past. He found himself in the library, surrounded by the gentle rustling of pages and the unmistakable scent of old books. Everything felt incredibly vivid and lifelike, as if he could reach out and touch the newspaper pages between his fingers.

In that precise moment, Coby's mind flickered, recalling the date on the newspaper article in vivid detail. The article, which detailed the enigmatic happenings surrounding Giles' tragic end, had a distinct aroma of aged paper and ink. Gracie's mention of a month, filled with vibrant autumn foliage, brought back memories so intense that they transformed the present surroundings into a hazy, ethereal state. Coby remembered capturing the article on his phone, the sound of the camera shutter freezing that moment in digital form. But what truly resonated was the precise date – October – an indelible imprint etched in his mind. The article, a relic from nine years ago, hit him like a sudden bolt of lightning, shattering his belief that Ewan could be Giles' son. The realisation pierced his senses, leaving a lingering taste of bitter truth. Ewan's birth, which occurred ten months after Giles' perplexing demise, added another layer of complexity to the tangled web of family connections.

Coby almost uttered his thoughts aloud, but he caught himself. Suddenly, the locals' derogatory term for Gracie, "tart," clicked in his mind.

Coby finally understood why Ewan's distinct features stood out. The fiery red hair, a stark contrast to Gile's pitch black hair, caught the light in a mesmerising way. His rounder frame gave him a softness that was accentuated by his freckles, sprinkled across his cheeks like stars in a clear night sky. And then there were his mesmerising emerald eyes, twinkling mischievously and betraying a hint of mystery. It was as if Ewan himself had a secret, clear in his knowing smile.

Gracie's gentle touch on Coby's arm sent a shiver down his spine, her delicate fingers leaving a lingering warmth.

"Is something wrong?" she asked, her voice drifting to him through a distant fog of thoughts. The sound was muffled, barely reaching his ears, as his own inner turmoil consumed him. Startled, he flinched and involuntarily jerked his hand away, a wave of repulsion washing over him. Gracie raised her eyebrows, suspicion clouding her expression. "Can I have more, mum!" Ewan's eager voice echoed down the staircase, resonating through the hallway as Janie hurried after him. The abruptness of the interruption hit Coby with a sharp blow, causing a jolt of recognition to course through him. Ewan's accent, tinged with a hint of English, evoked a sense of familiarity, but he couldn't quite pinpoint it.

Gracie lined a platter with a selection of treats, their sweet aroma wafting through the air. "Later, when we gather to sing for Uncle Coby, we can enjoy some cake together, alright?"

"Yes, mum," Ewan replied, his words slightly muffled by the food in his mouth. "Thanks, Uncle Coby," he added before swiftly making his way out of the room, Janie by his side. The sound of their footsteps echoed softly in the hallway.

Coby furrowed his brow in deep thought, a smile tugging at his lips. Ewan's voice echoed with "Uncle Coby" instead of the usual formal "Mister," immediately capturing his attention.

"He has a keen appetite," Coby finally remarked, his words hanging in the air. The contrast between Ewan's voracious appetite and his supposed father's slender frame struck him as peculiar. Gracie visibly recoiled at his observation, a flicker of unease crossing her face.

"Yes," she responded tersely, her voice holding a note of tension. She quickly changed the subject, asking, "How is your new book coming along?" The obvious question confirmed Coby's suspicions.

In an effort to ward off the impending uncomfortable silence, Coby willingly went along with the diversion. "Very well, thanks for asking," he replied casually.

Gracie furrowed her brow, suspicion lingering in her gaze. Her eyes, usually dreamy and distant, now fixed on him with intensity, urging him to share more details.

Coby casually shrugged, his eyes gleaming mischievously. "I have made remarkable progress and startling discoveries," he teased, "but you'll have to wait until it's published."

Her excitement palpable, Gracie exclaimed, "I can't wait!" With a playful slap on Coby's shoulder, she flashed him an impish smile, mischief dancing in her eyes.

Coby carefully took the empty glass from her, feeling the coolness of her fingers sending a jolt through his hand, and swiftly headed to the kitchen. The sound of the fizzy Irn-Bru filled the air as Gracie poured Ewan a glass, the bubbles dancing and popping. Holding her Drambuie, she looked at her son with adoration as he sat on the step, completely captivated by the mesmerising sunset. Gracie's intense gaze erased any lingering thoughts Coby had about the enigmatic man who fathered her son.

Taking a sip of his whisky, Coby wondered what thoughts were running through her mind. He felt a warm sense of comfort wash over him, a stark contrast to the constant barking of orders from Elaine. The mere act of being near Gracie filled him with an indescribable happiness. For the first time since he arrived, he felt a sense of hope that perhaps the future held better things for both of them. With that in mind, he decided to hold on to the good news he had to share for a little longer, relishing the growing excitement.

As the night grew darker, the melodious tunes of ABBA resonated through the room, filling the air with nostalgia. The timeless pop anthems brought a warm smile to their faces, as if transported to another era. Despite the absence of others, Coby felt a profound sense of contentment in the presence of his current company. He had always prioritised substance over sheer volume.

Gracie's fondness for the Drambuie was clear in the way she savoured each sip. The delightful aroma of the liqueur filled the air, creating a harmonious blend with the surroundings. The sound of their glasses clinking shattered the icy silence, instantly thawing the distance between them and igniting a newfound connection. Gracie found her rhythm, tapping her foot in sync with the lively tunes that filled the room, while her animated conversations captivated Coby's attention.

Gracie's eyes, filled with memories of her love for Giles, shone with a mixture of joy and sorrow as they continued their heartfelt conversations. The corners of her lips curled into a wistful smile, while her gaze seemed to wander into the distant past, reliving the moments they had shared.

Similarly, Coby's face radiated with a warm nostalgia as he fondly reminisced about his time with Elaine. The lines on his forehead softened, and a gentle glow of contentment spread across his features. His eyes, filled with gratitude, sparkled with an unmistakable twinkle, reflecting the cherished memories he held dear.

Gracie and Coby found solace and comfort in their discussions, their voices filling the air with a mix of nostalgia and longing.

Chapter Thirteen

Amidst the enchanting ambiance, the ethereal quartet, always present and vigilant, joyously celebrated Coby's birthday. They seamlessly merged into the dance, their spectral forms gracefully swaying to the melody, their movements a mesmerising sight. Yet, their mischievous glee was most apparent when they playfully tormented Ewan. Their laughter echoed, reverberating through Coby's ears, as Ewan's complexion paled, a clear victim of their pranks. Mockingly, they extended their spectral fingers towards Ewan's ashen face, playfully labelling him the "Alabaster starry face."

With Gracie rushing to the bathroom, Coby tentatively approached the apparitions, taking care not to disturb their ethereal presence. He engaged them in a hushed conversation, his voice a gentle plea. With kindness, he requested they treat the young lad with care, urging them to be lenient. Their reaction was a collective gasp, followed by a chorus of mischievous giggles, their antics reminiscent of misbehaving children.

A fresh scent, reminiscent of the wild, filled the air, instantly capturing Coby's attention. It was a raw and primal musk, conjuring images of deer wandering through dense forests. Amidst the urban setting, it felt strangely out of place, yet undeniably powerful. Suddenly, an icy coldness descended, causing a shiver to race down Coby's spine.

The ethereal quartet sensed an impending doom, huddling together like frightened sheep seeking shelter from a relentless hailstorm. Darkness consumed the room, and time seemed to freeze momentarily. In that fleeting moment, Coby's ears caught a faint whooshing sound, like the whisper of the wind, as a man materialised before his eyes. It was Giles, Gracie's deceased husband, his ghostly figure bearing the unmistakable mark of the fatal bullet that pierced his heart.

Dressed in his camouflaged hunting attire, Giles lurked above the ethereal foursome, their hisses and shrieks echoing through the air, as he stared them down with a menacing intensity. Jane, Vivienne, and Josephine scattered into the murky shadows like ethereal wisps of smoke. Sandra, however, stood her ground, her gaze unwavering, her eyes radiating with a malevolent glint. A knowing smile curled upon her lips, and Giles acknowledged it with a fleeting glance, revealing a shared wisdom between them.

Giles turned his gaze towards his wife, his eyes filled with longing, before disappearing into the mysterious depths of the shadows beyond the front door. The musky scent hung in the air, a lingering reminder of the ethereal presence that had recently moved through.

Coby's frown lines deepened, and his intense eyes widened in disbelief at what he had just witnessed. Giles, with an otherworldly presence, appeared to exist beyond the confines of his surroundings. The air crackled with mystery and anticipation as he wondered where Giles' domain could be. Perhaps he lingered in the shadows of the quaint cottage, where echoes of his and Gracie's laughter still resonated.

Within these boundaries, the haunting image of Giles seemed to wander aimlessly, casting a shadow of unease. Coby's voice barely carried the word "phantom," the disbelief clear in his tone. The word hung in the chilly air, causing Gracie to gaze at him with curiosity, sensing his distant thoughts. She rose from her seat and closed the creaky front door, the sound reverberating through the room, a sudden interruption to Coby's musings. Involuntarily, he repeated the word "phantom," this time as an exclamation. Gracie looked at him in surprise, her brows furrowed with confusion.

"What did you say?" she asked, trying to make sense of his sudden detachment. Realising his slip, Coby quickly composed himself. Gracie, her arms wrapped around her body, rubbed them up and down to ward off the cold. The gesture was a physical manifestation of her concern for Coby's well-being. With a nurturing touch, she placed an assortment of treats on a delicate plate and handed it to him.

Noting the pallor on his face, she affectionately remarked, her voice radiating warmth. "You look like a ghost. Come on, have something to eat now."

Absentmindedly, Coby took a bite of the chocolate pastry, savouring the delectable flavours that danced upon his tongue. The opulent and smooth flavour engulfed his senses, momentarily transporting him away from the ethereal moment.

"Ewan!" Gracie called out, her voice breaking the silence. Her son emerged from the shadows, accompanied by Janie, his loyal companion. The flickering candlelight illuminated their faces as Gracie ignited the candles on the birthday cake. Together, they harmoniously chanted the familiar melody, their voices blending in celebration of Coby's special day. With the room resonating with the chorus, the apparitions of Jane, Josephine, and Vivienne materialised once again, their ethereal figures blending harmoniously with the jubilant atmosphere. Jane added own unique twist to the traditional chant, incorporating snippets of a Scottish clan's battle cry, their voices merging seamlessly with the rhythm.

Coby's laughter erupted, a melodic sound that filled the room, while Gracie, unable to comprehend the source of amusement, watched in puzzlement. Ewan eagerly took his slice of cake, balancing it precariously on his plate piled high with treats, as he scampered up the stairs. Coby imagined the sound of laughter filling the house as he shared his bounty with Janie, their hunting games coming to life. Coby thought the evening couldn't be more perfect, with the sound of laughter and the aroma of his favourite foods filling the air. His eyes lingered on Gracie, drawn to her enchanting presence and the alluring temptation of her lips. Sensing his desires, she leaned in close, her lips moist and inviting, tempting him to savour their intoxicating taste.

Just as their lips grazed, the sound of the knocker echoed through the hallway, jolting them out of their passionate moment. They exchanged a curious glance, their eyes wide with anticipation, just before the front door creaked open, its hinges groaning in protest. The unmistakable white top hat, adorned with a black ribbon, announced Alistair Sinclair's untimely entry. He cautiously poked his head through the narrow gap in the door, his menacing grin spreading wide, exposing a set of discoloured teeth. Gracie's gasp pierced the silence, her scream of terror echoing through the air and causing

Coby's heart to race.

She forcefully snatched the half-empty whisky glass from the table and flung it in Alistair's direction. Alistair's eyes widened in astonishment as the glass shattered upon impact, the sharp fragments of crystal colliding with the wooden frame and filling the air with a cacophony of splintering sounds. Alistair cried out in pain as the shards of glass and burning liquid pierced his skin and blinded him. A strong smell of whisky permeated the air, blending with the metallic tang of fear.

Lost in his agony, Alistair stumbled backward, his balance betraying him. The room filled with a resounding thud as he crashed onto the floor. Coby, overcome with concern, rushed to his aid, dropping to his knees beside him. He extended a hand, helping Alistair to his unsteady feet. The once immaculate white suit now bore traces of dust, evidence of his sudden tumble.

"I beg your pardon," Alistair muttered, his voice tinged with both anguish and annoyance. "I thought this was an open invitation." He retrieved his walking stick and top hat from the floor, hastily making his way down the grand staircase towards his sleek Range Rover, its metallic body glimmering under the moonlight. The engine roared to life, its powerful rumble filling the night air, as he sped off, the tires spinning and leaving tracks in the gravel.

Breathing heavily, Coby turned to Gracie, confusion etched on his face as he rejoined her. She was frantically gathering her belongings, preparing to leave the scene of chaos and uncertainty.

"What was that about?" Coby asked, his voice filled with a mix of concern and bewilderment as they stood amidst the aftermath of Alistair Sinclair's unexpected intrusion.

"I am sorry!" she spat, her voice dripping with venom. The words slashed through the air like a poisonous blade as she declared, "I cannot be your friend any longer." Her eyes burned with anger and hurt, tears threatening to spill over. Overwhelmed by a torrent of emotions, her trembling hands flew to her eyes, the sound of her sobs echoing in the room.

The weight of her pain brought her to her knees, her body convulsing with each heart-wrenching sob. Coby, feeling the intensity of her despair, wrapped his arm around her shoulders, pulling her into an embrace radiating warmth and comfort. He could feel the violent tremors coursing through her fragile frame, her sadness stirring a whirlwind of emotions within him. Despite his desire to comfort her and reveal his surprise, he held back, allowing her to find solace at her own pace. Amid her tearful confessions, her uncontrollable sobs muffled her words, making it difficult for him to make out what she was saying. Leaning in closer, he caught fragments of her broken plea.

"He," Gracie choked, sobbing uncontrollably, "He," her voice hitched as she took a shuddering breath, mustering the strength to divulge her secret, "He raped me," she whispered, the words barely escaping her lips, her voice a haunting melody of remorse and anguish. The revelation hung heavy in the air, disbelief flooding Coby's mind.

"What!" Coby exclaimed, his voice a crescendo of incredulity, the shock reverberating through the room like a thunderclap. The ethereal trinity leaned in closer, their murmurs of astonishment a chorus that pierced the silence. Their eyes, like flickering embers, filled with sadness as they gathered around Gracie.

Summoning her inner strength, Gracie untangled herself from her contorted position, her eyes locked on Coby. Her eyes, red and glossy, mirrored a profound sadness that words alone could not express. She nodded her head, her silent repetition a testament to the weight of her words. Her body trembled with a potent blend of fear, anger, and anguish, her muscles quivering with the intensity of her emotions. The colour drained from her face, leaving her complexion pale and lifeless. Each breath she took seemed laboured, as if the air itself had turned heavy and suffocating.

Coby watched in both awe and distress as Gracie's entire being seemed to crumble under the weight of her confession. He could see the toll it had taken on her physically, the lines of exhaustion etched deeply into her once vibrant features. Her shoulders slumped, burdened by the weight of her secret, and her hands now hung limply by her sides.

His outstretched arms enveloped her, and he immediately noticed the clammy, hot sensation of her skin against his hands. He could feel the rapid, erratic heartbeat pulsating through her chest, as if it were desperately trying to escape the torment within. The tremors that had wracked her body now seemed to have subsided, leaving her drained and fragile.

Gracie's tear-stained eyes met Coby's, a mix of vulnerability and determination shining through. She had summoned the courage to share her deepest pain, to lay bare the darkness that had haunted her. And in that moment, Coby understood the enormity of what she had just entrusted him with.

Silence enveloped the room as they both processed the magnitude of her revelation. The weight of her words hung in the air, suffocating and oppressive. Coby's mind raced, his heart torn between a desire to comfort and protect her and an overwhelming rage at the injustice she had suffered.

But above all, Coby knew that in this fragile moment, his role was not to offer immediate solutions. It was to be a pillar of support, a source of strength for Gracie as she navigated the painful aftermath of her confession. And so, with a gentle squeeze of his arm around her, he silently conveyed his unwavering commitment to stand by her side through the storm that lay ahead.

Without the need to urge her on, she laid it all bare. Tears streamed down her face as she sniffled, her voice trembling between her gasps, barely above a whisper. The air was thick with the scent of sorrow and vulnerability.

"After Giles died," she managed to say, her voice choked with emotion. "He... he..." Her words trailed off, lost in the weight of her grief. She took a deep breath, trying to steady herself.

"Alistair came to my house to offer his condolences." She paused, her eyes scanning the room, making sure her son was not within earshot. "I was vulnerable, and he brought a bottle of his fancy wine." Gracie's voice quivered as she spoke, the memories weighing heavily on her shoulders. "I got tipsy, because I had not eaten in days. And then he forced himself..." The words hung in the air, a painful confession that she had carried for far too long.

Coby had heard enough. He knew where this was going, and the thought of the grim details made him cringe. The room seemed to close in on him, suffocating him with the weight of Gracie's pain.

"I can't even imagine what you've been through," he interrupted, his voice filled with compassion. "But please know, I'm here for you."

A thin smile played on Gracie's lips, and for a moment, the room seemed to brighten. It was the kindest words she had heard in a long while, a glimmer of hope in the darkness.

Coby sometimes heard how the workers talked to her, taunting her, making suggestive remarks. It aggravated him that people would treat a woman in dire need, the way they did. He had a word with their supervisor, and the taunting ceased. The room felt a little lighter, the air less suffocating.

"I... I didn't know who else to turn to, Coby," Gracie whispered, her voice filled with regret. Her words were barely audible, choked by the lump in her throat, burdened by the weight of her secret. Coby gently stroked her hair, relishing the softness of the silky strands. He looked into her eyes, seeing the pain and vulnerability reflected in them.

"It's just... it's been eating me alive, Coby," she confessed, her voice barely above a whisper. "I couldn't keep it a secret any longer. I needed someone to know."

"Mum!" Ewan's voice boomed from the top of the staircase, jolting them out of their embrace. The sound reverberated through the room, breaking the heavy silence.

The shattered remnants of their magic spell left them exposed, with Ewan's presence looming over them. Coby watched in awe as Gracie's eyes sparkled with determination, her posture straightened, and her shoulders squared. With a sigh, she wiped away her tears and swiftly jumped up. Her hands moved effortlessly as she carefully assembled a slice of cake and a selection of treats onto a paper plate. The sound of Ewan's feet thumping against the stairs filled the room as he eagerly descended, his excitement palpable. He snatched the delectable treats from Gracie's hand, his joy infectious.

Meanwhile, Coby refilled their drinks, the clinking of glasses filling the room. He cranked up the volume, and the familiar tunes filled the room, creating a soothing ambiance. Despite the broken magic spell, he felt a glimmer of hope that he could restore it. A surprise he had in store, a glimmer of happiness amidst the darkness.

"Gracie, there's something I have been eager to show you," Coby said, his voice a soft murmur as he gently took Gracie's hand. Guiding her towards his office, Gracie's hand felt stiff in his, her reluctance clear in each hesitant step she took. The ghostly figures floated behind them, their otherworldly presence creating an air of intrigue.

"Shut your eyes," Coby whispered, his words barely audible. Gracie obeyed, her eyelids shutting tightly, transforming her into a picture of delicate beauty, akin to a slumbering princess from a fairytale. With great care, he gently arranged her hands, palms up, and silently retrieved the brand new laptop from his drawer. He savoured the moment, prolonging her anticipation, noticing her eyelids twitching to steal a glance.

"Don't look!" he warned with a mischievous grin, gently placing the laptop in her eager hands. Gracie's eyes flew open in surprise as she felt the sleek design in her hands, her brow furrowing in confusion.

"I'm confused," she uttered, her voice tinged with a curious tone.

"I need a research assistant," Coby declared, his voice brimming with determination. "Although it's only part-time, the pay is good." Pausing for effect, he felt a wave of relief wash over him as he witnessed the joy that spread across Gracie's flawless face. "I had thought about placing an ad in the newspapers, but ever since I met you, I... I..." he struggled to find the right words to convey his feelings.

Gracie's face beamed with unadulterated joy, her excitement palpable in the air. Setting the laptop aside, she leaped into his arms, peppering his face with tender kisses. "Coby!" she exclaimed, her voice filled with uncontainable happiness. "You don't know how much this means to me!"

The sheer magnitude of the response caught Coby off guard. His heart swelled with joy as he retrieved a stack of documents from his drawer, handing them over to Gracie. "Mrs Drummond, here is your contract. I am pleased to have you join my team." Extending his hand in agreement, he awaited her response.

Instead, Gracie's joyful shriek pierced the air, her excitement contagious. Pulling him into a warm embrace, she showered him with affectionate kisses, overwhelming him with her love and gratitude. The ethereal trinity stood in silence, their eyes filled with a bittersweet mix of awe, joy, and sadness.

Chapter Fourteen

Sundays were always a sensory delight for Coby. He relished the quiet absence of bustling workers and chattering people around him, allowing him to fully immerse himself in his writing. Elaine used to find solace in the rhythmic chants and hymns of the church, while Coby preferred the tranquillity of silent contemplation.

Coby's gaze flickered between the foreboding manila envelope bearing his name, and the gift Gracie had brought him for his birthday. The anticipation tightened his chest.

"Let's start with the bad news," he whispered, quickly ripping open the envelope. The soft rustling of the paper filled the air as he revealed the contents within. The conditions of his divorce decree lay before him, a heavy burden that made his heart sink. Without dwelling on it, he hastily skimmed the document once before signing it. After all, he was the one who had walked out on Elaine. With a sense of accomplishment, he placed the signed document in his outbox.

His future hinged on the success of his latest book, a thought that weighed heavily on his mind. If things took a turn for the worst, he could always sell the estate. But what would become of Gracie and her precious son, Ewan? An inner storm brewed, leaving him struggling to "get it together," as Elaine used to say.

Yearning for a moment of respite, Coby eagerly tore open the gift from Gracie. His breath hitched in his throat as his eyes fell upon a beautiful framed photograph. It depicted Gracie and Ewan standing side by side, bathed in sunlight reflected off a serene lake. The sight brought tears of joy to his eyes, and he carefully placed the photograph next to his monitor. Now, he could steal glances at them amidst his work, finding solace in their presence.

Coby quickly composed an email to his former real estate agent, urgently requesting the sale of his beloved sanctuary in Peebles. It was a decision that required little contemplation, as he knew it had to be done.

Now, as he sat in his dimly lit study, Coby's focus shifted to his true purpose. The apparitions that lingered in his thoughts had become the central topic of his latest work. With the excitement of the previous day's events still fresh in his memory, he eagerly positioned his fingers on the keys of his keyboard and began typing 'Josephine banana' into the search bar. With each keystroke, the gentle hum of his computer filled the room, creating a soothing atmosphere.

A moment of anticipation passed before a startling discovery awaited him. The search results unveiled a list of videos, each with its own tantalising title. One particular video caught his attention immediately. The title read 'Josephine Barker's banana dance.' Intrigued, Coby clicked on it, and the room filled with the lively rhythm of jazz music. The screen displayed the iconic Josephine Barker, her vibrant energy radiating through the grainy footage. Her poised figure, adorned in a scandalous banana skirt, further emphasised her no-nonsense attitude. From his encounters with her apparition, he could discern that Josephine was undeniably genuine, perhaps just a year shy of her actual age.

Coby's extensive and quick research revealed that Josephine Barker had died from natural causes, adding to the perplexity of her presence as an apparition. Yet he knew that the notion of 'unfinished business' was nothing more than a myth. Josephine must have had a compelling reason for staying behind, and he was determined to uncover it. What became clear was that music and dance were integral to the ethereal trinity, acting as a valuable key. As he pondered this, a memory resurfaced – a case he had previously worked on. It involved a grieving mother who had lost her son. Even after her own passing, she stubbornly remained in the realm of the living, her spirit determined to find him before crossing over. Coby's involvement in that discovery had given him an immense sense of accomplishment. Since then, he had delved into countless enigmas, uncovering the eerie ties between apparitions and their haunting locales across the globe.

The pieces of the ethereal puzzle slowly came together, each one fitting into place like a delicate whisper. Coby's attention turned towards Vivienne, captivated by her mesmerising can-can rendition. He marvelled at the way she effortlessly adjusted her dance routine to match the rhythm of the music, her graceful movements a symphony of elegance. Frustrated by his unsuccessful attempts to find information about, he typed 'Vivienne can-can' into the search bar, only to be met with empty results. Undeterred, he tried 'Vivienne Moulin Rouge,' hoping for a breakthrough, but again, the search yielded no answers. His frustration grew, but his determination remained unshaken.

He delved deeper, searching for 'famous Moulin Rouge dancers,' scouring through a list of images, hoping to catch a glimpse of the mysterious figure that had captured his attention. Hours turned into an endless stream as he meticulously compared each image to the spectral vision of Vivienne etched in his mind. And then, as if guided by fate, he struck gold. It was her playful smile, a glimmer of mischief in her eyes, that betrayed her true identity. The replica captured every eerie detail of the spectre that plagued his sanctuary. Vivienne's hair was an exquisite display, with spectral ribbons and ethereal flowers intricately woven into an elaborate updo. The otherworldly light illuminated the petals of the flowers, creating a magical and enchanting glow around her ethereal appearance. Her dress, adorned with delicate lace, showcased her refined taste and elegance, the intricate patterns a testament to her timeless allure.

Finally, he had her full name, Vivienne LeClaire, a name that rolled off the tongue like a melody. With anticipation in his eyes, he entered her name into the search bar. A quick search result gave him all the information he needed, and it deeply intrigued him. His eyes caught the first title that showed up in the search results, 'MYSTERY IN MONTMARTRE: THE ENIGMATIC DEMISE OF VIVIENNE LECLAIRE, JEWEL OF THE MOULIN ROUGE.'

Leaning in close, Coby could feel his heart race with excitement as he delved into the article, completely absorbed.

In the heart of Montmartre, beneath the glimmering lights of the Moulin Rouge, everyone's lips once danced with the name Vivienne LeClaire. She was the jewel of the cabaret, captivating audiences with every twirl and pirouette, embodying the intoxicating allure of the can-can. But beneath the sequins and feathers, Vivienne concealed secrets darker than the Parisian night.

One winter's evening, she mysteriously vanished. The following morning, the city awoke to shocking news – Vivienne LeClaire, the beloved dancer, had been found dead. The circumstances surrounding her demise were shrouded in mystery, a puzzle as intricate as the labyrinthine streets of Montmartre itself.

Her lifeless body was discovered in an obscure alley, a crimson stain marring the cobblestone. Beside her lay a single white rose, its pristine petals providing a stark contrast against the grim tableau. It was a symbol, a message, but from whom? And why?

As news of her tragic death spread through the city, whispers of foul play began to circulate. The police were bewildered, and the public was horrified. Who would want to harm the darling of the Moulin Rouge? And more importantly, why?

In life, Vivienne had remained an enigma, a woman who danced in the limelight while evading prying eyes. In death, she became a legend, her story echoing through the ages, serving as a poignant reminder of the fragility concealed beneath the glittering facade of the showbiz world.

Vivienne LeClaire's untimely end remains one of Paris' most intriguing unsolved mysteries. They say her spirit still haunts the Moulin Rouge, forever etched as a spectral dancer in the heart of the city she adored.

With a showman's flair, Coby let out a playful whistle and made his way towards the chaotic whiteboard. He felt a flicker of curiosity as he pondered the mysterious connection between Vivienne, Josephine, and Jane. His stately home, with its captivating presence of haunting spirits, exceeded his expectations and sent shivers down his spine. As he surveyed the room, the ethereal ambiance seemed to whisper secrets that were slowly unravelling. The haunting melody of Sandra's voice echoed in his mind, guiding him towards understanding her tragic demise and the motives behind it. Unexpectedly, the enigmatic presence of the Phantom of Giles added another layer to the puzzle.

Lost in thought, Coby meticulously categorised the chronicles on his whiteboard, searching for simplicity. His previous experiences had taught him that by delving into one mystery, he often stumbled upon threads that tied together the enigmatic events. Focusing his attention on Sandra, he resolved to unravel her story.

Immersed in his research, Coby scoured the internet for details about Sandra's untimely end. The images and information he stumbled upon created a vivid, mental snapshot. The memory of his encounter with Sandra left a lingering sense of a hidden love affair with Lord Lucas. Yet, this tale had hidden depths waiting to be discovered. One particular fact caught his attention – conflicting accounts from close family members claiming Lord Lucas had taken his own life in Newhaven.

With a heavy sigh, Coby shifted his focus to his emails, hoping for a response from his contact at New Scotland Yard. Disappointment washed over him as he saw no new messages. With determination, he crafted a new email, meticulously including essential details in his inquiry.

Despite Sandra, the nanny, preparing tea, he couldn't help but wonder how the kitchen lights were switched off. Moreover, how could the killer have silently and effortlessly placed her lifeless body into a sack without any assistance? If the car Lord Lucas had used to flee was a borrowed car, it raises the question of who placed the piece of lead pipe in the back. It was during the investigation that the discovery of the so-called murder weapon finally surfaced, but by then, Lord Lucas had already fled.

Coby's sense of urgency compelled him to take swift and decisive action. He set his plan in motion, his eyes filled with unwavering determination, propelling him forward towards his goal. He followed the dimly lit corridor, the flickering light casting eerie shadows on the peeling walls. The musty smell of old dampness filled his nostrils as he made his way to the trapdoor. Step by step, he made his way down the spiral staircase and into the dimly lit abyss of the basement. With a simple flick of the switch, the room was bathed in light, yet an unsettling silence filled the space. While walking down the labyrinth corridor, he came across Spectral Vision, who was sitting on the bottom step of the buttery, accompanied by the ghostly presence of Josephine. Their ethereal presence filled the room, emanating a luminous glow and creating eerie shadows on the walls.

Coby whispered, "Morning ladies," careful not to startle them, and cautiously approached. The apparitions, known for their ability to startle others, seemed surprised by his abrupt interruption. Their eyes, like glowing embers, seemed to penetrate deep into his core.

He asked Josephine to find out from Sandra if she had any information about what had happened to her lover, Lord Lucas, and if she had any visions of him in the spiritual world. Sandra leaned forward, her finger tracing delicate patterns in the layer of dust, her unique way of conveying messages. Coby pondered why she avoided direct conversation, her eyes betraying the deep-seated distrust she harboured towards humans. As he inched closer, he deciphered the first word she wrote: 'R-I-C-H-I-E.'

Furrowing his brow, he felt a sense of unease as he prepared to retrace his steps. Josephine's menacing hiss pierced the air, freezing him in place. Sandra's finger continued, slowly forming the letters in the dust. The word below the first one read 'S-I-N-K.'

"Richie sink," Coby whispered, etching the phrase into his memory. Expressing his gratitude, he promised to host a party soon. Sinister smiles stretched across their lips, their ember eyes gleaming with twisted joy. Coby hurried back to his study, his footsteps light and energetic. During his research, Coby stumbled upon the perfect endearment for someone with the name Richard John Biggans – 'Richie.' The term of endearment rolled off his tongue, a harmonious combination of elegance and affection, sure to bring a smile to the affluent man's face. A new question arose, lingering in the air. Despite the deaths of Lord and Lady Lucas, Sandra's apparition persisted in haunting the manor, a ghostly reminder of past secrets. Coby decided – he would be the one to reveal the truth Sandra so desperately desired.

Coby hurried to his car, the old leather seats creaking as he sat down and reached for the worn map tucked in the glove box. His finger traced a quick route from Inverness to Newhaven Harbour, following the winding highway. After a brief calculation, he realised it would take him a little over three hours to reach his destination. With a great sense of urgency, he packed an overnight bag, the fabric rustling as he hastily shoved his laptop and map into the bag.

And that is when it struck him. Janie was missing. He let out a concerned whistle; the sound echoing through the empty rooms as he checked her usual hiding place, but she was nowhere to be found. Ewan's name sprang into his mind, and with a determined expression, he locked the house and activated the alarm; the beep resonating in the air.

Coby hastily tossed his bag into his car and followed the gravel route, listening to the crunch beneath his tires. There was Janie, fully immersed in a hunting game with Ewan, her joyful barks resonating through the woods. The sight of them together filled Coby with a great sense of joy, a warm feeling spreading through his chest.

"Good morning, Uncle Coby," Ewan exclaimed, his voice filled with infectious excitement.

Hearing Ewan affectionately call him uncle Coby brought a deep sense of joy to him. "Morning yourself," Coby said, his voice filled with warmth and a smile playing on his lips.

Just then, Gracie's alluring silhouette emerged through the back door, the gentle click of the door grabbing his focus.

The sight of her made Coby's heart flutter, a rush of emotions coursing through him. "Good morning!" Gracie bellowed, her voice carrying a hint of playfulness.

"Morning yourself," Coby said, his voice filled with warmth. "I'm on my way to Edinburgh. Would you mind watching Janie while I'm gone?" He asked, stepping closer, inhaling Gracie's intoxicating floral fragrance, the scent enveloping him in a sweet embrace.

"Of course—" Gracie started, but Ewan quickly interrupted, his voice eager and flushed with excitement. "Mum, can I go with?"

Gracie and Ewan locked their unwavering gazes onto Coby, their eyes filled with a mixture of curiosity and intrigue. Coby welcomed the company, grateful for the lively atmosphere. With the holiday season upon them, he knew Gracie deserved some well-deserved "me" time.

"Sure," he responded, a smile gracing his face, "But keep in mind we might be out of town for a couple of days."

Ewan's excitement burst forth with a joyful cry, his arms enveloping Coby in an embrace. In response, Janie barked in giddy anticipation, her tail wagging in a silent celebration. Gracie nodded in agreement, her head moving in a silent affirmation, before swiftly making her way into the house.

Inside, the scent of anticipation hung in the air as Gracie deftly packed an overnight bag for her son. The aroma of delectable treats wafted from the plastic container she filled, ensuring a delicious journey ahead. Coby entrusted her with his set of house keys, along with the code for the alarm system. He left a generous amount of cash, ensuring that Gracie would have everything she needed.

The hum of the engine filled the air as they embarked on their long drive, the sound of tires on the road accompanying them. With the wind tousling their hair, they set off on their adventure, a rush of freedom and excitement pulsating in their veins.

They reached the picturesque city of Inverness pretty soon, the charming buildings and cobblestone streets unfolding before their eyes. Coby made a quick stop, the aroma of freshly brewed coffee wafting through the air as he bought a strong takeaway coffee for himself. Understanding the growing young lad's appetite, he also grabbed two bottles of Irn-Bru, the fizzy orange drink that had a distinct tang. With a quick glimpse of the stunning glimmering loch, the Volvo seamlessly merged onto the trunk road. It's a crucial connection that stretches from the scenic Highlands down to the bustling Central Belt. The winding path to Perth buzzed with the constant rumble of cars and trucks, creating a symphony of sound.

While driving, Coby felt an inexplicable sense of ease in young Ewan's presence, as if they were lifelong friends. Unable to resist, he stole quick glances at the young lad beside him, feeling a deep fondness for him.

"Why did you become a writer?" Ewan asked, his voice breaking through the roar of the engine.

"Ach," Coby said, adopting a parentese tone. "I studied criminology at Uni," he tried to explain, but Ewan quickly interrupted him. Coby patiently explained what criminology meant before continuing, "And I became a policeman, advancing to Chief Inspector."

Ewan went off-topic briefly, his curiosity piqued as he asked if Coby had ever seen a dead body. Coby assured him, "yes, many," before continuing his story. "While I was an inspector, or investigator as they call 'em in the movies, I saw things other officers could not see..." Ewan interrupted again, this time asking what he could see. Coby replied, "I will tell you later," before continuing, "And so, I shared my experiences with the deceased's..."

"What does the deceased mean?" Ewan asked, and Coby remembered he was speaking to a young lad. He corrected himself with a reassuring smile, "dead people," and carried on. "I shared what I saw with their loved ones, and I could see how much it meant to them. It was a simple decision," Coby said, pulling aside to allow a speeding car from behind to overtake them. He suddenly realised his slow pace, creeping at forty miles per hour in a fifty zone, and sped up.

"I left the force and became a writer to share my experiences with others."

"Wow!" Ewan exclaimed, his eyebrows shooting up in awe as he glanced at the breathtaking sunset painting the sky in hues of orange and pink. The cool breeze brushed against their faces, carrying with it the faint scent of blooming flowers from a nearby field. "I am also going to write one day," Ewan added, his voice filled with determination.

"Good idea," Coby reassured, a smile playing on his lips as he admired the vibrant colours of the sunset. "Realising I would write about the supernatural. I did a philosophy degree while I wrote my stories."

Ewan's curiosity piqued, but he struggled to pronounce the word 'philosophy'. Patiently, Coby explained its meaning, his voice accompanied by the soothing sound of the wind rustling through the trees.

Ewan's eyes widened with curiosity as he listened intently. "But what does supernatural mean?" he asked, his brow furrowed in confusion.

Coby seized the opportunity to answer, taking in the sight of Ewan's eager expression. "Supernatural," he began, his voice carrying a hint of mystery, "means to see things outside our world."

"Like ghosts!" Ewan exclaimed, a trace of disbelief in his tone as he glanced around the car, half-expecting to see a spectre lurking in the shadows. Coby nodded, his smile reassuring and knowing. "Yes," he affirmed, his voice steady.

Ewan's conviction shone through as he exclaimed, "I knew it!"

The car continued to glide along the road, the engine's rhythmic chugging blending with the cool breeze that now drowned out their conversation. The silence was peaceful, allowing them to appreciate the beauty of the moment.

Suddenly, Ewan posed a question that made Coby's excitement soar. "Is a ghost what happens to us when we die?" he asked cautiously, his voice betraying a hint of fear.

Coby's eyes sparkled with anticipation as he prepared to delve into the realm of the supernatural. He launched into an explanation, his words tumbling out in a torrent of enthusiasm.

"Yes, and no," he replied, his voice filled with intrigue. He explained the latter, his words accompanied by the mesmerising play of shadows and sunlight dancing across the car's interior. "I believe," he began, his gaze locking with Ewan's, "when we die," he continued, adopting a spooky tone. "Your soul leaves your body, what we call the terminal breath we take, the final exhale. A whisper of farewell." Ewan sat transfixed, his attention focused on every word.

"And then!" Coby exclaimed, his voice startling the young lad. Ewan's eyes widened, his grip on his drink tightening as he leaned in closer.

"Your soul darts through the mortal landscape, its speed rivalling that of lightning, in search of a host," Coby continued, while the air carried a faint scent of anticipation.

"What is a host?" Ewan asked eagerly, his furrowed brow and inquisitive eyes revealing his serious curiosity.

Coby explained, "A newborn baby." He then elaborated with excitement, "A maternity ward at a hospital would be a good choice." Ewan's intense focus and the way his expression showed genuine interest mesmerised Coby.

"It hovers over the baby, waiting, waiting," Coby continued, pausing for effect, "and then when the baby gasps for air, taking its inaugural breath, it enters, and there you have a new life," he explained, his tone tinged with enthusiasm. "Thousands try, but some fail, just like sperm fights in a swim to the womb. The survival of the fittest."

Ewan sat frozen in his seat, the straw of his drink lingering in his mouth as he absorbed Coby's words, his senses heightened by the captivating tale.

Ewan's voice carried a mix of wonder and understanding as Coby's explanations slowly permeated his thoughts. "Now I know what ghosts are!" he exclaimed. Whispers of realisation escaped his lips, "It is the souls that did not make it."

The crisp wind whistled through the open windows, sending a slight chill down their spines. Coby, his face adorned with a gentle smile, neither confirmed nor denied the young lad's theory, allowing him to uncover the truth for himself.

Lost in his thoughts, Ewan murmured almost inaudibly, his words blending with the rustling of leaves outside. "I wonder if my dad made it." A pang of longing echoed in his voice, overshadowed by the cool breeze that swept through the car.

But Coby, always skilled at diverting attention, quickly shifted Ewan's focus elsewhere. "Look!" he exclaimed, his voice piercing the silence and instantly changing the mood. His finger extended, directing Ewan's gaze to a magnificent castle adorned with many towers and turrets, all built with vibrant red bricks. Surrounding the castle, a meticulously maintained lawn showcased intricate patterns, the lush green grass radiating vibrancy. As Coby pointed, he could almost sense the gentle caress of the breeze, hear the soft rustle of leaves, and catch the refreshing scent of freshly cut grass, all embraced by the warm, comforting touch of the sun.

"Scone Palace, the crowning place of Scottish Kings," Coby explained. His words hung in the air, infused with a palpable surge of excitement that matched the awe in his eyes.

Ewan's jaw practically hit the floor as his gaze settled upon the castle, his senses overwhelmed by its grandeur. It stood tall, an architectural masterpiece nestled amidst a picturesque landscape. The sight before Ewan left him in awe. Coby quietly wondered if he had ever laid eyes on something so awe-inspiring. And amidst the wonder, a flicker of uncertainty lingered – did he ever have the chance to experience such beauty beyond the walls of his home?

Before Coby knew it, the bustling streets of the small city of Perth surrounded them. The tantalising aroma of freshly baked pastries filled the air as Ewan devoured most of the mouthwatering treats, prompting a quick pit stop for more food and drinks. Politely, Ewan requested another round of Irn-Bru before rushing off to the public restrooms. Meanwhile, Coby took advantage of the moment to stretch his stiff legs from the arduous journey. As daylight gradually surrendered to moonlight, determination pushed him forward. The Volvo effortlessly blended into the busy flow of traffic on the motorway connecting Perth to Edinburgh, its engine emitting a soothing hum as it sped up to match the new speed limit.

Drowsiness stealthily enveloped them, casting a hushed spell over their surroundings. Recognising the need for rest, Coby halted their journey. They found a cosy two-bed room at a delightful guest house in Rosyth, a picturesque town on the Firth of Forth in Fife. He eagerly expected Ewan's awe at the majestic Queensferry Crossing, set against a breathtaking sunrise.

Carrying Ewan's weary, slumbering body, he stepped into the cosy guesthouse, the aroma of fresh linens enveloping his senses. Gently placing him on the plush bed, the lad scarcely stirred, his peaceful form bringing tears of joy to Coby's eyes. Determined to share their location, he swiftly sent Gracie a text, the sound of his fingers dancing on the phone's screen filling the quiet room. A flurry of kisses in her response made his heart skip a beat.

Seeking solace, he ventured into the enchanting guesthouse's ancient pub, the warm glow of flickering candles casting a tranquil ambiance. Nestling into a worn leather chair, he savoured the rich aroma of a double whisky, its amber hues swirling in the glass. The tantalising scent of bangers and mash wafted from the kitchen, teasing his appetite. With another sip of his drink, he settled in to watch the gripping last moments of the football game on the small television. Contentment washed over him as he made his way back to their room, the soft carpet beneath his feet adding to the soothing atmosphere.

Chapter Fifteen

With their bellies pleasantly full from devouring a delectable full English breakfast, Coby and Ewan embarked on their journey. The sound of the rumbling engine drowned out all other noises as they smoothly glided along the open road. During their pit stop for petrol, Coby excitedly shared the addictive crunch of peanut brittle with Ewan. The sweet aroma of roasted peanuts filled the air, tickling their noses with its mouthwatering scent. Ewan, overwhelmed by this new sensory delight, couldn't help but send his mum a text, expressing his joy and excitement over discovering a newfound treat he dubbed "sticky peanuts."

Ewan's mind, refreshed from a restful night's sleep, was now brimming with curiosity. He bombarded Coby with an incessant barrage of thought-provoking questions. Among them, the young lad pondered about the whereabouts of his father, wondering if he resided in heaven. Coby, mindful of the sensitivity of the topic, deferred the answer to Ewan's mother. But it was the next question that caught Coby off guard. Ewan inquired about the distinction between sperm and a soul.

Coby had already explained the concept of a soul, and he left the intricate subject of 'sperm' for Ewan's mother to address. However, Ewan persisted with his questioning, responding to each answer with a resolute "why?"

Just as the weight of these profound inquiries overwhelmed Coby, a sight of awe-inspiring beauty came to their rescue. As they approached the outskirts of Edinburgh, the majestic Queensferry Crossing came into view. Its towering spires pierced the sky, a modern marvel of steel and concrete suspended over the glassy surface of the River Forth. The early morning sun painted the structure in hues of gold and orange, casting long, dancing shadows on the rippling water below.

Ewan was awestruck, his eyes wide as he took in the spectacle. The sight of the colossal bridge seemed to lift the weight of his questions, replacing it with a sense of wonder and awe. His small hand tightened around Coby's, a silent testament to the impact of the sight before them.

The hum of the Volvo's engine, the soft rustling of the wind against the car windows, and the distant cries of seagulls filled the air, creating a symphony of sounds that underscored their shared moment of marvel.

As they drove across the bridge, Ewan pressed his hand against the cool window, tracing the lines of the crossing with his fingers. The sight of the sprawling cityscape of Edinburgh unfolding before them brought a fresh wave of excitement. The mix of historic charm and modern vibrancy of the city seemed to pulse with life, promising adventures yet to come.

Finally, Coby found a quaint two-bed room in a cosy inn nestled along Edinburgh's waterfront, near the Leith Newhaven Ferry Landing. The location was simply perfect, offering a picturesque setting for their stay.

After Coby had texted Gracie to let her know they had arrived safely, he navigated the ancient city's winding streets until he reached the bustling heart. The aroma of freshly popped popcorn wafted through the air as he drove Ewan to the cinema. With a sense of generosity, Coby slipped a thick wad of cash into Ewan's pocket, the crisp bills rustling softly as they made contact. He reassured Ewan that he could indulge in as many movies and as much popcorn as his heart desired.

Ewan's eyes sparkled with anticipation as he eagerly inquired about Irn-Bru, his signature radiant smile lighting up his face. Coby's warm reassurance brought a sense of comfort as he tousled the lad's vibrant red hair affectionately.

However, it was only later, amidst the historical charm of the Port O'Leith Motor Boat Club, that Coby realised his dreadful mistake. Surrounded by locals and regulars, he bombarded them with a barrage of questions, hoping to uncover information about Lord Lucas's whereabouts. An elderly man, his pipe emitting a cloud of white smoke, fixed Coby with a knowing gaze. With casual nonchalance, he uttered the unexpected revelation, "U'r at the wrong port, O'l chap."

Coby furrowed his brow in confusion, his mind racing. Retrieving his phone, he hastily typed 'Newhaven UK' into the search bar. Newhaven Fort stood tall in East Sussex, the very place Lord Lucas sought refuge after Sandra's tragic end. Not Newhaven Harbour in Edinburgh. Embarrassment flooded Coby's cheeks, turning them a deep shade of crimson as he excused himself from the boat club. The sound of laughter and jeers followed him as he hurriedly made his way to the inn, collecting their belongings with a sense of urgency.

Coby's heart raced with worry as he sped towards the cinemas, the adrenaline pumping through his veins. Upon arrival, he approached the usher, his voice filled with urgency as he explained the family emergency. The usher nodded, acknowledging his words. "Yea mon, mi sight him," the usher remarked, absentmindedly running his fingers through his tangled dreadlocks. "Mi see dis likkle yute wid four boxes a popcorn," he said, flashing a charming smile. Coby's face lit up with a smile as he heard the description, leaving no doubt that it was Ewan.

Following the trail of popcorn scattered on the floor, Coby and the usher made their way through the dimly lit cinema. And there, amidst the flickering screen and the captivating scenes, they found Ewan. His eyes were filled with awe, his mouth stuffed with popcorn, his cheeks bulging like a chipmunk.

With Ewan and his buckets of buttery popcorn seated beside Coby, he eagerly explained his mistake. Speeding through the city, Coby's fingers moved swiftly, dialling the airport's number. He anxiously inquired about flights to Gatwick, the anticipation clear in his voice. The polite lady on the other end of the line calmly informed him that there were only four seats available on Highland's Airlines flight EG945, leaving in just forty-five minutes.

Coby's heart raced as he exclaimed, "Please reserve two seats!" The sound of his urgency reverberated through the car as he firmly pressed his foot down on the gas pedal, propelling them forward. "Mister McTavish, and son," he responded after a brief pause, his voice filled with hopeful anticipation, before abruptly ending the call.

Ewan's initial disappointment quickly transformed into elation when he learned he was now Coby's son. His eyes, sparkling with affection, widened as he gazed at his new dad. "I've never been on a plane!" he exclaimed, his voice filled with excitement. Coby's determination intensified, causing him to drive even faster, the rush of adrenaline coursing through his veins. As they sped down the road, Ewan leaned out of the window, the rush of wind slapping his face and bringing tears to his eyes.

Amidst the thrill of the moment, Coby's mind couldn't help but ponder over a pressing problem. Neither he nor Ewan had their passports with them. Coby reached for his driver's license, the worn edges and faded image of his younger self staring back at him. "That'll have to do," he reassured himself, a sense of determination filling his voice as a massive passenger jet soared into the cerulean horizon.

In his days as a police officer, Coby had frequented Edinburgh airport countless times, becoming intimately familiar with its ins and outs. The memories of those visits intertwined with the strands of grey hair on his head. He knew a trick, a hidden pathway that would lead them to the long-term parking bays. Manoeuvring his Volvo through the bustling airport streets, he skilfully guided them towards their destination. Finally, they arrived at a secluded parking bay, tucked away just beyond a service lift that emerged in the heart of the bustling terminal.

With a determined expression, Coby firmly gripped the handle and pulled open the smooth, frameless tailgate of the sleek Volvo, retrieving their bags. Time seemed to slip away like sand through his fingers as he glanced at his watch, realising they only had fifteen precious minutes left. Ewan clutched his one remaining bucket of buttery popcorn close to his chest, the rich aroma wafting up, tempting his senses. They hurriedly made their way towards Highland's Airline terminal, the sound of bustling footsteps and echoing announcements filling the air. The curious and judgmental gazes of nosy mothers cast a shadow over them, their eyes like prying spotlights. Coby's tummy fluttered with nerves, but he mustered up the courage to approach the check-in lady, his palms slightly sweaty. He reminded her of their booking under the name McTavish, hoping for a smooth transition. Her reassuring smile and kind words, "Under

UK law, children under the care of an adult do not require a passport," brought tears of joy to his eyes, like a shimmering waterfall cascading down. Ewan's head swivelled in every direction, his eyes wide open, eagerly taking in the sights and sounds of the bustling airport. His senses heightened like that of a vigilant owl, absorbing the cacophony of voices, the hum of rolling suitcases, and the bright, vibrant colours of signs and advertisements.

As they nervously waited for their boarding call, Coby frantically dialled Gracie's number. His voice filled with anticipation as he eagerly shared their revised plans. Ewan, unable to contain his excitement, swiftly grabbed the phone from Coby's hand.

"We're going to take to the skies!" he exclaimed, his words reverberating through the air, drawing the attention of passersby. Onlooker cast curious glances at the father and son duo, their eyes filled with intrigue, while the distant hum of airport activity provided a constant background soundtrack.

"That one is absolutely stunning," Ewan exclaimed, his voice brimming with excitement, as he eagerly pointed towards a ravishing flight attendant with raven hair, her smile captivating. With each graceful step, the sound of her heels reverberated through the cabin, creating a rhythmic echo. Her maroon skirt, a tantalising touch too short, flirtatiously showcased her milky legs above the smooth, white stockings. Ewan's fingers clumsily fumbled with his seatbelt, until the flight attendant, her perfume wafting in the air, gracefully intervened. Her delicate touch produced a satisfying click as the buckle fastened securely. Coby's gaze was fixed on them, and he couldn't help but notice the mischievous smirk playing on Ewan's lips as he shamelessly stared down the attendant's dress, taking in a generous view of her alluring cleavage.

As they listened to the takeoff instructions, the anticipation built up within them. With precision, the plane aligned itself on the runway, its nose pointing dead centre towards the stark white lines. Coby knew what was about to happen, and he fixed his gaze on young Ewan beside him, his eyes widening with awe. The engines roared to life, filling the cabin with a powerful rumble, and the vibrations reverberated through their bodies. Ewan couldn't contain his excitement and let out a joyful, "whoo!" as the g-force thrust him back against his seat, his cheeks bouncing like a playful puppy.

The aircraft gracefully ascended into the cerulean sky, and the soothing voice of the pilot resonated over the intercom, accompanied by the familiar ding sound. Slightly tilting to the left, the plane offered Ewan a breathtaking panoramic view of Edinburgh, with its picturesque harbour spreading out below. The pilot set the course for London Gatwick Airport, and as lunchtime approached, the cabin crew served light snacks. Ewan eagerly savoured his portion of shepherd's pie and Irn-Bru, his eyes widening with delight. The raven-haired flight attendant leaned in close to serve him, her presence captivating him. He couldn't help but take a lingering gaze on her curvaceous bosom, and in return, she bestowed upon him an enchanting smile, clearly relishing the attention.

As the fasten seatbelt lights illuminated once more, signalling the approach of landing, the cabin crew diligently prepared the cabin. Coby observed Ewan bracing himself as the aircraft descended towards the earth, his knuckles turning white from gripping his seat tightly. With skilful expertise, the pilot gently touched down on the smooth tarmac, and the plane leisurely taxied towards its designated gate.

The young man, his blemished skin contrasting with his pearly white teeth, handed Coby the keys to their rented car. Ewan leaned in closer and whispered, "Why does he talk so funny?" Coby gently nudged him, reminding him to be quiet, as they were now in England, where the melodic cadence of the locals' speech filled the air.

With a grunt of exertion, Coby forcefully wedged their precious belongings into the cramped trunk. The items rattled and clanged as they set off on the journey towards Newhaven, creating a symphony of metallic echoes.

Making a swift pit stop in Crawley, Coby could hear the soft hum of the petrol station as they filled up the small tank. The scent of petrol filled the air, blending with the irresistible smell of snacks that made Ewan's mouth water. Coby took a moment to explain, his words lingering in the air like a heavy fog, as he tried to make sense of the absence of Irn-Bru in this unfamiliar part of the world. Despite Ewan's initial understanding, disappointment clouded his speckled face. Coby thought the familiar sound of his mother's voice would bring him comfort, so he dialled her number.

Gracie's voice on the phone brought a wave of joy to Ewan's senses. The sound of her laughter was like sweet music, and the playful kisses she sent caused a delightful tingling sensation in Coby's stomach, like a flutter of butterflies taking flight. With the cheap rental car filled up, they could hear the engine purring as they hit the road.

They eagerly arrived at the Newhaven marina, where Coby had booked a charming two-bed room on the wharf. With a sense of relief, Coby parked the old, rattling car in the designated parking bay, glad to be free from its noisy engine. Ewan couldn't resist teasing him about the car's condition, but Coby brushed it off, knowing that it had served them well on their journey. The sight of the bustling marina filled him with excitement for the adventures that awaited him. As he carried their belonging towards the room, he could hear the gentle sounds of the waves lapping against the dock, creating a soothing melody. The salty sea air filled his nostrils, invigorating his senses and adding a touch of freshness to the atmosphere. The piercing squawks of seagulls filled the air, evoking a sense of nostalgia and belonging.

Coby hurriedly made his way to the front desk to handle the financial matters, while Ewan comfortably settled onto a bed with a perfect view of the television. Inside the room, Coby noticed an adult channel playing on the television and quickly turned it off, not wanting any distractions from their new adventure. He scowled at young Ewan, who was peacefully slumbering with a mischievous grin on his face. Determined to explore their new surroundings, he wasted no time and set off towards the seaside town. The beauty of the seaside captivated him as he took in the breathtaking views of the vast expanse of water.

Being a whisky enthusiast, Coby knew exactly where to go to learn more about the local area – the pub. As he strolled along the wharf, he spotted the unmistakable signs of a pub: 'The Mariner's Inn'. A warm, golden glow enveloped the entrance, emanating from the overhead sign and lantern.

The contrast of the dark night against the illuminated signage added to the charm of the pub. Above the doorway, a traditional lantern hung, casting a soft glow that further enhanced the welcoming atmosphere. The bold, golden letters that displayed the whisky specials caught Coby's attention, and his excitement bubbled up inside him.

A surge of excitement washed over him when he noticed a group of players huddled around the dartboard, their passionate energy palpable in their animated gestures. The air was filled with the joyful sound of laughter and friendly banter, creating a vibrant and jovial atmosphere. Eager to join in on the fun, Coby couldn't wait to interact with the friendly locals and discover more about the town.

Seated on the polished wooden barstool, the rich aroma of hops and barley permeated the air as he requested a double whisky special. With each sip, he relished the refreshing flavour, the sound of darts hitting the bristle board creating a lively atmosphere. As he played back his voicemail, Gracie's urgent voice resonated, carrying a palpable sense of concern. The mere mention of Alistair Sinclair, a name that reverberated throughout the town inquiring about Coby's whereabouts, sparked intrigue.

Dismissing the news with a nonchalant shrug, he shifted his attention to the dart game unfolding before him. The locals' initial excitement gradually faded as they marvelled at Coby's exceptional skill, their enthusiasm giving way to a mix of awe and admiration. Determined to win them over, he adjusted his play, strategically allowing them to take the lead. The atmosphere became alive with the sound of laughter, the clinking of glasses, and the pleasant aroma of drinks. Engaging in casual conversation, the locals revealed themselves to be true gentlemen, creating an enjoyable and relaxed ambiance.

In their playful conversation, Coby stumbled upon the secret of the ancient fortress, located just a stone's throw away. Whispers in town hinted at the fort being a popular gathering spot for ethereal entities. Excitedly, the group shared stories of famous ghost hunters who flocked to this sought-after destination. The stories echoed in Coby's mind, eliciting a mischievous grin that curled his lips. With the image of Ewan slumbering in front of the flickering television in his mind, he set off on his adventure, feeling a thrilling sensation coursing through his veins.

Luck was on Coby's side when he stumbled upon the fort's extended hours, discovering it remained open until eight in the evening. With a mix of excitement and bone-chilling dread, he stepped into the abyss of the Newhaven fort. The dimly lit tunnels, with their brick walls adorned in faded white paint, emitted an eerie and cold sensation, sending shivers down his spine. As he delved further into the labyrinth, eerie whispers echoed through the archways, intensifying the suspense.

Navigating the pitch-dark tunnels with the beam of his phone's flashlight, the cool air brushed against his skin, causing goosebumps to rise. He didn't have to search for them; the footsteps found him. The unmistakable sound echoed closely behind him, creating a shiver that made his hands tremble as he tightly gripped his phone.

With determination fuelling his every step, he pressed on, refusing to succumb to intimidation. He searched for a hidden nook where he could interact with the ghost without any eavesdroppers. Suddenly, an unseen force caused his phone's flashlight to flicker, momentarily plunging him into darkness. His breath hitched, adrenaline pumping through his veins.

Trembling, he shook his phone, coaxing the flashlight back to life as he ventured further into the dimly lit passageways. The air grew colder, sending a shiver down his spine, while a soft whisper filled his ears with chiding hisses, urging him to "get out." Ignoring the prickling of goosebumps on his skin, Coby hastened his pace, the sound of his footsteps echoing off the walls of the subterranean tunnels.

"Get out," the spectre urgently breathed, its words laced with foreboding. In the darkest corner he could find, Coby spun around and boldly confronted the apparition.

"Hello," he greeted politely, "I mean you and your brethren no harm; I only seek your wise counsel." As if summoned by his words, the apparition materialised as a resolute soldier, standing tall in his military attire. His uniform, a blend of khaki, olive, and slate grey, seamlessly blended with the natural tones of the hidden tunnels.

Coby could feel his heart racing, the adrenaline coursing through his veins, as he locked eyes with the resolute soldier. The soldier's piercing gaze seared into him, imprinting a lasting impression on his very being and engulfing him in an overwhelming wave of fear. The weight of history and the stories that these tunnels held were palpable in the air.

Coby couldn't help but notice the soldier's face, weathered and worn, a testament to a life of duty and honour. His eyes, a deep shade of grey, held a wisdom that spoke of a lifetime of experiences. The soldier's presence exuded an aura of authority and strength, commanding respect even in his ethereal form.

Despite being faded, the soldier's uniform kept the scars of past battles. The patches, badges, and insignias showcased his rank and dedication to duty. It was a reminder of the soldier's unwavering commitment to his cause, even in the face of the unknown.

The dim light of Coby's phone flashlight cast eerie shadows on the soldier's face, accentuating the contours and scars that told tales of bravery and sacrifice. The air around them seemed to grow heavier, as if the spirit of the soldier was channelling the weight of the fort's history.

Coby's voice quivered slightly as he spoke, trying to maintain his composure in the presence of such a formidable apparition. "I seek your guidance," he whispered, his voice carrying both respect and a genuine desire for knowledge. He brought up Lord Lucas's picture on his phone and showed it to the soldier, who squinted to get a better look. "I want to understand if this man is a familiar face in your circles," Coby muttered, his voice filled with reverence and a genuine curiosity.

The soldier's stern expression softened, and a glimmer of recognition flickered in his eyes. It was as if he could see the sincerity in Coby's intentions and admired his bravery in venturing into the unknown. Slowly, the soldier spoke, his voice filled with echoes of the past and a sense of duty that transcended time. "Yes," he exhaled, his words reverberating through Coby's entire being. His voice dripping with secrecy, he hissed in a soft whisper, "The others call him the gambling man."

Coby knew he had found his man. His intuition never failed him. But he remained oblivious, his excitement bubbling beneath the surface. And so, in the depths of the fort's hidden tunnels, Coby found himself immersed in a conversation that bridged the gap between the living and the departed. The soldier's words reverberated with profound wisdom, unveiling long-guarded secrets.

The air around them seemed to shift and grow heavy as they spoke, filled with the weight of the soldier's tales and the unanswered questions about the missing man. Coby listened intently, his mind and heart open to the lessons and knowledge that the apparition imparted. In that moment, he realised he had stumbled upon something far greater than he could have ever imagined – a connection to the past that would forever shape his understanding of the present.

He warmly thanked the soldier, his voice resonating with heartfelt gratitude for sharing his deeply cherished stories. Promising liberation, Coby leaned in closer, his eyes sparkling with unwavering resolve, as he divulged the soldier's authentic encounters of sorrow. The apparition, its otherworldly form shimmering in the soft, muted glow, nodded appreciatively, its voice a gentle whisper of gratefulness. Leading him back to the entrance, its presence gradually dissolved into the enveloping cloak of shadows, dissipating like a delicate wisp of smoke.

With a buoyant spring in his step, Coby's whistled melody floated through the tranquil night air, reaching far and wide as he hurried back to The Mariner's Inn. A peculiar sensation, akin to the gentle prickle of a refreshing breeze, cascaded down his spine, causing him to abruptly halt in his tracks. Spinning on his heels, his eyes darted frantically in every direction, until finally he glimpsed the figure of the vanished man, hunched and defeated, sloshing dismally along the jetty before vanishing beneath the water's surface. The scent of dampness and salt permeated the atmosphere, mingling subtly with a tinge of resignation.

An exquisite shiver, akin to tiny electric shocks, rippled across Coby's arms as a blend of awe and exhilaration surged through his veins. A thin, triumphant smile tugged at the corners of his lips, revealing a sly satisfaction, as he confidently strode into the inn. The harmonious symphony of clinking glasses and jovial chatter enveloped him, creating an atmosphere of jubilant celebration. With an air of self-assurance, he approached the bar, his voice resolute as he ordered a double whisky, the amber liquid glinting alluringly in the dim, atmospheric glow.

Chapter Sixteen

Gracie's heart swelled with joy as she watched Coby and Ewan pull up, the gentle hum of the engine growing fainter as they parked near the charming cottage. Janie couldn't contain her excitement and barked ecstatically, her tail wagging with fervour. Gracie showered her son's face with kisses, her happiness clear in each tender touch. Yet, it was Coby who received a longer, more affectionate kiss, a display of pride from Ewan's mother. Janie and Ewan quickly reunited, their animated conversation filling the air as they ventured into the nearby woods. Ewan's voice reverberated with excitement as he passionately described his thrilling journey.

Coby's heart swelled with tenderness as he witnessed Ewan and Janie's reunion, feeling as if a warm embrace of affection engulfed him. In that moment, he invited Gracie and Ewan for dinner, although Gracie insisted on taking charge of the cooking. With a contented smile, Coby drove back to his stately home, admiring the picturesque view of the winding gravel path that led to his manor. He tossed his suitcase on his bed and hurried to his study. As he entered the room, a subtle change in the air caught his attention, accompanied by the scent of freshly cleaned surfaces. It became apparent that someone had taken the time to tidy the house during his absence, prompting Coby to remind himself to express his gratitude and compensate Gracie for her kindness. A surge of determination coursed through his veins, urging him to open his draft and immerse himself in the haunting tale of Sandra River's tragic demise. Eager to share his progress, he sent a copy to his editor, who promptly responded with words of praise and anticipation, igniting a radiant smile on Coby's lips.

Engrossed in his emails, he let out an audible gasp; the sound reverberating in the room's stillness. His eyes widened, taking in the words from his contact at New Scotland Yard. The sight of their agreement to the essential details he had listed brought a sense of relief. But it was the postscript at the bottom of the email that made his heart race and his eyes grow as wide as saucers.

With anticipation, he clicked on the link provided; the hand cursor hovering over it. The screen flickered to life, revealing the webpage of a venerable newspaper. An article from days long past filled the display, its vintage hues casting an alluring glow that bathed the room in warm, nostalgic light. With eager anticipation, he quickly scanned the article, absorbing the information as if his life depended on it. The abandoned car of Lord Lucas stood in solitary silence, its grimy windows and dull, lifeless exterior creating an unsettling atmosphere. A reporter beat the police to the scene and meticulously documented his discovery with vivid descriptions.

Coby eagerly read on, his eyes fixated on every word on the screen, while the air filled with an electrifying scent of excitement. The words describing the three Cluedo cards found inside the car – 'Mrs Peacock,' 'the lead pipe,' and 'the kitchen' – drew a chilling parallel to the real-life murder. The gravity of the situation sank in, intensifying his desire to uncover the truth.

Driven by curiosity, Coby quickly searched for more information, the sound of his fingers tapping on the keyboard filling the room. The click of the mouse led him to a startling discovery about the character of Mrs Peacock in the game, her portrayal as a grande dame. His voice barely above a whisper, he murmured, the words laced with astonishment.

The pounding of his heart matched his racing thoughts, reverberating in his ears. The soldier's words in the dark subterranean tunnels beneath the Newhaven fort came back to haunt him, the memory confirming his suspicions. Excitement and trepidation intertwined inside him, their contrasting emotions settling heavily upon him.

With a surge of triumph, Coby's arms shot up in the air, the feeling of victory coursing through his veins. The room seemed to brighten, a sense of accomplishment filling the space. "Checkmate," he exclaimed, the words a testament to his determination and unwavering pursuit of the truth.

With determination fuelling his every step, Coby made his way to Sandra River, eager to put his theory to the test. Following his routine path across the grand hallway, Coby traversed the dimly lit corridor and descended the spiral staircase into the basement. He flicked the switch, illuminating the dim passages that led to the buttery. Goosebumps prickled along Coby's arms, a physical manifestation of the thrill that coursed through him. The atmosphere was electric, with an unseen force crackling through the air. Each intake of breath felt charged with possibility, as if he were inhaling the very essence of his investigation.

He neared the buttery, his heart racing with the anticipation of encountering Sandra's otherworldly presence. And there she was, perched on the bottom step, her delicate finger tracing intricate patterns in the layer of dust. The enchanting melody of her lullaby enveloped Coby's senses, evoking a profound sense of nostalgia and connection. With a warm smile, he greeted her cautiously, his voice filled with a hint of hesitation.

Sandra's gaze bore into him, her eyes ablaze with intensity, and he hurriedly spilled the details of his findings. With each word he uttered, the burden of sorrow lifted from her eyes, making way for a glimmer of hope. With no warning, her ethereal figure glowed with a dazzling, otherworldly white radiance before effortlessly merging into the encompassing darkness, accompanied by a mesmerising chorus of enchanting, celestial voices disappearing like a fleeting whisper of mist. Coby let out a dramatic sigh, filling the room with his discontent as she pondered on the possibility of sharing the joyous news with her mystical sisters. He walked with a spring in his step, whistling a cheerful melody as he made his way back through the dimly lit passageway. Just as he turned on his heel, the ethereal trinity appeared, their ghostly figures flickering before his eyes, emanating a sense of satisfaction. Gasping in shock, Coby jumped with a start. "Stop doing that!" he exclaimed, her face flushed with anger. Behind him, he heard their ethereal giggles, delicate and reminiscent of a symphony of tinkling bells.

With Sandra's melancholic tale behind them, he could now focus entirely on the enigmatic trinity of apparitions. His intuition told him they held a deep connection to Giles's perplexing demise, and by unravelling their secrets, he could release Giles's lingering spirit.

In his office, the spectral trio appeared, their ghostly presence filling the room with an otherworldly aura. The monochrome reflections they cast created eerie shadows that seemed to dance against the walls. They eagerly gathered around his laptop, their eyes locked on the screen, their anticipation growing with each passing moment, eagerly awaiting their chance to be captured by what Jane referred to as the "magical eye." Coby, however, lacked the strength to explain to them that the camera was incapable of capturing their ethereal forms. Suddenly, a realisation dawned upon him. He had a friend who was a skilled composite artist and used to work with him. With a newfound sense of excitement, he decided to call his friend.

A mischievous smile played upon his lips, for he now possessed a potentially powerful bargaining tool. Inspiration struck him like a speeding city bus, and he hastily made his way to his bedroom. Retrieving a full-length mirror, he carefully balanced it against his desk, positioning himself in front of it to reveal his reflection. The apparitions gasped and whispered in awe, their murmurs carrying a soft hissing sound. Coby directed the mirror's reflection towards them, and in perfect unison, they turned their gazes, only to see the grand hallway behind them. Their lips parted in unison, releasing gasps that transformed into ethereal hisses, filling the air with a symphony of whispers.

"You see," Coby said with a menacing sparkle in his eyes, "unlike the living, you don't reflect light." The spectral trio furrowed their brows in confusion, their elegant monochrome faces displaying a collective bewilderment. Their eyes darted back and forth, searching for answers in the air.

"But don't stress," Coby began, his words hanging in the air as he noticed their oddly arched eyebrows. With precision, he tilted his laptop, positioning the camera lens to face the ghostly trio. Standing before them, he set the timer and flashed a smile for the camera. The brilliant light of the flash filled the room, accompanied by the satisfying click of the shutter. The ghostly trio let out a collective hiss and gasp, their astonishment causing whispers of disbelief to fill the air. Coby turned the screen to show them the captured image, only to be met with tangible disappointment and anger etched across their elegant monochrome faces.

"Do you like that?" he asked, his voice tinged with excitement, a hint of anticipation. Their ghostly heads floated up and down, displaying clear amazement, while their glowing eyes widened with wonder. Curiosity and possibility hung in the air, filling the room with anticipation.

Coby's voice held a playful tone as he suggested, "If you provide me with something, I can do the same for you." He waited, watching their expressions closely. True to form, Jane's lips parted, and she let out a soft breath, her eyes never leaving him, eager to discover what he would bring to the table. Coby's brow furrowed in deep thought, his mind working furiously, contemplating how to use his hand wisely.

"My friend will capture your image," he began, his voice resolute, yet brimming with curiosity, "but there are questions burning inside me that demand answers." Taking a moment to collect his thoughts, he swiftly added, "You," as he pointed towards them, his finger cutting through the air, "are to answer my questions, while I," he pointed at himself, his finger now directed inward, "will capture your image with the help of my friend."

The divine trio remained silent, their stillness filling the atmosphere, their unwavering stare unbroken. Finally, with a whoosh that echoed like a distant whisper, Jane took a step forward, causing Coby's heart to flutter in his chest.

"Ask," she breathed, her voice barely a whisper, the sound reverberating off the walls, causing an icy shiver to run through Coby. Coby's eyes locked with Jane's mesmerising ember eyes, their intense gaze pulling him in deeper and deeper. However, his negotiation was abruptly halted by the unmistakable sound of tires crunching on the gravel outside, shattering the silence.

The spectral trinity hissed and gasped, their faces filled with dread, their features contorted with fear. The sound of their hissing voices filled the room as they warned, "Sassenach!"

They vanished into the shadows, their presence evaporating like a fleeting puff of fog. Coby instinctively understood who the uninvited guest was, feeling his anger bubbling just below the surface, his blood pulsating with fury.

He hurried to the foreboding front door, the creaking hinges echoing in his ears as he swung it open. Alistair Sinclair ascended the staircase, his footsteps echoing on the steps. The sight of Alistair's signature knowing smile sent a shiver down his spine, like stiff fingers tracing his back. "What do you want?" Coby demanded, his tone sharp and impatient.

"I have a warning," Alistair casually mentioned, the subtle aroma of tobacco surrounding him, while he raised his white top hat.

Coby's frustration boiled over, and he swung the door shut in Alistair's face. Alistair, with unwavering determination, wedged his boot into the gap, keeping the door from shutting completely.

"I beg you, Mister McTavish, please lend me your ear and hear me out," Alistair implored, his voice filled with a touch of desperation.

Reluctantly, Coby swung the doors open again, his scowl etched deep into his features. His eyes met Alistair's, and he could see the concern etched across the old man's face, like cracks on a weathered painting. Curiosity tugged at him, like an invisible force pulling him closer.

Coby's impatience was palpable as he snapped, "You only have one minute."

Alistair removed his hat, revealing a sheen of sweat on his brow, the scent of anxiety lingering in the air. He fixed Coby with a stern gaze, his eyes piercing through him.

"Be cautious of Gracie Drummond," Alistair warned with unwavering conviction, his voice carrying a hint of urgency. "The townspeople are buzzing with rumours about her alleged romantic involvement with a wealthy British aristocrat."

Coby remained silent, feeling the weight of Alistair's unease settle on him like a suffocating fog. The atmosphere between them crackled with anticipation, as if a storm was brewing and about to unleash its power.

"Some people say they carefully orchestrated the assassination of her husband," Alistair finally revealed, his words lingering in the air like the scent of a forbidden secret. He turned his back on Coby, descending the stairs with a sense of purpose.

"Be warned," he cautioned, his voice growing fainter as he moved further away. "Every step you take echoes in my ears." With that, he casually got into his sleek Range Rover and sped off, leaving Coby's heart pounding in his chest. In that moment, a realisation struck Coby like a bolt of lightning. Alistair Sinclair's features outshone Ewan's in every way. Ewan's fiery red hair, and plump cheeks sprinkled with freckles, stood in stark contrast to Alistair's wispy white hair and slender frame.

The realisation struck Coby with a force that made his knees weak and his breath catch. The path ahead was uncertain and treacherous, but he couldn't deny the pull of curiosity and the need to uncover the truth that tugged at him relentlessly. Taking a deep breath, he steeled himself, feeling a newfound determination coursing through his veins. With every fibre of his being, he vowed to delve deeper into the secrets of Gracie Drummond, determined to uncover the truth that lay hidden beneath the surface of their small town.

Coby called Larry, his talented composite artist friend, in the Northern Constabulary and could hear bustling police radios in the background. It took a bit of persuasion, but a bottle of expensive whisky, good food, and free boarding secured a deal. He crossed the task off his list, the satisfying sound of a pen scratching against paper, checked his watch, and hurried into town.

His mind raced with thoughts as he carefully manoeuvred along the winding road into Serenity Falls. The vibrant green foliage surrounding him created a lush, immersive environment as he continued on his way. Gracie's version of the events clashed with Alistair's, their voices reverberating in Coby's mind. But what bothered him the most was Ewan. His polite, happy mannered ways were indeed very opposite to Alistair's. Coby decided that there is no way that Ewan could be Alistair's son. This revelation cast question marks over Gracie's head, and he decided to confront her face to face. During their recent adventure to Newhaven, he developed a deep affection for Ewan, the warmth of their connection lingering in his heart. On the other hand, Gracie took meticulous care of his stately home while he was away, leaving the air filled with the crisp scent of freshly polished furniture. A surge of inspiration hit him, a burst of energy coursing through his veins.

He stopped at the florist and bought a bouquet of vibrant flowers, their colours popping against the green backdrop. The nosy auburn-haired lady, her voice inquisitive, insisted on knowing who the flowers were for. In the end, Coby, unable to withstand her persistent questioning any longer, snapped. "For my mother!" he lied, the frustration clear in his voice.

With a quick visit to the liquor store, he stocked up on Irn-Bru for Ewan and two bottles of Drambuie, the clinking of glass bottles filling the air. From the local chip shop, he indulged in the irresistible temptation of three portions of pizza crunch, the sizzling sound of frying oil tantalising his senses. Aware of Ewan's voracious appetite, he couldn't resist ordering two heaping portions of perfectly deep-fried golden delicious chips. Coby stole a quick glance at his watch before sneaking in a rapid-fire dart game at the lively Stag's Head Inn, where the clatter of darts hitting the board and the boisterous cheers of the regulars created a lively atmosphere. The locals expressed their joy at seeing him again and raised their glasses to celebrate the safe return of the local dart champ.

Just like luck would have it, Coby noticed a redheaded man, perched on a barstool, with a sinister glint in his eyes. His mind played tricks on him, and every redheaded man he saw became a haunting reminder of Ewan's possible biological father. Coby casually shrugged off the idea, the weight of his thoughts weighing heavily on his shoulders, as he plunged into his dart game, his eyes fixated with determination. After narrowly winning, he quickly downed his pint and made his way home.

Chapter Seventeen

The powerful rumble of the Volvo engine echoed as it ascended the steep driveway of Coby's grand estate. His heart fluttered at the sight of Gracie and Ewan perched gracefully on the staircase. The setting sun painted their faces with a warm, saffron glow, accentuating Gracie's radiant beauty. Her hair, dark and silky, caught the sunlight and shimmered, giving her an ethereal aura like a celestial being. In that moment, Coby's worries about Alistair's warning disappeared like a distant memory. Beside her, Ewan sat, his fingers gently gliding through Janie's silky, golden fur. Gracie greeted Coby with a warm hug and a tender kiss, electrifying his entire body with the taste of her lips. Coby revealed the vibrant bouquet of wildflowers, filling the air with their sweet, fragrant scent, causing Gracie to gasp and shriek in surprise. Her embrace tightened around him, and she lovingly planted soft kisses all over his face.

"I appreciate you looking after my place," he said, blushing and giving a bashful smile.

Gracie playfully sealed his adorable look with a gentle kiss, teasing in a seductive voice, "Nothing beats the thrill of spending someone else's money." Coby chuckled, his laughter filling the air, before playfully slapping her on her soft, inviting backside.

While Coby and Ewan unpacked the groceries, Gracie carefully arranged a table for two, placing the silverware with precision. She adorned it with a row of flickering candles, casting dancing shadows against the walls, imbuing the room with a romantic ambiance. Drawn by the mesmerising music and the dancing candles, the ethereal trinity materialised, their presence filling the room with an otherworldly energy. Fixated on the flickering flames, their eyes glimmered like embers, casting an icy embrace over the hallway.

Gracie transferred the pizza crunch and chips to elegant ceramic dishes, placing them on the dining table. She joined Coby in the kitchen, where he prepared their drinks. Meanwhile, the tantalising aroma of the food enticed Ewan into the hallway. The sight of the golden, crispy chips tempted him irresistibly. His fingers reached out, capturing a fry, bringing it to his mouth. Janie inhaled deeply, extinguishing the candles as her icy breath brushed against Ewan's fingers, sending a shiver down his spine. Ewan's face turned ghostly pale with shock, his voice quivering as he desperately gasped, "Mum!"

Instead of consoling her son, Gracie scolded him with a wagging finger, her voice filled with sternness. "I caught you red-handed, attempting to swipe a chip, you mischievous little scoundrel."

Ewan's cheeks turned a deep shade of crimson as he hurriedly retreated outside, accompanied by Janie's excited barks. A knowing smile graced Coby's lips as he raised his crystal whisky glass in a toast. While Coby and Gracie indulged in their mouthwatering meal, Ewan ate in solitude, his gaze fixed on the distant horizon. Coby knew he had a sneaky way of sharing his food with the eager Janie, their secret pact clear in Ewan's consistent request for seconds.

With each passing drink and the advancing evening, Coby found it increasingly difficult to silence Alistair's voice reverberating in his head. The warning echoed in his mind, overpowering the vibrant music that filled the air, distracting him from fully engaging in Gracie's captivating stories. He grew distant, his attention drifting away, and he did not savour the affectionate gestures Gracie bestowed upon him. Normally, he would yearn for her touch, but tonight it was different. At one point, Gracie sensed his discomfort and gently placed her hand on his leg, the warmth of her touch seeping through his jeans, but he brushed it off, his mind consumed by his internal turmoil.

"What is the matter?" Gracie eventually asked, her voice as gentle as a summer breeze. Glossy eyes accompanied her tender gaze, reflecting the amber glow of the Drambuie in their glasses.

Coby could not bear the sight of her, his heart heavy with the weight of his confession. With a heavy sigh, he broke down, his words tumbling out, carried by a mix of emotions. Gracie, stunned into disbelief, took his hand, their fingers intertwining gently.

"Listen, Coby," she started, her voice filled with vulnerability. "I've already shared with you the details of what took place. The grief of losing my husband made me vulnerable and easily deceived." Gracie let out a deep breath, her voice trembling with sadness, "since I hadn't eaten for days, they got me drunk."

"What do you mean by 'they'?" Coby snapped, his tone laced with disbelief, the sound of his voice cutting through the air like a sharp blade.

"Hold on, cowboy," Gracie assuaged, her touch offering a reassuring anchor. She gently squeezed his hand, her touch a comforting embrace amidst the storm brewing within him. "I recall little of that dreadful evening, but the more I pondered, the more convinced I became that I heard voices, not just Alistair's." She paused, allowing her words to sink in. "The following morning, I found myself without clothes, with the chilling touch of the bedsheets enveloping my body. I saw familiar marks of intimacy on the bed linens." Gracie halted, her grip tightening on her glass, the scent of the alcohol mingling with the tension in the air. She closed her eyes, her hand trembling, her vulnerability palpable. "Before long, I started experiencing morning sickness, and I realised that I was pregnant." She closed her eyes and took a long sip of her drink, her hand trembling. "Since Giles was already deceased, it was impossible for the child to be his."

Anger coursed through Coby's veins, intensifying with each beat of his heart like an inferno. The weight of betrayal bore down on him, his emotions swirling in a tempest of fury and disbelief. His fingers curled tightly around his crystal whisky glass, the coolness offering a brief respite from the seething heat within him. And then, in an instant, the glass snapped into shards in his hand, the sharp sound of its destruction echoing through the room. Blood dripped from the deep cut on his finger, the metallic tang mingling with the scent of whisky, staining the polished marble floor, collecting in a crimson puddle. Gracie's gasp echoed through the room as she swiftly jumped up, her determined steps carrying her to the kitchen.

"Where's your first aid kit?" she urgently asked, the sound of her footsteps echoing on the tiled floor.

"In my study," Coby said, his eyes wandering over her graceful form in the kitchen, the gentle sunlight streaming through the window and casting a cosy radiance on her delicate features. He felt a pang of guilt stab his heart, his chest tightening as if weighted by the burden of his actions. Gracie hurried to his study, the sound of her hurried footsteps reverberating through the hallway. The rustling of papers and clinking of objects filled the room, a symphony of busyness. She returned with the first aid kit and kitchen towels, their pristine white fabric contrasting against the crimson stain on Coby's shirt. She tenderly tended to his wound, the cool touch of the cloth soothing his skin. With each gentle stroke, the spills on the floor disappeared, the faint scent of cleaning solution mingling with the lingering aroma of whiskey. Coby watched her work, his eyes tracing every movement, every act of care, and a deep sense of admiration filled his heart, a warmth spreading through his veins like a comforting embrace. He had never experienced the privilege of someone as caring as her in his life, the feeling foreign yet undeniably comforting.

"Mum!" The sudden bellow of Ewan's voice shattered the peaceful atmosphere, startling Coby out of his deep thoughts. Ewan's figure slowly came into focus, his silhouette framed against the backdrop of the hallway, the dim light casting shadows on his face. Coby noticed him cradling a lifeless pheasant, the feathers ruffled and motionless, dangling from his hand by its lifeless legs.

Gracie's brow furrowed in thought, her expression a canvas of contemplation, and she scolded her son, the words piercing the air like a stern reprimand. Ewan recognised the weight of her gaze, the intensity of her disapproval, and hurried outside, the sound of the door closing behind him echoing faintly. Janie, their loyal companion, wagged her tail by Ewan's side, the rhythmic thumping against the floor a testament to her unwavering loyalty. Gracie and Coby exchanged a knowing glance, their eyes filled with unspoken affection, a silent understanding passing between them.

"Now is not the time for him to boast about his hunting skills," she commented, her voice carrying a gentle yet firm tone, while her warm smile radiated love. The words struck a nerve within Coby, memories flooding his mind, his thoughts transported back to the day he first stepped foot into his new stately home.

As if a curtain had been lifted, he found himself back in the library, the scent of aged paper and leather permeating the air, evoking a rich and earthy aroma that whispered tales of history and wisdom. The memory of his first encounter with the dusty library remained etched in his mind – his eyes widening in awe as he explored the manor's labyrinth of rooms, stumbling upon the treasure trove of knowledge. Out of nowhere, his face brightened with a remarkable revelation, his eyes flickering with an exhilarating surge of excitement.

"Hold on," Coby murmured, his voice filled with surprise, barely audible in the hallway. Gracie watched him intently, her eyes filled with curiosity, her gaze a gentle prodding for him to share his revelation. Coby leaped up, his movement swift and decisive, his hand reaching out to grab hers, their fingers intertwining as if forging a connection. With a sense of purpose, he pulled her along the labyrinth of corridors towards the library, the sound of their footsteps echoing through the empty spaces, the harmony of their strides resonating in perfect synchrony. With each deliberate step, Gracie's heels clicked loudly against the polished marble floor, emphasising her determination. They reached the library, and as the heavy oak door swung open, the scent of old books and leather engulfed them, a nostalgic perfume that transported them to another time. The shelves, filled with ancient books, invited them closer, their weathered spines telling stories of countless readers.

"What is your quest?" Gracie asked, her voice filled with curiosity, a hint of excitement in her eyes. Coby tore his gaze away from the old books, their musty scent filling the air, and his anticipation palpable in his glowing eyes.

"Don't forget," he said, raising his eyebrows in a questioning manner, "you mentioned that your deceased husband, Giles, managed the estate, right?" Gracie nodded, her eyes welling up with tears, each drop a testament to the love she still felt for her deceased husband.

"Um," Coby began, his voice echoing through the deserted library, the words resounding against the walls, "he died in a tragic hunting accident, and you just mentioned hearing voices, not just Alistair's voice." He paused, allowing the silence to fill the room as his words hung in the air. Gracie watched him intently, her eyes wide with awe.

"Each property keeps hunting records, a hunting ledger," Coby added, his voice brimming with enthusiasm. As he spoke, he could see

Gracie's eyes glowing, the realisation slowly dawning on her.

"This document would act as a register of previous participants, recording not only their names but also a wide range of details that enhance the intricate story of the manor's past," Coby assured, a smile tugging at his lips as he retrieved his phone and began scrolling through the collection of images. When he came across an image of him and Ewan on their recent adventure, a brief smile played on his face, reflecting the joy of that moment. Undeterred, he continued scrolling, aware of Gracie's anticipation. His eyes lit up when he found the image of the article he took in the library.

Gracie noticed what he was doing and quickly joined him, her eyes fixated on the phone screen, captivated by the images. Her voice was soft and grave as she reminded him, "Giles died on the seventh of October." Coby checked her words against the date in the article on the image. The date was a perfect match, the ninth of October, exactly nine years ago, just two days after his passing.

With a surge of inspiration, both of them knew what to do, a shared understanding passing between them with no need for words. They embarked on a search for the Estate's hunting ledger, their hands brushing against the spines of every book, the sound of pages rustling filling the room. Running his fingers along the spines, Coby could almost hear the stories they held, patiently waiting to be unravelled. He had to stand on a footstool to reach the higher shelves, his heart racing with anticipation. Gracie hurried to the lounge, the sound of her footsteps echoing, fetching a chair and standing on it. Together, they searched every corner of the shelves, every nook and cranny, their fingers skimming over every book.

Coby's heart jolted, a sharp pang that made his breath catch in his chest, as Gracie's voice reverberated through the room. "I found it!" she cried out, the sound echoing in his mind. A surge of relief and excitement rushed through Coby like a powerful wave crashing over him. He hurried towards Gracie, his eyes fixated on the large ledger she held in her hands. The sight of it left him breathless, a testament to the grandeur of Hemlock Manor. The leather binding, adorned with gleaming gold, showcased the formal name of the manor. As Coby touched the cover, he felt the smoothness of the leather against his fingertips, while the embossed coat of arms captivated his gaze. The visual elements were vivid, bursting with colours that seemed to come alive. The blue and white crisscross pattern on the cover added a tactile sense of texture, inviting Coby to run his hand over its intricate design. At the centre, a shield boasted a mesmerising blue and white diamond pattern. Above the shield, a knight's helmet, adorned with mantling decorated with the same blue and white motifs, stood proudly. Perched atop the helmet, a golden lion roared fiercely, emanating a sense of majestic power. Two banners, elegantly displayed, held carefully crafted text; one proclaimed "Àrd agus Brònach" above, while the one below simply read "Ledger." The overall design was intricate and elaborate, a testament to the heraldic symbolism that Hemlock Manor held dear.

With a slow, deliberate motion, Gracie opened it, and the soft rustle of the pages filled the room. The scent of aged paper wafted towards them, mingling with the excitement in the room. The faded ink on the pages told stories of thrilling hunts and the bonds formed around roaring fires. Each entry read like a short story, a frozen moment in time. A testament to Giles's attention to detail, the dates and names of participants were meticulously inscribed. Coby's eyes flicked between Gracie's captivating gaze and the words on the pages, his heart swelling with a mix of emotions. As Gracie flipped through the pages, he could almost hear the whisper of time passing, with each turn revealing another month gone by. Her pace slowed as she reached the fifth of October, the sixth, and beyond... "No!" she exclaimed, her voice filled with dismay. Coby's heart sank, his knees feeling weak beneath him. The walls of the library seemed to close in, suffocating him. The torn parchment only had a fragment of the date remaining – the seventh of October. A fleeting glance passed between them, their eyes filled with unspoken understanding.

"My familiarity with Giles was strong," Gracie declared, her tear-filled eyes shining in the soft glow of the flickering candlelight. Memories of her late husband stirred a mix of sorrow and longing within her core.

"Do you think Giles made a backup?" Coby asked incredulously, his voice cutting through the silence of the ancient library. The air grew frigid, sending a shiver down Coby's spine, as a cloud of miseries seemed to settle over the room. He could feel the prickling sensation across his skin, causing him to tense up in anticipation.

A soft whoosh, which brought with it a chilling breeze, pierced the air. Giles's ghost materialised beside Gracie, his monochrome eyes locked onto the ledger, specifically the conspicuous absence of a single page. The ghostly figure softly hissed, "It was a terrible day," as the sound echoed through the book-filled shelves.

"Yes," Gracie whispered, barely audible, "and the young apprentice surely knows the details."

"Do you know the name of the apprentice?" Coby asked eagerly, his voice tinged with excitement.

Overwhelmed with emotion, Gracie found herself speechless. Beside her, Giles's ghostly presence sent chills down Coby's spine as he whispered the name "Barclay" in a haunting, hissing voice.

In a sudden flash of realisation, Gracie's face lit up with a new found brightness, as if a light bulb had switched on inside her. "Yes!" she exclaimed, her voice filled with excitement. "Barclay Gillies - that was his name." Disappointment quickly replaced her initial elation, clear from the sudden downturn of her expression.

"But he went away with the other employees when the owners left," she murmured, her voice filled with a sense of resignation. Gile's apparition floated above Gracie, emanating an aura of affection.

Coby's voice was filled with curiosity as he asked, "Why did they depart in such haste?" Involuntarily, Coby shuddered as Giles shot him a frosty glare, tinged with frostiness.

Gracie's furrowed brow betrayed her deep contemplation as she replied with a sigh, "Och," her voice filled with a tinge of unease. "They claimed the place was haunted after that fateful day, prompting them to pack up and leave." Giles shook his head in disagreement, his ethereal form trembling as he pointed a spectral finger inward. Coby's lips curved into a thin smile, but his heart pounded in his chest, the tension in the air palpable.

"Who do you mean when you say 'they'?" Coby asked, his voice casual but filled with weight, allowing the words to linger like a dense cloud.

"Roy and Bonnie Sinclair," Gracie absentmindedly replied, her gaze fixated on the weathered ledger in her hands. The words hit Coby like a thunderous train, knocking the wind out of him. The world around him spun out of control, and he fought against the urge to collapse under the weight of the revelation.

"Are they..." Coby's mouth was parched, his tongue sticking to the roof of his mouth as he fought to speak. "Are they family of Alistair Sinclair?" he asked, his eyes tightly shut, bracing himself for the answer he feared.

"Yes." Gracie's words pierced his ears like a painful thud, each syllable seeping into his very being. "They are his children." Giles's ghost effortlessly merged with the inky darkness, vanishing amidst a soft murmur, engulfing Coby in a maelstrom of emotions.

Before they bid their farewell, Gracie made a solemn promise to search every nook and cranny of the cottage for a backup of the hunting ledger. With a gentle touch, she greeted Coby, leaving a tender kiss on his lips that sent a flutter through his chest. As the front door slammed shut, he swiftly made his way to his study, sinking into the tranquillity that enveloped him, accompanied by the aroma of a well-aged whisky. With nimble fingers, he diligently scoured the depths of the internet, befriending every Barclay Gillies he could find on social media. Under the watchful gaze of the otherworldly trio, he shuffled through the dimly lit corridors, his footsteps echoing softly.

"See you later, gators!" he playfully called out to them, as he reached his bedroom and extinguished the lights. In the silence that followed, he caught their mischievous giggles and murmurs of anticipation, intertwining with the stillness of the air before they disappeared into the darkness like wisps of smoke.

Chapter Eighteen

Coby woke abruptly, his eyes fixated on the white ceiling above. Memories from the previous day flooded his mind, filling him with a sense of excitement. With a burst of energy, he sprang out of bed, the floor beneath his feet cool and smooth. While humming a cheerful tune, he slipped into his clothes, relishing the sensation of the soft fabric against his skin.

The sound of a lively Celtic melody filled the air, harmonising with the clink of the toaster as he inserted two slices of slightly stale bread. He heated the leftover macaroni pie in the microwave, and the scent of toasted bread mingled with its aroma. The warm, cheesy pie melted onto the toast, creating a mouthwatering combination of flavours.

While he waited for his coffee to brew, the kitchen filled with the mouthwatering scent of a perfectly fried egg and the symphony of sizzling and brewing. Placing the fried eggs on top of the macaroni pie, he drizzled them with English mustard, the tangy scent tickling his nose.

His taste buds encountered a scorching sensation as he took a sip of the hot coffee, leading him to sputter it out. Undeterred, he eagerly devoured his breakfast, relishing every bite. Thoughts of Janie crossed his mind, imagining her adorable puppy face begging for food.

With a contented pat on his full belly, he strolled into his study, whistling a lively tune. The ethereal trio gathered around Stanley's upside-down sketch. It did not surprise him; they were exactly where he thought they would be.

"Good morning, ladies," Coby sang out in a voice that was high-pitched and melodic. Ignoring his presence, their longing gazes remained fixed on the sketch. He playfully pretended to smack each apparition on their bottoms, but his hand passed through their ethereal forms.

Chuckling heartily, he sank into his plush leather chair, placing his coffee next to the framed photograph of Gracie and Ewan. The sight of them made his heart flutter, his eyes gleaming mischievously. Jane's solemn stare met his, her eyes filled with pleading.

"Alright, alright," Coby reassured, flipping Stanley's sketch over to reveal their ethereal likeness, captured in delicate detail. The lines on the paper seemed to come alive, as if they could step out at any moment. Their responses were filled with such intense emotion that it rendered him utterly speechless.

Vivienne's ghostly figure let out a high-pitched scream of delight. The sound bounced off the walls and rang in Coby's ears. Their hands flew to their cheeks in unison, their astonishment palpable. Whispered hisses filled the air as they engaged in an animated discussion, a blend of English and French harmonising like a melodic symphony. Words poured forth, their disbelief clear as they exchanged fleeting glances. Jane's spectral image pointed at the sketch, and that's when Coby heard it. The unmistakable mention of "Moulin Rouge" several times. Leaning back in his chair, he listened intently, a mischievous smile playing on his lips.

Coby's mind conjured an image of cabaret dancing, complete with the rhythmic clacking of heels on the wooden stage. Just as he was lost in thought, the sound of tires crunching over gravel outside broke the silence. He turned his gaze towards the windows and spotted Alistair Sinclair's Range Rover pulling up, uninvited. Ignoring the ghostly trinity's animated discussion, Coby remained seated. Alistair knocked on the hallway's wooden door, creating a resounding echo of metal meeting wood.

"Come in!" Coby called out, and the ominous doors creaked open, followed by the thudding of Alistair's walking stick against the marble floor.

In the study doorway, Alistair lifted his white top hat, casting a shadow over his face, and greeted Coby with a stern "Morning."

Coby responded with a coy smile and asked, "Whisky?"

Alistair eagerly nodded and sauntered into the study, the tap-tap of his walking stick echoing through the room. Coby headed straight for the sideboard, where the scent of aged Scottish whisky wafted through the air, enveloping the room in its rich aroma. Meanwhile, Alistair's gaze fell upon the sketch, showcasing the allure of the ethereal threesome. His eyes widened with shock, and his trembling hands betrayed his astonishment. He let out a startled gasp, his face draining of colour as he collapsed into a pitiful heap on the floor. Startled by the thud, Coby swiftly turned around, initially unable to locate Alistair's sprawled frame behind the desk. His brow furrowed in confusion, as if the man had vanished. "Unbelievable," Coby murmured, his eyes wide with astonishment as he carefully set the two crystal glasses aside.

In the dimly lit room, the supernal trio, their ethereal forms softly glowing, suddenly noticed Alistair Sinclair lying sprawled on the floor. Startled, they leaped aside, emitting high-pitched shrieks of terror that reverberated through the air. Their fingers, translucent and bathed in an otherworldly glow, ominously pointed towards the motionless figure. Whispers of astonishment and eerie hisses filled the room, creating an unsettling atmosphere.

Coby's heart raced in his chest, his wide eyes fixated on the spectral beings as they gracefully moved their fingers, creating an otherworldly spectacle. Alistair's unconscious form was a shocking sight that made his breath catch in his throat. He knelt down beside him, the coolness of the floor seeping through his jeans, and urgently shook him by the shoulder. "Alistair," he murmured, his voice filled with concern, repeating his name again and again, his hands trembling with worry. Alistair groaned softly, his body stirring in response to the persistent shaking. The air was filled with the murmurs of the apparitions, their whispers echoing like eerie hisses from a distant realm.

Coby swiftly retrieved his phone from his pocket, his fingers instinctively finding the national emergency number. But before he could make the call, a murmur, barely audible yet strangely captivating, filled the air, distracting him from his task. Intrigued, he set his phone aside and focused his gaze on Alistair, eager to hear what he had to say. "What was that?" he asked, his voice filled with curiosity and a touch of unease.

Alistair's eyes snapped open, startling Coby as he jumped back, his heart racing. "The silence isn't always your friend!" Alistair exclaimed, his voice filled with urgency and a touch of desperation. With shaky legs, he quickly stood up, his knees trembling beneath him, and stumbled his way out of the room. Coby's ears were met with the resounding thud of the front door slamming shut. Through the window, he watched as Alistair Sinclair hastily jumped into his Range Rover, the engine roaring to life. The tires screeched loudly against the rough gravel, leaving behind deep tracks as the car surged forward. Coby stood there, his face a mixture of awe and disbelief, as he watched Alistair's car speed down the driveway.

With Alistair gone, the spectral threesome huddled closely together, their excited whispers creating a lively atmosphere. The silence was shattered by their hollow, eerie laughter, its echoes bouncing off the walls. Jane, her spectral finger trembling, pointed directly at the image of her own likeness on the sketch, her whispers of "mine" growing more desperate with each repetition. Coby noticed the profound sadness in her eyes, as if the weight of longing hung heavy in the air. He watched as she cradled an invisible baby, swaying rhythmically with a tenderness that tugged at his heart.

Coby spoke, his voice as gentle as a summer breeze, acknowledging Jane's claim on the sketch. However, his words seemed to awaken something within her, causing her spectral eyes to flash open, glowing like smouldering embers. The sight sent a jolt of fear through Coby's body, causing him to grip his chair tightly, his knuckles turning white. Jane's hissed reply, "Mine," sent shivers down his spine, as fear gripped his heart.

With a stammer and a dry mouth, Coby nervously asked about the baby's name, his voice noticeably trembling. Sensing the shift in the atmosphere, Josephine and Vivienne turned their attention to Jane, their eyes locked on her. The room seemed to come alive with an unsettling symphony, a blend of palpable tension and the soft, ghostly sounds of coos and whispers. Jane's piercing shriek of "Mine" filled the air, causing Coby to wince and almost lose his balance on the chair. Her finger, filled with menace, pointed upwards, guiding Coby's gaze to the rolling hills outside the window. His eyes nervously flickered back and forth between her menacing finger and the breathtaking panorama stretching out before him.

Coby furrowed his brow, deep in thought, as he gazed at the plush hills, their vibrant green captivating his eyes. "Mine," he whispered to himself, the word escaping his lips repeatedly like a soft breeze. A flicker of joy ignited in his face, illuminating his features, as a realisation dawned on him.

"Oh, it's a mine!" Coby exclaimed, his voice booming through the air, startling the ethereal trinity, whose hisses filled the silence with menace. Sheepishly, he offered an apologetic "Sorry!" and noticed Jane subtly nodding her head in understanding.

At last, a clue had emerged, sparking a surge of inspiration that coursed through his veins like an electric current. His fingers glided effortlessly over the keyboard, the soft clicks of each keystroke echoing in the room. He delved into a search, seeking everything he could find about Scottish mines. The screen before him overflowed with information, a vast sea of knowledge about the popularity of coal mines and gold mines. Yet, upon further investigation, he realised that coal mines were not present in the Highlands, and he swiftly scratched them off his list. "We are left with gold mines," he murmured, his voice barely audible, as if afraid to disturb the tranquillity of the moment. In response, Jane's hissed reply of "mine" caught him off guard, her head bobbing with a sense of affirmation.

However, his efforts to find information about gold mining in or around Serenity Falls proved fruitless. The dates of the Scottish gold rush in the late nineteenth century aligned with the apparitions' dresses from that era, further cementing his theory. Frustration settled heavily on his shoulders like a weight, a tangible burden that dampened his spirits. Despite his exhaustive searches, he had reached a dead end, leaving him grappling with the mystery that shrouded Serenity Falls. An idea hit him like a speeding bus, the force of it crashing into his mind.

"The library!" Coby exclaimed, his voice filled with excitement. "Goodbye, ladies," he playfully taunted the ghostly figures, their shimmering ethereal shapes waving back as he bid them farewell. He downed his whisky in one gulp, feeling the burn as it slid down his throat, and stormed out of the room. The Volvo engine roared in protest as he put his foot down, the sound reverberating through the air. He sped down the steep driveway. At the junction of the driveway and the main road, he abruptly hit the brakes. The piercing sound of screeching tires echoed, and the pungent odour of burning rubber permeated the air

* * *

A smile graced Coby's lips when he stepped into the library, the familiar scent of old books embracing him. Glancing around, he felt a wave of relief wash over him as he saw that the microfilm reader was unoccupied. The impolite librarian lady handed him boxes filled with microfilm, her face contorted with annoyance. With the soft hum of the reader filling the air, he began his search. The historic newspaper images flashed before his eyes, their black and white forms dancing across the screen. He went way back, delving into the past, searching for anything related to the word 'mine.'

Layer by layer, Coby fed the microfilm through the reader, the rhythmic ticking of the seconds transforming into a seemingly endless passage of time. The air in the room hung stagnant, broken only by the occasional cough or the rustling of pages. Now and then, the screech of a chair against the floor broke the silence, indicating the presence or absence of other customers.

From afar, the piercing wail of a siren filled the air, marking the conclusion of lunchtime. Coby's eyes remained fixated on the screen, his focus unwavering. He flicked through the ancient newspaper images, scanning every headline and article for the words 'gold' or 'mine.' Suddenly, an image of a young family flashed before him, catching his attention. At first, he didn't fully register her presence, his mind consumed by the search terms. But then, the significance hit him like a lightning bolt, and he hurriedly clicked back to the article with the photograph of the family. Against the dark background, the monochrome photograph seemed to come alive, its sharp lines and shadows creating a sense of depth and nostalgia. The figures within seemed frozen in time, their stories trapped in the grayscale world that surrounded them. Each shadow held a secret, each highlight a revelation, weaving together a tapestry of forgotten tales as intriguing as they were elusive.

"My god!" Coby exclaimed, his outburst earning him disapproving glances from other library-goers. He quickly raised his hand in apology, his gaze lingering on the captivating image. "That is Jane," he whispered, his voice filled with a mix of disbelief and awe. Jane stood side by side with a man and a young boy in the vintage image, their eyes filled with happiness. A small house stood behind them, its chimney releasing billows of smoke into the air. With a gentle swipe,

Coby cleared the smudges from his reading glasses, exposing his teary-eyed expression. The intense focus made his eyes burn with discomfort.

His gaze was instantly captivated by the bold headline that screamed, 'SERENITY FALLS SHROUDED IN GRIEF: GOLDMINE COLLAPSE ROBS BELOVED TEACHER OF FAMILY.' Coby leaned in close, his eyes scanning the words with anticipation as he delved into the depths of the article.

Once a town filled with dreams of prosperity, Serenity Falls now stands engulfed in a heavy pall of sorrow. The collapse of the goldmine, which was once the heart of this bustling gold rush town, has claimed many lives and shattered countless dreams.

One of the affected individuals is Jane Baines, a beloved local schoolteacher, who tragically lost her dear husband, Irvine, and their cherished son, Archie, in this unfortunate incident. Mrs Baines, known for her unwavering dedication to her students, was already grappling with the loss of her vocation when Lord Henderson Sinclair, a wealthy British aristocrat, closed the school to exploit the young boys as labourers in the mines.

Sinclair's arrival had initially brought hope and anticipation to Serenity Falls, as he promised commercial gold mining and prosperity for all. However, beneath the glittering surface of this gold rush, a darker tale unfolded. Sinclair's ruthless industrialisation not only deprived the town's children of education but also resulted in a disaster that robbed the town of its joy and claimed the lives of many of its inhabitants.

The tragic accident has left the town in mourning, with lingering questions about Sinclair's practices and the true cost of the gold rush. As Serenity Falls grieves its losses, the residents come together in solidarity, united by their collective pain, serving as a stark reminder that not everything that glitters is gold.

On Sunday, the community will hold a memorial service for the deceased at the local cemetery. As they gather to remember Irvine and Archie and to support Jane in her time of grief, the spirit of Serenity Falls remains unbroken, albeit bruised. This devastating event serves as a poignant reminder that the relentless pursuit of wealth can sometimes come at a terrible price.

Coby's body trembled with disbelief, his exclamation echoing through the silent library. Tears welled up in his eyes, blurring his vision as a dark sorrow gripped his heart. The weight of his emotions played a tumultuous rollercoaster within him, like a wild ride through a stormy sea.

As his thoughts drifted to Jane, he could almost hear the haunting silence that surrounded her, a silence filled with the absence of her beloved family. The heavy aroma of loss seemed to permeate every corner of the room.

Amidst the whirlwind of emotions, one name towered above all else, like a blazing inferno against the night sky - Lord Henderson Sinclair. The mere thought of him sent shivers down Coby's spine, his intuition screaming with certainty that this evildoer was undeniably connected to Alistair Sinclair. It was as if the very air whispered the truth, carrying the scent of greed and entitlement.

With a resolute determination, Coby was willing to stake everything on his conviction, even his cherished hat. He knew, without a shadow of doubt, that the heartless aristocrat was none other than Alistair's father, the puppeteer behind this tragic web of deceit and loss.

Coby's heavy sigh reverberated through the narrow confines of the Library, creating an echo that lingered in the air. He had reached his limit, feeling mentally and physically exhausted. Before he could continue his grim research, there was something he needed to understand.

With a fresh coffee and a rich dark chocolate in hand, he convinced the librarian to share directions to the cemetery. With a grateful smile on her face, she eagerly shared the intricate details. Coby expressed his appreciation with a winsome smile and made his way towards the outskirts of the small town. With a quick stop at the local florist, he followed the cobblestone road, taking in the sight of the well-kept cemetery. Its old stone walls stood proudly, nestled between two lush, rolling hills.

The air was filled with the sweet sounds of lambs bleating and sheep softly baaing as they grazed upon the rolling hills. On top of a hill, an ancient tractor chugged along, its rhythmic rumble fading into the distance. The sound of Coby's footsteps reverberated through the air as he stepped through the rusted, creaking metal gates, creating a symphony of echoes along the gravel path. His eyes scanned every name etched into the weathered headstones, desperately searching the small cemetery for the elusive pair of similar names. The task proved more challenging than he had expected, leaving his lips yearning for the taste of aged whisky. Instinctively, he licked his parched lips, feeling the dryness.

Finally, after meticulously searching, Coby's eyes landed on a single row of graves, each one perfectly aligned with the next. Standing before the weathered and towering communal grave marker, he ran his finger along the fading names etched into the fieldstone, feeling the rough texture beneath his touch. Each name shared a common thread – the deceased date. It was a poignant reminder of lives cut short, dreams left unfulfilled, and families torn apart. Coby's discovery was both fascinating and dreadful. Tears welled up in his eyes, and he felt the tight lump of sorrow forming in his throat, a physical manifestation of his emotions.

With a heavy heart, Coby knelt beside the graves of Irvine Baines and Archie Baines, feeling the weight of their absence and the solemnity of the moment. Carefully, he placed the vibrant bouquet of wildflowers next to the two resting places, feeling the weight of remorse weighing him down. On his knees, he sat there as time stretched on, feeling the frigid, damp ground penetrate his very core. Finally, he mustered the strength to rise, his weary body aching with every movement. Determined, he embarked on a relentless search for the grave of the sinister man, Lord Henderson Sinclair.

He meticulously searched every corner of the cemetery, the unmistakable smell of moist soil and decomposing foliage permeating the air. His hands brushed against the rough edges of headstones, his fingertips tracing the carved names and dates. Despite his relentless search, the elusive grave continued to evade his grasp, leaving him feeling exasperated and bewildered.

An insistent intuition tugged at him, insisting that there was something he needed to investigate elsewhere. An unsettling feeling whispered in his ear, urging him to make his way towards his stately home. Forgoing his customary stop at the Stag's Head Inn, Coby trudged forward, the heavy weight of the unknown pressing on his mind.

On a whim, he took a quick detour and stood in front of Gracie's enchanting cottage, its colourful exterior inviting him inside. The scent of lavender infused the air, soothing his restless mind. Gracie, her warm smile lighting up her face and her kind eyes full of compassion, provided him with the much-needed information he sought. Despite the short distance, she insisted on joining him, her presence providing a reassuring comfort.

Ewan bid them a brief farewell, choosing to remain with Janie. Together, Gracie and Coby ventured along the winding gravel path, the crunch of stones beneath their feet punctuating the silence. With each step up the hill, the soothing sound of a nearby brook grew louder, creating a peaceful atmosphere.

Gracie felt a shiver run down her spine as a fateful wind blew through the desolate wasteland, causing her to rub her arms for warmth. The small graveyard came into view, enclosed by weathered wrought iron fencing that emitted a faint metallic scent.

The air was filled with an unsettling aura as a figure dressed in a haunting white cloak glided before a towering tombstone. The wraith-like figure, with her head bowed, emitted a sorrowful wail as it mourned for the soul of the passing wicked. Coby was accustomed to seeing them, a common sight near the graves of the revered. Their incessant weeping resonated through the air, casting a sombre mood. Whenever Coby spoke of them, he would always use the word 'weepers', evoking a sense of sadness and melancholy.

The heavy gate swung open with a creak, its protesting noise breaking the eerie stillness of the graveyard. Coby stepped inside, the uneven ground beneath his feet causing a slight unsteadiness. As he stood beside the wraith, a wave of conflicting emotions washed over him – a mix of both dread and relief. Up close, he could hear her pleas echoing softly, like a mournful melody.

Just as he had expected, the towering marble headstone of Lord Henderson Sinclair stood before him, casting a solemn shadow. Over the passage of time, Lord Sinclair's headstone remained a steadfast presence in the peaceful graveyard, emanating stories of honour, duty, and unyielding devotion through its engraved words. His name, 'Lord Henderson Alistair Sinclair', shimmered in elegant gold letters against the dark backdrop.

The cool touch of the marble sent a shiver down Coby's spine as he traced his fingers over the engraved dates, marking the beginning and end of a mortal existence. The faint aroma of freshly cut flowers danced in the air, intermingling with the gentle hint of earth and passaging years. Delicately etched below the dates, the biblical verse, 'The LORD is my shepherd, I shall not want,' served as a whispered promise in stone. A dedication to his influential role caught Coby's attention at the bottom, with the title 'Devoted servant to his people and his land'. Coby couldn't help but scoff, the bitter truth weighing heavily on his mind. Lord Sinclair's insatiable greed had led to the downfall of many and, ultimately, his own demise.

As he prepared to depart, he found himself drawn to the captivating gaze of Gracie's enchanting sapphire eyes, unable to look away. The gentle breeze caressed her hair, playfully swirling dark strands across her forehead, and she gracefully brushed them away. It added a whimsical touch to her presence, causing Coby's heart to flutter in his chest. Walking alongside the babbling brook, their synchronised steps created a rhythmic crunch of gravel beneath their feet.

They eventually arrived at Gracie's charming abode, where Coby settled himself at the small, round table in the rustic kitchen. Gracie, observing his pallor, poured him a meticulously crafted, strong whisky. The air was filled with the enticing aromas of slow-cooked pheasant and the earthy fragrance of freshly harvested vegetables. Coby's eyes widened as Gracie placed a tantalising pheasant pie in front of him, its flaky crust begging to be devoured. With Janie's beseeching eyes fixed upon him, her tail wagging in a slow rhythm, Coby eagerly devoured each morsel, savouring the taste. Satisfied and satiated, he divulged all that he had discovered about Jane, painting a vivid picture of her grief and the tragic events that befell her beloved husband and son.

Gracie, unsurprised by the revelation, shared her own experiences of her late husband working under the imposing presence of the Sinclair family. The haunting enigma of why Lord Henderson Sinclair's title had not been passed down to his son, Alistair Sinclair, gnawed at Coby's conscience. It was a riddle wrapped in a mystery, a piece of the puzzle just out of reach. He felt it – a burning desire, a relentless determination simmering within him. In his quest, he would leave no stone unturned, no shadow unexplored. He made a solemn vow, not just to himself, but to the memory of the fallen Baines – he would unearth the truth, no matter how deep it was buried.

Chapter Nineteen

The gloomy, colourless day filled the air with a heavy sense of melancholy. Coby's attentive gaze carefully scanned his study, meticulously assessing every detail to ensure it was flawless for Gracie's arrival. He brought in a new desk, complete with a plush leather chair, creating a cosy and professional workspace. Gracie arrived early, adorned in a vibrant floral dress that caught his eye. The aroma of freshly brewed coffee filled the air as she handed Coby a cup, its rich and delightful taste bringing a smile to his face. Working side by side in silence, he admired Gracie's meticulous nature and swift understanding. She was a refreshing change from Elaine, who would idle away and incessantly chatter. In front of the cosy fireplace, Janie snuggled up, basking in its soothing ambiance. Coby could hear the soft, rhythmic sound of her breathing as her chest rose and fell. The sight of Gracie and Janie warmed his heart, and he gladly embraced their company.

In his plush leather seat, Coby leaned back, his gaze absentmindedly fixed on the screen. However, he couldn't help but steal furtive glances at Gracie, his heart swelling with pride. Gracie rewarded his flirtatious curiosity with a knowing smile, her eyes twinkling mischievously.

Having unravelled most of the truth surrounding Jane Baines, Coby meticulously documented the details in his draft, which he promptly shared with his editor. John Drake, his editor, had informed him of his abrupt break in Paris, where he was honing his French skills. He expressed immense admiration for Coby's progress. With Gracie by his side, Coby shared the grim discoveries on his social media platforms, urging for further information and offering a generous reward.

As expected, many fans swiftly responded, divulging intimate details for a signed copy of his books. Gracie laughed heartily, unaware of the modern social media norms. Together, they set up an email account for her, and Coby involved her in every reply and new message. When she reminded Coby about missing attachments, they laughed, creating a joyful ambiance that filled the air. In an email to his researchers, Coby pleaded for information, promising an increased hourly payment rate. The researchers promptly replied, assuring him they were on the task.

Coby now found himself at a dead end, left with nothing to do but wait. He had long since become desensitised to the alluring temptation of a cigarette, having kicked the habit. However, he openly confessed to experiencing the craving during monotonous moments like these. The endless frustration consumed him as he eavesdropped on the animated conversations of the ethereal trinity, perpetually gathered around the sketches of their images. Their discussions alternated between English and French, with only fragments reaching his ears. He yearned to unravel the enigmatic events that connected them in this eternal afterlife sanctuary. Coby listened intently, narrowing his eyes, hoping to catch repeated phrases. The air remained still, only interrupted by the steady ticking of the grandfather clock. The apparitions often whispered "Moulin Rouge," their words hissing softly. Coby jotted it down, followed by a question mark, pondering its significance.

Their discussion was impressive, with Vivienne's flawless French, answered in English by Jane, as if the language boundaries did not affect them in the afterlife realm. Josephine chimed in with a medley of English and French terms, and Jane would nod her head in understanding. Their conversation felt strange, like a never-ending loop, repeating the same ideas trapped within the confines of a timeless bubble.

Coby, aware of the significant meaning behind it, strained his mind, hoping to unravel their secrets. A phrase caught his attention, and he knew it was in French, because Vivienne repeated it often. With excitement, she would point at the images of Jane and Josephine in the sketch, gesturing and saying, "*dance avek mwa.*"

Coby jotted it down and typed the phrase into the search bar. He ended up with a list of music videos and played the first one. The video opened, revealing a stunning dark-haired woman wearing a glossy, dark blouse and proudly displaying a beauty mark on her left cheek. With a seductive tone, she serenaded "*dance avek mwa*," her flawless French accent lingering in the air. A steady whoosh sound accompanied her serenade, as the seductive melodies of a piano grew more intense.

The sounds immediately captured the apparitions' attention, and they rushed towards the origin, gathering closely around the screen. Coby restarted the video, and the sweet melody filled the air, creating a serene ambiance. In the video, the ballet dancer, dressed in sleek black attire, entered a small room with a mirrored wall, captivating viewers with a mesmerising performance. Beside Coby, the apparitions let out astonished gasps, their excited murmurs filling the room with ethereal whispers.

Jane sprung into action, her body undulating with a graceful fluidity that brought her desires to life. The familiarity of the moment washed over Coby as he listened to the soft melody playing in the background and watched Jane gracefully move across the floor in her ballet dance. It was a surreal echo of a memory he couldn't quite place, a sensation of Déjà vu that sent shivers down his spine.

The room pulsed with an electric energy, as if the air itself was alive with the emotions evoked by Jane's dance. Coby's breath hitched in his throat, caught in the enchanting spell woven by Jane's fluid movements and the captivating music. He couldn't tear his gaze away, completely captivated by the raw expression of desire and passion that emanated from every step, every leap, and every twirl.

Josephine and Vivienne, equally captivated, observed with awe-struck expressions and hushed voices, their spectral figures shimmering in harmony with the heightened atmosphere. The emotions portrayed in the dance seemed to reverberate through their very souls, transporting them back to a distant era.

The piano melody swelled to a crescendo, and Coby's emotions mirrored the intensifying energy, reaching a frenzied state. With his surroundings blurring into a whirlwind of colours and sensations, the room seemed to spin around him. Excitement surged through him, making his heart race.

And then, as the last note of the melody faded away, the room fell into a profound silence. Coby's jaw dropped in astonishment, unable to utter a single word. The echoes of the dance lingered in the air, intertwining with the stillness of the room, leaving behind a profound sense of longing and nostalgia.

In that moment, he realised the significance of the memory that had stirred within him. It wasn't just a simple déjà vu; it felt like he had lived this moment before, down to the tiniest details.

Coby's brow furrowed, the creases on his forehead deepening as he delved into his thoughts, a whirlwind of memories swirling in his mind. His eyes locked onto the spectral trio, his unwavering gaze consuming his every thought. He hurriedly made his way to the sideboard and poured himself a generous glass of whisky. The amber liquid shimmered in the soft light, its rich aroma wafting through the air. With the weight of the glass in his hand, he allowed himself to reminisce, his mind drifting back to his encounters with the ethereal trio.

Following Coby's lead, Gracie reached for a bottle of Drambuie and she poured herself a tot. The sweet, honeyed scent permeated the room, mingling with the intoxicating aroma of the whisky. The air became thick with the combined fragrances, evoking a sense of nostalgia and anticipation.

Suddenly, a vivid memory jolted Coby upright. He squeezed his eyes shut, feeling the rush of emotions as the weight of the memory enveloped him like a comforting embrace. As the evening of his birthday arrived, memories flooded back to him. The music filled the air, mingling with the sounds of laughter and conversation. "And the dancing!" he exclaimed, causing Gracie to jump and almost spill her drink. Coby's breath hitched, his chest tightening as he struggled to capture every detail of the memory. His hands trembled as he desperately attempted to assemble the scattered fragments, his anxiety palpable.

Gradually, the puzzle pieces clicked together, forming a complete picture. The apparition's mention of the "Moulin Rouge," the vibrant imagery of Vivienne's expert rendition of the can-can dance to the rhythm of Dire Straits' "Walk of Life." The music reverberated in his ears, the beats pulsating through his veins. With his eyes closed, he could see Vivienne twirling and spinning, her graceful movements etching themselves into his mind.

The flashback was a whirlwind of sensations, blurring the boundaries of time with its vividness and intensity. Transported back to that special moment, Coby relived it with every fibre of his being, the present surroundings fading into a distant, hazy dream. The image of Vivienne's lifeless body, illuminated only by the faint glow of the alley lights, struck him with an overwhelming sense of dread. He quickly clicked on the saved article in his bookmarks. His eyes widened like saucers as he reached the chilling ending of the grim article. In a soft murmur, barely above a whisper, Coby read aloud, "They say her spirit still haunts the Moulin Rouge. Forever etched as a spectral dancer in the heart of the city she adored."

The connection was so intense that it sent a shiver down his spine, making his skin break out in goosebumps. One thing puzzled him, though – the haunting echo of Vivienne's words etched into his mind. "*Danse avek mwa,*" Coby murmured to himself, his voice barely audible amidst the silence. The haunting echo of those words lingered in his mind.

"Come dance with me," Gracie said, her voice cutting through the silence and catching Coby off guard. Teetering on the edge of his seat, he felt his muscles strain as he fought to stay upright. His brow furrowed with confusion as he sharply snapped, "What did you say?"

Gracie curved her lips into a knowing smile, her eyes locked on him, radiating elegance. "Danse avek mwa is a French term that means 'Dance with me' in English," she repeated, her voice melodic and calming.

Coby's frustration melted away, and he sprung up energetically. "Well then," he exclaimed with a triumphant fist pumping the air, "We'll head to Paris!" Gracie wasted no time and swiftly made all the arrangements, ensuring everything was in order.

In the end, Coby embarked on a solo journey to France. Ewan, unable to travel without a passport, had no choice but to stay behind. Gracie, with her natural nurturing instincts, decided to stay behind and care for her son and their beloved companion, Janie. Gracie used the money she had saved to book Coby a first-class seat, promising a train ride of pure indulgence. With the morning sun streaming into the room, Coby woke up to find Gracie by his side, gently assisting him in packing his bags.

The container she prepared overflowed with delectable snacks, their enticing aroma filling the air. However, as they prepared to depart, Coby witnessed a side of Ewan he had never seen before. Frustration and anger consumed the young lad, clear in his scowl and inflated cheeks. Coby couldn't help but chuckle, unknowingly fuelling the fire burning within Ewan's childish heart. With Janie barking excitedly, they drove off, beginning their scenic journey to Inverness.

Inverness beckoned with its picturesque landscape, where rolling hills and vibrant greenery created a symphony of colours and scents. Their arrival at the station triggered a wave of departure anxiety, Coby's heart pounding with a whirlwind of emotions. The towering structure of Inverness railway station stood tall, bustling with people and echoing with the symphony of sounds – the clatter of luggage, the chatter of passengers, and the distant whistle of a departing train. It was a stark contrast to the peaceful tranquillity of his stately home.

With a final tearful hug from Gracie and a solemn nod from Ewan, Coby stepped onto Platform one. Awaiting him was the gleaming LNER train, its metallic body shimmering under the morning sun, reflecting the vibrant hues of the surrounding landscape. Its imposing figure stood like a majestic beast, ready to devour the miles between him and his destination.

The train journey was a visual spectacle, the Scottish countryside unfolding outside the window like a mesmerising symphony. The rhythmic clatter of wheels on tracks created a soothing melody, accompanied by the gentle hum of the engine. Coby was entranced by the rhythmic clickety-clack of the rails. Slumber enveloped him, and his mind slipped into a state of tranquillity. His mind wandered and came to rest on the bittersweet recollections of his dad, filling his heart with warmth and longing. While they took their morning runs together, the rhythmic breathing of his dad echoed in his mind. A speeding bus tragically took the life of Payton McTavish, his dad, mentor, and life coach. By a stroke of luck, Coby narrowly escaped with his life. After they buried his dearest dad, Coby started hearing faint whispers beside him while he was running. He knew who it was, but the mysterious presence lurking in the shadows made him too afraid to meet his gaze. Whenever Coby celebrated his victory in a marathon, he would playfully insist that his mentor's unseen presence had propelled him to success. His dad's ethereal approval filled him with a sense of comfort, like a gentle embrace on a chilly day. On that day, his dad's voice slowly faded away, leaving him to sprint blindly through the encroaching darkness. Coby ran alone through life, his footsteps echoing in the silence.

Just as Coby was getting lost in his thoughts, the train abruptly jerked, snapping him back to reality. His eyes darted back and forth, desperately searching the empty seat for any trace of his father's essence. But all he found was an empty space, devoid of the warmth and guidance his dad had always provided. A knot formed in his throat, making it difficult to swallow as a wave of grief washed over him.

The once serene train compartment now felt suffocating, as if the air had turned heavy with the weight of his emotions. The rhythmic clatter of the wheels on the tracks had transformed into an unsettling cacophony, a stark contrast to the soothing melody it had once been.

Coby's sense of direction wavered, and a feeling of unease washed over him. The familiar whispers that used to keep him company during his runs were now gone, leaving behind an eerie silence. The mysterious presence that had lingered in the shadows had vanished, leaving him alone to face the harsh realities of life. He felt a deep yearning for his dad's guidance, a longing for the sound of his voice and the reassurance it had always brought.

The train journey, once a visual spectacle, now felt like a cruel reminder of his loss. The Scottish countryside, which had unfolded outside the window like a mesmerising symphony, now seemed dull. Coby was no longer captivated by the vibrant greens and majestic landscapes, as they only served as reminders of the moments he had shared with his dad.

As the train continued its journey, Coby's gaze remained fixed on the passing scenery, his mind wandering amidst a sea of memories and unanswered questions. The haunting echo of the once familiar clickety-clack of the rails plagued his thoughts, serving as a poignant symbol of the irreparable loss he had endured.

After nearly eight hours, the train pulled into King's Cross, London, signalling the end of the first leg of his journey. The momentary gap before his next departure was a whirlwind of activity. Coby navigated through the throngs of people, their voices blending into an unintelligible murmur. The sight of St Pancras International's iconic Gothic facade was a welcome sight amidst the chaotic urban atmosphere. Its intricate details and towering presence added a touch of grandeur to the bustling station.

On Platform six, the Eurostar awaited him, its sleek design and modern amenities a testament to the luxury Gracie had promised. Boarding the train, he settled into his plush first-class seat, enveloped by the softness of the upholstery. The gentle hum of the train became a soothing lullaby as it began its journey under the English Channel.

Two hours later, the train emerged from the darkness into the enchanting cityscape of Paris. The sight of Gare du Nord, the heartbeat of the city's transportation network, filled Coby's senses with awe. The grand architecture of the station, with its intricate details and bustling energy, was like a portal into the heart of the city.

Stepping onto the platform, Coby instantly felt the vibrant pulse of Paris, its rhythm resonating within him. The city's energy filled the air, a medley of scents wafting through – the warm aroma of freshly baked bread, the enticing smell of aromatic coffee, and a subtle hint of perfume. The sensory feast heightened his anticipation as he prepared to unravel the mysteries of Montmartre.

In the distance, Vivienne's spectral figure seemed to dance in the dimly lit alleyways of his mind, her words echoing in his ears, "Danse avek mwa." With renewed determination, Coby set off, ready to uncover the truth about Vivienne LeClaire, forever etched as a spectral dancer in the heart of the city she adored.

As Coby stepped out of the bustling Gare du Nord, Paris greeted him with a symphony of vibrant sights, sounds, and sensations, instantly awakening his senses. The city was a mesmerising fusion of the past and present, with its pulse resonating like a captivating symphony in the twilight atmosphere. Hailing a taxi, he couldn't help but notice the vibrant yellow car standing out like a sunflower amidst the sea of concrete.

The taxi ride to Montmartre was a chaotic whirlwind of honking horns and screeching brakes. The city unfurled like a grand tapestry, bathed in the warm glow of the setting sun. As the taxi weaved through the labyrinthine streets, he passed charming cafés brimming with laughter and clinking glasses, stone buildings whispering tales of centuries past, and cobblestone paths echoing with the footsteps of countless artists, dreamers, and lovers who had once walked them.

Arriving at his temporary refuge, a quaint hotel nestled in the heart of Montmartre, Coby marvelled at its charming exterior, a mix of worn brick and faded paint that spoke of its age and character. Gracie had chosen well; it exuded the simple comfort and warmth of a home, a stark contrast to the opulence of his train journey.

Entering the dimly lit lobby, Coby was greeted by the soft echo of Edith Piaf's voice, her melancholic melody seeping from an old radio perched on the reception desk. The scent of aged wood and a faint trace of lavender embraced Coby as he entered the dimly lit lobby.

His room, modest yet cosy, was adorned with vintage furniture and faded photographs, showcasing the district's glory days. Opening the window, he was greeted with the enchanting view of the majestic Sacré-Cœur Basilica, its silhouette illuminated against the twilight sky.

Collapsing onto the bed, he felt an overwhelming wave of exhaustion while the distant sounds of Parisian nightlife acted as a soothing lullaby, coaxing him into a deep sleep. Closing his eyes, Vivienne's enigmatic figure flickered in the shadows of his mind. The quest to decipher her mystery had begun, and Montmartre, with its enchanting allure, was the ideal stage for this unfolding drama.

Chapter Twenty

The soft cooing of pigeons penetrated Coby's deep slumber, their soothing melodies slowly bringing him back to consciousness. The radiant sun ascended over the bustling metropolis, casting long shadows that stretched across the cityscape and brought Coby back to reality. Memories of his reason to visit the city flooded back, igniting his determination to unravel the mysteries surrounding Vivienne LeClaire's untimely demise. His heart pounded, a wild drumbeat echoing the rhythm of the city below. He rushed onto the narrow balcony, the sound of flapping wings filling the air, determined to shoo the pesky pigeons away. The warming rays of the sun caressed his face, casting a cool, comforting glow as he stretched his arms and luxuriated in the vibrant sights, intoxicating smells, and captivating views of his new surroundings.

A charming café caught his eye, beckoning him downstairs for a delightful breakfast. However, his phone chimed urgently, causing him to rush back inside. "Oh, no!" Coby exclaimed, noticing eight missed calls from Gracie. In his exhaustion, he had neglected to inform her of his safe arrival, leaving her worried and unaware of his gratitude for the flawless arrangements. Swiftly, he composed a message, expressing his heartfelt thanks and ending it with three kisses, since he wasn't sure how to convey hugs through text. Gracie responded with a cheerful grin and a cascade of kisses.

Just as he was about to use the cramped bathroom, Coby's phone rang, bringing a smile to his face as he saw John Drake's name on the screen. Eagerly, he answered the call, sharing the name of his hotel and agreeing to meet John at the café downstairs. With some careful manoeuvring, he discovered the peculiar bathroom configuration, where the door had to be closed before the shower door could be opened. He managed to fit himself into the narrow space between the toilet and shower, shutting the bathroom door that opened inward, and at last entered the revitalising shower. The steaming hot water enveloped his body, creating a soothing and rejuvenating sensation.

Edith Piaf's timeless voice continued to resonate from the small radio as Coby stepped through the lobby. He caught sight of his editor, standing across the bustling city street, a mischievous glint in his eyes and a grin on his face. "John, you rascal," Coby exclaimed, his footsteps hurriedly echoing along the bustling pavement.

With the events of the day ahead clouding his mind, Coby failed to notice the cars zooming by, their exhaust fumes mingling with the scent of freshly brewed coffee from the nearby café. With only a quick glance to the left, he recklessly dashed across the tarmac, narrowly evading a collision with vehicles hurtling towards him from the right. The screeching tires and blaring horns created a deafening cacophony that assaulted his ears, causing him to come to an abrupt halt in the middle of the road, frozen with fear. The angry drivers leaned out of their car windows, their voices piercing the air as they hurled a relentless barrage of insults at him in rapid-fire French. Overwhelmed, he shouted back at them, "Oh, get over yourselves!" as his heart pounded in his chest, and he hastened towards the safety of the sidewalk.

John pulled Coby into a tight embrace, their bodies pressed together. Coby felt a slight discomfort as he noticed John's peculiar dress sense – a men's sarong and a golf tee shirt. He subtly held back, hoping to avoid any contact between their hips. John released his grip and placed his hands on Coby's shoulders. Coby could feel John's fiery blue eyes scanning him from head to toe.

"You look great, buddy," John said, his balding head emphasising the wrinkles on his forehead as he arched his eyebrows and gave Coby a playful pat on the back. Coby was taken aback and would have preferred a simple handshake.

"Good to see you," he managed, giving John a pat on the back. They settled into narrow seats around a small, round table on the bustling sidewalk. The table was situated under a vibrant red and white striped awning, bearing the name of the café.

The cobble street was alive with activity, and the air was filled with the irresistible scent of freshly baked goods. Charming A-frames lined the street, displaying mouthwatering specials in French, luring visitors in. The hum of conversation surrounded them, occasionally interrupted by laughter and the sound of cups and saucers clinking. A waiter rushed over to their table, skilfully flicking his wrist to place two menus on it, before swiftly making his way back to his spot. Like a vigilant guardian, he stood there, his eyes scanning the surroundings of the café.

John's French skills came in handy as he called the waiter over and ordered two bottomless coffees and croissant breakfasts. They had to raise their voices to be heard over the unrelenting noise of the city. Coby quickly realised that car horns were a popular form of communication among the French. Another waiter arrived, placing their unadorned croissants and pale scrambled eggs on the table. Their waiter returned, carrying a tray with steaming coffee and orange juice, placing it aside before scurrying off.

The aroma of the freshly baked golden croissant filled the air, tempting Coby's taste buds. He persuaded John to request a dollop of velvety cream cheese from their waiter, enhancing the overall breakfast experience. Coby devoured every morsel, savouring the taste and feeling a sense of relief wash over him after the long journey the previous day. There was a distinct air of anticipation surrounding John, giving the impression that he was in a hurry. John's eyes darted to his watch repeatedly as he devoured his food and gulped down his coffee and orange juice.

"Let me see," John mumbled with a mouthful of food, eagerly rubbing his hands together in anticipation.

Surprised, Coby's eyes darted around the table, desperately searching for a napkin to wipe his sticky fingers. Failing to find one, he resorted to rubbing his hands on his worn jeans. With a quick swipe on his phone, his heart skipped a beat as he scrolled through the images, catching a glimpse of Gracie and Ewan. Finally, he found the sketch he had taken, showcasing the ethereal trinity. Zooming in on Vivienne's face, he proudly showed the image to John. With confidence, he declared, "That's the one."

"Hmm," John mumbled, his gaze fixed on the image, his furrowed brow showing deep thought. "Vivienne Lecrerc."

"LeClaire," Coby corrected, his voice filled with certainty, "they found her dead body in a secluded alley somewhere in Montmartre."

Raising an eyebrow, John's eyes squinted as he studied the image. Absentmindedly, he asked, "Do you have any other information about her?" There was a touch of curiosity in his voice.

A knowing smile danced on Coby's lips, captivated by the unexpected question. "She was a dancer at the Moulin Rouge," he hesitated before uncertainly adding, "I suppose."

John habitually bit his thumbnail, creating an unsettling sound that sent a shiver down Coby's spine. "Okay," he exclaimed, accidentally calling the waiter over, who promptly came to their table before being dismissed. "Coby," he cautioned, locking eyes with him, "we must avoid any encounters with the French police." Coby nodded in agreement, fully comprehending the seriousness conveyed in John's voice.

"In this area, there are three libraries," John said, his deep bass voice resonating as he made a sweeping circular motion with his hand to emphasise his point.

"That's useful," Coby added.

John nodded without paying attention. "Tonight," John announced with unwavering resolve, "we shall pay a visit to the Moulin Rouge."

Coby's face lit up with a radiant smile, clearly delighted by John's masterful planning. "We need to hurry," he declared. "I have a tight budget, and I'll be heading back to Inverness tomorrow morning."

"You got it!" John exclaimed, summoning their waiter, who hurried over with the bill folder in hand. They split the bill, and Coby couldn't help but question the exorbitant total listed under the 'Extras' column. John patiently explained that things worked differently in the Parisian lifestyle. "See," he said, gesturing towards the bill, "the prices vary based on your seating location."

Coby's eyebrows shot up in astonishment, his eyes growing wider. He made a mental note to steer clear of the pricier outdoor seating areas at cafes whenever he brought Gracie along. Gradually, the enchanting synergy of the city began to captivate him, but he understood that truly immersing himself would require patience and time.

John had a hired car, a sleek black hatchback, because he somehow convinced his boss that his trip to the city was work related. They sank into the snug seats of the tiny two-seater, feeling the cramped space around them. John tapped buttons on the touch screen, the soft glow illuminating the car's interior, showing a map with a blue car icon. A female voice, crisp and clear, blared over the speakers, guiding John through the labyrinth of the Parisian city's veins. Coby marvelled at John's skilful navigation as the car weaved through the bustling traffic, horns honking and engines roaring. The city appeared to lack the road rules Coby was accustomed to, adding an element of excitement and uncertainty to their journey.

Coby counted three U-turns in total as they wound their way around the railway tracks, running parallel to the main road they followed. He heard the female navigator announcing the word 'destination,' her seductive French accent adding a touch of allure to the instructions. John smoothly pulled into an undercover parking bay, the potent scent of petrol filling the air. They waited for a machine to spit out a ticket, the mechanical whirring adding to the background symphony of the city. "I'll cover the first two hours," John declared with confidence, his voice unwavering, as the parking bay barriers rose, allowing them entry.

They walked a short distance to the library, the sleek glass facade reflecting the soft hues of the sky and surrounding environment. The building emanated an aura of sophistication and innovation, its modern design drawing the attention of passersby. On one side, the visual art displayed a burst of creativity, with the name 'Bibliotheque Goutte d'Or' written in modern, rounded script.

They approached the entrance, ascending a staircase that felt cool and smooth beneath their feet. John increased his pace, taking charge, his footsteps echoing in the quiet space. They entered the building, the air-conditioning providing a refreshing respite from the summer heat. John confidently approached a lady seated behind a reception area, the curved red partition adding a touch of elegance to the space.

Perched on her nose, her sleek tortoise rimmed glasses reflected the fluorescent lights as she peered at John, offering a welcoming smile. Coby listened intently, the sounds of hushed conversations and rustling papers filling the air, trying to make out the unfamiliar word the receptionist mentioned. Suddenly, the receptionist's face lit up, her eyes widening with recognition, and she shot Coby a curious glance.

She repeated the word 'wee,' several times, her head bobbing feverishly, a mix of excitement and intrigue clear in her expression.

The receptionist gracefully moved away from her desk, smoothing her skirt over her knees before gesturing for them to follow. The corridors echoed with the rhythmic clacking of her heels, while the tantalising scent of freshly brewed coffee filled the air from a nearby cafeteria. As she shot glances at Coby, her auburn hair fanned out, adding a touch of allure to her swaying hips. Coby couldn't help but feel a pang of regret for not wearing his wedding ring, nervously smiling back at her.

They entered the elevator and descended into the depths of the building. Stepping out, she flicked a switch, illuminating the frigid corridor with fluorescent lights in a sequential pattern. They finally arrived at a door labelled 'archives nationales' in bold black letters against a cream-coloured background. With a swipe of her access card, a short beep and a green light illuminated, granting them entry. Inside, she flipped the switch, instantly illuminating the large rectangular carpeted room with a burst of bright light.

At the centre of the room, there stood an oblong table, while towering metallic shelves filled with an endless number of boxes surrounded it. The receptionist switched to broken English, addressing Coby and saying, "Vivienne LeClaire, you want, wee." From then on, she punctuated every question she asked with the word 'wee,' adding a playful touch to her conversations. Coby couldn't help but break into a wide grin, his happiness clear to all. She nodded and led them to a terminal, where she powered it on, casting a soft amber glow that illuminated the dark square screen filled with characters.

Her slender fingers, adorned with perfectly manicured nails, danced across the small keyboard. Enthusiastically, she mentioned something about "Montmartre and Jewel," bobbing her head and emphasising the word 'wee' at the end of the sentence. Against the side of the metal shelves, a rolling ladder with hooks teetered on the edge. She gracefully moved the ladder, swaying her backside as she ascended the steps. John cleared his throat, and Coby patiently waited.

The receptionist pleaded for help, her eyes filled with desperation, prompting John to spring into action. He hurried over and securely held the ladder in place as she retrieved a large box and handed them to him, who carefully placed them on the long table.

After getting down from the ladder, she carefully opened the box and began explaining its contents to John in fluent French. He nodded his head in agreement, and rewarded her with two pecks on her cheeks. She did the same to him, and Coby, who quickly wiped the red lipstick stains from his cheeks. Her footsteps echoed through the empty hallway, gradually fading away.

John sank into the plush seat, its cushioning enveloping him in comfort. He gestured for Coby to join him, the motion smooth and inviting. Together, they delved into the box's contents, their fingers grazing the worn edges of the items. The air was heavy with the scent of aged paper, mingling with the faint aroma of history. The rustle of vintage newspapers and the delicate crinkle of ancient documents echoed softly in the quiet room. Despite the language barrier, Coby's eyes scanned each item intently, his determination driving him to search for the elusive name Vivienne LeClaire.

The seconds stretched out like never-ending hours, each one feeling longer as they meticulously sifted through the contents. The low hum of the air conditioner provided a constant background noise, while the fluorescent lights buzzed above them. John eventually excused himself and returned with two steaming takeout coffees, their invigorating aroma filling the air, accompanied by the mouthwatering scent of tomato and cheese sandwiches.

The receptionist frequently checked in, her footsteps soft against the cold floor. Sitting close to Coby, the nostalgic scent of her lavender perfume overwhelmed him, instantly transporting him back to his childhood.

In a sudden burst of energy, John's voice shattered the eerie silence, brimming with uncontainable excitement. Coby leaped up from his seat, his heart pounding in his chest, and hurried to his editor's side. Spread out before them, a captivating vintage monochrome image of a young woman unfolded. Her lifeless form sprawled against the cold, unforgiving street, dark bloodstains blemishing the weathered cobblestone. Adorning her motionless body, a single rose lay delicately, its vibrant hues lost within the confines of the black-and-white photograph. As Coby took in the scene, his senses heightened, his heart racing faster with every passing second. The sheer improbability of it all sent his excitement skyrocketing, almost beyond belief.

John slowly translated the accompanying French article, his words providing little new information. But now, Coby had a visual of Vivienne, even in death. He pulled out his phone, capturing several snapshots of the image, zooming in to reveal the terror etched on her face before her tragic end. And now, he knew the name of the street. A triumphant fist pump escaped Coby's lips as he exclaimed, "Yes!"

Before leaving, they tidied up the room, the sound of shuffling papers and the clatter of objects resonating in the otherwise silent space. They approached the receptionist's desk, its polished surface reflecting the bright overhead lights. To show his appreciation, Coby treated her to a chocolate and coffee, the sweet scent of cocoa intermingling with the delicate aroma of lavender. As he presented the gifts, she jumped up with excitement, wrapping her arms around him and delicately kissing both of his cheeks. The flutter of his heart matched the warmth that spread up his cheeks, a mixture of appreciation and a newfound connection.

When they reached the parking lot, the fluorescent lights buzzed overhead, casting a harsh glow on the cracked surface. They split the bill, and a sinking feeling settled in Coby's heart as he saw the exorbitant fee displayed on the ticket. John skilfully manoeuvred the cramped hatchback along the narrow, bustling streets of Paris. The scent of freshly baked baguettes wafted through the open windows, mingling with the distant aroma of brewing coffee. The female navigator's voice filled the car, guiding them through the labyrinthine roads towards their destination, *Rue des Rêveries*.

To avoid the steep parking fees, John remained in the car, the seats creaking slightly as he adjusted his position. Coby hopped out, his footsteps echoing on the cobblestones as he entered the dimly lit alley. The setting sun painted a golden hue on the rattling treetops, creating a mesmerising display of dancing shadows on the old stone walls. The alley was nestled between an antique furniture shop, and a stone-faced catholic church, its ancient stones holding the weight of centuries.

Coby's spine tingled with a shiver as he stood in the exact location where Vivienne LeClaire had met her tragic demise. The air was heavy with a sombre stillness, broken only by the distant sound of traffic and the occasional meow of an alleycat. None of the articles they had uncovered revealed any clues about the capture of her killer. The thought lingered, a haunting presence in Coby's mind, that the perpetrator could still be lurking in the shadows of this very city.

Now, only a large dumpster overflowing with discarded debris stood as a testament to the once vibrant alley. The scent of decay mingled with the faint odour of old food, carried by a gentle breeze. Coby closed his eyes, savouring the memories of the Jewel of Moulin Rouge, her enchanting aura lingering in his mind. The memory of Vivienne's spirit hung in the air, forever intertwined with this place of sorrow and grief.

As he settled back into the cramped seats of the car, it felt like John could almost hear the faint whisper of his cravings for a taste of whiskey. They didn't exchange a single word, but their unspoken understanding guided John's skilful navigation through the vibrant and bustling city streets. The pulsating lights and distant sounds of laughter filled the air as they effortlessly found a parking spot. The two companions embarked on a short walk, their footsteps echoing on the pavement, leading them to a hidden gem called Dirty Dick, a cocktail bar. Coby's eyebrows shot up in astonishment, while John's mischievous grin revealed a glimmer of wickedness in his eyes.

***

John stood outside Coby's hotel, the clock striking eight as he waited in his finely tailored evening suit. The soft glow of the streetlights cast a warm ambiance on the city, illuminating the pavement. Coby appeared, his casual attire contrasting with John's elegant outfit. John's smile was charming, his breath carrying a hint of brandy that lingered in the air.

As they set off on their adventure, John's unwavering confidence emanated through his expert manoeuvres behind the wheel. The cacophony of blaring horns and the sight of cars darting through the congested traffic transformed the atmosphere into a chaotic symphony, evoking memories of a vibrant Parisian street. Coby's knuckles clenched, turning pale as he tightly gripped the seat, his body electrified with the rush of adrenaline.

After a brief drive, they reached Rue Mansart and discovered a convenient parking spot in a hidden bay. They strolled towards the Moulin Rouge, and as they rounded the corner, Coby's breath caught in his throat at the magnificent spectacle before him. The iconic red edifice pulsated with energy and vitality, its radiant lights casting a mesmerising glow upon the night sky. The rhythmic throb of the music filled the air, blending with the faint scent of excitement and anticipation. With its colossal blades poised to spin in perfect harmony with the pulsating beat of the night, the red windmill, an emblem of the establishment, proudly towered against the sprawling backdrop of the cityscape.

The bold red letters spelling out 'Moulin Rouge' created a visual symphony, their vibrant hue catching the eye and igniting a sense of excitement and allure. Coby could sense the excitement in the atmosphere, with the subtle aroma of perfume blending with the lingering echoes of music and dance that had filled this iconic venue. The red facade captured the essence of the Moulin Rouge, its colour pulsating with energy, a beacon that drew in the curious and the captivated.

As they neared the venue, the buzz of excitement emanating from the line of people waiting outside set the tone for the lively ambiance of the area. Conversations buzzed through the air, intermingling with the faint sounds of laughter in the distance. Potted plants lined the pavement, their fresh fragrance adding a touch of natural beauty to the scene, as if nature itself had adorned this legendary place. The partly cloudy sky above added an air of mystery and intrigue, casting shadows that danced along the streets, as if holding secrets waiting to be unveiled. The cool breeze brushed against Coby's skin, carrying with it a hint of excitement and adventure.

Their turn finally arrived, and Coby and John stood at the front of the line, anticipation bubbling within them. The hostess, a vision of allure with vibrant red lips and a dress that mirrored the hues of their surroundings, greeted them with a striking smile. As she exchanged a few words in melodic French with John, the air filled with the soft whispers of their conversation. With a graceful wave of her hand, she motioned for them to follow her. She had a peculiar fondness for using the term "wee," infusing her speech with a whimsical charm.

Surprisingly, instead of leading them to the bathrooms as Coby had expected, the hostess guided them past the familiar toilet signs and down a labyrinth of corridors. The scent of perfume lingered in the air as they walked, mingling with the faint aroma of freshly polished wood. The grandeur of the Moulin Rouge became clear, its spaciousness a testament to the ingenuity of French design.

Eventually, their journey led them to a windowed counter that looked like a ticket booth, complete with a small glass pane and a sliding window. As they approached, a fierce, redheaded woman with crimson-stained lips and a charming beauty spot on her upper lip warmly welcomed them. Her wide smile was contagious as she chatted briefly with the hostess, spreading warmth to those around her. Her teeth, weathered by the passage of time, held a story of years gone by. With expressive hand gestures, she pointed in different directions, passionately explaining something to John.

With a quick flick of her wrist, she slid two lanyards, each attached to a press pass, across the counter. John's excitement was palpable as he eagerly snatched them, passing one to Coby. The weight of the lanyard against their necks was a comforting reminder of the newfound freedom they possessed.

"We have the freedom to go anywhere now!" John exclaimed, his eyes gleaming mischievously as he flapped his arms like a bird taking flight. With a playful blow of kisses to the hostess and the booth lady, he confidently strode down a corridor, with Coby trailing a short distance behind. Their hearts filled with anticipation of the adventures that awaited them.

Coby's eyes grew wide as he understood what John meant. Quietly, they disappeared behind a heavy maroon curtain, surrounded by the echoing resonance of a lively French man's voice and the melodious sounds of an organ. The sound of the laughter reverberated in the air, reaching the high ceiling above. The duo then veered to the right, traversing a seemingly endless corridor that led them to a grand staircase adorned with a luxurious crimson carpet. Coby couldn't help but feel that they had reached the prestigious VIP section.

The moment Coby and his companions entered the exclusive cocktail bar, the sight of elegantly attired guests instantly captivated them. The clusters of people were seated gracefully on barstools covered in luxurious crimson velvet, their backs adorned with shiny brass accents. Amidst the crowd, a petite bar stood, where a skilled bartender with slicked-back dark hair and a meticulously curled moustache expertly served drinks. Coby, feeling self-conscious in his casual jeans and flannel shirt, confidently shrugged off the disdainful glances of the crowd.

Sensing Coby's unease, John gently clutched his arm and led him to a quiet corner next to the bustling bar counter. Engaging in a swift, polite conversation in French, John motioned for two exquisite crystal glasses. With utmost precision, the skilled bartender placed the glasses before them, their delicate chimes filling the air. Pouring a measure of a luscious, well-aged French Armagnac, its rich, mahogany colour, hinted at its potent allure.

"Cheers!" John exclaimed, quickly finishing his drink and expressing his contentment by smacking his lips. Coby hesitantly raised the glass to his lips, feeling the fiery elixir cascade down his throat, leaving a scorching sensation that stole his breath away and caused his eyes to sting. John laughed at Coby's reaction, leading the way along a dimly lit corridor, their journey continuing.

Coby's breath hitched in his throat as they stepped into a long corridor. Life-size framed portraits of classical Moulin Rouge dancers adorned the walls. Their vibrant colours and intricate designs captivated his gaze. The dimly lit light cast flickering shadows, adding an air of mystery to the scene. A soft creaking sound echoed with each cautious step on the wooden floor, heightening the anticipation. The scent of old paper and dust mingled in the air, hinting at the passage of time. John, with his fluent French, translated the meaning behind the words on the posters, further immersing Coby in the experience.

Coby's heart skipped a beat as he spotted the monochrome picture of Josephine Barker, as if he was in a dream. The grayscale tones of the picture created a nostalgic atmosphere, transporting him back in time. Catching the dim light and reflecting it like tiny stars, the beads on her outfit glistened and sparkled. The sight of her clad in her iconic banana skirt and metallic brassiere exuded rebellion and a no-nonsense attitude. Her graceful movements, frozen in the poster, evoked a sense of elegance and mystique. It was as if time had stood still, encapsulating her essence. The monochrome photograph, with its timeless beauty, had a captivating allure that could captivate anyone who laid eyes on it.

Coby pulled out his phone, the sleek screen illuminating with an image of Josephine Barker. With careful precision, he captured multiple snapshots, preserving the moment. Sliding his phone back into his pocket, he continued along, his eyes fixated on the captivating posters that surrounded him.

Suddenly, the young dancer in one of the framed pictures flashed Coby a mischievous grin, a playful twinkle in her eyes. His eyes widened in awe, and a smile of astonishment spread across his lips. His eyes shimmered with anticipation, as he tried to soak in every minute detail of the portrait in front of him.

It depicted Vivienne LeClaire, her presence dominating the composition. Two life-size images of her stood side by side, capturing her essence from different perspectives. On the left, a black-and-white photograph showcased her mid-pose as a dancer, her left leg elegantly raised. Her hair, meticulously styled in an elaborate updo, caught Coby's attention with its delicate ribbons and vibrant flowers. Vivienne's signature smile held a hint of mischief, her eyes glinting with a touch of intrigue. Adorned in a layered dress that appeared to be in perpetual motion, she held her right hand gracefully above her head, while the left hand delicately grasped a section of her dress. The backdrop featured a gradient of black and white, with her shadow gracefully cast upon the stage floor.

On the right, a vibrant coloured picture presented an illustrated version of Vivienne in the midst of a dance. The text at the top read

'Bijou,' while the bottom proclaimed "Joyau du moulin rouge." To her left, elegant cursive text spelled out 'La Joie du Cabaret.' Her white dress, similar to the left image, possessed a stylised flair with visible ruffles and layers. Mimicking the black-and-white photograph, she raised one arm in a poised gesture. The image flawlessly portrayed her otherworldly aura in the physical realm.

John, ever the translator, began deciphering the text for Coby, starting from the top and moving clockwise. "Jewel," he pointed to the bottom text, "Joy of the cabaret," he gestured towards the text on her left. "Come smell her lilac," he concluded, his gestures inviting Coby to experience the scent.

A crashing wave of nostalgia suddenly overwhelmed Coby, sweeping him back in time. As if a mystical curtain had been lifted, he found himself transported into his study, surrounded by the familiar scents that filled the room. The musty aroma of old books mixed with the faint hint of ink, evoking memories of countless hours spent immersed in the captivating article, 'Mystery in Montmartre: The Enigmatic Demise of Vivienne LeClaire, Jewel of the Moulin Rouge.' The silence that once filled the peaceful haven now seemed to amplify in his ears, broken only by the gentle sound of pages turning. Amidst it all, he could almost catch a whiff of Vivienne's alluring lilac perfume, as if her ethereal presence still lingered in the air, enticing him further into the past.

"I really need a drink," John murmured, his voice barely penetrating Coby's daydream, sounding far away and muted. Coby, lost in his own thoughts, gazed sheepishly at a vibrant poster on the wall. John extended his arm and lightly shook Coby's shoulder, bringing him back from his daydream. Coby blinked, his eyes meeting John's in a curious glance as he slowly returned to the present moment.

Feeling a surge of inspiration, Coby swiftly pulled out his phone, the sleek device fitting perfectly in the palm of his hand. He centred Vivienne's image on the screen, capturing her essence in a series of snapshots. The soft click of the camera echoed in the air, capturing the memory forever.

With John leading the way, Coby obediently followed behind, their footsteps echoing on the staircase as they ascended to the top of the iconic Moulin Rouge. They emerged onto the "Toit," a chic rooftop bar where shimmering lights created a magical ambiance. The ambiance was electric, as the vibrant energy of the surrounding Pigalle district permeated the air.

As they neared the bar, the air became infused with the alluring fragrance of cocktails and mouthwatering tapas, intermingling with the intoxicating scent of aged whisky. The illuminated wings of the cabaret watched over them, casting a mesmerising glow. John, appreciating Coby's accomplishment, ordered two neat double shots of the finest aged whisky.

Their glasses clinked together, the sound resonating through the air, symbolising their unbreakable friendship. The smooth whisky warmed their bodies and added to the shared moment of celebration. Together, they basked in the enchanting atmosphere of the Moulin Rouge, savouring every sip and cherishing the memories they had created.

Chapter Twenty-One

As Coby stepped out of the towering structure of the Inverness railway station, a colourless sky that seemed to stretch endlessly above him greeted him. The sight of Gracie and Ewan waiting for him brought a rush of emotions, their smiles stirring something deep within him. Gracie, adorned in a vibrant floral dress, looked absolutely enchanting, and his heart skipped a beat at the sight of her. Overwhelmed with excitement, he brought two fingers to his lips, kissed them, and touched the soil as a tribute to his home country. With a gentle pull, Gracie enveloped Coby in a warm embrace, her lips meeting his in a tender kiss. The lingering taste of her cherry balm filled his senses. The scent of her jasmine perfume wafted delicately, filling his senses with sweet promises.

Ewan swiftly snatched Coby's small suitcase from his weary hand and dragged it towards the car, his eagerness clear. Exhausted from the long journey, Coby settled into the passenger seat, his body sinking into the soft cushion. Gracie, with a warm smile, offered to take the wheel. Ewan leaned forward between the front seats, his eyes filled with anticipation as Coby shared every intricate detail of his journey. Gracie's genuine happiness shone through as she listened, and her hand gently rested on his leg, sending a thrilling ripple of excitement through his body.

Serenity Falls welcomed them with a breathtaking sight - a picturesque landscape and ancient buildings that seemed to whisper tales from centuries past. Gracie slowed down, not for a flock of sheep as one might expect, but for a crowd of passionate protesters chanting slogans. Holding their placards high above their heads, they marched down the cobblestone street, their passionate chants and demands filling the air. Gracie skilfully navigated the car through the noisy crowd of protestors. Coby's eyes carefully scanned the placards, each one emblazoned with bold messages protesting the reopening of a silica sand mine. He glimpsed a placard that read 'Ashes to ashes, dust to dust, don't turn our town into dusk,' and it brought a smile to his face, a sense of belonging washing over him.

The engine of the Volvo roared as they slowly ascended the steep driveway towards his stately home. His heart fluttered with excitement at the sight of the majestic manor. Through his recent discoveries, he had unravelled the hidden secrets that had shrouded his home for so long, and now he had found a sense of inner peace by purchasing the estate. Janie, their loyal companion, barked excitedly upon their arrival, her joyful whimpers piercing through Coby's heart. He lovingly patted her soft coat all over and showered her face and long snout with affectionate kisses. Ewan dragged the suitcase up the grand staircase, while Gracie carefully unpacked his few belongings. Her laughter filled the air as Coby shared the amusing tale of his visit to the iconic Moulin Rouge, dressed only in jeans and a flannel shirt.

After savouring the rich aroma of freshly brewed coffee and indulging in a hearty serving of flavourful pheasant pie, Coby and Gracie entered his study, their personal haven. His heart skipped a beat as he took in the sight of his office, now transformed beyond recognition. Gracie's feminine touch had worked wonders, creating a cosy and inviting workspace. Vibrant flowers adorned the windowsills in window boxes, infusing the urban landscape with the beauty of nature. She rearranged their desks side by side, ensuring convenience and accessibility to everything they needed. However, as Coby's gaze darted around the room, he couldn't spot the ethereal trinity. Gracie had securely stored the sketches in a cupboard, and he knew that their captivating allure was now missing. Determined to address it later, he focused on his plan.

Wasting no time, he condensed his research onto the whiteboard, the vivid colours contrasting against the pristine backdrop. Deep in thought, his brow furrowed as he stepped back, absorbing every intricate detail. Puzzle pieces fell into place, yet more questions arose. Music and dance, he realised, were somehow intricately linked to the spectral trio. Now, he knew that Vivienne and Josephine were famous for their mesmerising cabaret performances, while Jane had a preference for a distinct style of dance. The answer to a burning question eluded him, like a stubbornly elusive dream. How did their spectral forms find themselves within the walls of his expansive estate, and what was the reason behind their presence? Engrossed in deep thought, he scanned the names on the board, his eyes briefly lingering on each one until he reached Jane Baines, where he promptly marked a bold red question mark. A subtle feeling told him she held the key to unravelling all the mysteries.

While Jane meticulously searched the online directories and tirelessly dialled every number for Baines she found, Coby decided to venture to the Inverness library. Even though he didn't know Jane's maiden name, he could sense that Gracie was wasting her time, but her eagerness to help never wavered. The task of finding her relatives would prove to be a challenging endeavour. Coby had already exhausted the resources of the local library, gathering all the information he could about Jane and her enigmatic past. Now, he felt the need to expand his horizons, to delve even deeper into the mystery.

Ewan, with pleading eyes, begged to accompany him on this journey, and after Gracie gave her approval, Coby relented. Excitement hung heavy in the air as Coby turned the key in the ignition of his Volvo, the engine's purr echoing his resolute determination. Before hitting the road, they made a quick stop at Serenity Falls to stock up on Irn-Bru for Ewan. Together, they embarked on their journey; the anticipation causing Coby's heart to pound in his chest as he skilfully navigated the winding road towards Inverness.

Ewan eagerly sipped his Irn-Bru, his head swivelling in every direction as he absorbed every detail of their surroundings. "Uncle Coby," he eventually spoke up as they entered the monotonous final stretch of their journey. His voice, tinged with youthful curiosity, hinted at a lingering question.

"Yes," Coby replied firmly, encouraging him to ask his pressing query.

"Do you remember when you told me what happens to a person's soul after they die?" Ewan asked cautiously, his words laced with intrigue.

Coby had an inkling of where this was leading. "Oh yes, I remember," he answered, popping a bubblegum into his mouth casually.

"So, what if a woman's soul ends up in a baby boy?" Ewan asked casually. Fixing his penetrating gaze on Coby, his eyes revealed an intelligent expression that couldn't be ignored. Coby chuckled, appreciating the astuteness of the question.

"That's a fantastic question, my lad," he answered, as the magnificent sight of Inverness loch unfolded before them, its glistening waters bathed in the sun's brilliance. "You know how often that happens, don't you?"

Ewan nodded in agreement, his brow furrowed with intense concentration, as Coby playfully ruffled his vibrant red hair. Following Ewan's directions through his intermittent hiccups, Coby manoeuvred the cobblestone streets of Inverness until they arrived at the public library. The friendly lady's voice chimed in, announcing their arrival, and Coby parked the car in one of the many available parking bays. He shut off the engine and briefly daydreamed about parking in Paris, a luxury for the lucky ones. A scoff escaped his lips, quickly replaced by a bright smile that lit up his face.

The sight of the public library left Coby breathless as he stood there, taking in every detail. The grandeur of the building, which resembled Greek Revival style, etched itself into Coby's memory. Six grand columns, each exuding a sense of majesty, graced the entrance. Beautiful wreaths adorned the pediment above, lending an elegant charm to the facade. The building's overall design commanded attention, exuding an aura of historical significance. Coby couldn't help but notice the rough texture of the weathered stone as they approached, a reminder of its age and unwavering durability. Like silent guards, the two green doors stood in stark contrast to the weathered grey stone, their faded paint hinting at years of wear and tear.

The stillness of the air-conditioned library engulfed them as Coby pushed open one of the creaking green doors. The scent of books and polished wood filled the air, creating a comforting atmosphere. Ewan's face lit up upon seeing the vibrant children's section, adorned with colourful couches, and he eagerly darted off. Behind the counter, a young lady with cascading platinum blonde hair greeted Coby affectionately, her smile warming his heart. He quickly explained his case, and she responded with a smile, her sleek glasses reflecting the blue light of the monitor. Peering over her glasses, she walked to a set of drawers, rummaged through them, and handed Coby a reel of microfilm, its metallic surface glinting in the dim light.

"I believe everything you need is in there," she said with a friendly wink, gesturing towards the reader.

Coby expressed his gratitude and explored the outskirts of the vast library, taking in its many attractions. He settled into a cushioned chair before the microfilm reader, feeling its plushness beneath him. With a flick of the switch, the reader hummed to life, filling the air with a gentle buzzing sound. Once again, his search for Jane Baines began, meticulously scanning every heading and article in his quest to find her name. Luck seemed to be on his side as he effortlessly flicked through the timeworn newspaper articles, drawn in by the captivating images.

His heart skipped a beat as he caught a glimpse of Jane's name in bold letters on the heading. He leaned in close, the sound of pages turning filling his ears as he perused every intricate detail. The anticipation of the story made his palms tingle, as if he was about to embark on an unlikely journey himself. Before delving into the depths of the article, his gaze couldn't help but linger on the striking monochrome image. The black-and-white photograph showcased Jane, gracefully positioned in front of a formation of soldiers. Their Scottish army attire was impeccable - kilts swaying, long socks neatly pulled up, shoes gleaming, and shirts impeccably ironed with perfectly tied ties. Jane, the focal point, exuded elegance as she stood centred amidst the soldiers. A Tam-o'-shanter playfully adorned her head, tilted to the side. Delicate ballet flats complemented her ensemble, a flowing skirt and crisp shirt, evoking the essence of a ballet dancer. A delicate amulet hung from her neck, adding an air of mystery to her appearance.

Amidst the allure of the image and the promise of a dance with destiny, Coby felt his heart race with excitement and his mind filled with wonder. The captivating heading, 'A DANCE WITH DESTINY: JANE BAINES AND THE BLACK WATCH'S UNLIKELY JOURNEY TO PARIS,' immediately captured his attention. Eager to uncover the story behind it, he delved into the article, eager to indulge in the words that awaited him.

In a time consumed by conflict, an unlikely heroine emerged from the Highlands. Jane Baines, known for her exceptional Highland Dancing skills, became a symbol of hope and resilience for the men of the Black Watch.

After losing her husband and son in a tragic mine accident, Baines found solace in dance. Her captivating performances showcased not only her talent but also her indomitable spirit. Recognising her unique gift, the Black Watch invited her to join them as their dance mascot, a ritual performed before every conflict.

When the regiment was called upon to assist in a conflict in France, they brought Baines along. Her entrancing dances were believed to bring good luck. It was a dangerous and uncertain journey that would forever change Baines' life.

Arriving in Paris, a city teeming with life amidst the chaos of war, the Black Watch, accompanied by Baines, was captivated by her performances. Her dance became a beacon of hope not only for the regiment but also for the local populace.

During this time, Baines crossed paths with renowned cabaret dancers at the famous Moulin Rouge. Despite the tumultuous circumstances, a bond was formed, uniting the women through their shared love for dance against the backdrop of conflict.

However, Baines' documented journey ends with the Black Watch's return from France, leaving many questions unanswered about her fate. What remains clear is that Baines' story is one of courage, resilience, and the power of dance. Her legacy lives on in the annals of the Black Watch and in the heart of the Highlands.

"Oh, my goodness!" Coby exclaimed, his voice barely above a whisper, a wide grin lighting up his face. The faint sound of his words echoed through the stillness of the room, the air heavy with anticipation. As the weight of the revelation settled upon him, his heart raced, its thumping rhythm filling his ears. A shiver ran down his back, sending a wave of goosebumps along his arms, as he made the unsettling connection that mascot, in Latin, means spectre. The camera lens wobbled in his grasp, the faint click of the shutter momentarily drowned out by the rush of blood in his ears. His vision blurred for a fleeting moment before he steadied himself, the world coming back into focus. He knew these snapshots were more than just pictures; they were tangible proof of a connection that transcended the physical world. The excitement that surged through Coby's veins manifested itself in subtle, yet unmistakable ways. Goosebumps prickled along his arms, raising the tiny hairs on his skin as if they were trying to reach out and touch the truth. His fingertips tingled with an electric energy, as if the discovery he held in his hands had charged them with its essence, leaving a faint scent of possibility lingering in the air.

But amidst the euphoria, a bittersweet realisation crept in. The dead end revealed in the article cast a shadow over Coby's elation. France, a distant land filled with its own mysteries, now stood as an insurmountable barrier to unravelling the full extent of Jane's journey. The excitement waned, leaving a faint trace of disappointment in its wake.

Coby's mind raced, desperately searching for a way to continue the quest. He knew he couldn't let this setback deter him. There had to be more to uncover, more threads to pull at, until the tapestry of Jane's story was fully revealed. With renewed determination, he rewound the microfilm reel, ready to embark on a new chapter in his own search for the truth.

A surge of determination propelled him forward. Coby leaped up and hurried to the front desk, his heart pounding in his chest. The sound of his hurried footsteps echoed through the air as he approached the friendly, whose warm smile radiated a sense of comfort. Her mention of the Highlands Archive Centre, with its modern digital channels for accessing family history records, sparked hope in him.

With a crumpled twenty-pound bill in hand, Coby eagerly dropped it into the donations box, eliciting a grateful smile from the lady. She then recommended a visit to the Highlander's Museum, where a remarkable collection of wartime artifacts awaited him. His heart swelled with joy at the proximity of both the archive centre and the museum. In his excitement, Coby momentarily forgot about Ewan, who was engrossed in a captivating, spooky book, completely oblivious to his surroundings in the children's section.

Coby's first destination was the archive centre, a modern building adorned with a combination of wooden and red panel exteriors. Surrounded by lush greenery and rocks, it stood as a testament to history. With a screech, he came to a halt outside the entrance and hurried inside. Approaching the counter, he presented his case to the auburn-haired lady, her hair neatly parted down the middle. Coby winced as her high-pitched voice cut through the air, causing a slight discomfort in his ears. After paying the research fee, he wasted no time and ascended the stairs to the first floor, where the family history room awaited.

The research assistant, stationed in the small room, greeted him with a warm smile as he settled into the plush chairs before the workstations. The overwhelming scent of her perfume filled the room, momentarily taking his breath away. He longed for a breath of fresh air, wishing he could open the windows. The sight of the wall to ceiling bookshelves, lined with family genealogy encyclopaedias, was both impressive and overwhelming.

Coby shared the names of Jane's husband and beloved son, Irvine and Archie Baines, as he brought up the article detailing their demise. The research assistant, her long nails tapping on the keyboard, diligently searched through countless records. However, the fee Coby had paid only granted him an hour of research time. Reluctantly, she took down his email address, promising to share any newfound information about Jane Baines. Defeated, Coby rose from his chair and left the room. Despite the weight of disappointment, he pressed on to his final destination – the Highlanders' Museum.

Coby's hand trembled as he reached for his phone, the smooth surface cold against his fingertips. With a racing heart, he dialled Jane's number, the sound of each digit pressing against the silence, creating an anxious symphony. The ringing pierced through the air, echoing in his ears like a haunting melody. Anxiety hung heavy, filling the car with a palpable tension, as he nervously awaited her answer.

"Hello?" Jane's voice flowed through the line, laced with concern, like a gentle breeze carrying a hint of worry.

Coby's eyes widened, his breath catching in his throat, as a wave of fear washed over him, its taste bitter on his tongue. The realisation of his grave mistake swallowed him whole, his mind spinning with panic.

Summoning every ounce of courage he could muster, he forced himself to fabricate a lie, the words straining against the truth in his voice. "Ewan? Oh, he's behaving himself just fine," he stammered, his strained voice betraying his inner turmoil. Desperation clawed at him, urging him to end the conversation, to avoid any further probing.

With haste, he hung up, his fingers fumbling to disconnect the call, desperate to escape the weight of his guilt and the impending questions that threatened to expose his negligence.

As he tore through the labyrinthine cobblestone streets, the rhythmic clatter of the tires echoed hauntingly in his ears. The car jolted over each stone, setting off a staccato symphony that resonated throughout, a melodic composition that hinted at the history of well-worn routes and timeless expeditions. The sound was a constant companion, a pulsating cadence that underscored the urgency of his pursuit. His heart raced in his chest, synchronised with the rhythmic clattering of the tires. Tension hung heavy in the air, suffocating Coby's thoughts with guilt.

At long last, he made it to the library, where he found Ewan hunched over on the low stoop, looking defeated. The redheaded lad, his hands buried in his face, was a poignant sight that tugged at Coby's heartstrings. A surge of pity coursed through Coby, making his chest feel heavy with empathy.

Determined to make amends, Coby pulled up beside Ewan, the screeching of his brakes piercing the silence. A sense of relief washed over the lad's face as he saw Coby's arrival. A glimmer of hope sparkled in his eyes.

Coby quickly explained his plan, the words rushing out of his mouth. The promise of a mobile phone hung in the air, as tangible as the summer breeze. Ewan's head bobbed with excitement, his enthusiasm palpable. He vowed to keep the secret locked away, sealing it with a silent promise.

The scene was a whirlwind of emotions – fear, relief, and determination filled the air. Coby and Ewan's unspoken connection grew stronger as they carried the weight of their shared secret.

Stepping into the hallowed halls of the Highlanders' Museum, Coby could hear the faint whispers of past warriors and the clinking of armour. Time seemed to freeze within these ancient walls, as the faint scent of aged parchment and wood polish filled the air. Each artifact, meticulously displayed, whispered stories of bravery and sacrifice by the Highland regiments.

Among the thousands of artifacts, Coby's gaze fixated on an old photograph, its worn edges tinged with sepia. The stern and resolute faces of men in quilted uniforms stared back at him, while a woman, Jane Baines, stood tall and determined, her eyes filled with unwavering resolve. Her ghostly presence, felt in his stately home, became undeniable as he saw her face captured in time. The rhythmic beat of the drums and the haunting melody of the bagpipes echoed in Coby's mind as he closed his eyes, creating a vivid image of the regiment parading through the streets of Paris.

Beneath the photograph, a small plaque revealed the truth he had been seeking: Jane Baines had indeed journeyed to France with the Black Watch in the early 20th century. Coby's heart raced within his chest; the evidence he had longed for now in his grasp.

Continuing his exploration, Coby's footsteps reverberated through the eerily quiet halls, creating a symphony of echoes. As he ventured further, he stumbled upon a glass case, delicately preserving a pair of weathered dancing shoes. The vibrant colours that once adorned them had faded over time, now bearing the marks of countless rehearsals and performances.

His eyes widened in astonishment, capturing the dance of light as it reflected off the worn leather. In that moment, he recognised these ballet flats as the very ones Jane had worn in the photograph from the library article. The shoes seemed to emanate a subtle energy, pulsating with the echoes of Jane's graceful movements. Through the passage of time, her indomitable spirit had left an indelible mark on them.

As Coby's gaze lingered, a faint scent of rosin filled the air, a nostalgic reminder of countless ballet studios. His fingertips tingled with anticipation, yearning to extend his hand and caress the worn material. These shoes, mere objects at first glance, now stood as powerful symbols of courage and resilience. They were a testament to Jane's unwavering determination, her spirit shining through despite the hardships she had endured.

So close, yet just out of reach, the shoes beckoned to him, evoking a mixture of longing and admiration. Coby's heart raced with the desire to bridge the physical distance and connect with the profound story they held.

As Coby stood before the glass case, his breath became shallow, his chest rising and falling rapidly. His eyes remained fixed on the worn ballet flats, their presence seeming to radiate an ethereal aura. The vibrant memories of Jane's journey, captured within their faded exterior, seemed to seep into Coby's very being. A surge of emotion welled up within him, a blend of awe and admiration for the woman who had once worn these shoes.

Time seemed to stand still as Coby wrestled with his own longing to touch the shoes, to hold a tangible connection to the bravery and resilience that they represented. His fingertips twitched, an unconscious impulse to reach out and grasp the worn material, to feel the echoes of Jane's graceful movements beneath his own touch.

The air around him seemed charged with an intangible energy, as if the very essence of Jane's spirit lingered in the room. It was a moment of profound connection, where the boundaries of time and space blurred, and he felt as though he stood on the precipice of unravelling the untold stories that lay hidden within these shoes.

With a deep breath, Coby finally mustered the courage to extend his hand towards the glass case. His fingertips hesitated just inches from the worn leather, as if engaged in a wordless dialog with the lingering echoes of the past. In that suspended moment, a surge of excitement coursed through him, as if he stood on the brink of uncovering a hidden truth that would redefine his perception of Jane Baines.

"No touching!" A man's deep voice exclaimed from behind Coby, causing him to jolt out of his fixation. He quickly scanned his surroundings, his eyes darting from one object to another, before finally settling on Ewan. A mischievous smile adorned Ewan's face as the security guard gently took hold of his arm and guided him towards the exit. Ewan's eyes widened in astonishment as Coby dropped a double figure note into the donations box, the crisp paper crinkling softly under his touch.

A renewed sense of purpose coursed through Coby's veins, invigorating every fibre of his being. The visit to the museum had provided him with valuable clues, yet there were still gaps in Jane's story that yearned to be filled. Determined, he vowed to unravel the mystery of Jane Baines, refusing to rest until he uncovered the truth.

Coby made a hasty stop at a bustling electronics store, its vibrant lights illuminating the aisles filled with gleaming gadgets. As they stepped inside, a wave of the clean, metallic scent of newly unpacked electronics hit their nostrils. A salesman, his dark hair slicked back, skilfully demonstrated the exquisite range of phones, his fingers gliding across the screens like a serpent in motion. Ewan, his eyes alight with understanding, opted for a compact and stylish design.

Leaving the store, they made a brief detour to a quaint shop, the aroma of freshly brewed Irn-Bru wafting through the air. With their refreshing beverages in hand, they embarked on their journey home, meandering along the winding and picturesque route. Ewan swiftly acquainted himself with his new gadget, bombarding Coby's ears with an enthusiastic barrage of its features. At every turn in the road, Ewan eagerly leaned out of the window, mesmerised by the breathtaking scenery that stretched out before him. He couldn't resist capturing its beauty with his brand-new phone's camera, a pure expression of joy radiating from his face.

Suddenly, Ewan's voice broke the tranquillity of the moment, causing Coby to flinch. "How come some people can see ghosts?" Ewan inquired, his brow furrowed in contemplation, his eyes shimmering with curiosity. Coby took a moment, his thoughts racing, before responding.

Gripping the steering wheel tightly, Coby prepared himself to answer the question. "Because," he said, as he delicately tousled Ewan's vibrant red hair, "there are only a handful of people who genuinely want to see them, with no trace of uncertainty."

Ewan pondered this, his face a canvas of deep thought and fascination. He couldn't hold in his excitement as he asked, "Can you see ghosts?"

Coby, with a clear conviction, responded cautiously, "What is your reason for asking?" The screeching of tires filled the air as Coby slammed on the brakes, narrowly avoiding a flock of sheep crossing the road. The shepherd, with his trusty border collies, guided the last of the flock, their barks echoing in the distance. Coby resumed their journey, his pace steady and deliberate.

"My mom doesn't believe in ghosts," Ewan said, his voice tinged with frustration, "but the man I spoke to felt more like a ghost than my real dad."

Coby understood the turmoil in Ewan's words, a pang of empathy coursing through him. He also knew he had to tread lightly, aware of the sensitivity surrounding the topic of Ewan's real father.

"We share something in common," Coby started, locking eyes with Ewan. "I lost my father as a child and always yearned to see him again." He winked at Ewan, his eyes glinting mischievously as he whispered, "and just maybe I saw him again, lurking in the shadows," his voice taking on a haunting tone.

With a sudden burst of excitement, Ewan's hands shot up in the air, proclaiming, "I knew it!"

Coby couldn't help but smile, his eyes shining with the shared understanding. A sense of relief washed over him as he realised their secret was safe, and he could finally breathe easily.

Chapter Twenty-Two

Instead of accepting Gracie's dinner suggestion, Coby politely asked for a raincheck, and they both agreed to reschedule for the next evening. He desperately needed to get some writing done. Gracie left him a generous dinner serving for the evening, complete with a mouthwatering, golden-baked pie and the tantalising aroma of the warm, savoury filling. She took her son's hand, their footsteps crunching on the gravel pathway as they left for their charming cottage. Coby embraced the break after his tiresome journey and headed to his bedroom.

A change of clothing would make a world of difference for him. He ran the hot water of the shower, feeling the steam rise and hearing the soothing sound of water cascading down. As he undressed, the air turned frigid, causing goosebumps to form on his skin. Before him, Jane's ghostly figure materialised, casting eerie shadows on the walls with her pale silhouette. He gasped, feeling a mix of surprise and embarrassment, and quickly cupped his hands over his privates to hide his nudity. Jane's lips curved into a thin smile, and in an instant, she disappeared into the darkness, leaving behind only a whisper of her presence.

Coby couldn't help but notice that Jane appeared alone for the first time. There were no spectral companions by her side. It piqued his curiosity about what she was up to. His brow furrowed in deep thought, and he shrugged it off, relishing the hot water cascading over his body and the steam enveloping his senses. With some time to spare before dinner, he made his way to his study, ready to tackle his tasks.

Huddled around his desk were the apparitions of Jane, Josephine, and Vivienne, their ghostly presence sending a chill down his spine. He knew exactly what they were after, but he had an even more delightful surprise in mind. They watched him with eyes filled with an impossible-to-hide longing. Without hesitation, Coby swiftly transferred the photos he captured of Vivienne and Josephine in the Moulin Rouge to his email. After visiting the Highlanders' museum, he immediately emailed the image he captured of Jane, eager to share the memory. He carefully selected the three most captivating images of them and sent them to the printer. With a whir, it sprang to life, filling the room with its mechanical hum as it diligently printed out the glossy images. Sneaking up behind the apparitions, he carefully arranged the printed photos on his desk, relishing the satisfying sound of each photo sliding into place.

Witnessing their reactions was like watching a captivating spectacle. In unison, they pointed their long, slender, and bony spectral fingers at their own likenesses, their pale forms shimmering in the dim light. Gasps of surprise escaped their ethereal lips, filling the air with a soft, breathless sound. A haunting chorus of hisses followed their murmurs of astonishment.

Coby braced himself, feeling a mix of anticipation and curiosity. He knew something extraordinary was about to unfold. And then, their animated discussions began, their voices blending together in a fusion of English and French. The words hung in the air, a tapestry of languages, each syllable vibrating with energy and meaning.

A satisfied smile crossed Coby's lips as he absorbed the scene before him, their presence enveloping him in a warm embrace. Time seemed to warp as the seconds transformed into hours, and he diligently captured every detail he had learned in his draft. A sense of accomplishment washed over him, tingling through his veins, as he shared the draft with John Drake, his trusted editor.

In the room, the grandfather clock chimed nine o'clock, its deep dongs filling the silence with a haunting resonance. Coby, feeling a surge of weariness, slowly rose from his seat, his body protesting the long hours of focused work.

He greeted the spectral trinity, their ghostly forms still engrossed in their own images, their translucent figures shimmering in the subdued light. With a sense of hunger gnawing at his stomach, he made his way to the kitchen. The aroma of the freshly baked shepherd's pie filled the air, its savoury scent mingling with the faint hint of herbs and spices.

Coby savoured every bite of the delicious, flaky pie, the tender meat and rich flavours dancing on his tongue. To complement the meal, he poured a glass of whisky, its amber hue glinting in the soft light. With each sip, the warmth spread through his body, soothing him and adding a touch of contentment to the evening.

Finally satiated, Coby made his way to bed, a smile of fulfilment gracing his face. Throughout the day, Coby had experienced extraordinary encounters and accomplishments, and as he drifted off to sleep, a sense of gratitude filled his heart for the spectral presence that had enriched his life.

With a sudden jolt, Coby awoke from his sleep, his face creased with worry. The full moon, veiled by passing dark clouds, cast intermittent shadows that enveloped the room in fleeting darkness. Straining his senses, he sat upright in bed, his ears keenly attuned. His eyes darted frantically around the room, searching for the source of his disturbance. And then it came again—a soft whimpering, echoing through the grand halls of the immense mansion. In the dimly lit room, he reached into his nightstand drawer and pulled out a flashlight, its cold metal handle providing reassurance. He tapped his palm forcefully, and the device sprang to life, emitting a brilliant beam that cut through the darkness of his bedroom. In the distance, the feverish barking of Janie pierced through the serene silence of the woods.

With each step he took on the creaking wooden stairs, the steady thumping of his own feet synchronised perfectly with the ticking of the grandfather clock. The silence in the air was unsettling, broken only by sporadic hoots from an owl. Upon reaching the landing, he paused, straining his ears for any sound. The eerie circles cast by the flashlight seemed to dance on the newly painted walls. And then it came again—the soft whimpering, growing louder with each step he took, sending a shiver down his spine. Summoning his courage, Coby continued down the dark hallway, drawn towards the sorrowful cries. The haunting sobs echoed through the air, growing louder with each passing moment. With bated breath, Coby entered the room; the flashlight illuminating every crevice and corner. In the dimly lit room, nestled in a secluded corner, he found his eyes drawn to the ethereal figure of a youthful woman, radiating an otherworldly glow from her bare skin. Her lustrous, ebony locks flowed gracefully, draping delicately over her exposed chest.

She shot him a quick, fiery glare, her eyes burning with intensity at his intrusion. Her lips emitted a high-pitched shriek, and a hiss followed as the beam of the flashlight revealed her face, igniting her eyes with a fiery rage. The piercing sound of her soft whimpering grew louder, escalating into pitiful sobs that reverberated through the room like a mournful melody. With each step Coby took towards her, she instinctively curled herself tighter into the corner, seeking refuge in the small crevice. Her arms wrapped protectively around her trembling body, forming a shield against the unseen horrors that haunted her. Her knees were drawn up to her chest, and her head bowed low, as though bracing herself for an imminent blow. The sight of her fearful huddle stirred a deep well of sympathy within him, as if he could almost feel the weight of the invisible torment that had brought her to such a state of terror. In a gentle tone, he hushed her, his voice filled with reassurance.

"Don't be afraid, I am here to offer my help," Coby cooed, and with a sense of relief, he turned off the flashlight, allowing the room to be bathed in her eerie, otherworldly glow. He extended his hand, an offering of comfort, but knew he couldn't touch her trembling body.

As he reached out, a sudden gust of wind rattled the windows, sending shivers down his spine. Shadows danced on the walls, twisting and contorting in a macabre ballet. The air grew heavy with an oppressive silence, broken only by the faint sound of her laboured breaths.

With caution, he took a step closer, his heart pounding in his chest. A chilling breeze brushed against his skin, carrying the scent of decay and despair. The room seemed to pulse with a malevolent energy, as if it were alive, feeding off the fear that consumed her.

Coby's hand trembled as it hovered inches away from her quivering form. He could almost taste the desperation that radiated from her, like a bitter poison seeping into his veins. A flicker of determination ignited within him, fuelling his resolve to free her from the clutches of her torment.

Summoning every ounce of courage, he closed the gap between

them, his fingertips barely grazing the edge of her trembling shoulder. The air crackled with static electricity, causing his hair to stand on end. A surge of electricity coursed through his body, jolting him back as if he had been struck by lightning. The room erupted in a frenzy of swirling shadows, as though the darkness itself fought against his intrusion.

Despite the setback, Coby took a deep breath and composed himself before making another attempt. This time, he approached cautiously, hovering his hand gently over her back. In that moment, a profound sense of recognition passed between them, as if an ancient link had been awakened. Her sobs began to subside, replaced by a flicker of hope in her tear-stained eyes.

In that moment, Coby knew he had become her beacon of salvation, guiding her through the abyss of her darkest fears. Together, they would confront the unseen horrors that had held her captive, forging a path towards liberation.

Filled with resolute determination, he whispered, "I assure you, I will uncover the person who has wronged you."

They fearlessly ventured into unfamiliar territory, their intertwined fates linked by a mutual quest for redemption. In a split second, her ethereal figure disappeared, seamlessly merging with the shadows beneath his outstretched hand.

A heavy sense of disappointment weighed on Coby, his heart sinking as he let out a deep grunt that reverberated in his chest. He could practically taste her anticipation in the air, and if he had just a little more patience, he could have spoken to her. Frustration seeped through his veins as he muttered curses under his breath, his teeth gritted tightly together. Determined to proceed with caution if he ever crossed paths with her again, he knew she held the key to the valuable information he desperately sought, like a hidden treasure waiting to be discovered.

Defeated, he trudged down the stairs, his shoulders slumping with each step, and entered the kitchen. The flick of a switch illuminated the room, casting a warm glow as he poured himself a generous measure of whisky. The guilt of drinking alone in the early hours of the morning settled on his shoulders like a heavy burden, impossible to ignore. However, an idea ignited in his mind, and he confidently strode down the dim corridor, his flashlight casting a guiding beam with each bound.

The sound of the rusty hinges, protesting with a haunting creak, filled the air as he descended the spiralling staircase into the basement. The flip of a switch instantly illuminated the basement with a soft light. Straining his ears, he listened intently, and in the stillness, he could hear it. The enchanting melody of Sandra's Celtic tune wafted through the air, captivating him. It whispered tales of ancient lore and timeless love, weaving its way into his soul.

"The siren's call," Coby murmured, his voice filled with a smug self-confidence as he eagerly trailed her enchanting voice through the labyrinthine corridors. And there, on the bottom stair of the buttery, sat Sandra, her finger tracing intricate patterns in the layers of dust. Her otherworldly aura filled the room, casting ominous shadows that danced along the walls.

Taking a seat beside her, Coby basked in the sweet, eerie lullaby she sang. He watched her closely, completely enchanted by her presence. "I know you need my help," he said, his desire to run his fingers through her silky, ghostly hair almost tangible.

"You'll be free soon, like everyone else," he whispered. He stayed there until the sun rose, immersing himself in Sandra's celestial presence and the captivating symphony that enveloped them.

Chapter Twenty-Three

"Have you been drinking?" Gracie greeted Coby, her voice dripping with suspicion. The sound of her words hung in the air, creating a tension between them.

"Ach, just a wee drop!" he protested, throwing his hands up in the air. The scent of alcohol wafted through the room, mingling with the delicate aroma of Gracie's floral perfume. He playfully teased her, giving her backside a gentle slap. Gracie gasped playfully, jumping aside, her laughter filling the room like a melodic symphony.

Gracie busied herself with preparing a pot of coffee; the aroma filling the air. Listening intently, she could hear the rapid footsteps racing down the hallway and then retreating to the office. With a wave of her hand, she scoffed at the eerie sound, refusing to acknowledge its presence. Carefully balancing a tray of steaming coffee, she entered the study with a relaxed stride. Coby had fallen into a peaceful sleep, cocooned in a soft, cosy blanket. Gracie furrowed her brow at the crumpled blanket, wondering how it had ended up there.

She murmured with a touch of fear, her voice barely above a whisper, "Ewan's onto something. There must be spirits lurking in the shadows." Coby's rhythmic snores reverberated off the walls, breaking the serene silence that filled the room. Gracie couldn't help but smile at the sight of him peacefully sleeping, but she quickly pushed the distraction aside and refocused on her research.

Suddenly, a loud thud echoed through the room, startling Gracie. Her heart raced as her eyes darted between Coby and the bookshelf. Coby stirred and mumbled in his sleep, oblivious to the commotion.

Confusion etched itself across Gracie's face as she noticed a candlestick mysteriously dropped to the floor. She collected it and placed it back in its rightful spot, feeling a sense of unease that lingered in the air. A chill ran down her spine, causing goosebumps to form on her arms. She rubbed them vigorously, trying to dispel the eerie sensation.

With anticipation coursing through her veins, Gracie felt her heart pounding in her chest, like a drum beating in a crescendo. Her eyes widened in horror as she witnessed her stapler skid across the desk, the sound of its crash echoing through the room, creating a deafening clamour that reverberated in her ears. A terrified yell escaped her lips, piercing the air and shattering the once serene silence that enveloped the room. Meanwhile, Coby's eyes shot open, and as he inhaled deeply, he could feel the crisp morning air filling his lungs. Slowly, the spectral trio emerged, their monochrome images materialising in the soft glow of the morning sun that filtered through the windows, casting a gentle warmth upon the scene. Their laughter erupted mockingly, filling the surrounding space with haunting echoes.

"Good morning, ladies," Coby greeted, his parched lips yearning for a refreshing drink of water.

Gracie's suspicion seeped into her tone as she asked, "Who are you speaking to?"

A sheepish smile played on Coby's lips as he replied, "You."

Gracie shot him a scowl, her narrowed eyes filled with distrust as she poured his coffee. The sharp sound of tires crunching over the gravel outside immediately caught their attention. The spectral trio hurriedly made their way to the windows, their ghostly figures casting eerie shadows on the floor. With fearful anticipation in their glowing ember eyes, they menacingly whispered the word "Sassenach."

Coby felt a shiver run down his spine as he realised who they were directing their hostility towards. Anger surged within him, and he exchanged a quick, questioning glance with Gracie, their eyes silently communicating their thoughts. She responded with a nonchalant shrug, taking a sip of her coffee. The spectral trinity murmured with astonishment and exchanged hushed whispers of surprise, their long, bony fingers pointing accusingly at the Range Rover parked outside.

Bracing himself, Coby heard the distinct sound of a knock on the front door, the sharp sound of metal meeting wood.

"Come in!" he exclaimed, his tone dripping with frostiness. The ominous doors creaked open, and he could hear the distinct thudding of a walking stick against the marble floors of the grand hallway.

"Hello!" serenaded a woman's voice, her high lilting tenor filling the air. "Is anyone home?" Confusion furrowed Coby's brow as he tried to make sense of the situation.

"In here!" he called out, his voice echoing through the empty hallway. The sound of the walking stick grew louder, and a finely dressed elderly lady walked in, her silver hairdo catching the light and shimmering like bursts of fireworks. Before elegantly removing her crisp, white opera gloves, she tapped her walking stick twice on the wooden floor, creating a rhythmic sound. Coby stood up and confidently walked towards her, his footsteps echoing in the silence.

"Hello," he greeted, extending his hand. "Allow me to introduce myself. I'm Coby McTavish, and this is Gracie Drummond," he said, motioning towards Gracie. He gestured towards the worn leather Chesterfield couch, its soft cushions beckoning the lady to take a seat. She shook his hand, her touch delicate as she offered only her fingertips, before gracefully sinking into the leather couch, her weight causing it to protest with a low creak.

With a posh accent, she proudly declared, "I am Lady Morven Sinclair," placing a hand delicately over her chest. With her lips pressed tightly together, a hint of a sneer appeared at the corners of her mouth. Gliding towards the newcomer, the ethereal trinity's spectral eyes scanned her figure, capturing every intricate detail. Jane mockingly pointed a long, bony finger at Morven's hat. The vintage mauve wool piece sat jauntily on the side of her head, adding a touch of whimsy to her outfit. The spectral accomplices erupted with ethereal laughter, their haunting voices reverberating through the room.

Confusion etched itself across Coby's face. He did not understand why Morven referred to herself as a lady. He knew the Sinclair's had been stripped of their titles, a consequence of the mining scandal involving Lord Henderson Sinclair. It surprised him when he visited the small graveyard on the estate and noticed Henderson's title etched into the headstone.

Morven tapped her walking stick twice on the polished wooden floor, the sharp thumps reverberating through the room and jolting

Coby out of his wandering thoughts.

"Oh dear," Morven exclaimed, frustration evident in her voice, as she frantically fanned herself with delicate hands. "A lady is in desperate need of refreshment. Where, pray tell, is your staff?" In response, the ghostly trio emitted a menacing hiss, their fiery eyes illuminating the dimly lit room with an eerie glow.

Gracie's voice, laced with unmistakable irritation, declared, "I'll make some tea." She abruptly leaped up, causing her chair to scrape against the floor and adding to the cacophony. In a swift motion, she collected the tray, the sound of cups and saucers clinking echoing in the air, and stormed out, her frustration tangible. Coby could hear the clattering of pots and pans and the sound of Gracie's frustrated sighs as she moved around the kitchen in a rush.

"Why have you come here today?" Coby asked, his tone dripping with sarcasm. He directed his gaze at Morven, a smug smirk playing on his lips, as if he knew something she didn't. Her presence irked him, but he refused to show it.

Morven's face scrunched up in clear displeasure as she flinched at the sight of his nonchalant attitude. She brushed it off dismissively, swatting at it as if it were an annoying fly. "You should know that it is considered polite to introduce oneself to new neighbours," she replied with a snort, her voice laced with a touch of superiority.

Coby grappled with the temptation to retaliate against Morven by recounting her husband's betrayals. "Well then," he casually remarked, a hint of wickedness in his gaze, "I appreciate you stopping by." The ethereal trinity observed their exchange with unwavering focus, their eyes darting back and forth like spectators at a captivating tennis match. Gracie sauntered into the study, her footsteps echoing on the polished hardwood floor, and set the tray down on the low coffee table.

The pleasant sound of the teaspoon clinking against the teacup filled the room as Morven prepared her tea. However, she suddenly hesitated, her gaze becoming fixed on the sugar bowl. With a gesture towards the bowl, she inquired, "Do you happen to have any sugar cubes?"

Coby, showing his typical indifference, casually shook his head. "No," he replied, "if you happen to come by again, which hopefully won't be anytime soon, you can bring some."

Gracie flinched at Coby's pun, her laughter bubbling up and breaking through her composed facade. She quickly regained her composure when Morven shot her a disapproving look, her face becoming expressionless.

Morven's eyes shot up, her gaze scanning the ceiling. She waved her hand through the air, as if dismissing the surroundings. "You spent your money foolishly on this brothel," she said scornfully, her words filled with contempt.

Coby could feel a surge of anger welling up inside him, like a searing flame that spread from his chest, causing his cheeks to turn a deep shade of red. As he glanced towards Gracie, her intense gaze conveyed a stern warning. The room was enveloped in a heavy silence, the only sound being the rhythmic inhales and exhales of their breaths. With effort, Coby managed to muster a false smile, his eyes locked firmly with Morven's, a simmering intensity underlying his expression.

"Oh, what a wise investment," he sarcastically replied, "and how I thoroughly enjoy being surrounded by the legacy of your family's errors."

Gracie, with her teacup in hand, was in the middle of taking a sip when an uncontrollable laughter erupted from within. The sound echoed through the room, accompanied by the sight of her tea spewing out in a comical spray, creating a messy spectacle. Suddenly, Ewan burst into the room, his cheeks flushed with excitement, violating the unwritten rule of not entering the office during working hours.

"Mum!" he exclaimed, his voice filled with enthusiasm. "Look what I found." In his hand, he held two vintage ballet flats, their soft pink hue weathered from years of dancing. He carefully placed the worn shoes on his mother's desk. A soft gasp escaped from Jane's lips as she felt her ethereal presence gravitate towards the shoes. Recognition sparked in her eyes, gleaming brightly. She floated effortlessly towards Gracie's desk, her attention immediately captured by the pair of shoes that exuded an aura of mystery, causing her eyes to well up with sadness. Morven's eyes fixated on young Ewan, a flicker of recognition shining in her gaze. Lost in the depths of a distant memory, her brow furrowed deeply, showing the weight of her thoughts.

Gracie leaned forward, her eyes filled with curiosity and her voice dripping with affection, as she asked her son, "Where on earth did you stumble upon them?"

Ewan responded with a nonchalant shrug, rolling his eyes playfully. "Upstairs," he said, a wistful smile on his face, "where the grand piano had its own special place." Coby and Gracie exchanged a knowing glance, their eyes speaking volumes of their shared understanding.

Gracie raised her eyebrows and asked Ewan, "How did you figure out that it was a piano?" The room filled with anticipation as they awaited his response. Ewan simply shrugged, a hint of mischief in his eyes.

"I guessed," he stated nonchalantly before making his way out, joining Janie, who eagerly wagged her tail.

Morven's lips curled into a roguish grin, while a playful glint shone in her eyes. "Just look at the time already," she said, her voice dripping with irony. Coby escorted her to the front door, slamming it shut behind her, causing the windows to rattle with the force.

"Ewan!" Coby cried out, his voice filled with urgency, echoing through the old house. He could hear the rapid thumping of the young lad's heavy footsteps on the worn floorboards above, the sound reverberating in his ears.

"Yes, uncle Coby," Ewan responded, leaning over the creaking wooden railing. Coby's eyes quickly scanned the dimly lit hallway, finally spotting Ewan with his vibrant, fiery red hair standing out against the muted surroundings.

"Could you please guide me to the place where you discovered the shoes?" Coby asked, his voice filled with curiosity and anticipation, as he climbed the staircase that emitted soft creaks under his weight. Ewan eagerly nodded, his head bobbing up and down as he led Coby to a desolate room filled with a chilly breeze. The moment he stepped into the room, a rush of déjà vu flooded through Coby, instantly transporting him back to the haunting memory of the bare, ghostly figure. A shiver ran down his spine, a mix of both anticipation and familiarity.

Ewan pointed towards the secluded corner of the room, wagging his finger to indicate where he discovered the mysterious ballet flats. Astonishment washed over Coby's face, his eyes widening in disbelief as he realised he had overlooked the shoes during his last visit. He noticed the four deep grooves carved into the worn wooden floor, a testament to the weight of the grand piano that had once graced the room. A brilliant idea sprouted in his mind, filling him with a surge of inspiration that illuminated his radiant face.

"Good job," he praised Ewan, his voice filled with warmth as he affectionately tousled Ewan's vibrant red hair. With renewed determination, Coby hurried downstairs and into the study. Gracie met him with an expectant gaze, her eyes brimming with curiosity, eager to uncover the secrets he held.

"Are you able to play the piano?" Coby asked, his words rushed and urgent, a hint of desperation lingering in his tone. A puzzled expression washed over Gracie's face, her brows furrowing as she processed the unexpected question.

"Yes," she replied, her voice wavering with uncertainty, as if she was unsure of her own answer.

Coby's desperation surged, a knot tightening in his chest. The relentless ticking of the clock reverberated through his ears, intensifying the pressure as the deadline for his draft approached. The weight of unfinished tasks pressed against him, suffocating his thoughts. He had unravelled the mysteries surrounding Sandra's demise, but the ethereal trinity remained elusive, shrouded in enigma. And then there was the haunting image of the bare, whimpering young woman, etched in his mind like a ghostly apparition. Coby yearned to hold the key that would unlock their secrets, his fingers itching with anticipation.

Frustration radiated from him like an invisible aura, and Gracie, sensing his unease, kept their conversations to a minimum, her focus unwavering on her research. They shared little updates recently, both consumed by the task at hand. Yet, her presence proved invaluable, a lifeline in his race against time.

Coby's editor had just provided an update on his latest draft, showering it with praise as his magnum opus. Coby let out a theatrical sigh, his eyes scanning the influx of social media responses. "It's all bullshit!" he declared, his frustration overflowing, resulting in a disapproving scowl from Gracie. She had a strong aversion to swearing, especially when it occurred in the presence of her son. Coby halfheartedly apologised, his hand raised in a feeble attempt to appease her, before refocusing on his tasks. Through his experience, he had become adept at distinguishing the authentic social media responses from the fraudulent ones. Most of the people were mere attention-seekers, craving their own moment in the spotlight. He closed his eyes, mentally retracing his steps, ticking off the places he had visited. The libraries, the research centre, the Highlands museum, and even Paris all checked off in his mind's meticulous list.

Suddenly, Janie's excited barks pierced through the air, jolting Coby from his thoughts. He turned his gaze towards the windows and spotted a flatbed truck laboriously ascending the steep driveway. Its engine groaned in protest, burdened by its heavy load. A small, yellow crane stood between the cab and the flatbed, its metal frame perched precariously as if it were a mechanical sentinel keeping watch over the delivery.

A surge of delight washed over Coby as realisation dawned on him. It was the Steinway grand piano he had ordered from a second-hand dealer.

"The piano is here!" he exclaimed, his voice filled with excitement echoing throughout the room.

"Ewan!" Gracie called, her voice carrying a mixture of urgency and anticipation. She beckoned her son to join them, and together they hurried outside. With a flourish, Coby swung open both wooden doors, revealing a gateway to his musical dreams.

The old truck hissed, releasing a blast of compressed air as it came to a standstill at the bottom of the creaking staircase. Two burly men hopped out, their boots thudding against the ground as they busied themselves with unloading the cumbersome piano.

The bulky man, his voice carrying a distinct Irish accent, settled himself into a worn seat adorned with control levers. A mechanical whirr filled the air as the pneumatics came to life under his expert touch. With precision, he operated the crane, its steel arm extending and deftly clasping the piano. The small truck beneath him squeaked in protest as the piano swayed, but the man remained unfazed, navigating the contraption towards the entrance.

Together, the two men manoeuvred the sleek black piano into the grand hallway, its presence instantly adding an air of elegance to the space. Coby's eyes widened in disbelief as he watched the two men struggle under the weight, their muscles straining with every step. Gracie, her movements graceful and fluid, delicately brushed her hand over the piano's smooth design, her eyes shimmering with astonishment. With anticipation written all over her face, she gently lifted the fallboard and let her fingers hover over the delicate ivories. But Coby's sudden grip on her hand halted her, his touch firm and urgent.

"Please, not now," he pleaded, his voice soft and filled with longing. "Let's do it tonight."

Gracie fixed him with an endearing look, her eyes brimming with the same tenderness she reserved for her son, and nodded in quiet understanding. Coby's heart fluttered at the sight of her hair pulled back into a high ponytail, a rush of excitement and love coursing through him.

In gratitude for their help, Coby offered the driver of the truck and his assistant a generous swig of whisky, the scent mingling with the crisp air. Besides a generous tip, their exchange was punctuated by warm pats on the back, a fleeting moment of camaraderie. Janie barked excitedly as the truck's engine roared to life, and the men leaned out of the windows, waving goodbye as the truck descended the steep driveway, a sense of finality lingering in the air.

As Coby had predicted, the sudden presence of the grand piano in the dimly lit hallway captured the attention of the ethereal trinity. Intrigued, they materialised and were drawn towards the piano, their ethereal bodies gliding gracefully through the air. Their spectral gazes fixated on the magnificent instrument, and a sense of curiosity emanated from their otherworldly essence. In perfect harmony, their ethereal faces lit up with a surge of recognition as they comprehended the significance of the piano. Soft whispers and gentle hisses escaped their ghostly lips, filling the air with a melodic murmur of astonishment.

They gathered around the piano, their translucent figures huddled closely together, engrossed in animated conversations. The air became alive with the beautiful medley of their discussions, blending both English and French seamlessly. A sense of intrigue and wonder electrified the atmosphere. A mischievous smile danced on Coby's lips as he observed their astonishment, knowing that the piano would occupy their attention.

"Finally," he muttered under his breath, feeling a wave of relief, "I finally have my study all to myself."

Chapter Twenty-Four

As the twilight hues merged in a celestial ballet, Gracie and Ewan entered the grand hallway, their footsteps echoing softly. True to their agreement, they arrived on time, immediately grabbing Coby's attention. Gracie, adorned in a flowing black velvety dress, exuded an air of elegance that captivated the room. As she moved, the fabric whispered against her skin, adding a subtle touch of sensuality to her appearance.

Coby, who had been eagerly waiting, couldn't help but steal a sneak glance at Gracie's elegant leg, playfully revealed through the delicate slit in her dress. His eyes lingered for a moment, appreciating her beauty before he warmly greeted them. Gracie carefully held a steaming bowl of classic Scottish Broth, the rich smell of lamb bones and vegetables wafting through the air, enticing anyone nearby.

While Ewan and Janie hurried upstairs, Coby and Gracie focused on setting the table and preparing their drinks. Coby's choice was an aged whisky, the golden liquid shimmering in the dim light of the room. Gracie opted for her favourite, Drambuie, the sweet and aromatic liqueur adding a touch of warmth to their evening.

Ewan, in his mischievous nature, had recently developed a habit of teasingly calling Coby "dad." Coby jokingly reprimanded the young boy, suggesting that he should "go have fun with his furry companion." Ewan, finding amusement in Coby's reaction, couldn't resist teasing him further, playfully uttering phrases like "yes, dad." Gracie's response to this dynamic remained somewhat ambiguous to Coby, yet he couldn't overlook the subtle upward curve of her mouth and the distant expression in her eyes. These moments only deepened

Coby's love for her, as he yearned to be a part of her beautiful, small family and longed to give her a child of their own.

However, his mind involuntarily drifted back to that fateful, colourless day in high school. The football pitch had been drenched with rain, making it wet, muddy, and treacherously slippery. Coby, known as 'Bender' for his unique skill to curve the football into the nets, had positioned himself for a goal attempt. With the goalkeeper and the net within his sight, he expertly dribbled the ball, the sound of his cleats scraping against the wet grass filling the air. As he took a quick step back to build momentum, his body suddenly betrayed him, causing him to slip. The opposition's midfielder, already engaged in his defensive manoeuvre, collided with Coby in an unfortunate accident.

Instead of finding the ball, the tip of his boot collided with Coby's sensitive area, causing a searing pain to surge through his entire body. The pain was so intense that Coby blacked out, only to wake up in a sterile hospital room. The elderly doctor, whose touch Coby found oddly comforting, clasped his hand, his voice filled with concern. He explained that an emergency operation was necessary, and the news of Coby's possible infertility hung heavy in the air. In his youthful naivety, Coby retorted with a nonchalant "I don't mind," unaware of the eye rolls and scoffs it would elicit from the girls. Little did he know that his words would have such a profound impact on his life, resulting in three failed marriages.

Coby had to summon all his courage to share the intimate details with Gracie. The soft glow of candlelight illuminated the room, casting gentle shadows on the walls. He could hear the faint crackling of the fire in the background, its warmth permeating the air. The scent of vanilla from the scented candles filled his nostrils, adding a touch of sweetness to the moment.

Uncertainty lingered in his mind as he gazed into Gracie's eyes. Questioning whether she would be open to a long-term commitment, he couldn't help but feel a sense of unease lingering in the air. Though he knew her husband had passed many years ago, he had no idea how she felt about opening their lives to a stranger.

Their encounters had shared fleeting moments of intimacy, but he understood that such connections were ephemeral. It didn't necessarily imply a desire for marriage, but rather a need for affection.

Deep in introspection, he softly uttered, "Time is the ultimate judge."

Gracie's voice broke through his reverie, distant yet ethereal, as if floating in a dream. Startled, Coby shook his head to dismiss the daydream, and Gracie's radiant beauty gradually came into focus. Her gaze bore into him with an intensity that seemed to unravel his every secret.

Ewan's loud and commanding voice abruptly shattered their peaceful moment. He bellowed for his mother's attention, bringing them back to the present reality. Gracie elegantly served her son's meal, the clinking of dishes filling the air. Ewan hastily grabbed the soup bowl from his mother's hand and rushed up the stairs, with Janie's tail wagging eagerly at his side.

In that moment, Gracie pulled Coby into a warm embrace, her body pressed against his, and her lips met his with a passionate kiss. The weight of her longing was tangible, a desperate desire to unravel the enigma that he embodied.

The scent of the flavourful Scotch Broth filled the air as Ewan made his way down the stairs. Gracie and Coby relished the tender lamb, savouring every succulent bite as the mixed vegetables exploded with a medley of rich and delectable flavours. Coby immersed his traditional home-baked Scottish Bannocks deep into the broth, relishing the wholesome tastes of barley that accompanied the savoury soup. Gracie, witnessing his enjoyment, happily served him seconds and assured him that there would be plenty left over for breakfast.

With a contented smile, Coby patted his full belly and reclined in his chair. Swiftly, Ewan gathered the leftover bones and fed them to Janie, who eagerly gnawed on them in front of the crackling fireplace.

Gracie, adjusting her dress, revealed her slender legs, capturing Coby's attention. He shifted in his seat, feeling a surge of excitement. With a mischievous smile and a nod to her one-man audience, she lifted the fallboard of the Steinway grand piano and delicately placed her fingers on the ivory keys. Her elegant black nails created a striking contrast against the pristine white keys. As she kicked off her shoes and rested her feet on the pedals, Coby's heart fluttered, and his breath quickened. Like a skilled conductor, Gracie closed her eyes and hummed a bittersweet lullaby in her melodic soprano, her voice echoing through the majestic hallway. Coby sat up straight, anticipation coursing through him, as he felt the prickling of goosebumps on his skin.

Gracie's fingers danced across the ivories, the high notes filling the air with a melodious sound. With effortless grace, she sang the words to "Hee Balou, My Sweet Wee Donald – Bannocks o' Bear Meal" by Robert Burns, channelling the masterful performance of Gillian MacDonald.

The tender serenade, a gentle whisper of a mother's love, flowed with the rhythm of a rocking cradle. Gracie's voice, a river of emotion, washed over the melody. Coby felt tears welling in his eyes as the emotional lullaby penetrated his very being. During the chorus, Coby lifted his glass, his deep voice harmonising with the melody, as they sang, "Here's to the Highlandman's bannocks o' barley." Janie wagged her tail excitedly, her eyes fixed on the duo, and joined in with a howl that harmonised with the melody.

The haunting melody reached its last note, leaving Coby with tears streaming down his face. The sound gradually faded, leaving him with a lingering silence that made him acutely aware of the wetness on his cheeks. He hastily wiped them away. Gracie's voice, like a bird's call, had the power to draw out deep emotions from within her audience. It reminded Coby of the lore behind the sirens, those enchanting sea nymphs who lured unsuspecting sailors to their demise with their sweet songs.

Overwhelmed by the performance, Coby erupted in thunderous applause, his hands clapping together with a resounding noise. Janie barked excitedly, her tail wagging in anticipation of more. Gracie gracefully bowed and delicately rested her fingers on the piano keys.

The hallway was silent except for the comforting sound of the fireplace crackling in the background. With a mischievous wink, she began her rendition of "Blue Bells of Scotland" by Dora Jordan. The classical composition, devoid of lyrics, warmed the depths of Coby's soul. He knew that this timeless Scottish favourite dated back to 1801.

Yet, the true magic awaited its perfect moment, like a dream unfolding before him. Gracie paused, waiting for the applause to subside. Coby rose to his feet, giving her a standing ovation, chanting "encore" repeatedly. A radiant smile adorned her face as she elegantly bowed her head. Her finger landed on a high key, resonating through the air, and Coby's heart skipped a beat. He knew what was to come. With a graceful press of her foot on the sustain pedal, a high note reverberated through the air, its lingering ring captivating her audience's ears.

With a knowing smile, Gracie's fingers danced effortlessly over the ivory keys while she began to sing the beloved "Auld Lang Syne" by Robert Burns. Coby placed his hand over his heart, feeling the vibrations of the bass notes melding with Gracie's soprano voice. He closed his eyes, allowing the music to consume him, pouring his heart and soul into the song.

Suddenly, Janie's abrupt yelp shattered the peaceful atmosphere. Coby opened his eyes, startled by the interruption. His gaze followed Janie as she darted out of the hallway, her tail tucked between her legs. Confusion clouded Coby's mind as he turned his attention back to the grand piano. To his astonishment, the ethereal trinity materialised around it. Their eyes held a deep longing as they joined their unique voices, singing in both French and English, harmonising with the melody.

Pride and astonishment warred within Coby's expression as apparitions emerged from every corner, floating towards the sleek, black piano. He fixed his eyes on them, his expression showing a combination of wonder and nervousness. His eyes widened like saucers as the apparition he had encountered a few nights before gracefully descended the staircase, sending shivers down his spine. Out of respect, Coby looked away from her naked body, illuminated softly by the moonlight's gentle touch. She added her voice to the spectral trio, and as they sang, their harmonies reverberated through the hallway.

Gracie, completely unaware of the ethereal presence surrounding her, continued her serenade, her voice reverberating off the ornate walls of the room. Coby, overwhelmed by the sheer number of ghostly figures encircling Gracie and the grand piano, lost count. Suddenly, an overwhelming wave of nauseating brimstone assaulted Coby's senses, mingling with the putrid odour of decaying flesh.

The stench permeated the grand hallway, its foulness wafting through the atmosphere. Suddenly, a dense, dark fog materialised, engulfing the marble floor and filling the air with an eerie silence. The air was thick with fog, which amplified the crackling sound that echoed through the surroundings, intensifying the acrid bite of brimstone. Coby's eyes stung, and he instinctively pinched his nose to block out the repulsive smell. Amid the murky fog, a discoloured vortex materialised, emitting an eerie static sound that sent shivers down Coby's spine.

The vortex loomed menacingly, its swirling void appearing to devour everything in sight, causing Coby's eyes to widen in sheer disbelief. Gradually, the figure of a man emerged from the swirling vortex, his black coat billowing behind him. The man's eyes emitted an eerie saffron glow, like smouldering embers, as if flames were flickering within.

His furrowed brow etched a dark valley of disapproval across his face, while his limbs moved with a puppet-like quality. The fog gradually cleared, uncovering a chilling scene: two shadowy figures flanking the malevolent being. Their contorted shapes heightened the eerie sensation that hung in the frigid air.

Coby's body trembled involuntarily as he took in the sight, overwhelmed by an intense sense of foreboding. The newcomer's presence cast a gloomy shadow over Gracie's performance, saturating the air with a profound sorrow. The malevolent entity's presence sent a chill down the spines of every spectre near the grand piano, shattering the previously peaceful ambiance. Their wide-eyed gazes met his intense, fiery stare, and their screams of terror echoed through the air as they frantically scattered in all directions, desperate for safety. Despite the others backing down, Josephine Barker remained defiant, fearlessly locking eyes with the malevolent presence. In response, his head snapped back sharply as a maniacal laugh escaped his lips, sending shivers down Coby's spine.

Unfazed, Josephine remained motionless, her eyes emanating a serene tranquillity that provided Coby with a sliver of comfort. Gracie abruptly ceased her performance, her glossy eyes snapping open wide with terror, and she emitted a gut-wrenching scream that compelled Coby to cover his ears. Like a fleeting dream, the apparitions of Josephine and the wicked man vanished into the shadows, leaving the air filled with a mysterious stillness.

"What's troubling you?" Coby exclaimed, his voice filled with concern, as he rushed to Gracie's aid. He immediately wrapped his arm around her trembling shoulders, feeling her body quiver against his. The air was filled with tension as her eyes darted around, searching for something that wasn't there.

"I have no doubt that I saw a fleeting image of Alistair's dad, Lord Sinclair," she stated, her voice conveying a touch of suspicion. The room was hushed, with only the subtle crackle of the fireplace providing a gentle background noise. Gracie's gaze remained fixated, as if she could still see the ghostly figure lurking in the shadows.

"It has to be the nostalgia," she whispered, her words barely audible amidst the sound of her own breathing.

Coby furrowed his brow, his concern deepening. Gracie's last sentence lingered in his mind, leaving him with an uneasy feeling that there was something hidden within her words. The memory of Morven Sinclair's visit yesterday flooded his mind. There had been a strange familiarity between them, despite Gracie's initial annoyance. The echo of Morven's unkind words about Coby buying a brothel lingered in his ears, a bitter taste forming in the back of his throat.

Suddenly, a veil lifted, and Coby connected Morven's words with the apparitions that had appeared during Gracie's performance. It was as if the truth had been right in front of him all along. He could see the ethereal figures now, dressed in extravagant attire that glimmered like stars in the night sky. The memory of the bare apparition, her exposed figure illuminated against the walls, flooded his mind. It was the same room where the piano had once stood, a room that held secrets he had been blind to.

"I'm such an idiot," Coby muttered through gritted teeth, his frustration palpable. His hand slammed against his forehead, the sound reverberating through the room. "Och, my house used to be a kittle-hoosie," he uttered, the scent of longing and remorse wafting through the room.

Chapter Twenty-Five

The golden rays of sunlight filtered through the sheer curtains, gently caressing Coby's face as he slowly stirred from his slumber. He blinked his eyes open, feeling the warmth on his skin, and let out a contented yawn while stretching his arms. Memories from the previous evening flooded his mind, causing a smile to play on his lips. He woke up with a sense of anticipation, a positive energy coursing through him for the new day.

With a burst of energy, he leaped out of bed and eagerly got dressed, the fabric of his clothes brushing against his skin. A merry tune escaped his lips as he made his way into the kitchen, where the aroma of freshly brewed coffee filled the air. He spread creamy Crowdie cheese on slices of toasted bannocks, relishing the soft texture of the bread and the tangy taste of the cheese.

As Coby savoured his self-proclaimed 'bachelor's disjune,' he hummed the cheerful tune that had been echoing in his mind. Cradling his steaming cup of coffee, he made his way to his study, the sound of his whistling filling the hallway. The sleek black piano caught his attention, its glossy exterior mirroring the sunlight, and he couldn't help but feel a growing anticipation.

A mischievous smile played on his lips as he approached the piano, his fingers hovering above the keys. With no knowledge of how to play the instrument, he pressed down on random ivory, producing a discordant symphony of low notes that reverberated through the room. The three apparitions, Jane, Vivienne, and Gracie, gasped in surprise, their whispers of annoyance floating through the cool air.

Coby couldn't resist teasing them further, repeating the action and relishing their menacing hisses and bared teeth. The icy breath of the spirits grazed his face, and an unpleasant odour of decay filled his nostrils.

"Sorry!" Coby exclaimed in a playful tone, quickly retreating to his office just as the front doors ominously creaked open.

Gracie and Ewan entered, accompanied by Janie, who scurried to her hiding spot beneath the staircase. Gracie greeted him cheerfully, tossing her belongings onto her desk. Coby responded with a mischievous smirk, causing Gracie to furrow her brow inquisitively, her eyes narrowing with a mixture of concern and curiosity. "Oh," she gasped, figuring out what he was thinking, "I know what's on your mind." Her cheeks turned a shade of crimson, a soft flush spreading across them.

Coby playfully nodded his head, winking at her as she hurried off to the kitchen. He could hear the clamour of her morning routine as she efficiently went about her tasks. Glancing at his watch, he marvelled at Gracie's punctuality, recognising that she was the epitome of timeliness in everything she did.

Coby now understood what his manor house used to be many years ago, although he did not know the exact date range. The memory of the apparitions dressed like high fashion harlots lingered in his mind, evoking a sense of a bygone era before Roy and Bonnie Sinclair's arrival. The musty scent of old books and the creaking of floorboards as he walked through the halls gave him a sense of the house's age. At least this, coupled with the former name Hemlock Manor, gave him some clues. Without delay, he emailed John Drake requesting a month's extension on his final draft's submission deadline.

While they worked, Gracie and Coby exchanged fleeting glances, a silent understanding passing between them. The cosy sound of the fireplace crackling filled the room, setting the perfect ambiance for their shared moments. His eyes flitted between her azure eyes, their vibrant colour drawing him in, and her glossy lips hinting at a hidden desire. Every time she curled the corner of her mouth into a knowing smile, it felt as if a swarm of butterflies took flight in his stomach. Mischievous thoughts flooded his mind, and he pictured her balancing on the edge of his desk, her snug skirt hiked up to reveal her thighs. Coby's pulse quickened as he imagined the silky touch of her legs under his fingertips, and the warmth of her intimate embrace. Vivid images tormented his reverie, each detail becoming more vivid with each passing second.

Gracie gripped a fistful of his flannel shirt onto her slender fingers, the fabric soft against her touch, with her other hand tightly wound around his groin. She yanked him close, the sound of buttons popping echoing in the room, and kissed him passionately while she begged him to make love to her, right there on the desk. The scent of her perfume mingled with the musk of desire, creating an intoxicating aroma that enveloped them. With a groan of pleasure, she wiped away the dark tendrils clinging to her sweaty brow; her glistening skin, a testament to her exertion. They would have to be quick and take risks, their hearts pounding in anticipation of Ewan's imminent arrival. The thought of their bold nuances made Coby's breath quicken as excitement surged through him.

"I found something!" Gracie exclaimed, her voice filled with urgency, jolting Coby out of his lustful reverie. The suddenness of her words caused Coby to click his tongue in disappointment, and he quickly joined her side. Gracie's elegant finger glided over the screen as she read the email, her perfectly manicured nails tapping softly against the glass.

"He says he was a journalist," she started, her voice filled with curiosity, "and he was once an editor at The Kilted Mirror, a well-known daily newspaper."

Coby's eyes widened with astonishment, his breath hitching as he leaned in close to read the email. The intoxicating scent of Jane's floral perfume lingered in the air, heightening his excitement, but he quickly pushed the distracting thoughts from his mind.

"Sounds legitimate," Gracie remarked, her brow creasing as she pondered.

Coby's eyes widened in disbelief as they lingered on the intricate details at the bottom of the email. "Call him now!" he bellowed, his excitement reaching a fever pitch. He rushed to his bedroom, the floor creaking beneath his hurried footsteps, and began stuffing any clothing he could find lying around into his weathered tartan suitcase. The sound of fabric rustling filled the room as he strained to listen to Gracie's conversation, tossing his toothbrush and paste into a cosmetic bag. Gracie hung up the phone just as he forced the zipper closed, and he dragged his suitcase into the grand hallway. Setting it aside beside the large doors, the cold marble floor sent a shiver up his spine as he paced back and forth, his heart hammering in his chest.

"Coby!" Gracie called out, her voice filled with urgency.

"I'm here," Coby said, his voice echoing through the cosy study. Gracie flinched as he appeared out of nowhere, catching her completely off guard.

"His name is Jackson Kinney," she began, her gaze darting between the phone and Coby in the doorway, "and you won't believe what happened next," she exclaimed, increasing his anticipation. Coby's eyes were fixed on her lips, hoping they would move, and he raised his eyebrows, silently urging her to continue.

"He moved to Inverness, and I have his address!" she exclaimed with excitement, her eyes welling up with tears of joy, gleaming with glossy happiness.

"What?" Coby asked in disbelief, his voice filled with a mix of shock and excitement. He gently cradled her face in his hands and covered her cheeks with a cascade of grateful kisses. "We're going for a ride!"

Gracie leaped at the opportunity, not needing a second invitation, and quickly called out, "Ewan!" Her son, recognising the urgency in his mother's voice, appeared in the doorway, seemingly appearing out of thin air.

The powerful Volvo engine roared to life, its deep rumble vibrating through Gracie's and Ewan's bodies as they scrambled to find a seat. The old car lurched forward, causing a jolt of excitement to surge through them. Coby skilfully raced down the steep driveway, the tires gripping the cobbles with a satisfying screech.

Through the rearview mirror, Coby caught a glimpse of Janie frantically chasing after the car. Her paws skidded on the ground as she desperately tried to catch up. Ewan swiftly opened the door, and Janie jumped in, panting heavily and filling the air with the pungent scent of her decaying breath. Ewan instinctively rolled down the window, allowing a rush of wind to whip through the car, carrying away the odour.

Knowing the routine well, Coby made a quick stop at their favourite shop. As they stocked up on refreshments for their upcoming journey, the tantalising sight of Irn-Bru filled Ewan with delight. He savoured each sip, the fizzy liquid tickling his taste buds. Gracie's hand gently rested on Coby's leg, sending a tingling sensation through his body, a mix of excitement and anticipation. In the rearview mirror, Ewan's smiling face reflected his happiness, and his playful taunt brought a grin to Coby's lips. Janie, caught up in the playful atmosphere, let out a series of excited barks.

Navigating the winding road, Coby rounded a bend, only to abruptly brake as a flock of sheep crossed their path. The shepherd, trailing behind the last sheep, tipped his hat and offered a friendly smile to Gracie. Coby grunted in frustration, his knuckles turning white as he tightened his grip on the steering wheel, but he quickly regained his composure. He pressed his foot on the accelerator, and the car surged forward, the tires humming against the twists and turns of the road. Ewan's enthusiastic praise echoed in the car, accompanied by Janie's excited barking. Gracie's grip on Coby's leg tightened, her touch electrifying, sending waves of pleasure coursing through his body.

The sparkling lochs of Inverness shimmered on the horizon, their beauty beckoning to Coby. Thoughts and questions swirled in his mind, preparing for his upcoming meeting with Jackson Kinney. Ewan dutifully activated the maps app, and the voice of the female navigator filled the car with seductive English accents, guiding them through the cobblestone streets. Each bump and rattle of the tires on the uneven surface synced with Coby's racing heartbeat.

Finally, the Volvo approached the imposing green heavy metal gate. Gracie, understanding the importance of Coby's meeting, took Ewan sightseeing, leaving him alone with Jackson Kinney. Coby waved them goodbye, blowing kisses as they drove off. The anticipation of what awaited him behind the gate hung in the air, a mix of nerves and excitement intertwining.

Coby's eyes eagerly scanned the neatly printed names on the intercom, the sound of his breath quickening with anticipation. Finally, his gaze settled on the name 'Kinney' beside unit thirteen, and a surge of excitement pulsed through him. With a practiced touch, he pressed the button, feeling the cool metal beneath his fingertips.

A quivering voice, tinged with nerves, crackled through the intercom, causing Coby's ears to perk up. "Yes," the man responded, his voice betraying his unease.

"Hi," Coby greeted, his lips hovering near the intercom, his words carrying a hint of warmth. "My name is Coby McTavish and I'm here to see Mister Kinney, please." As he waited, he could hear the man's laboured breaths mingling with the faint hum of the intercom.

"You can come up," the man eventually responded, and the green gate opened smoothly with a gentle buzz and click. Coby stepped forward, his footsteps echoing softly against the glossy green corridor as he made his way up a flight of stairs. With determined eyes, he scanned the doors, searching for unit thirteen. Just as he was about to knock, the door swung open, revealing an old man leaning on a walking stick. Dressed in blue and white pyjamas, he greeted Coby with a nod, his movements slow and deliberate. Without a word, he gestured for Coby to follow, his unsteady legs guiding them down a dimly lit corridor.

Entering the living room, Coby's gaze wandered over the aged wooden furniture that adorned the space, each piece holding memories of years gone by. The old man sank into an ancient leather seat, the worn fabric creaking softly beneath his weight. A pungent aroma of stale tobacco hung in the air, mingling with the faint scent of whisky. Coby's eyes trailed over the walls, adorned with framed awards and qualifications, each testament to a life well-lived. His gaze then settled on a sideboard, its surface lined with liquor bottles and gleaming bronze horse riding medals, the only source of light filtering in through the nearby windows.

"I apologise for my casual outfit," the elderly man said, his voice weathered from a lifetime of indulgence. The sight of nicotine-stained fingers overwhelmed Coby's senses as the old man lit a cigarette, the acrid smoke curling lazily into the air.

"Hi, I am Coby McTavish," Coby introduced himself, extending his hand. The old man's touch sent a chill down his spine, the unexpected coldness a stark contrast to the warmth of the room. Jackson Kinney gestured for Coby to take a seat, his cigarette casting a hazy glow as he spoke.

"I'm 87 years old," he announced, seemingly aware of Coby's astonishment. Coby winced, his hand raised in apology. In response, Jackson pointed his cigarette towards the sideboard, silently requesting a refill. Coby nodded, his movements dutiful, and poured two generous shots, passing one to Jackson Kinney.

"My father," Jackson began, his voice trailing off as he leisurely lit another cigarette, the flame flickering and casting an amber glow in the dimly lit room. He gestured towards the framed photographs adorning the peeling wallpapered walls, the glass reflecting the soft glow of the flickering candle on the coffee table.

Coby's gaze followed, his eyes fixating on the photograph of a man resembling Jackson. Adorned in traditional Scottish military attire, the man in the picture stood with a regal air. The vibrant red coat caught Coby's attention, contrasting against the plain grey background. The white cross belts added a sense of formality, while the dark green kilt boasted intricate tartan patterns. Coby imagined the smooth texture of the chequered hose and the shiny black shoes, their metallic buckles gleaming under the light. Completing the ensemble was a tall black hat with a striking red topper, exuding an air of authority. Coby could sense the heaviness of the brown musket as the man gripped it tightly. The photograph captured the vibrant colours and the intricate details of the attire, creating a visual contrast that was impossible to ignore.

Jackson took a drag, and a thin trail of smoke curled from his lips. Coby smirked, his eyes filled with a sense of recognition, and he nodded his head in understanding, leaning in close to listen to the story.

"He was called Roy Kinney," Jackson continued, puffing out a white cloud of billowing smoke. His calm voice had an uncanny ability to elongate every moment. "A decorated soldier of the 42nd Royal Highland Regiment–"

"The Black Watch," Coby interrupted, his tone laced with disbelief. Jackson shot him an annoying glance before he continued.

"And... a Harvard professor and Scottish diplomat," Jackson added, his voice filled with a subtle pride. He continued, "A happily married father and devoted husband to my dearest mother," as he made the sign of the cross in the air, his movements slow and deliberate.

"However, everything changed when he reluctantly received an invitation to that cursed Hemlock Manor," Jackson muttered angrily, his teeth clenched in frustration.

"What happened next?" Coby asked, leaning in with curiosity. Jackson raised his hand, signalling for silence, and blew out a cloud of white smoke, the tendrils dancing in the air before dissipating.

"He met his mistress, Jane Baines," Jackson spat, his eyes burning into Coby's. Coby visibly flinched at the mention of Jane's name, and a tense silence settled heavily in the room. "After he passed away, I stumbled upon a collection of their intimate love letters," Jackson continued, pointing a cigarette at a pile of aged envelopes on the low coffee table. The envelopes were stained with cigarette burns, their edges yellowed with time.

Jackson's voice dripped with a bitter yet fascinated tone as he revealed, "Their affair lasted decades. I only discovered it after his passing, which happened shortly after my mother's."

Coby nodded enthusiastically, urging him to continue with his intriguing story. As an award-winning journalist, Jackson believed it was his duty to unveil the concealed truth and hidden secrets. His hand swept across the walls adorned with framed newspaper clippings, capturing moments of triumph and recognition in their captivating headlines.

Jackson's chest wheezed as he took a long drag of his cigarette, the smoke swirling around him. "As I began my research in France," he continued, "I held a strong belief that this country held the origins of everything. I diligently followed the path of Jane Baines, meticulously documenting her journey to the wretched brothel. It was precisely in this very place that my father had encountered her, during a grand hunting event attended by many high-ranking aristocrats."

The weight of those words hung in the air, enveloping Coby with a profound sense of revelation. His excitement was tangible as he sat on the edge of his seat, his eyes darting back and forth, eagerly absorbing every detail.

In a low whisper, Jackson murmured, "Long story short, I wrote an article about my discoveries. As a young journalist, I was eager to publish it. However, my editor declined, claiming that it mentioned the names of powerful men who commanded nations. Refusing to accept this outcome, I fought against it. I went over his head and shared my story with other newspapers." His words resonated in the room, brimming with the passion and determination that had fuelled his relentless pursuit of the truth.

"In the end, my conviction got me fired, but now it's all yours," Jackson said with determination. Coby's excitement overflowed, causing him to leap up and throw his arms victoriously into the air.

He carefully gathered the letters, feeling the weight of anticipation in his hands. Hesitantly, he opened the delicate flaps, the sound of paper rustling softly. As he read one or two of the intimate love notes, he could almost smell the lingering scent of secrecy and desire. Recognition flooded in his mind, and he couldn't help but recall the distinct aroma of Jane Baines' lotus flower perfume, which lingered in every corner of his grand estate.

Coby's heart raced in his chest, the adrenaline coursing through his veins like a roaring river. His palms became moist with sweat, and his fingers shook with a combination of anticipation and anxiety. His senses seemed to sharpen, every sound and scent amplified in the charged atmosphere of the room.

With each love note he read, his breath caught in his throat, his eyes widening in astonishment. The words on the page seemed to dance before him, each sentence igniting a spark of inspiration within him. Goosebumps prickled along his arms, a physical manifestation of the emotions that consumed him.

The rejected article, now discarded on the table, beckoned to him like a forbidden fruit. With trembling hands, Coby reached out and snatched it up, his fingers brushing against the smooth surface of the paper. He devoured the words hungrily, his mind racing to piece together the puzzle that lay before him.

His excitement was palpable, a tangible energy that seemed to fill the room. He could feel his cheeks flushed with a rosy hue, his eyes shining with a newfound determination. Each word he read fuelled his passion, his imagination running wild with possibilities.

Unable to contain himself any longer, Coby's hand instinctively reached for his phone, eager to capture this momentous occasion. But Jackson's raised hand halted him, freezing him in place. Coby looked up, meeting Jackson's unwavering gaze, and saw a flicker of amusement in his eyes.

"Take them all," Jackson said, his voice carrying a hint of nonchalance. His casual wave of the hand emphasised his confidence in Coby's abilities. "I know that with your skilled hand, you will weave the perfect story and unveil the truth, Mister Jones."

Coby's jaw dropped in astonishment, his eyes widening even further. The weight of Jackson's trust in him, the belief that he held the power to expose the hidden depths of this intriguing story, struck him. A mixture of gratitude and determination swelled within him, fuelling his resolve to do justice to these remarkable letters.

A dramatic exhale escaped Coby's lips, reverberating through the room like a gust of wind. His senses tingled with excitement, his thoughts racing as he strategized his next move. Jackson simply nodded, his smile knowing, as if he had expected this very reaction from Coby all along.

In that moment, Coby realised that this was not just a thrilling opportunity, but a turning point in his career. With renewed purpose, he pocketed the letters, his mind already envisioning the headlines and the impact his words would have. He vowed to unveil the truth and leave no stone unturned in his pursuit of it.

Chapter Twenty-Six

With each step down the squeaky clean stairs, Coby's urgency grew as he dialled Gracie's number. She promised not to delay him, her voice crackling through the phone. The distant sound of Ewan's fretful cries echoed in the background, adding a sense of urgency to the situation. Gracie abruptly cut short their sightseeing adventure and screeched to a halt just as Coby's feet touched the pavement. With a sense of urgency, he clambered into the car, Gracie making room for him in the passenger seat. With a quick stop to grab some refreshing drinks, Coby maneuvered the car onto the winding road that led back to Serenity Falls.

The scenic landscape passed by in a blur of vibrant colours, the verdant greens of the trees and the azure hues of the sky blending together. Gracie glanced at Coby, her eyes filled with curiosity, noticing the distant gaze in his eyes as they drove. Coby let out a tired sigh, his eyes twinkling mischievously as he winked at her, stealing a quick glance at Ewan through the rearview mirror.

"There's not really a lot to say," Coby spoke with a touch of enigma, leaving the words lingering in the atmosphere. The weight of the untold details about Gracie's husband's demise weighed heavily on him, but he couldn't reveal them in front of Ewan. Gracie, ever perceptive, picked up on his unspoken message and patiently remained silent until they arrived home.

The cheerful sounds of a Celtic tune filled the car, their voices blending in perfect harmony. This time, luck seemed to favour them as they drove along the road with no sheep blocking their path. Coby made a quick stop in Serenity Falls to pick up some essentials, the tantalising smell of freshly baked bread filling the car. The picturesque road, with its tall hemlock trees casting ominous shadows, stretched out before them, beckoning them towards Coby's stately home.

Out of nowhere, a sleek car raced past, its bright headlights momentarily blinding Coby. The engine roared with power as it sped past them, leaving behind a distant echo. Coby's brows furrowed in confusion as he glimpsed the car in the rearview mirror. It was a silver Porsche Carrera, a sight that stirred a familiar memory within him. He racked his brain, but the answer eluded him, and he opted to dismiss the nagging thoughts for now.

Coby's stomach growled, a reminder of his hunger, as he yearned for a taste of the hearty Scottish Broth awaiting them at home. With determination, he pressed down on the accelerator, the engine roaring with renewed vigour as they raced along the winding road for the last stretch. The Volvo slowly climbed up the steep driveway, its engine straining against the incline. The sinking sun bathed the well-tended lawn in long shadows, creating a melancholic atmosphere with its fading light. Coby's heart sank as he caught sight of a figure standing on the porch, her presence filling him with frustration.

Gracie's voice carried a tone of disbelief as she asked, "Who is that?" Coby grunted in response, his voice laced with frostiness.

"Elaine," he replied, his ex-wife's name dripping with disdain. Janie let out a series of excited barks at Misty, Elaine's posh Scoodle, who stood haughtily next to her. The tension in the air was palpable as Coby approached Elaine, his tone icy.

"What is this?" he asked, glaring at his ex-wife with a touch of anger in his voice. Elaine simply shrugged, dismissing his annoyance with a careless wave of her hand.

"Niall Preston, your friend, betrayed me and took everything I had," Elaine exclaimed, her face red with anger. The gentle breeze carried the scent of her perfume mixed with a tinge of bitterness, leaving Coby with no doubt that her words held some truth.

"You had nothing," Coby snapped, his voice filled with anger, forcefully opening the door and deactivating the blaring alarm. The piercing sound ceased, replaced by the heavy silence of tension. Ewan emerged from his hiding spot behind his mother, his footsteps muffled on the plush carpet as he dutifully carried Elaine's overweight suitcases into the house. Gracie, feeling a knot of anticipation in her stomach, waited until everyone was safely inside. With a sense of urgency, she hurried into the study and sank into the comfort of her plush leather chair.

The echoes of Coby and Elaine's furious argument reverberated through the house, their words like daggers being thrown, each one aimed with precision. The air was thick with their anger, tangible and suffocating. Coby insisted that Elaine could not stay, his voice filled with frustration, while Elaine defended herself, her voice strained with desperation, claiming she had nowhere else to go.

In the end, exhaustion won over pride, and Coby reluctantly showed her to a small room on the upper level. Frustrated, he stormed into the office, the sound of his heavy footsteps echoing in the room, and ordered furniture for Elaine online, determined to provide her at least with a bed.

A cacophony erupted from upstairs as Elaine angrily unpacked her belongings, the sound of things being tossed around in a fit of frustration. Her footsteps reverberated down the staircase, their rhythm echoing through the grand marble hallway, until they finally reached the small study. The tension in the room was palpable, a heavy weight pressing down on Gracie's chest.

"Could I please get a serving of coffee?" Elaine's voice cut through the silence, her piercing gaze darting between Gracie and Coby. Gracie, sensing the tension, rose from her seat, but Coby quickly gestured for her to remain seated, his scowl betraying his annoyance.

"You are not a maid," Coby said, his voice softening as he turned his gaze towards Gracie, his eyes filled with adoration.

He stared at Elaine with determination and said, "Gracie is the love of my life, and she is not at your disposal," his voice filled with love.

Elaine flinched, her hand flying theatrically to her heart, tears threatening to spill over. The room was suffocatingly silent, punctuated only by the sudden gasp that escaped her lips. Her furious eyes darted between Coby and Gracie, searching for a way to retaliate. With a scoff, she whirled around, her heels clicking heavily on the cold marble floors as she hurried towards the kitchen. Gracie and Coby exchanged a questioning gaze, their unspoken understanding bridging the gap between them. Coby could see the appreciation in Gracie's eyes, a warmth that made his heart flutter with hope.

"I'm sorry Ewan had to hear our argument," Coby apologised, his voice filled with remorse.

Gracie narrowed her eyes, her gaze fixed on him intently. The room fell silent as she contemplated his kindness towards her son. A wave of warmth and comfort washed over her, knowing that Coby had always been good to them. She knew that if someone provoked Coby, he would fiercely defend those he loved. It brought her immense solace, and in that very moment, she realised he was the man she loved. It was the first time since her husband's passing that she felt ready to open her heart again.

Rising from her chair, Gracie enveloped Coby in a tender embrace, her arms wrapping around him tightly. As she held him close, she whispered, "Tell me what you found," her fingertips gently stroking his hair. In a sudden realisation, Coby gasped, his eyes growing wide, before leaping to his feet and bolting outside.

Moments later, he returned with a stack of vintage envelopes tightly grasped in his hands. The scent of aged paper wafted in the air as he hurried back into his office. Fumbling through the envelopes, his fingers trembled with anticipation until he finally found the article bearing Jackson Kinney's name. Next to it, someone had boldly typed the word 'rejected' in capital letters, painted in vibrant red.

With a sense of reverence, Coby carefully unfolded the letter, revealing its contents to Gracie. The typewritten words seemed to echo through time, each letter imprinted on the yellowed parchment with a faded but still legible ink. Before them, the rhythmic pattern of the words danced, showcasing the vintage typewriter's character. The room filled with the imagined sounds of a bustling newsroom, the clacking of keys reverberating off the walls.

The document lay before Gracie, a relic of the past, each tactile sensation and visual detail capturing the essence of history. In a bygone era, the scent of aged paper mingled with the faint whisper of dried ink, taking them both back to a time where every keystroke held significance. It was a simple piece of paper, yet it held within it the power to captivate, to evoke a sense of nostalgia for a time long gone.

Gracie read it out loud, her voice filling the room with excitement, starting with the bold and captivating heading, "The Enigmatic Trio: A Story of Lies, Movement, and Tragedy at Hemlock Manor." Her eyes widened with eager anticipation as she spoke, and she discreetly stole a quick glance at Coby, hoping to catch his attention. In response, he nodded, a wordless affirmation that urged her to continue, his gaze fixed on her.

Biting her lip anxiously, Gracie continued reading with a furrowed brow. "Nestled in the heart of the English countryside, Hemlock Manor stands surrounded by towering, centuries-old trees, its presence as mysterious as the stories that echo through its history. Its stone walls hold secrets that have been whispered through its corridors for generations. Among these are tales of three extraordinary women, their lives intertwined by fate, passion, and an insatiable longing for freedom."

Gracie took a deep breath, feeling the weight of the letter in her hands, and pressed on, reading each word slowly. "Jane Baines, Vivienne LeClaire, and Josephine Barker, fondly remembered as the Enigmatic Trio, were more than just inhabitants of Hemlock Manor. They were its life, its soul, and ultimately, its victims. Their stories, buried deep in the manor's foundations, have been unearthed, shedding light on the chilling events that transpired within its walls. Jane Baines, a grieving widow and mother, found solace in the arms of Roy Kinney, a high-ranking member of the 42nd Royal Highland Regiment, also known as the Black Watch. Their illicit affair, spanning decades, unfolded amidst the backdrop of war-torn France. Jane, once a dancer for the regiment, met Vivienne LeClaire and Josephine Barker and together, they enthralled audiences with their mesmerising performances throughout Montmartre, Paris."

Coby's eyes were fixed on Gracie, captivated by her intense focus as she delved deeper into the story. "Their dance routines were so captivating that they immediately caught the eye of Lord Henderson Sinclair, who happened to be the owner of Hemlock Manor. He promised them a life of luxury and fame, luring them away from Paris to his stately home in Scotland. However, the promise was nothing more than a cruel ruse. Hemlock Manor, under Sinclair's rule, was not a haven for artists but a high-end brothel serving the whims of the elite. These were men whose names have the power to echo through history."

Gracie's hand shook with anticipation as she lifted the teacup to her lips before she continued reading the captivating article. "The estate manager of the manor, Giles Drummond, suspected foul play. His untimely death, ruled as an accident, sent a chilling message to the inhabitants of Hemlock Manor. Panic ensued and the dancers, realising the danger they were in, fled. Tragically, Vivienne LeClaire was found murdered in an alley, a rose – a sinister symbol of the Sinclair household, placed by her side."

Gracie's eyes filled with tears, on the brink of streaming down her cheeks, yet she pushed through, reading with a lump lodged in her throat. "Jane Baines, returning to the Black Watch under her Gaelic name, Sine Byrne, met a tragic end, too. The mystery surrounding her drowning during a channel crossing only intensified, sparking endless rumours of foul play. These revelations cast a long, dark shadow over Hemlock Manor's past. The Enigmatic Trio, once symbols of freedom and passion, became victims of deceit and violence. Their stories, hidden for so long, now echo through the manor's halls, a chilling reminder of the price they paid for their dreams. Their spirits, it is said, still haunt Hemlock Manor, dancing in its moonlit corridors, their laughter and whispers forever imprinted in its stone walls. The uncovering of these secrets marks a significant moment in Hemlock Manor's history. It lays bare the truth behind its facade, revealing a tale as chilling as it is captivating. As we delve deeper into its past, we can only hope to honour the memory of the Enigmatic Trio, their lives a testament to their resilience, their spirit, and their undying love for dance."

Coby enveloped Gracie in his arms, feeling the weight of her sobs reverberate through her trembling shoulders. The sight of her tear-stained face tugged at his heart, filling him with a pang of remorse. As he comforted her, his fingertips gently brushed against the silky strands of her hair, their velvety texture providing a soothing sensation.

Gracie, amidst tearful gasps, managed to speak, her voice choked with emotion. In between sniffling, she revealed, "I finally discovered the truth about Gile's death. I always suspected it was Henderson Sinclair." Her red, teary eyes met Coby's gaze, their intensity reflecting the deep pain she carried.

Recognising the need for solace, Coby granted Gracie time off, giving her the opportunity to find peace amidst her emotional turmoil. As the house fell into a hushed silence, he flung open his laptop; the keys clacking under his nimble fingers. The screen flickered to life, a digital canvas for his investigative journey.

Hours turned into days as Coby delved into the mysterious letters. He followed the breadcrumbs, connecting dots, and unravelling secrets hidden within the ink. The truth leapt off the pages, enticing him with each captivating clue.

Caffeine fuelled his sleepless nights, his eyes bloodshot but unyielding. His phone buzzed incessantly, messages from anonymous sources, each one leading him deeper into the labyrinth of deception.

Coby's fingers trembled with anticipation as he delicately unearthed a worn, sepia-toned photograph, the missing piece of the enigmatic puzzle. His gaze fixated on the image, his eyes widening in disbelief, as if time itself had come to a standstill. In the background, Hemlock Manor loomed like a stoic sentinel, its ominous doors bearing the weight of secrets. The air held a faint scent of aged paper and dust, adding to the mystique of the moment.

Before the grand residence, a group of women and men stood, frozen in time. Jane, Vivienne, and Josephine graced the foreground, their elegant attire mirroring that of their ghostly apparitions. They exuded an air of mystery, their presence both haunting and alluring. Behind them, a cluster of captivating women, adorned in high fashion garments, seemed to beckon with a seductive allure.

Surrounding the alluring women, the men of the era stood with an air of poise and superiority. They were aristocrats, members of the elite, their eyes gleaming with a sinister glint that sent shivers down Coby's spine. Among them stood Lord Henderson Sinclair, a man of power and influence, and another whose very name commanded nations.

This astounding discovery revealed a hidden truth, a revelation that had the potential to rock the world to its very core. The weight of the moment hung heavily in the air, as if the entire universe held its breath, awaiting the unveiling of secrets long kept hidden.

With a rush of excitement, Coby meticulously composed an article. His fingers flew across the keyboard as the rhythmic clatter of the keys resonated through the room, harmonising with the pulsating thuds of his heart. The scent of freshly printed ink permeated the air, a tangible manifestation of his unwavering determination. Swiftly, he shared his masterpiece, complete with a captivating photograph, with the Inverness printing press, envisioning its impact.

In a matter of moments, a reply arrived, gratitude and promise entwined within the words. The article, they assured, would grace the front page of every British newspaper come morning. Anticipation bubbled within him as he forwarded his work to his editor, John Drake.

With eagerness, Coby's eyes scanned the email, absorbing the essence of John's response. It read, "Good job, mate," injecting him with a surge of pride. The email continued, "Your greatest work. The editors are preparing the final draft. Congratulations."

As the sun rose on a new day, casting its warm glow upon the world, Coby stood tall, ready to face the challenges that awaited him. He had discovered his purpose, his passion intertwining with his duty to expose the darkest corners of society.

The headline, bold and commanding, demanded the attention of every passerby. He had unveiled the truth, and the powerful were held accountable. Justice, at long last, was served.

The world buzzed with the aftermath, whispers of Coby's name floating on the lips of all. Amidst the chaos, he remained grounded, his feet firmly planted on the path he had chosen. He knew this was just the beginning, a mere stepping stone to uncover greater truths. With unwavering resolve, he vowed to continue his quest for justice, his words becoming a beacon of truth in a world shrouded in deceit.

No longer just Mister Jones, an aspiring writer, he had transcended into Coby McTavish, a force to be reckoned with. A fearless seeker of truth, destined to leave an indelible mark on the world.

That night, Elm Brook Manor was alive with the sounds of laughter and joyous chatter. Ewan and Coby skilfully adorned the grand hallway with colourful balloons and shimmering trimmings, transforming it into a vibrant and festive space. Champagne bottles popped and the sweet scent of celebration filled the air. Gracie's nimble fingers danced across the piano keys, filling the room with cheery melodies that resonated in everyone's hearts.

A mouthwatering aroma of freshly baked pizza wafted through the air, enticing the guests with its delicious allure. The tables were adorned with an abundance of piping hot slices, enough to satisfy the hunger of every member of the 42nd Royal Highlands Regiment. The pizza spread was a visual feast, with a mouthwatering array of toppings and a tempting aroma.

As the evening unfolded, the ethereal trinity took centre stage, captivating Coby with their graceful dance performances. Their movements were like poetry in motion, enchanting everyone in the room. Their ethereal beauty mesmerised Coby, and he felt a sense of wonder and awe washing over him.

Sandra River's ethereal voice blended effortlessly with the hypnotic piano melody, creating a chilling harmony that sent shivers down the spines of all who listened. Meanwhile, Janie's mournful howls echoed through the surroundings, creating a spine-tingling backdrop that added to the eerie atmosphere. Gilles Drummond's spectral form materialised fleetingly, blending with the jubilant atmosphere. His eyes emitted a luminous glow, casting an otherworldly aura as he affectionately fixed his gaze upon Gracie. Like a wisp of smoke, he vanished into the enigmatic cloak of shadows, leaving only the faint sound of a whisper in his wake.

Amidst all the merriment and jubilation upstairs in her bedroom, Elaine sought solace, finding comfort in the silence of her locked room.

Coby's latest book, titled 'Hemlock Manor,' soared to unprecedented sales in a whirlwind of time. It swiftly claimed the top spot on all official bestseller lists across the globe, even in France. The book's translation transcended boundaries, becoming the most linguistically diverse in history. It was even translated into Etherealese, a language shared by ethereal beings, as if anticipating the need for a haunting presence lurking in an underground basement to delve into its pages. Coby, writing under his pen name, Mister Jones, earned the nickname 'Lightning Fingers' from the Ethereal Trinity.

With impeccable timing, a mere day after the book's publication, Coby summoned all the spectres to gather in his study. News of his extraordinary story spread like wildfire, prompting Interpol to reopen the haunting, cold case of Sandra River. Moving quickly, they traced Coby's trail of clues and he soon discovered that his contact shared his theory. Sandra River's ethereal presence briefly graced the surroundings, casting a mesmerising glow and filling the air with a joyous atmosphere, only to vanish like a wisp of mist.

The truth about Jane Baines and Vivienne LeClaire finally came to light, capturing headlines in both France and the United Kingdom. Alistair Sinclair and his wife, Morven, mysteriously vanished overnight, leaving no trace. The haunting spirit of Giles Drummond, too, disappeared without a single sighting. Jane and Vivienne's ethereal forms materialised in front of Coby, emanating a brilliant glow that momentarily blinded him, before vanishing into nothingness.

Only Josephine Barker remained behind, her presence a deliberate choice. Coby sensed that there was more to her story than she revealed, prompting him to conduct thorough research. Yet, he concluded, she stayed to ensure that Henderson Sinclair's haunting spectre caused no harm to those who came before her or those who would come after. Over time, she and Coby forged a deep friendship, their voices blending harmoniously as they gathered around the piano, their songs filling the night with a comforting pall.

Coby reassured Gracie that his spacious manor house was officially free from any eerie whispers or ghostly apparitions. With excitement, she and Ewan moved in with him, leaving behind their old lives. Meanwhile, Elaine took over the cosy cottage, its walls adorned with charming trinkets. Filled with affection, Ewan lovingly referred to Coby as dad, his words carrying a comforting warmth. Coby and Gracie, determined to preserve the magic of their relationship, decided not to bind themselves in the confines of marriage. Their pact proved successful, allowing their love to flourish. As night fell, Coby settled into his comfortable bed, the soft sheets embracing him. Suddenly, a piercing scream shattered the tranquillity echoing from the distant cottage where Elaine now lived. Ignoring the chaos, Coby closed his eyes with a serene smile, surrendering to sleep's gentle embrace.

One fateful day, Coby's eyes came across an intriguing article detailing the nearby haunted estate known as The Serpent's Manor among the locals. The mere mention of it sent chills down his spine. This eerie place seemed frozen in time, its ancient walls bathed in an ethereal glow cast by flickering candlelight. The air hung heavy with the scent of age-old books, mingled with the comforting aroma of crackling wood smoke. Yet, beneath it all, there lingered a chilling metallic tang, sending shivers down the bravest of souls. A mischievous smile danced upon Coby's lips, while a sinister glimmer ignited his eyes as he entertained the idea of acquiring the enigmatic manor.

Is it really the end?

Acknowledgments

In the quiet corners of my heart, where words are born from whispers of inspiration, I owe an immeasurable debt of gratitude to two extraordinary souls

To my wife, Marna, my Babalooba, who has been the beacon guiding me through the stormy seas of life. Her love is the wind in my sails, her faith in me is the compass that steers my course. She is the lighthouse promising safe harbor, even amidst the most tempestuous squalls. To her, I pledge my eternal love and gratitude.

Then there is Lettie van der Merwe, a woman of extraordinary strength and boundless love. She cradled my world in her seasoned hands, nurturing the seedling of my existence into the tree I am today. Her unwavering support and unconditional love have been my sanctuary, my refuge. In her honor, I strive to emulate her kindness and resilience in every line I write.

It is to these remarkable women that I dedicate my passion for writing. They are the ink that flows onto the parchment of my life, their love the tale that I yearn to tell. They are the heartbeat in every word, the soul in every sentence. And as long as my pen dances across the page, their spirit will live on in my stories.

From the terrestrial cradle of Earth, amidst the constellation of ordinary lives, a writer was born. His name is Iwan Ross. Iwan's journey into the realm of letters began in the hallowed halls of academia, his passion for writing emerging as a beacon amidst the shadows of youthful uncertainty. Yet, he chose to let time season his talent, to let experience shape his voice. Like a fine wine maturing in an oak barrel, he waited patiently to pen his first novel, allowing life's trials and triumphs to ferment his creativity.

Bearing the dual mantles of a solutions engineer by day and an author by twilight, Iwan navigates the labyrinth of life with a pen in one hand and technology in the other. His qualifications as a feature journalist and copy-editor lend him a unique perspective, enabling him to weave intricate narratives that blur the lines between fact and fiction, reality and fantasy.

Raised single-handedly by a mother whose love knew no bounds, her resilience sculpted Iwan, her strength becoming his own. The absence of a father was not a void, but a catalyst, pushing him to explore the uncharted territories of life on his own terms. It taught him to appreciate the true essence of womanhood, to respect and understand it, adding a rich layer of depth to his characters and narratives.

In a world where words hold the power to illuminate the darkest corners, Iwan Ross stands as a torchbearer, his pen lighting up the canvas of literature one stroke at a time. His journey is not just about telling stories, it's about unraveling the threads of human emotions and weaving them into a tapestry that resonates with readers long after the last page has been turned.

Printed in Great Britain
by Amazon

39544961R00142